Book

Billionaire

Quadruplet Alphas

A ROMANCE NOVEL

written by

JOANNA J

Copyright © 2022 Joanna J

Joanna J has asserted her right under the laws of Singapore, to be identified as the Author of the Work.

All rights reserved.

No part of this book may be reproduced or transmitted in any form by any means, graphic, electronic, or mechanical, including photocopying, recording, taping or by any information storage retrieval system without the written permission from the copyright holder.

This is a work of fiction. Names, characters, businesses, places, events, and incidents are either the products of the author's imagination or used in a fictitious manner: Any resemblance to actual persons, living or dead, or actual events is purely coincidental.

Design and composition by CRATER PTE.LTD.

First Edition, 2022.
Published by CRATER PTE.LTD.
Singapore

AUTHOR'S NOTES

Writing has always been therapeutic for me. Writing was my escape from reality, especially whilst I was working as a young doctor during a difficult time. I made a little fantasy world, one where immortality was within reach, good triumphed over evil, and true love prevailed. I wrote because stories demand to be told. They wind their way into my mind and trickle out through my fingertips. I hunched over my desk every night, writing about werewolves and witches. My curious cats and my loyal little dog were my honorary co-writers: Noddy, Winky, Dobby, and Minnie, respectively. They dutifully kept me company throughout the night. They were silent sources of comfort and inspiration. The support from my parents remained steadfast. They have always been there for me at every stage of my life: at every parent-teacher meeting, after every exam, before every job interview and during the writing of every book. A few of my closest relatives and friends checked on me regularly as well.

My editor at Dreame/Stary Writing, Mona, was always there to assist and warmly encourage me. The readers brightened my days with their enthusiasm and support. Each and every single reader means so much to me. I am so grateful to everyone involved in making this possible. I am thankful for the many opportunities made possible by the entire team at Dreame/Stary Writing. I remember watching the read count of my books on the app increase. I was ecstatic. People were actually reading something I had written! I began to receive messages on social media from readers who said my writing had helped them cope in some small way.

I felt so honoured. I continued to post chapters on the app. After about one and a half years, I had written three books. Billionaire Quadruplet Alphas was my fourth book on the app. I knew I wanted to write a modern fairytale, one that encapsulated all the themes I grew up loving and reading regularly. I am so happy to see it in print. Please note that this book is a work of fiction. All the characters, places and names are fictional and derived from my imagination. Any similarities between this book and any true life story are merely coincidental. This book is not based on real events from my life or anyone else's.

Joanna J.

TABLE OF CONTENTS

AUTHOR'S NOTES iii
Chapter 1 1
Chapter 2 8
Chapter 3 12
Chapter 4 18
Chapter 5 23
Chapter 6 31
Chapter 7 35
Chapter 8 40
Chapter 9 44
Chapter 10 57
Chapter 11 57
Chapter 12 61
Chapter 13 66
Chapter 14 70
Chapter 15 74
Chapter 16 79
Chapter 17 85
Chapter 18 92
Chapter 19 97
Chapter 20 101
Chapter 21 108
Chapter 22 112
Chapter 23 117
Chapter 24 123
Chapter 25 126

Chapter 26 130
Chapter 27 134
Chapter 28 157
Chapter 29 146
Chapter 30 152
Chapter 31 157
Chapter 32 163
Chapter 33 166
Chapter 34 169
Chapter 35 173
Chapter 36 178
Chapter 37 184
Chapter 38 191
Chapter 39 198
Chapter 40 202
Chapter 41 206
Chapter 42 211
Chapter 43 216
Chapter 44 222
Chapter 45 228
Chapter 46 233
Chapter 47 241
Chapter 48 246
Chapter 49 256
Chapter 50 261
Chapter 51 271
Chapter 52 281
ABOUT THE AUTHOR 287
ABOUT DREAME 288

Chapter 1

Monday 7th September, 2020

Hannah Star's Point of View

The castle loomed before me. It was perched precariously on Mount Viper, the highest point on the Viper Moon pack lands.

Like most teenaged members of the Viper Moon Pack, I attended Viper Moon Academy, an elite boarding school located on the top of Mount Viper. However, *unlike* most teens there, my family was not able to afford the tuition and boarding fees. I was a scholarship student, and money wasn't the only thing I currently lacked.

Our werewolf pack was known for two things: its incredible wealth and the deadly venomous bites of its wolves. I had neither. I was from one of the few poor families in our elitist pack and I was in the ten percent of venom-less wolf families in our pack.

I sighed as I trudged up the vast sloping driveway, keeping my eyes downcast on the smooth dark pitch. I was wheeling my suitcase along behind me. It contained my few possessions, namely several well-worn articles of clothing and a few dog-eared books I had read over and over.

I tried not to look at all the Glossy People arriving via limousines and sports cars while I arrived on foot. I drowned out the laughter and loud music of those excited for senior year by keeping myself focused on the pitch. I reached the stone steps that led to the huge double doors of the castle.

The school had been built in 1836, and it was all grey stone with domed towers, pointed roofs and stained glass windows. It was breathtaking to behold. I especially loved how enchanting it looked during autumn and winter. We were on the brink of autumn. Summer's flowers wilted as the green leaves turned yellow and orange before cascading to earth.

I tried to hoist my suitcase up the steps, and as usual, I could barely manage. I was petite for a she-wolf at only five feet and four inches. I had golden skin and dark brown eyes with waist-length loosely curled chocolate brown hair. My name was Hannah Star, but my few friends called me Star. I looked around, hoping to spot Jillian or Toby but no such luck. I sighed.

Before I could attempt to lift my luggage again, a strong-looking hand grasped the handle. I jumped, startled, looking up to find one of the Quadruplet Alphas. The Quadruplet Alphas, or the Quads as they were called, were set to inherit the Viper Moon Pack. They had yet to take over from their father, Alpha Quaid Quinn, but they were still referred to as Alphas in the interim upon their request. They were dashingly handsome and obscenely rich and they knew it too. They were identical with each of them boasting a height of six foot four inches and a leanly muscled physique. They had thick light ash-brown hair that almost reached their shoulders, astonishingly green eyes, and chiseled faces with high cheekbones, thick eyebrows, long lashes and strong jaws. They had slightly full lips and straight pointed noses that were often up in the air while everyone else's noses were up their butts. They were coddled and spoilt by the entire faculty at the school, upon their parents request, and the student population fawned over them too, *especially* the she-wolves. Their names were Jonah, Noah, Elijah and Isaiah Quinn.

Needless to say, I was shocked to see one of them lifting my suitcase up the stone steps for me. He carried it effortlessly. He was in a navy blazer with a white fitted tee-shirt underneath and navy pants with designer shoes. I was sure the clothes were designer as well but I was not too great at recognising high-end logos. I was not familiar with most of it. I scampered after the Quad, glancing around for his other three brothers. He put my suitcase down on the doorstep and turned to face me.

"Where to?" He asked smiling as though I were a lady of the house and he was my butler.

"Um, I..., I'm going to my dorm," I said sheepishly, suddenly feeling self-conscious about the runs in my black stockings under my grey tweed skirt. I had paired the skirt with a similar blazer and a white shirt underneath. My dark brown curly hair hung loose all around me. I knew it was tousled and windswept. I tied to smooth it hastily.

"Lead the way," he said.

Chapter 1

I scurried forwards, opening heavy doors for him as we went along and trying to ignore the looks of disdain and envy many she-wolves gave me. I led him up a winding staircase past some oil paintings. The castle's ceilings were extremely high and it was a bit chilly in the later months of the year. I was on the first floor girls 'dormitory near the very end of the hallway. I shared a room with another scholarship student, my friend Jillian. I knocked on the door in case she was there already and changing.

"This is where I leave you, then," said the Quad matter-of-factly, putting his hands in his pocket.

I looked up at his face. Now that we were standing still I could really appreciate how much he towered over me. I took a step back. He had a powerful alpha aura despite having not claimed the position yet along with his three brothers.

"Thank you! Thank you so much!" I said, truly grateful.

He turned to leave.

"My name is Hannah!" I called down the hallway.

"Noah!" He called back, grinning.

My heart fluttered. I grinned nervously and waved as he turned around and walked away.

The door flung open and Jillian launched herself at me. She was pale with strawberry blonde hair in loose ringlets down to her shoulders. Her eyes were a light haunting blue. She was dressed in a pink sweater and jeans. She was even tinier than I was at only four feet and eleven and a half inches. She constantly reminded everyone of that half of an inch. I followed her into our dorm. Her side was entirely decorated in all things pink and fluffy. My side was adorned with every shade of purple I could get my hands on.

"What took you so long?" She whined.

My grandmother could not afford to give me enough money for the bus or a taxi so I had to walk most of the way. Thankfully it was too chilly out to make me sweat and a good samaritan in his off-roading vehicle gave me a lift up the mountain. He had dropped me off just about half a mile from the gates. I couldn't tell Jillian all of that.

"You know I walk slow," I replied with a dull excuse.

She shrugged.

"There's gonna be a party tonight you know!" She said excitedly.

I was certainly not into parties.

"It would be a great opportunity to meet our mates! All the young Viper Moon men will be there!" She shrieked, beside herself with excitement.

"I can't find my mate right now. I'm not eighteen yet," I reminded her.

I would turn eighteen on the 12th of September which was this coming Saturday. A lot of students at the school had lavish, excessive birthday parties especially for their eighteenth birthday as that was when one could realise who your fated mate was. Werewolves mated for life so it was a very special and significant birthday. Gillian was already eighteen and had yet to find her mate but she was an open book and a hopeless romantic. I, on the other hand, hid and buried my feelings.

"We're going ok. That's final!" Squeaked Jillian. I sighed outwardly but smiled inwardly.

I wore a mini red velvet dress with long lantern sleeves and opaque black tights with black velvet ankle boots. I bundled myself up in a black coat.

We were getting a ride with Toby, our other friend. Tobias picked us up in his car. He was not a scholarship student like Jillian and I were. His family owned a potato company that sold their produce to all the big potato chip brands. He loved to dance and sing karaoke and party till dawn, the complete opposite to me. He was only an inch or two taller than me with big blue eyes under round-rimmed glasses. He had light brown almost dark blonde wavy hair.

"Girls!" He squealed excitedly as he got out of his jaguar to greet us near the school's entrance. We hugged and all piled into the car.

"Whose party is it?" I asked, suddenly realising I should have asked that from the moment Jillian had brought it up. Tobias looked at me in the rearview mirror. His baby blue rimmed glasses matched his blazer and pants perfectly. He had a pastel pink tee shirt underneath. Jillian looked back at me, her shimmery gold crop top catching the light. She had paired it with pale skinny jeans and high heels.

"Angelique's," she mumbled quickly.

"Stop the car!" I said.

"Star!" Chastised Toby.

"Stop it right now!" I yelled.

The car screeched to a halt in the darkness. Angelique had ruined almost every school year for me by doing something terrible to me. She was five feet and nine inches of leggy blonde evil incarnate and she happened to be my cousin on my father's side. Tobias and Jillian knew how I felt about her. She even denied the fact that we were cousins at school but was sickly sweet to me outside of school at family gatherings.

I got out and stepped into the darkness, hugging myself tightly. The wind howled like a wolf at the full moon. The mountain road was lonely. It winded all the way down. We were going to the Valley for the party.

"Star, Star come on!" Called Toby.

"Get back in the car, Star!" Said Jillian. "Star!" She shrieked.

Chapter 1

I continued to stumble over some rocks by the mountain side. I froze when I saw it. A huge snow-white wolf crouching in the darkness. It almost glowed. It had huge yellow eyes which it turned upon me. I slowly backed away. It was massive. I could tell even from yards away. I got back into the car slowly.

"Drive," I said softly, not wanting to make any sudden movements in case the wolf launched itself at the car.

"What's gotten into you? You look like you've seen a ghost," mumbled Toby, starting the car and driving away. I breathed a sigh of relief.

"There was a huge wolf back there," I explained to them.

They glanced at each other. "We're just glad you've decided to come. You sure it wasn't one of us, a werewolf."

"Either it was just a huge regular wolf or a rogue. I didn't recognise its smell," I said,

"We're here!" Squealed Jillian.

We pulled into the gated community. The guard made a call to someone and let us continue on. We reached the last house on the street. House was an understatement. We reached the last sprawling mansion on the street. The driveway was filled with cars. We spotted people partying, dancing, laughing and drinking even on the porch with the loud music emanating from inside.

We went around to the back. There were a couple people in a massive jacuzzi. There was a huge pool but it was devoid of people in this cold weather. I spotted my darling cousin Angelique making out with Jonah in the hot tub and I felt a pang of jealousy. Where had that come from? My inner wolf was growling. She was furious. What was with her? She had begun to show herself little by little as I got closer to my eighteenth birthday. I couldn't communicate with her effectively yet.

My eyes trailed across the other occupants of the jacuzzi. The huge tub contained all four Quads and four girls including Angelique. About two dozen teenagers were on the back porch, some playing beer pong and others surrounding the hot tub to fawn over the Glossy people, the shiny rich pretty people with their ugly interiors. Angelique's interior was the ugliest.

I felt a pair of eyes on me. Noah. The Quad who had helped me with my luggage earlier. Strangely I was able to pick him out, deciphering him from the other three. He smiled slightly at me. I smiled and waved. Jillian and Tobias tried to drag me inside to do shots but I refused. I stayed on the back porch and edged a little close to the jacuzzi. Angelique broke apart from Jonah and spotted me. She smirked.

"Hey there, uh, Moon?" She asked. She knew exactly what my name was. My father and her mother were brother and sister. Jonah snickered and I felt sick for some reason. I refused to correct her.

"Hi, Angelique," I said politely.

My eyes were on Noah. Angelique caught this. She placed a manicured hand on his bare wet shoulder.

"What brings you here, Cloud?" She said, making Jonah laugh again.

Ugh. I glared at Jonah and his eyes widened as if worried he'd upset me. He quickly recovered his haughty expression. Noah had been glaring at him too but he was now focused on me.

"Tobias insisted I come," I murmured.

"Ohhh, yeah, Toby," she said chuckling. "You must be thrilled, huh, to get to see how the other half lives?" She asked snidely.

I frowned and chose to ignore her.

"Hey, Noah, thanks for the other day," I said smiling.

"What happened the other day?" Asked Angelique quickly.

Why was she acting like she owned the Quads? Identical multiples were technically one fertilised egg that was split into parts for example, two for twins, three for triplets and four for quadruplets. Each part essentially becomes a whole new person, identical to the rest, a naturally occurring clone. Thus, they usually shared a single mate. The Quads despite being eighteen hadn't found their mate yet. Multiples usually didn't share girlfriends prior to the mate-bond so it was weird for Angelique to be possessive of Noah when she had been making out furiously with Jonah a few minutes ago.

"He..." I began.

"Nothing!" Said Noah quickly.

A sharp lancing pain sliced through me. That stung!

Was Noah ashamed of me? I thought.

I actually looked nice tonight. I was on scholarship though. Maybe he only wanted to rub shoulders with his fellow elites. I frowned at him sadly. I saw him wince a little at my expression before I walked away, heading inside the house.

The party raged on and I spotted all the Quads towel drying their hair, dressed in grey sweatpants and grey tee shirts now. I averted my eyes.

"Hey, Hannah!" Said a familiar voice. Noah.

"Yeah," I mumbled.

"Let's keep our business to ourselves. It's no one else's concern," he said simply.

I took that to mean "don't tell people I associate myself with the likes of you." I nodded and began to walk away but he grasped my arm. Jonah noticed and came over.

Chapter 1

"I thought you didn't know her, little bro," said Jonah.

The Quads in birth order were Jonah, Noah, Elijah and Isaiah.

"I don't," insisted Noah, relinquishing my arm as if it had electrocuted him.

"I was just telling her to keep her distance," Noah said.

I felt like he had splashed ice-cold water in my face. My jaw dropped.

"Run along ok, Cloud," said Jonah. "You weren't invited."

Elijah and Isaiah had sauntered over to us. They just stared at me blankly. All eight eyes were on me. My brain was foggy.

"I told you to go," said Noah, waving his hand in my face.

I stood rooted to the spot as though transfixed. My wolf was purring. How could she be happy around these monsters?

"Hey!" Snapped Isaiah. "The eldest Alpha told you to fuck off!"

I winced at him swearing at me like that. Jonah, Elijah and Isaiah laughed at my expense.

"Seriously, bye," sneered Elijah.

I looked at Noah, knowing full well that my eyes were glassy, shimmering with tears. I bit my lip, not wanting to cry in front of the Quads.

"Are you seriously about to cry?" Asked Isaiah incredulously.

Noah stiffened. Jonah stopped laughing. Elijah took a step closer to me, and I instinctively took a step back. I gulped and took a deep breath.

"No," I said softly and walked away.

Chapter 2

Tuesday 8th September, 2020

Hanna Star's Point of View

The day that dawned was grey and bleak with an overcast sky. It was the first official day of classes. After the Quads had told me to fuck off last night, I had tried to find Toby to drive me home but he had been chatting up some guy. Jillian had been in this rich guy's lap. She had introduced him to me as Chet. He was actually best friends with the Quads and their next door neighbour. He was tall with olive skin, black wavy hair and dark brown eyes. He had dropped us both back to the boarding school in his corvette.

I sighed as I dragged myself out of bed. I had brought a bucket to Jillian's bedside because she kept vomiting. She had been drunk last night and was still hungover this morning.

"Who was that guy, really, Jillian?" I asked, sweeping her strawberry blond ringlets out of her eyes.

She had been too drunk last night to explain properly. She shot up into a sitting position making me jump.

"What?" I squealed.

"He's my mate" she said softly. "Last night, I met my mate!"

She squealed then frowned. "But I was so drunk I hardly got to talk to him. What happened?"

"He took us home," I said smiling.

I was happy for her even if it meant I would have to see the two-faced Quads more often now. Jillian hugged me.

Chapter 2

"Chet is so wonderful, Star! I can't wait for you to find your mate and then we can double date!" Exclaimed Jillian.

I smiled. Truth be told, I could not picture myself having a mate. The way werewolf guys doted on their she-wolf mates. I just could not fathom any guy liking me that much. I knew that probably sounded pathetic and hopelessly insecure but it was true. I really could not picture it. I sighed.

Our first class of senior year was Lupine English Literature, one of my favourites. I sat in the front and listened with rapt attention. I had to keep my grades up as I was on scholarship and my grandmother really could not afford this place. My parents had been killed by rogues when I was little and Granny Hella had raised me. We were really close. We didn't have much but we had each other.

The Quads walked in late with the same four girls from the hot tub the other night. I made sure *not* to make eye contact with any of them though I could feel their eyes on me. Jillian was next to me, grinning widely. I looked up and immediately regretted doing so as I locked eyes with Noah. His expression was impassive. Chet was next to him beaming at Jillian. Chet came and sat next to Jillian, wrapping his arms around her.

"You ok?" He murmured practically pulling her onto his lap.

Chet and Jillian had both turned eighteen over the break so even though they had never acknowledged each other's existence before they were joined at the hip now. The Quads were eighteen as well but had yet to find their mates.

Angelique strutted into class in impossibly high heels that were not regulation. We had to wear uniforms that consisted of knee-length grey pleated skirts, grey blazers, white shirts and grey bowties. The guys wore grey blazers and pants with white shirts and regular ties. We all had to wear black, white or grey flat shoes and socks. Angelique's heels were red stilettos paired with shimmery fishnet stockings. Jonah whistled at her which made my heart contract painfully. Ugh. Why was I so jealous of stupid Angelique all of a sudden? She sat between the Quads with two of them on either side of her. She was keeping their attention with some long ridiculous story about being asked to model in Paris but turning it down to go model in Milan instead.

I could feel Noah's eyes on me. If I'd been a braver girl, I would've told him off. He was acting so strangely, nice one minute, then mean the next. I would rather he just ignored me. It occurred to me that Angelique was eighteen already too, meaning that the Quads were definitely not her mates as she would've felt the mate-bond already. I smiled at this but then stopped myself. Why did I care?

"...Friday at 9pm. You're gonna love it!" Said Chet as class had just finished.

Jillian nudged me. "Aren't you excited?"

Huh. I hadn't been listening to the teacher and I hadn't been listening to Jillian and Chet either.

"My parents' cabin, in the woods," said Chet. "We're gonna spend a weekend there. We'll be back by Sunday night!"

"Saturday is Star's birthday!" Exclaimed Jillian.

"Awesome! There's no better place to celebrate!" Said Chet.

"*That* is coming with us to the lake, Chet," said Angelique.

Jonah stifled a laugh. Noah just frowned at me while Elijah and Isaiah sneered.

"If Star isn't welcome then I have no business being there," snapped Jillian defending me.

My heart soared. Noah smiled a little.

"I was just kidding, Jilli-bear!" Exclaimed Angelique.

Jilli-bear? I almost vomited.

I was on my way out of class. Angelique and three of the Quads were ahead of me along with Jillian and Chet who were holding hands. Suddenly, someone grabbed my hand. Tingles shot through my arm. I looked up. Noah had me pressed into the wall of one of the school buildings. The others disappeared from view. For one intense split second I thought he was going to kiss me but he didn't.

"Don't come to the Cabin this weekend!" He whispered fiercely.

My heart throbbed.

"Why not?" I whispered trying to not sound so broken.

"Because Angelique will just use this as an opportunity to humiliate you and Jonah will go along with it," he snarled as though that were obvious.

"Why does Jonah hate me so much?" I asked, feeling helpless and hopeless all of a sudden.

"Jonah?" Inquired Noah frowning. "He doesn't hate you. He just laughs at all of Angelique's antics. A better question would be why does Angie hate you so much?"

"Oh, she's my cousin. My Dad and her mother were brother and sister," I said.

"Were?" Asked Noah.

"My Dad's dead," I said softly.

He loosened his hold on me a little.

"Sorry to hear that," he mumbled.

"It was a long time ago," I said.

"So Angie doesn't want you to tell people you're related?" Asked Noah. "Why?"

Chapter 2

"The same reason you didn't want anyone to know you helped me with my luggage... ashamed of me I guess," I snapped and tried to brush past him.

He gripped my arms and really pinned me to the wall. This time he put one knee between my legs. His hips pressed against my tummy as I was considerably shorter than him. His palms were on either side of my head and his nose was buried in my curls. He sniffed the top of my head and I shivered. I squirmed, wanting to escape but me fighting him was like a butterfly raging against a bear: nonsensical, pointless. I sighed, relaxing into this weird embrace. He seemed satisfied when I became limp in his arms, submitting to him. He finally stepped back.

"I expect to not see you there! Don't disobey me!" He ordered.

I glared at him. "It's for your own good, Hannah," he said softly and walked away.

Chapter 3

Friday 11th September, 2020

Star's Point of View

I was not about to let Noah boss me around. I was going to the Cabin. Jillian would be there and it was her mate's cabin so I felt safe enough.

After classes, I showered and dressed in a mini black dress with puff sleeves over black stockings and high-heeled Mary Janes. I actually took the time to do my makeup: cat eyes and red lipstick. I felt a little strange with it on.

"Wow!" Exclaimed Jillian.

I smiled at her. We went down to the foyer where Chet was waiting. I was sad that Toby wasn't coming. It would just be me, Jillian, the Quads and Devilique.

"Excited for your birthday tomorrow?" Asked Chet while he lifted my suitcase into the trunk of his car.

No.

"Yes," I lied.

"You might find your mate soon," commented Chet.

Hopefully not.

"Hopefully," I said.

I really didn't need some guy rejecting me right now when I was already dreading this school year. Things at home had become abysmal financially. Granny told me not to come home for Halloween or Christmas because she couldn't afford to feed me, and she was too proud to ask the

Chapter 3

pack for help, even though the pack leaders gave money to less fortunate members all the time. That's what the pack was for. It was supposed to be like a family. I had nothing really to offer my mate besides love and my company. I sighed. I got in the backseat and off we went.

Chet drove his car really fast to impress Jillian who squealed in delight, enjoying the wind in her hair. I spotted two other sports cars. One was being driven by Jonah and Angelique was in the passenger seat. I felt nauseated again. It was a Maserati according to Jillian. The other car was a luxury vehicle I did not recognise but it was gorgeous. It was matte black. Noah was driving it, and Elijah and Isaiah were in the backseat playing on their phones. Noah was racing Chet and grinning but then he spotted me in the backseat of Chet's car and his whole demeanour changed. He frowned.

When we got to the Cabin, I was scared to face Noah. The "Cabin" was a huge vacation home in the woods with a dock and a private lake. It had three storeys not including the attic and the basement. It was decorated in warm colours: creams, mustard yellows, antique golds, chocolate browns and muted reds. The colour palette was reminiscent of Fall. The kitchen was bigger than my entire house. There was a huge living room, a television room with a huge flat screen television and comfy sofas, a games room with a pool table and another big television with game consoles, an indoor pool and jacuzzi, an outdoor pool and outdoor jacuzzi with a patio and brick oven, seven bedrooms and eight bathrooms.

There was a housekeeper named Lana, a middle aged woman with a heart shaped face and a no-nonsense tone that did not suit her face. She gazed disdainfully at Jillian and me. Certain staff members of the elite families hated to wait on poor friends of the aristocracy. A maid in the Alpha's house ranked higher than most low-ranking members of the pack. Staff like that also seemed to dislike rich guys accepting girls with no family money as their mates. Lana was definitely the type.

"Careful! That crystal vase is extremely expensive!" said Lana patronisingly.

"It says it's for her," I said indignantly.

The vase contained three dozen long-stem pink roses and the huge heart shaped tag read *"For Jillian, my mate, my love, my life."*

Lana scowled at the note and said, "I wasn't talking to you, dear-heart. Know your place."

Whoa. Before I could angrily protest, Noah came into the kitchen. Lana beamed at him. "Oh, Alpha..."

"Just a moment, Lana," said Noah quickly and to Lana's outrage, he grabbed my hand and marched me into the pantry shutting the door behind us.

"I told you not to come!" snapped Noah.

His eyes were black. This was ridiculous.

"Jillian is my best friend and Chet is her mate," I said simply. "You're a stranger who won't even admit that we spoke once! Why should I listen to you?"

Noah frowned as if truly upset by my words. He quickly recovered.

"I'm your alpha!" He said.

Oh yeah. There was that. He wasn't officially Alpha yet though. I sighed, tired of being scolded by everyone.

"Ok, Alpha, I'm sorry. It won't happen again..."

Noah's expression softened. He grabbed my hand. His thumb began stroking my wrist. He sighed.

"You don't have to call me alpha," he murmured.

"But I have to obey you so I may as well start now," I said, fatigued.

Noah got annoyed.

"Fine! Suit yourself!" He snapped.

He stormed out of the pantry. I sauntered out, sighing to myself already not looking forward to my birthday tomorrow. I knew I would not get any presents. Granny was flat out broke. Jillian might get me something even though I told her not to waste her time or money on me.

Lana begrudgingly led me to the room I'd be staying in. I could hear screams and giggles outside. Jonah, Noah and Angelique were playing in the lake. The boys were in their swim trunks, their perfect abs were on display and glimmering in the sun. Angie was in a sparkly gold bikini. I had to admit I was envious of her confidence and her sample size figure. I felt self conscious about my body. I was curvy. Jillian, who was almost as skinny as Angie, always lamented the fact that I had the boobs and hips that she wanted. I would happily trade figures with her honestly. My peers habitually teased me and insinuated that I was fat though I had a normal weight for my height.

I changed into my bathing suit: a black bikini with puff sleeves and high waisted bottoms. I put a kimono on over it and sat at the window seat on the landing of the stairs. I could see the dock and the lake from here. Angie was on Jonah's shoulders and Jillian was kissing Chet while they cuddled in a beach blanket on the shore. The water and lakeside were gorgeous and pristine like something from a post card. Noah splashed Jonah and Angie with water and then he splashed Jillian who retaliated. I couldn't go out there like this. I sighed.

"Why so glum?" Said a voice.

I looked up. Isaiah. Ugh. The meanest of the Quads. I ignored him.

"Hey! I'm talking to you!" He said.

Chapter 3

I was compelled to look at him. "Didn't you tell me to fuck off the other day?"

He smirked and chuckled a little as though that were funny.

"I was really drunk when I said that!" He admitted.

That was no excuse. He sat on the sill next to me. I felt his eyes trailing over my form. I instinctively covered up before he could insult my body.

"What're you hiding for?" He asked.

"I just... I know you guys don't want me here but I came to support my best friend ok. She's always been there for me and she's really excited to find her mate," I explained.

"I never said I didn't want you," Isaiah said.

"Here?!" I added the missing word for him.

He didn't say anything in response to that.

"You're turning eighteen tomorrow. We gotta stay up till midnight and ring it in," said Isaiah matter-of-factly.

"Um, ok," I said cautiously, remembering what Noah had said about Angie using this opportunity to try to humiliate me.

"Ok," said Isaiah getting up and holding out his hand.

I tried to shake the hand but he hoisted me up and pulled me out of the house.

"Hey, n-no please I can't swim!" I cried.

Noah looked up worried. Angie looked pissed off to see me actually here, encroaching on her quadruplet quality time. Jillian cheered when she saw me and Chet grinned. Isaiah pulled me along the dock. The dive from here would be into very deep water. He pulled me right in with him. I screamed and swallowed mouthfuls of water, spluttering. Before I could thrash about too much, Isaiah had me in his arms, bridal style, while he treaded water with me. I kept my arms around his neck, holding on for dear life. Noah was staring at me, his eyes displayed anger and something else...

"Put your legs around me. It'll be easier," said Isaiah.

I did as I was told without thinking too much about it. I faced him with my arms around his neck and my legs around his waist. He swam with me this way quite effortlessly. I was staring straight into his green eyes.

"I like your bathing suit... how it has little frilly sleeves," chuckled Isaiah.

"I don't like my arms," I blurted out. "So I always wear sleeves."

"What's wrong with your arms?" He asked.

"They're huge!" I cried.

Why was I telling him all these things? How was I comfortable with the meanest Quad?

He snickered. Here came the insult.

"You're tiny. You're insane. What're you talking about?" he chuckled. The insult wasn't very insulting. Tiny? Was *he* insane?

I suddenly became aware of his body and mine. I was a foot shorter and he must have weighed at least a hundred pounds more than me but it was all lean muscle. He was broad shouldered. His biceps and triceps were bulging. I could feel his rock hard abs against my soft tummy under the water. His chest was hard. He caught me staring and laughed. He flexed his pecs like those male exotic dancers did and I blushed deeply. His arms were around my waist. I wiggled in his grip a bit. That was when I felt it, a huge hard bulge poking me nestled against my bikini bottoms. I gasped and Isaiah smirked.

"See, I'm not lying," he said. "I like what I see." His voice was husky. It made my stomach clench. Heat ignited in my lower belly.

Isaiah rocked his hips against me a little.

"Don't," I protested weakly.

He stopped immediately to my relief. I didn't wanna be used by him and his brothers and go back to school on Monday feeling like a stupid slut.

"May I ask why?" He said rather politely.

I said the only thing I could think of. "I'm saving myself for my mate."

"So you're a virgin?" He said, his green eyes darkening.

"You knew that already. Can't you smell it?" I asked.

Alphas and other powerful wolves could smell if a she-wolf was mated or unmarked.

"Yeah I can smell it," he said softly.

Water splashed in my face. I squealed. I had been so engrossed in my strangely captivating and intimate conversation with Isaiah I had forgotten we were here with others. Angie had splashed me. She tossed her head back laughing.

"Clingy much?" She said snidely at my embrace of Isaiah.

He was still holding me in the deep cool water and didn't seem willing to let me go anytime soon. He had me thinking all kind of dirty thoughts I usually didn't think, like what would he say about my other body parts. What part on me would be his favourite? Which part of him would be my favourite? I already had a strong contender making itself known as it continued to poke against my bikini bottoms. My core started to get wet in anticipation of him. Oh no. This was embarrassing. Everyone would smell my body overreacting to Isaiah's touch. I bit my lip.

"Hey! Come on, come over here, we're having a splash war," said Angie, just as bossy as when we were kids.

She *knew* I couldn't swim.

"She can't swim!" called Isaiah.

Chapter 3

"So both of you come here then!" Angie practically growled.

"Fuck off!" Called Isaiah, eliciting laughter from Jonah.

Maybe, that was his catch phrase or something. I had taken things so harshly the other night.

"Sorry," I whispered to him, blushing.

"For what?" He asked, looking truly confused.

"For spoiling your fun," I said sheepishly, frowning.

He had to babysit me because I couldn't swim. He chuckled.

"You *are* my fun, you little idiot," he said.

"Hey!" I squealed at being called idiot.

"What?" Growled Isaiah, making me tremble as he pressed his nose against mine and allowed his eyes to turn black.

He edged even closer, his eyes half-closed and his lips parted,

"Don't kiss me," I whispered.

"Why not, Star?" He whispered.

He knew my nickname.

"I'm saving it all for my mate," I said, using the same excuse.

"Damn, that's one lucky mate!" growled Isaiah playfully.

I giggled. I stayed like that for a very long time just holding onto Isaiah, enjoying the water and the feel of his body. Something hit me. How did I not think of this before?

"Hey, you probably have a girlfriend?" I said sadly.

"No," he snickered.

"What about Angie?" I asked.

"She's Jonah's whatever the hell they are. They don't use labels or whatever," he muttered.

So, she did not have a claim on all four of them. She was barely holding on to her claim of the one. I smiled. I didn't care what Noah said. I was already here and like Isaiah said I should ring in my birthday and have some fun!

Chapter 4

Almost Saturday 12th September, 2020.

Star's Point of View

After Isaiah and I had gotten so close in the lake, I found myself avoiding him. The worst part was that he didn't seem to mind. He carried on as if everything were normal. Isaiah was ignoring me while I ignored him. Noah was still furious with me. Jonah and Angie were making out on the couch which always made me feel nauseated. Elijah was helping Isaiah ignore me. They did a few shots together. Werewolves were very good at holding their liquor so they were calm even after about five shots each. It was minutes to midnight. Jillian kept glancing at me from over Chet's shoulder. There was music playing now in the huge living room and Chet and Jillian, and Jonah and Angie were slow dancing to it.

Elijah offered me a shot. I had never actually drank alcohol before.

"I don't think she drinks," said Isaiah, eyeing me.

I ignored him and took the shot Elijah was handing me. I downed it and made a face. It burned! I coughed a little and sniffed.

"Whoa," was all I could say.

Elijah laughed. Isaiah grinned.

"Why do people drink? It's awful," I said.

"Do another," instructed Elijah.

Noah was looking at me disdainfully. I narrowed my eyes at him and downed another. I felt a little different after this one, less uptight. I wanted one more. Elijah poured me another one. I downed my third shot. I giggled. Jillian was grinning at me.

Chapter 4

Suddenly, Lana appeared, wheeling a huge purple birthday cake into the room with sparklers on top. The cake had seven round tiers all covered in edible flowers. Lana begrudgingly placed it beside me. The group started singing Happy Birthday to me. I smiled and swayed a little, feeling tipsy. It was minutes to midnight. I cut the cake with Jillian. We fed each other cake. It was delicious.

My heart started to race. I ran outside before the stroke of midnight. I could hear Jillian calling me, telling me to wait. I ran to the lake. The moon was high in the sky. Werewolves no longer needed a full moon, or any moon really. It was midnight. I screamed. My bones cracked in and out of place, reshaping themselves. I sank onto my knees. I put my palms on the cool floor. I was on all fours as fur sprouted all over me. It hurt! I tried to scream but all that came out was a howl that cut through the night. I had shifted.

I ran through the nearby woods as if on the wings of the wind. It was exhilarating. I felt like a shadow, like a ghost, a phantom of the night. Untouchable. I belonged there in the woods in the dead of night. I was unafraid. Everything was clear and sharp. Every smell and sight was easily discernible. I breathed in the smell of the forest flowers and the bark of trees and the fertile earth. I sighed happily. My wolf was satisfied. She caught another smell. It was intense and nearby. I ran towards it. It was delicious. A strange musky smell, clean and sharp and distinctly masculine. It made my mouth water. I came back to the house. I shifted. Shit! I did not have clothes to put back on. I had shredded them when I shifted. My clothes were upstairs in the room I was staying in.

I hugged myself and walked towards the house hoping to see Jillian. I passed by the outdoor pool. The jacuzzi was nearby. The autumn air nipped at me. I wondered if anyone was in the water. I would welcome some warmth. The delicious smell was growing stronger. I found the source. Jonah! He was in the jacuzzi and he smelt wonderful.

Mate.

My wolf stirred and then she howled in pain. Jonah was holding Angie. They were locked in a fiery embrace. I stifled a sob but the strangled noise that escaped me disturbed them. They broke apart. Jonah stared at me like he'd never seen me before. Angie looked at me incredulously.

"Put some clothes on!" She said snidely. "No one wants to see that."

I hugged myself tightly.

"Star," said Jonah, his voice hoarse. He was heartbreakingly handsome. I didn't want to look at him anymore. I ran into the house.

"Star!" He ran after me.

"Where are you going?" Cried Angie, following Jonah.

I could hear both of their wet footsteps slapping against the tiles as I ducked inside. I ran up the staircase. Isaiah was on the landing, sitting on the window seat where we had first properly talked earlier. He looked up at me. His eyes widened. He had a knowing smile on his face. I dashed by him. He looked just like Jonah and smelled just as wonderful. I needed to get away from him too. I ran to my room and shut the door just in time to lock Isaiah out. He banged on the door.

"Star! Star! Come on! Just get dressed and come out ok! I'm waiting right here. Couldn't you tell earlier? Didn't you feel something... between us? Come out, Baby! Why're you hiding?" Isaiah called at the door.

I breathed a sigh of relief when he stopped talking and moved away from the door. I quickly got dressed in whatever was closest, cotton underwear, a pink nightgown with short sleeves and a fuzzy pink jacket over it. I put on some socks. I really didn't care how I looked anymore. I just wanted to go to bed so this trip could be over soon.

"Star, it's Jonah. Look, I'm sorry. Let's talk," said Jonah from the other side of the door. Isaiah was back as well.

"Sorry?" He said to his brother. "What did you do to her?" He snarled.

"Nothing," replied Jonah. "She saw me with Angie."

I heard scuffling noises like the brothers were shoving each other. More voices. Elijah and Noah were there now too. Jillian came to the door with Chet. Angie's voice rang out the loudest.

"You guys are fighting over that loser? Seriously?" Asked Angie.

I heard a growl that I recognised immediately as Isaiah. I was suddenly able to tell them apart easily.

"Star, can we talk, honey?" Came Jillian's voice.

"No, please, not right now," I said, through tears, my voice cracking.

I knew I was being childish but the sight of Jonah and Angie had shattered me without warning. I did not think I could feel so deeply. I hardly knew Jonah. A small part of me wished I could let Isaiah come in, maybe even Noah, just to talk for a bit. Suddenly the door opened. Noah! He had the key.

"Noah!" Chastised Chet, for using the master key. "Not cool, bro."

Noah walked up to me. We stared at each other.

"You should leave," said Noah. Huh.

"WHAT?" Snarled Isaiah, storming into the room and grabbing me.

Tingles shot through me where he touched me. He put me behind him and faced his brother. Elijah entered and stood in front of me too.

Jonah came in and stood with Noah.

"She can go and we'll talk about this later," said Jonah, stamping on my already shattered heart.

Chapter 4

I gripped Isaiah's elbow and his warmth and the feel of his skin comforted me immediately.

"She's our mate. She's not going anywhere. Let your whore leave," said Elijah, referencing Angie.

Jonah growled. He was defending Angie. My heart throbbed.

"I'll go!" I managed to say. "It's clear you guys don't want me."

"How exactly is that clear, Princess? I've just asked my brother to get rid of his whore so you'll stop crying!" Said Elijah, cupping my face in his huge warm hands.

Warmth spread through me. He used his thumbs to wipe my tears.

"Baby, relax, Elijah and I are not gonna let you walk out of here," cooed Isaiah, his hand finding my lower back as he drew me close.

Their warmth was so intoxicating, I couldn't pull away.

Noah and Jonah were gazing at me intensely. Noah shook his head as if to clear it.

"Inviting her here was a mistake," said Noah.

Isaiah shoved him. Jonah grabbed the scruff of Isaiah's shirt. Elijah shoved Jonah away from Isaiah. The four brothers were at odds, the elder two against the younger two.

"Noah, I thought we were ok," I said in a small voice.

He had been the first of them to be nice to me.

His face softened. "Star, I'm doing what's best for you, trust me."

"And I get that Jonah wants to be with Angie," I said, sniffling. I wasn't an idiot.

"It's not that," said Jonah softly.

"Ugh! Would you and Noah just get the fuck out of here? You're upsetting our mate. She's not leaving tonight. Over my dead body!" Said Elijah.

His elder two brothers glared at him but it was two against two. Angie pulled Jonah away. I winced but Isaiah held me tightly. I glared at Noah. I felt betrayed by him. He sighed and kept his eyes on me until the very last moment when he shut the door.

I burst into tears, bitter sobs making my body shudder. It was all too much and all so sudden. I was confused about so many different things. I knew with multiples they all had to accept you for you to be fully marked and mated especially as they were alphas and would need to agree upon a luna. Isaiah and Elijah immediately wrapped themselves around me. Somehow, I ended up under the covers in my bed sandwiched between two of the Quads. I cried into my pillow while they massaged my shoulders and back, ran their fingers through my hair, and kissed my tear-streaked cheeks and my marking spots, making me shiver. Their body heat and scents soothed me. Sleep came quickly

Chapter 5

Saturday 12th September, 2020.

Star's Point of View

I woke up entangled with Isaiah and Elijah. My right leg was over Elijah's waist and his head was nestled in my bosom. Isaiah was spooning me from behind. His arm was over me and his face was buried in my hair as if he'd been sniffing me whole night. It was late Saturday morning so it was still my birthday. Most of my birthday was before me actually. I sighed.

I would need to make lists to keep up with all these mates. It was a good thing I was a journal fanatic with a decent stationery collection that I literally could not afford. I would use every dollar that wasn't spent on food on pretty notebooks especially if I could get them on sale. Here was what I knew for sure:

Isaiah - the youngest. He definitely wanted me. He must have sensed our mate bond early on the day before my birthday when we "swam" together.

Elijah - the second youngest. His desire for me was sudden but strong. He was the most impulsive one. I could tell by his drinking habits and how he could go from sneering at me at the party to fighting his elder brothers over me with nothing in between. He was one of those alphas who wanted their mate. End of story. No questions asked. He even called Jonah's non-mate girlfriend "his whore". Alphas who were really pro mate thought other relationships were basically pointless.

Noah - the second eldest. The most confusing one. He was the first to be nice to me without reason and now that he had an excuse to interact with me, he wanted nothing to do with me. He seemed to have mysterious reasons for not wanting me around at all even as a friend. He said it was for my own good so he was the one with secrets.

Jonah - the eldest. He had the most straightforward reason for not wanting me: Angie, my evil cousin and his girlfriend.

I wrote my notes down and wondered what to do. Part of me wanted to get dressed and peace out, but that would upset Isaiah and Elijah who were actually already fighting for me. This was horrible to admit but my Granny and I were on the brink of of being destitute, and my mates were billionaires. Maybe I should at least see if I could help my grandmother. I knew she couldn't afford groceries this month so I wasn't sure what she was eating. The neighbours checked on her from time to time. I felt a pang of guilt. I was here sobbing over not having all four of my mates but I did have two and food and shelter. My grandmother needed me.

Elijah stirred. The impulsive one.

"Princess?" He said groggily.

I blushed.

"Um, yeah," I murmured.

He sat up. "Hey, birthday girl!"

He looked at me so intensely. His green eyes lit up. His light brown hair was ruffled. He looked so damn cute.

He frowned looking really sad all of a sudden. My wolf whimpered.

"Princess," he paused looking ashamed. "My brothers were such assholes to you last night and ugh I was an asshole to you at that party earlier this week. I didn't get you anything for your birthday. I didn't know you were my mate!"

Elijah looked heartbroken.

"It's ok," I mumbled.

I hadn't been expecting anything. In fact, I'd actually been expecting nothing.

"Let's go shopping as soon as the malls open!" He said.

I had a thought. "Um, do you have your own car?"

He laughed. "Several," he said, grinning.

His face fell suddenly.

"Fuck! We carpooled with my dick of a brother Noah. Lemme just message my chauffeur to come get us," said Elijah.

"There's no need!" Said Isaiah, startling us.

We had not realised he was awake. He blinked, stretching.

Chapter 5

"I had my car brought here last night after the fight," said Isaiah, looking embarrassed too. "Baby, I'm so sorry about that, and I didn't get you anything either and I was a huge asshole at the party too," mumbled Isaiah, rubbing the back of his neck.

How do I ask for groceries for my birthday? Ugh. My cheeks burned with shame. Their elder brothers were probably already inclined to think I was a gold digger or something just because I was poor.

The guys got up and kissed my cheeks in unison: Isaiah on the right and Elijah on the left. I should approach them respectfully as Alphas. That was the sort of thing alphas did for any struggling member of the pack. I wouldn't ask for it as a birthday present. That would be weird.

"Alpha Isaiah and Alpha Elijah, I..." I began but Elijah cut me off.

"Oh my God!" He exclaimed, his face falling. "You're rejecting us!"

Huh! He rushed over to me and literally got on his knees. Isaiah did too.

"Baby, don't go! Noah and Jonah are being cagey now but they'll come around! You'll be our Luna, and everything will be fine! I know I was such a jerk before. I'm so sorry for telling you to fuck off. I'm just crass like that when I'm partying. I'm gonna make it up to you! You cannot leave! I would die! I'm gonna kill my brothers for this!" Isaiah said all of this so quickly and took my hands in his.

"Everything he said times two!" Added Elijah kissing the knee that was closer to him. "I have always wanted my mate. I know it's corny but it's true! Don't let my elder brothers scare you. And don't worry about Angie! She's a ho. She'll survive trust me! Plus, do you think she'd reject her mate when she finds him for Jonah? No! Jonah is not thinking this through! He's gonna regret it and come crying to you! He cries you know! He's the eldest but he's the most sensitive!" Said Elijah without pausing to take a breath.

I was in shock at having two arrogant future alphas literally grovelling before me.

"I...it's ok... I...I'll stay but um, I just have to do some groceries but I uh forgot my wallet," I managed to lie halfheartedly.

Elijah took his wallet out and produced his credit card, handing it to me. Isaiah gave me cash. I looked at it. It was a thousand dollars. What the fuck!

"I can go to the ATM for more! Take one of my cards too," said Isaiah, handing me another platinum credit card.

"Okay, I'm fine with this! Thanks!" I said quickly before they could give me anything else.

I ran out of the room. My hands were trembling. Then, like an idiot, I remembered I needed a ride. I sighed.

Jonah appeared in the hallway. He had rushed out of his room. Had he smelled me? He looked at me with wide eyes. His hair was ruffled and there was a hickey on his neck that I didn't remember being there yesterday! He gave me a guilty look. I glared at him coldly. Angie appeared, looking smug but her eyes looked tired. She put a hand on Jonah's shoulder, her fingers caressing his neck. I felt emboldened by Isaiah and Elijah and their very generous behaviour. They would defend me for sure. Noah entered the hallway as though he had been waiting too.

"You need to leave," Noah said, fixing me with a determined stare.

Elijah and Isaiah followed me out of the room. Isaiah growled at those words.

Jonah added, "Now! Sorry, Star."

"I am leaving!" I said boldly.

Jonah and Noah winced like I'd slapped them. Isaiah and Elijah looked heartbroken. Noah was eyeing the money and credit cards in my hands. I blushed but quickly recovered.

"Isaiah, Elijah and I have some business to attend to. We'll pack up my stuff and go, so you won't have to see me around, okay, Noah and Jonah. That should make you happy!" I snapped at them.

Elijah and Isaiah grinned, looking so relieved. Noah and Jonah both sighed.

"I'll explain later at school," mumbled Jonah.

"No need to explain to that low life," said Angie.

Jonah flinched but didn't defend me. Isaiah and Elijah weren't listening, they were just looking at me as though kinda turned on by my sudden sassiness.

"Yeah, later, but go now," said Noah sternly.

"There will be no later!" I pronounced.

Everyone gasped.

"You two stay away from me until I am ready to talk to you," I said to Noah and Jonah.

They looked crestfallen. Noah paled and Jonah's eyes looked glassy. I remembered what his brother had said about him being a cryer.

"Angie, my cousin!" I said.

She growled. The Quads looked shocked. I wasn't keeping that secret anymore.

"You stay away from me indefinitely!" I said.

She gasped and I flounced away. Isaiah and Elijah followed me.

I went back to my room and packed quickly. I put the money and credit cards in my little crossbody bag. I showered extremely quickly and put on a sundress. I put on some mascara, and I tried to fix my long loosely curled hair that I had neglected to detangle last night. I sighed and left the

Chapter 5

bathroom. I saw Elijah and Isaiah sitting on my bed which Lana had begrudgingly made. The guys looked so handsome in simple grey sweatpants and black T shirts. Their hair was still a little damp from their showers. I had the urge to finish drying it for them. The mate-bond was in effect so I would want to nurture and groom them whilst they would want to protect and put pups in me. The mate-bond was kinda sexist but we were part wolf so what did you expect?

"I can't believe our brothers would want you kicked out and on your birthday too!" Grumbled Elijah.

"That's okay, Elijah," I said brightly, wanting to at least be happy about the good side of this.

I had two boyfriends now essentially after having zero of them for my whole life. My wolf was angry though. She insisted I go immediately to try to entice my other two mates and break their resolve. She needed all four quadruples to feel complete. I placated her by telling her I'd take them back easily if they came to us. She was confident they would, and I was pretty sure they would not.

"Call me Eli," said Elijah. "Please don't ever call me Alpha again! You scared the shit out of me. I thought you were giving me your official rejection statement."

I smiled shyly and nodded. "Ok, Eli," I said.

Eli walked up to me. He towered over me. I could tell he wanted to kiss me but I wasn't ready. I wrapped my arms around his waist and buried my face in his shirt. Tingles ran through me. He massaged my back and held me close.

"You can call me Zaya instead of Isaiah," said Isaiah. "Let's get out of here. I don't wanna be around those pricks right now," Zaya said, taking out his car keys.

I followed Eli and Zaya down the stairs. I spotted Jillian and Chet at the breakfast table.

"Jillian!" I screeched and launched myself at her.

We hugged. Chet smiled. He came over and ruffled my hair and then pulled Jillian close to him.

"Thanks for inviting me Jillian and for the birthday cake. It was delicious. Chet thanks so much for having me. Your vacation home is lovely! I'm sorry to leave early!" I said.

"Leave early?" Chet repeated sounding confused.

"But why?" Whined Jillian. "Are you ok? Aren't you glad our mates are best friends?"

Jonah was looking at me from the breakfast table. Angie was massaging his shoulders. I tried not to look. Noah was staring at me. I was tired of covering for people who didn't give a shit about me.

"I would be but Jonah and Noah don't want me as their mate," I said blatantly.

Chet immediately got angry. Jillian was furious.

"So my best friend isn't good enough for you guys?" She huffed, folding her arms.

Noah looked defiant. Jonah looked guilty.

"Of course she's not. She's fat and poor," said Angie snidely.

That didn't even hurt anymore. I was already numb from Jonah and Noah crushing me.

"We never explicitly rejected you, Star!" Said Noah.

"Please call me Hannah, Alpha Noah. Star is an informal nickname my friends call me," I said with as much venom in my voice as I could muster.

Noah looked furious.

"That's enough!" Roared Jonah. "You will have respect for all four of us as your alphas and mates!"

"Jonah, what are you talking about? You don't want her as your mate remember?" Piped up Angie.

I wasn't gonna stand there so a guy who had a girlfriend already could tell me how much he didn't want me.

"I do respect you, Alpha Jonah. I'm leaving now," I said in a gentler voice.

I followed Eli and Zaya to the driveway. Zaya had a luxury vehicle too, but his was red not matte black like Noah's.

Jonah came running after me. Was there no end to this drama? Noah trudged along behind him.

"Star!" Jonah said, out of breath.

I lowered the backseat window.

"I'm not...we're not rejecting you. There's...it's complicated," Jonah said.

"Save it for Facebook profile, Jonah!" Yelled Zaya and he sped off before Jonah or Noah could say anything else.

Eli roared with laughter. They were both up front. I smiled at them in the rearview mirror.

"Hey, pretty princess," said Eli, looking back at me in a way that made heat flood my lower torso.

"I remember," said Zaya loudly as if he were narrating a story, "a young girl, of but seventeen, one day shy of her eighteenth birthday."

Eli grinned.

Zaya continued, "Who was saving herself for her mates down to her very first kiss."

I blushed deeply and avoided their gaze.

Chapter 5

Zaya drove really fast but both he and Eli seemed incredibly calm.

"She can only have one first kiss, Bro," said Eli.

"Oh, you can have her first kiss, Bro!" Said Zaya. "That's not the first I'm claiming. I'll be her first, alright." Zaya winked at me in the rearview mirror, switching from green to black eyes.

They quickly turned green again. He had such good control of his wolf to do that at will.

Eli laughed. "Stop, you're scaring her," he chuckled.

"Don't be ridiculous!" Said Zaya. "Our Luna is brave."

Zaya smirked and so did Eli.

My face was hot. I tried to look nonchalant. The younger two Quads were a lot wilder than their elder brothers. They were not the stiff snobs I was expecting. They were cocky but in a sort of fun way.

"Where to, princess?" Said Eli.

"Any grocery store, please," I said softly, still feeling a little out of sorts.

"God, you're so spoilt!" Snapped Eli suddenly.

I jumped then realised he was grinning. Zaya was laughing.

"When we said we'd take you shopping for your birthday, Baby, we meant like Dolce and Gabbana," chuckled Zaya.

"Yeah, not like butter and bread!" Exclaimed Eli.

They laughed. I giggled a little.

"Aww, so cute!" Said Eli doing the same thing Zaya had done where he flashed me his black eyes on purpose for a split second.

I was so amazed by this. I had been told the Quads were really powerful werewolves. Supposedly, they all had unique powers but that was part of the rumour mill. No one knew what powers they had for sure. There was also a rumour that the Quinn family was cursed. I could never get details on the curse though. Maybe, it was another stupid rumour, or, maybe, I just wasn't popular enough to be worth telling. I felt bold all of a sudden.

"They say your family is cursed at school!" I said, smiling at them slightly.

"Yeah the Quad curse," said Eli seriously. "Half of us were cursed to be assholes for all eternity."

Zaya burst into laughter.

"Only a beautiful virgin can break the curse with her tender love," Eli said.

"So I should give your brothers a chance then?" I said, grinning.

"No you break the curse by sleeping with the cooler brothers first!" Insisted Eli. "Princess, you need to pay attention when I'm telling you stories."

"You need to have respect for all of your mates and alphas, Star!" Roared Zaya, mocking Jonah's words from earlier.

Eli was beside himself with laughter, and I actually laughed too. A lot. I felt so much better. I couldn't believe how fun the younger two were. They were always huge groups of pretty girls laughing while they surrounded the younger two, but I assumed that was because they were rich and handsome not that they were actually funny. I guess I thought billionaire heirs didn't need humour, they had cash and credit. However, Zaya and Eli were the full package. They definitely offset my other two dreary mates nicely.

Chapter 6

Saturday 12th September, 2020.

Star's Point of View

Zaya pulled into a spot at the grocery store parking lot in one swift motion. He hopped out. I tried to get out too, but he locked the door with his remote. He stared at me, until I frowned and moved my hand away from the door. He then unlocked it and opened it for me. I got out and glared at him, but then I broke into a smile.

"You don't open doors, Baby, you just be sexy and cute. See, there, you have two jobs already," said Zaya.

"Poor Princess, working hard for the money," Eli half-sang.

They seemed to be in a great mood after having found their mate, despite their elder brothers not being on board. I was worried grocery shopping would be awkward, but Eli pushed the cart and Zaya threw a lot of random stuff in the cart that he wanted me to try. I was a little worried about the lie that I had "forgotten" my wallet. I hoped they wouldn't expect me to pay them back as I saw the growing pile of stuff. They knew I was doing groceries for my grandmother.

"Our grandmother likes this! Yours might too!" Said Zaya, adding a bottle of top of the line champagne into the cart.

I grabbed his wrist.

"Hey, I... that's really expensive," I said, avoiding his eyes.

"Baby," breathed Zaya, against my forehead, ruffling wisps of my hair. He kissed the top of my head and ran his fingers through my tangled curls. "I know. It's a gift ok from me and Eli to your Granny so she'll like us."

I smiled.

"And she'll let us have her sweet little granddaughter's hand in marriage," said Eli nonchalantly.

Marriage?! I was not ready for that. Was I?

We finished grocery shopping. I couldn't even stand to look at the bill. I went in my purse for the cash or credit cards they had given me but Eli was already swiping a different card he had. They put the groceries in the car. I tried to give them back the credit cards and cash from before.

"That's for you to shop for your birthday, Princess, remember?" Said Eli.

I frowned, feeling guilty.

"You're upset cause we're asking you to pick out your own gifts and that's not thoughtful, I know. I promise we're gonna give you the kind of birthday surprises you deserve, ok, Princess?" Said Eli, looking at me, his green eyes wide.

Eli was always misinterpreting my reactions to things.

"Ok," I said softly.

I liked being called Princess by Eli and Baby by Zaya more than I was willing to admit. I did not want to ruin the fun but I had to ask.

"Why do you think your brothers don't want me?" I asked, looking at two of my mates. They looked at me with worried faces.

"I…I get it…if it's cause I'm not rich or fancy or, you know, popular at school," I said softly.

"Our brothers are not that dumb, Princess. I know they act like they are but they have more depth than that, trust me," said Eli.

I wanted to drop off the groceries right away but, if truth be told, I was embarrassed for the two alpha quads to see where I lived. It was not a sprawling mansion and they usually acted so pompous. I was worried I was about to be made fun of.

"I want to just drop of these groceries," I said meekly.

"Yeah, Princess, where to?" Said Eli.

I explained to Zaya and Eli how to get to my house. We pulled up in front of the small wooden cottage where I lived with my maternal Granny. We didn't have much but we had each other. I went up to the door and knocked.

Granny came to the door in her nightgown with rollers in her hair. She squeaked in surprise at seeing the two alphas behind me. She hurried back inside, slamming the door in our faces. After a minute or two, the door creaked open and Granny came into view again. This time, she was wearing a house dress and her hair was in a neat bun.

"Welcome, Alphas!" She said. "Please come in."

Zaya and Eli followed me inside.

Chapter 6

"Do excuse the mess, Alphas!" Exclaimed Granny.

The house was small but there was no mess. Everything was in its proper place.

"Granny, this is Isaiah and Elijah," I said, after my mates gave me pointed looks.

Granny looked shocked at me addressing the alphas so informally.

"And guys, this is Granny!" I said sweetly, gesturing towards her

Granny looked so confused.

"Zaya and Eli, do you mind getting the stuff?" I asked with a small smile.

The alphas raced each other to the car and started carrying armfuls of stuff inside the cottage. When they were done, they bear hugged my Granny just before we left.

"The alphas are your... friends?" Asked Granny incredulously.

"Um, no, they're my mates," I said softly, still feeling shy about it, especially as two of the Quads didn't want me.

That night, the two younger Quads insisted that I sleep near to them in their private suite. I spent a ridiculous amount of time changing and fixing my hair and makeup. I was so nervous to have a sleepover with them even though I had fallen asleep between them before. Their private suite at the school was shared by all four of them. Each had his own bedroom and bathroom, but there was a shared living room area, a library to study in, and common kitchen and dining areas. The rooms were so lavishly decorated, I was afraid to touch anything.

"We didn't even get a chance to take you shopping properly today!" Exclaimed Eli.

I was sitting on his bed hiding in his room because I had heard Jonah's and Angie's voices. Jonah was laughing and Angie was giggling. I felt sick to my stomach. I didn't want to have to see them together so I remained hidden.

"It's time for dinner, Baby," Zaya said.

"Um, may I eat in here?" I asked politely.

"Uh, wouldn't you rather be comfortable outside?" Asked Eli, raising his brows.

"I'm comfortable inside," I said meekly.

They both sighed.

"You can't avoid Jonah forever, Princess, he's our brother and he's your mate whether he's being an ass about it or not. The wolf bond is eternal," Eli said.

I grumbled inwardly but smiled outwardly and went to get ready for dinner. I entered the huge dining area. There was a crystal chandelier overhead and a huge centrepiece: a crystal vase filled with white and pink roses. The table and chairs were carved from black wood. Eli pulled out a chair for me. I sat stiffly, keeping myself from locking eyes with Angelique at all costs.

Jonah was at the opposite end of the dining table. Angie was in his lap. Following my entrance, Jonah tried to put Angie in her own chair but she had refused, keeping her arms locked around his neck. I rolled my eyes.

"What's your problem, Star?" Sneered Angie.

I didn't answer. Eli and Zaya glared at her. Just then, Noah walked in, dressed for dinner. He seemed shocked to see me. I sighed inwardly. I wasn't sure how much more of this I could take. Eli and Zaya sat on either side of me in very close proximity. Servers came out in their uniforms and brought the first course, which looked and smelled amazing, but I couldn't enjoy it. I had a few bites before I gave up.

Angie kept nuzzling Jonah which was annoying. I had a thought. Two can play at that game. Eli had left for fencing practice, and Noah had gone to study in the Quads 'private library, so it was just Angie and Jonah, and me and Zaya.

I climbed into Zaya's lap, catching him off guard. He smiled. He was clearly pleasantly surprised. I leant my forehead against his, cupping his face in my hands and brushing my nose against his. I felt my heart flutter as I looked into his dark green eyes. I barely had time to drown in them before his lips were on mine, insistent but gentle. Tingles shot through me at every place that he touched and a heat arose in my lower belly. I moaned a little into his mouth, parting my lips just long enough for him to slip his tongue inside. He explored my mouth gently as he tightened his hold on me. I tangled my hands in his silky hair while he gripped my waist. I pulled away when I felt myself becoming breathless. I was panting and so was he. I had honestly forgotten all about Angie and Jonah until I glanced across the table. Their faces were comical, mouths agape in total shock. I giggled, but Zaya silenced me with another more urgent kiss.

Chapter 7

Monday 14th September, 2020.

Star's Point of View

On Saturday night, I slept between Zaya and Eli in their deluxe private suite at our elite boarding school. Zaya and I had kissed earlier that night and Jonah had honestly seemed a bit jealous. I could not help but be smug about it. Being around Jonah and Noah too much was a little too depressing for me. It felt like I was being rejected over and over again. Thus, on Sunday morning, I told Zaya and Eli that I wanted to return to my normal dorm room with my best friend Jillian. They seemed sad, but they allowed it. Eli helped me carry my luggage from the trip from their suite to my dorm. It was so reminiscent of Noah helping me out on the first day. I felt a pang in my chest. Why did Noah hate me all of a sudden? What sort of Alpha was Jonah to not even consider giving his fated mate a chance? He still clung to Angie.

Monday finally reared its sleepy dreary head. I tumbled out of bed, tangled up in my covers. I grumbled to myself as I trudged into the bathroom. I showered slowly, brushed my teeth and dressed. I had never rolled up my skirt at the waist before like most of the she-wolves did, so that it would be shorter and sexier, stopping at mid-thigh. I usually wore my skirts just below the knees, as per regulation. I wore a loose shirt whereas other girls had their school shirts fitted. I usually wore my long curly hair in a bun and no makeup. I did wear perfume though. I couldn't get enough of the stuff. Eli had gotten me a designer perfume on Sunday as a late birthday present, along with an iPhone, because he wanted us to have the same phone, so we could play all the same games and be friends on all the same apps. He said those were "the first two" of my gifts, but I had insisted on no more gifts. Zaya had gotten me a yellow gold opal ring with a diamond band that he had insisted I wear on the ring finger of my left hand, my wedding finger. I supposed it was meant to be a promise ring, but I was shocked at how fast he wanted to move.

I looked at Jillian. She had woken up late and was scrambling to get ready. She put her strawberry blonde curls in pigtails and hiked her skirt up by rolling it at the waist so that it hit at her mid-thighs. Her shirt was fitted and she was wearing mascara, eyeliner, blush and a lip stain. She looked really cute.

"Chet is a lucky guy!" I exclaimed.

"So are the Quads, though Jonah and Noah are jerks," grumbled Jillian. "You need my help. We need to make them squirm."

"What do you mean?" I asked, looking at my opal ring sparkling on my finger.

Zaya had made me promise to never take it off not even to shower. It was comfortable so I agreed. He claimed he had payed a high witch to enchant it so it would cast a protection circle around me. He was probably just joking. Zaya and Eli joked all the time.

"Just, trust me, ok?" Said Jillian.

I nodded. She grinned.

Jillian made me wear my hair down. She rolled my skirt at the waist, making it much short. I rolled it back down a little so that it would be just an inch or two above my knees. She pursed her lips at me, clearly annoyed. I grinned sheepishly. She fixed the skirt again, making it even shorter. She gave me one of her fitted shirts. Thankfully, she gave me the loosest one she owned, which was still fitted, but not too tight. I had some wiggle room. She made me change out of my loafers and into some high-heeled Mary Janes. I hoped I wouldn't fall on my face in front of the whole class. She did my makeup similar to hers. I looked in the mirror and smiled. Wow. I actually felt pretty.

"Thanks," I said sincerely.

She shrugged. "Let's go!"

We were late due to my last-minute makeover. I walked into the classroom to a chorus of whispers. People were talking about me. News that I might be the fated mate of the Quadruplet Alphas had spread. Girls stared at me with envy in their eyes. Others smiled and waved as if we had always been friends. Guys who had never noticed my existence winked at me. The seats in class were on rising rows like a movie theatre so that the last row was the highest up and the front row was the lowest. I spotted the Quads sitting in their usual middle row, dead centre of the class. Angie was sitting next to Jonah. He had his arm around her but was staring at me.

Chapter 7

Noah was staring too, or, perhaps, glaring was the right word. Ugh! What was his problem? Eli and Zaya grinned at me. They had saved me a seat between them in the same row as their brothers, Angie and a few other snotty popular pretty people.

The teacher had not noticed that Jillian and I were late as his back was turned while he wrote on the board. He had not taken attendance yet. His name was Mr. Damocles. He was the strictest teacher at the school. His wrath was legendary. He was average height for a werewolf which was still a bit tall for humans. He was fit and slender. He had dark hair, hazel eyes and a ruddy complexion. He usually covered his two sleeves of tattoos with blazers and shirts. He taught history and he also coached rugby at the school. Jillian quickly and quietly walked up the stairs to the middle row with the Quads and sat next to Chet who was on the other side of Jonah. I started up the stairs when Angie cleared her throat loudly. Mr Damocles looked around, frowning, and spotted me. He was livid.

"Late, Miss...remind of your name," he muttered.

"Star," said Angie, smiling.

"Thank you, Angie," said Mr Damocles.

Angie was always in his good graces. He favoured her.

"Not only are you late, Miss Star, but you are also inappropriately dressed. That uniform is not regulation!" He snapped.

Angie was dressed the same way, as was Jillian, and around ten of the fifteen girls in class today.

"Do you enjoy making a spectacle of yourself, MISS STAR, hmmm?!" He bellowed, making me tremble.

The room was silent and tense. I held back tears.

"Clearly, you like attention!" He growled, slamming his long ruler on the desk and making me jump.

"I'm...s-s-sorry, M-mis-," I began.

"SPIT IT OUT!" bellowed Mr Damocles, making me flinch and shut my eyes tightly.

"That's enough," demanded Jonah, the eldest alpha.

No one dared to defy him, not even teachers. Only the other three younger alphas could ignore his commands. Mr Damocles stiffened, shocked at Jonah defending me. The class actually gasped in unison. Angie scowled. She was seething. Even I was extremely surprised.

"Let's move on," said Mr Damocles curtly. "Take your seat, Miss Star."

I still hesitated a little, not sure if I wanted to sit with the Quads. My cheeks burned with shame. I spotted Zaya and Eli motioning for me to come up the stairs.

"You know what, never mind, Miss Star, kindly leave my class," said Mr Damocles, losing his patience again.

Everyone gasped. All four of my mates stiffened.

"That's bullshit!" Said Zaya.

"Excuse, me, future Alpha Isaiah, would your father approve of this behaviour and language?" Asked Damocles.

Before I could hear the rest of the argument, I just left the class, sighing. I went to the nearest girls 'bathroom to cry. I felt so embarrassed. There was a knock on my stall door. Huh? I opened it hesitantly.

Jonah?

"Hey," he said, gazing at me intensely.

He took out a handkerchief and dried my tears.

"Damocles is a jerk, ok," said Jonah.

So are you! I thought, but "Ok," was all I mumbled out loud.

"You ok?" Asked Jonah.

I shrugged.

"Did Zaya get in trouble?" I asked.

"No, Damocles isn't crazy. Zaya is Dad's favourite actually," Jonah said matter-of-factly.

He did not seem bothered by that fact.

"Zaya is your favourite too, huh?" He asked.

Now, he sounded really jealous. His green eyes darkened a little. I moved to walk away, but he grabbed my arm, pulling me back to him, flush against him.

"Hey!" I said furiously. "Go aw..."

He silenced me with his lips. They came crashing down against mine. I squealed in surprise but my wolf was elated. I moved my lips against his instinctively. He grabbed the backs of my thighs and lifted me easily, hurtling back into the stall and pressing me into the wall. Heat was coursing through me. I could feel his muscles hard and taut under his shirt. I could feel the huge bulge in his pants pressing against me. He nipped my bottom lip, making me gasp, so that he could slide his tongue into my mouth. I came to my senses. I kneed him in the groin. He dropped me and stumbled backwards.

"Argh!" He yelled. "What the fuck, Star!"

I slapped him, like those girls who got kissed by cowboys in westerns.

His face barely moved an inch but he flashed me angry black eyes.

"I'm the Alpha *and* the eldest! How dare you?" He snarled.

"How dare you kiss me without warning like that, and while your girlfriend, my cousin, is back in class waiting on you?" I shrieked indignantly.

He was a gross person, but he was a great kisser honestly. He smirked.

Chapter 7

"As if you don't want me," he said.

Ugh!

"I really, really don't!" I snapped, brushing past him.

"You'll regret walking away from me," he warned.

"I'm no one's sidepiece!" I snapped.

"Star," he protested, looking hurt. "You're not my sidepiece. You're my mate."

"So how come Angie gets to be your real girlfriend and all I get are scraps?" I yelled.

"Because I don't really care about her," he mumbled. "It's a douchebag move, but I can't be public with you. You'll get hurt."

"Yet your younger brothers accept me," I muttered.

"They don't know what Noah and I know. You can't have all of us until..." he began, trailing off.

"Until what?" I prompted.

I couldn't have all of them? Regardless of what the issue was, there was no need for him to flaunt Angie in my face.

"Excuse me? Until what?" I asked sternly.

"Don't you ever slap me again. And keep your voice at a reasonable volume when you talk to me! Understood, mon ciel étoilé?!" Said Jonah in an indecipherable tone.

I had no idea if he were serious or not, angry or playful, displeased or pleased.

"I won't slap you so long as you don't grab me like that," I said softly, wanting to let bygones be bygones.

I knew the Quads 'mother was French. I wondered what the French he had used meant. It sounded like a term of endearment. My heart fluttered. My wolf was excited but I felt disgusted with myself.

"May I go now?" I asked.

"Yes, Ma Louloutte!" He said, gesturing with his hand. "Après Vous!"

That definitely meant "after you" but I wasn't sure about the other word. It sounded like yet another term of endearment.

I stormed past him and opened the bathroom door to find myself face to face with Angie. She spotted Jonah just behind me. I glanced at him and realised there was some lipstick on his mouth and the collar of his shirt. I gulped.

Chapter 8

Monday 14th September, 2020.

Star's Point of View

Angie was livid. Before I could even explain myself, she tackled me. I shrieked and threw my hands up instinctively to protect my face. Angie rained her fists down on me. I could feel the impact of them on my arms as I blocked my face. She was screaming hysterically. All of this happened quickly, in just a few seconds at most. I was expecting to feel her fists connect with me again, but I felt nothing. The pressure of her on top of me was gone. I looked up confused. Jonah had grabbed her and pulled her off of me. She thrashed against him as he pinned her arms to her sides. She was kicking and screaming, flinging her legs up in the air. Her shoe flew off and hit me in the shoulder.

"ANGIE! STOP!" Roared Jonah in his alpha voice.

She was compelled to stop. She stilled in his arms, panting. He released her tentatively. She ran to get the shoe that had flew off. I scrambled away from her as she bent to pick it up.

"You're a disgusting slut!" She snapped at me.

I wanted to scream at her, to hit her back, or to yell the truth, that *he* had kissed *me*. I looked at Jonah, wondering if he would tell the truth. Angie put on her shoe and stormed away from me. She stopped at the doorway.

"Are you coming or not, Jonah?" Asked Angie.

Jonah stared at me then back at Angie,

"Jonah!" She shrieked.

"I..." said Jonah.

Chapter 8

"If you even have to second-guess it, then you belong with her," I told him.

She glared at me. Jonah's face fell. He offered his hand to me to help me up. I refused to take it, getting to my feet on my own and straightening my uniform.

"Star?" Said Jonah.

"I asked you to stop calling me that," I said softly, fighting back tears.

I couldn't hold them back anymore and they spilled out of my eyes and down my cheeks. Angie was still waiting at the door for Jonah.

"Angie, go ahead without me," said Jonah.

"If I walk out of here, we're over," she snapped.

Jonah sighed. "Just go," he said.

Her eyes widened. She stomped away on her heels.

Jonah approached me, but I dodged him. I ran out of the bathroom. I just wanted to get away from him and his crazy girlfriend, or ex girlfriend, whatever she was. It wasn't as though they hadn't broken up before. They'd been on-again off-again for almost a year. I walked quickly down the hallway. I probably looked as bad as I felt. I rounded a corner and walked right into Noah. He caught me by the shoulders so I wouldn't fall. His eyes softened when he saw that I had been crying.

"We need to talk," he said in a serious tone.

"Please, just leave me alone. I get it ok, you and Jonah don't want me as your mate, you just enjoying playing games and torturing me," I said, tears falling all over again.

"What?" Asked Noah. "No, of course not!"

He pulled out a handkerchief and started drying my eyes. I flinched because my cheeks felt raw. Angie must have caught me in the face once, before I blocked her.

"What happened?" Asked Noah, noticing my strange movement.

"Your brother's girlfriend attacked me in the girls 'bathroom because your brother chose to follow me in there! I never encouraged or instigated any of that!" I retorted.

Noah snarled. "Angie hit you?"

I nodded.

"And what did Jonah do?" Asked Noah.

"He pulled her off of me," I said, sniffling.

Noah held the handkerchief against my nose so I could blow my nose in it.

Just then, Jonah came up to us. Speak of the devil.

"Could you please stop running away from me, Ma Louloutte? I need to talk to you!" Said Jonah.

"Me too!" Exclaimed Noah.

41

I was tired of fighting with them. They wouldn't leave me be until they had said whatever it was they wanted to say.

"Ok," I said, wanting to get it over with.

"Where are Zaya and Eli?" I asked.

"They're in Visual Arts Class," said Noah as though that were obvious.

It dawned on me that I really knew nothing about the Quads, not even the subjects they took or what their schedules were like.

I followed the elder two. They led me to the gardens. Our school had beautiful sprawling grounds filled with flowering plants. There was a maze made of garden hedges with benches dotting the path every twenty-five feet or so. Jonah and Noah sat on a bench in the shade of the hedge. They motioned for me to sit between them.

"You ok?" Asked Noah, referencing the fight.

"No," I muttered.

It came out like a strangled little cry. Noah put an arm around me and drew me close. I tried to steady my breathing.

"I'm really sorry about Angie, Star!" Murmured Jonah, putting his arm around me too and burying his nose in my hair.

I wanted to slap both of their hands away, but their warmth helped me to relax.

"Hurry up," I found myself saying. "Just reject me and let's move on from this!" I snapped, folding my arms and pouting.

I knew I was being childish, but they were confusing, rude and impossible to please.

"I wonder if she has all this attitude with her Zaya and her Eli?" Asked Jonah, the jealousy evident in his voice.

"How can you be jealous when you have a girlfriend?" I demanded.

Were Noah and Jonah nuts?

"We... want to keep you safe... that's all," murmured Noah.

"Yeah," said Jonah, sighing.

"From what?" I asked.

"From our family curse," said Noah, lowering his voice and leaning in.

I rolled my eyes and got up to leave. Both Quads pulled me back to the bench.

"Please hear us out," said Jonah.

"You think we don't know how ridiculous it all sounds," said Noah, looking away from me.

He was staring at the nearby fountain. There was a stone mermaid perched in the midst of a bubbling pool. Water spouted from the mouths of several stone fishes surrounding her.

Chapter 8

"Long ago, our ancestor, Alpha Alto, was fated to a high witch named Georgianna," said Noah.

I resisted the urge to roll my eyes. Didn't all "curses" start with a "witch" and "long ago"?

"The witch, Georgianna, was discouraged from marrying the alpha, Alto, by our ancestors but they were in love. Defiantly, they got engaged. At their engagement feast, the younger brother of the alpha and next in line, Oleander, poisoned Alto with silver and wolfsbane in his wedding goblet rather than let a witch become luna. Losing a mate is the most painful thing, a fate worse than death. The witch was determined to make sure none of the sons of Oleander would ever experience true love or get to fulfil their mate bond. She put a curse on the entire bloodline to stop them all from finding love and happiness in the same way it was denied her," said Jonah.

I sighed.

"The curse begins from the moment the alpha lays eyes on his mate and future luna. The curse claims the lives of several people close to the luna until it is satiated enough, and once the luna is engaged, the curse claims her life," explained Noah.

"But in the story, the alpha dies not the luna?" I asked, not that it mattered because it was all bullshit anyway.

"If the curse were to claim the alpha and not the luna, she wouldn't be able to punish the same bloodline over and over again, because the last son would just die out. By killing his luna instead he's forced to settle for someone else just for the sake of continuing his bloodline and is successfully denied love for another generation," Jonah concluded.

"I get it, guys, I'm not your type. See, wasn't that easier and less ridiculous?" I snapped, getting to my feet.

"Star, please!" Said Noah, pulling me back onto the bench.

"That makes no sense! So how are your parents together, then?" I asked.

"Our father never married our mother. They did have us, but he avoided marrying her legally to spare her the final step. They just had a ceremony saying they loved each other. Most of her friends are dead and well she didn't have a big family to begin with," explained Jonah.

A chill crept through me. I thought of my grandmother all alone now. I looked at each of the elder Quads in turn, waiting for them to burst into laughter or smirk or snort.

"So what do you suggest I do then?" I asked.

Whether I believed it or not, it was no use continuing to avoid the inevitable. Obviously, the elder Quads had something in mind.

"We want to break the curse," said Jonah.

Chapter 9

Monday 14th September, 2020.

Star's Point of View

My head was spinning. Were my mates playing mind games with me? They wanted to break the curse. I wasn't even sure if the curse was real, and if they were being genuine. This was not a fun game, but I would play along.

"How do you plan on breaking the curse, might I ask?" I said, making sure they got the idea that I only half-believed them.

"By satisfying the witch somehow," Noah said.

I sighed. "How?" I asked, entertaining their nonsense.

"By marrying someone we don't love right off the bat and tricking the witch into thinking she's the one," said Jonah.

"You mean..." I gasped.

Was Jonah that callous? Would he sacrifice Angie like that?

"We're not gonna let the other girl get killed! We're just gonna use her as bait to trap the evil spirit of the witch, and then, the good witch we hired will purify the bad witch!" Explained Noah.

"Purify?" I said.

"She'll get rid of Georgianna's old evil energy, free her and free us," Noah explained.

I felt sick. First of all, Jonah was saying he would marry Angie and wanted his brothers to marry her too, to fool some ancient witch into thinking she was the one. Then, while risking my cousin's life, they would exorcise the old evil witch. They were both delusional: Noah and Jonah. Great, two of my four mates were psychotic.

Chapter 9

"It's been really great talking to you guys," I said, plastering a smile on my face and attempting to look serene. "Good luck," I said.

I tried to leave, but they both held onto me again. I wanted to scream, but I spotted Zaya and Eli coming up to us. Thank goodness.

"Zaya! Eli!" I cried desperately.

They were with me in a flash. Zaya wrapped his arms around me. Eli patted my head.

"Baby, we're so sorry! Damocles is such a jerk!" Zaya murmured into my hair.

"He's a douchebag, but he'll pay for this!" Eli said, sneering wickedly.

Zaya and Eli exchanged conspiratorial glances. Were all the Quads a bit villainous?

"Please, don't," I said.

I trusted Eli and Zaya to listen to me way more than the elder two. Eli and Zaya looked at each other.

"You mean that, Princess?" Asked Eli, his green eyes wide and worried.

"Really, Baby?" Asked Zaya, biting his lip nervously.

"Yes, I do!" I insisted.

"We can't undo it you see!" Eli admitted.

Zaya nudged him to be quiet. I spotted that!

"Can't undo what?" I demanded.

What had they done?

"We set up his car!" Eli said.

"To do what? Crash?" I asked, panicking.

"No, just to stall, that's all!" Said Zaya, stroking my cheek.

"Sorry, Princess, we should've checked with you first!" Eli said.

Zaya nodded fervently. I sighed. I hoped Damocles was ok.

Tuesday 15th September, 2020.

Damocles went to his car after class. That little Moon, or whatever her name was, irritated him. He got into his car and sped off. He was shocked Cloud, of all people, had been fated to the Quads. She was poor and seemingly weak.

"Her? Luna? Really?" He grumbled to himself.

The engine started to splutter. Ugh! This car was brand new! Couldn't it run on a quarter-tank of gas? How could it do this to him? This was not his day.

He went to get gas. He filled up the tank. The engine was still spluttering. It hadn't been the almost empty tank then? It was something else. He was truly frustrated now.

He parked at a diner where the waitress was young and cute and had huge...personality. Her huge personality bounced up and down as she walked briskly towards him. He stared, licking his lips. He ordered a milkshake.

"Squeezed not stirred," he specified.

She didn't like that joke. She frowned. He tried to tug on the strap of her apron playfully, but she huffed off. What a bitch!

He drank his milkshake and ate his heart attack burger with the double bacon, double cheese, fried egg, onion rings and three beef patties with a side of chilli cheese fries. He couldn't enjoy it. He was still pissed at that waitress. The other one was friendlier. Where was she? He payed the bill with exact change, no tip, and complained to the manager that he didn't wanna pay the service charge because she'd been rude to him. The manager ended up giving him the meal free and apologised. The waitress stormed off. Ha!

He went to his car. He drove a while. The sun was setting. The engine spluttered. Ugh! The car stopped dead in his tracks. Ian Damocles was so pissed. He got out. There was a gas station a few yards away. Awesome! He walked over. There was no-one there. It said there was a mechanic here on the sign. There was a sign saying the attendant would be back in ten minutes. He waited. Night fell. He had waited about twenty-five minutes. He was pissed when he saw the attendant. The attendant called the mechanic who must have been nearby. He showed up in five minutes and fixed the car. Wires had been cut! The car had been tampered with. Ian roared with anger. He sped off. The car was out of control all of a sudden. The radio turned on and off. The windshield wipers were moving haphazardly. The speedometer and the gas meter were reading wrong values. He didn't see the truck until it was almost too late. He swerved and ran off the road.

Jillian was shaking me awake. I screamed. I looked at the clock. Three in the morning.

"Star! Star! You were having a horrible nightmare!" Jillian said.

She hugged me. I was drenched in sweat.

"Damocles is dead," I said.

That must have happened last night, or in the wee hours of the morning!

She paled. "No! No, it was a dream!" Said Jillian.

"I saw it. I saw him get in a car accident, but it actually wasn't the Quads' fault. The car was like possessed. His first name is Ian! He's a jerk!

Chapter 9

He harasses women. I could feel what it was like to be him, like I knew what he was thinking!" I explained.

She stared at me. "Go to sleep, ok."

She got into bed with me. I was trembling. She made up a story and told it to me. It was about an emperor who was in love with identical twin concubines who even he could not tell apart, one good, one evil. I didn't get to hear the ending! I was so frazzled, but I was exhausted too! I fell into a fitful sleep.

I went to school a total mess. After third period, during recess, I was leaning on a random wall, with my eyes closed, when Eli grabbed me.

"Eli!" I said.

He crashed his lips against mine. He kissed me like his life depended on it! He had me feeling wide awake in no time. His hands roamed my body, making me moan and whimper. He planted hot open-mouthed kisses along my jaw and neck. He sucked my marking spot. I gasped and pushed him away.

"Princess, I never meant for that to happen, please believe me!" Eli said. "Please, please, please," he begged, kissing me in between every please.

My wolf was excited. I was worried.

"What happened?!" I demanded.

Eli was panting. He kissed me again, savouring it as though he wouldn't get to kiss me anymore.

"Princess, Damocles got in a car accident sometime last night, or, maybe, this morning. They found him after sunset dead," whispered Eli.

Chapter 10

Tuesday 15th September, 2020.

Star's Point of View

My dream had been real! What if Jonah and Noah had been telling the truth?! Was the curse real? It was supposed to claim people surrounding the intended Luna, but Damocles wasn't close to me? I had disliked him and he had disliked me. Any on-looker could have seen that unless…Jonah and Noah's weird plan was already working, and the curse was mistaking Angelique for their Luna. Angelique had certainly liked Damocles, and she had been his favourite! Could a curse be fooled?

My heart was racing. Eli kept me in his arms, holding me close to him. His warmth was so comforting. I was trying not to fall apart. If curses could be fooled, how come I had still been the recipient of the premonition? I wished Angelique and I were cool enough with each other that I could ask her if she'd had any nightmares recently. I sighed, trying to relax in Eli's arms.

I spotted Angelique! She was with Jonah and Noah. Ugh. My stomach did a somersault. Were they really going to pretend to be with her? I didn't think my heart could survive the Quads marrying her, even if it were under some guise to protect me. That was cruel towards Angelique also. Maybe, Jonah would tell me if Angelique had had any nightmares recently. Regardless, I had to try! I took a deep breath, and went over to their table!

"Star, wait!" Cried Eli.

Chapter 10

"I believe you! We'll talk more about it soon!" I said to Eli, giving him a peck on the lips just as Noah looked up from his seat.

I could feel Noah glaring daggers at me. Eli insisted on holding my hand, fingers interlaced, as we walked over to their table.

"Do you have a problem, Moon?" Noah snapped as I approached them.

Wow. We were back to rudely calling me the wrong name. He wanted to confuse the curse by making it seem as though the bond with me wasn't unanimous so I wouldn't seem like the true fated mate. What better way to play along than to totally ignore Jonah and Noah's very existence, and to not even tell them about it so their reactions would be legit? I felt like a bit of an evil genius with that plan. It helped me get a little revenge on the elder two, while playing it safe and not hurting the younger two. If I was pretending to not be their mate, I couldn't act jealous of Angelique. I took another deep breath, because she was in Jonah's arms.

"Angelique, I wanted to talk to you," I said as cheerfully as I could.

She looked at me like I was nuts, which is exactly what I had been expecting.

"Um, no thanks, Cloud," she snarled.

"I deserve that," I lied, keeping my tone even.

Angelique reacted to my even tone as though I had slapped her. Jonah looked dumbfounded and even Noah seemed upset.

"I'm really sorry about what happened in the bathroom! That was wrong of me! I overstepped a boundary, and I don't expect forgiveness, but hopefully, we can be civil. We are related after all!" I reminded her, ignoring the bad taste that fake apology left in my mouth.

Jonah's grip slackened around Angelique. She didn't seem to notice. She had assumed a smug expression.

"Perhaps," she said haughtily.

Eli was staring at me, mouth agape. Jonah looked really worried and Noah seemed confused. I decided to lay it on thick.

"Jonah and Noah are all yours," I said, feeling sick.

Angelique looked at me in disbelief, her eyes wide. Jonah flinched and removed his arms from around her entirely, but she still didn't notice. His eyes pleaded with me. Noah was taking slow measured breaths as though fending off a panic attack. My wolf was upset. She wanted to comfort and reassure her mates, but I knew they sorta deserved this.

"But Eli and Zaya are mine!" I said, making that clear.

I wasn't going to pretend to have no connection to all of the Quads. My wolf couldn't handle that. She relaxed a little but she felt incomplete.

Angelique shrugged. "Fine," she said, rolling her eyes.

"So, can we talk?" I reiterated.

"We just did!" She snapped.

I sighed. "About something else? Something private!"

"Not right now," she said with a gloating smile.

I reined in my snarling she-wolf.

"Cool. Later then?" I asked.

"Don't think we're friends now!" She scoffed. "You're still a broke fat looser!" She said.

I saw Jonah's eyes turn black, but he quickly regained his composure, turning them back to green. Wow. Angelique's hatred for me ran so deep! Why?! Was there something I was missing? Had our parents, who had been siblings, hated each other too? Her parents never helped out my Granny despite being loaded, while Granny and I were on food stamps half the time, but I had always assumed that was because she was my maternal grandmother, whereas my father was the one related to Angelique's mom. Eli was glaring at Angelique. He put his arms around me protectively. I tried to recover from the insult. I really needed Angelique to cooperate.

"Then, you shouldn't consider me a threat," I tried.

I instantly realised that I had touched a nerve.

"I don't!" She said, turning red and standing up. "You? A threat? To *me*? As if! You're nothing compared to me. The Quads all refused to even be caught dead with you before the supposed mate bond!" She snarled, putting air quotes around the words "mate bond" as though it was ridiculous for me to be fated to the Quads.

She had a distinct sort of voice that carried so everyone in the dining hall stopped eating, laughing and talking to listen and stare, especially since this drama involved the Quads, their future alphas and current school heartthrobs. Angelique continued her verbal attack on me.

"Even with the mate bond, two of them still don't want anything to do with you. And the younger two only care about you cause you're a pathetic virgin, and they love deflowering naive girls like you!" She spat.

Eli growled, his eyes black. Okay, that really stung.

"The same Eli, who told you to fuck off before the mate bond brainwashed him into feeling sorry for your poor handout-needy ass, is defending you now?" Scoffed Angelique.

Technically, it was Zaya who had told me to fuck off, but Eli had been mean too. She laughed coldly. The old me would have cried hands down, just like I had wanted to cry when the Quads were so mean to me at the party, but the new me had a very important task at hand.

"If you're done, I'll just ask you what I came here to ask you since you clearly don't care to have any privacy. Did you have any nightmares last night?" I asked.

She looked at me with wide eyes.

Chapter 10

"You're such a freak!" She said, her voice rising in pitch somewhat hysterically, which made me think she had had nightmares.

I'd known her my whole life. She was deflecting. She was scared!

"Were they realistic?" I enquired, furrowing my brow.

"Fuck off! You stupid bitch!" She screeched.

There were gasps.

"Angelique!" Bellowed Zaya who had just walked into the dining hall.

Angelique was seething. Zaya came over and glared at her with black eyes. He put me behind him, but I peaked out at Angelique.

She spoke through gritted teeth," Keep your crazy mate away from me!"

Zaya and Eli both snarled.

"Don't feel flattered by these two defending you. They laughed at you behind your back, saying you asked for grocery money for your birthday, and that you live in a shack, and will probably give it up to them soon!" She said snidely with a coldhearted laugh.

I exhaled sharply. How had she known about the groceries? She could have guessed about the state of my house and my lack of experience because of past knowledge, but the grocery shopping trip on my birthday was specific. They must have told her something, or, at least, told their elder brothers, and, perhaps, Jonah told her. I felt my eyes burn a little as they filled with tears. Maybe, I was way out of my league here if they all discussed me behind my back.

All the Quads were staring at me now with wide frightened eyes. Practically the whole school was looking at me. I was tired, so tired. I composed myself enough to answer her.

"Ok, Angelique, you win. I hope you're happy," I said softly so that only Angelique herself and the Quads heard.

Everyone else was craning their necks and straining their ears, their curiosity piqued. I extricated myself from Zaya and Eli and left the dining hall. I could hear footsteps behind me. They probably belonged to Zaya and Eli. I couldn't stop myself from glancing back. I was startled seeing all four Quads following me. I broke into a run. I just didn't want to play this game anymore. It was cruel on all sides. The Quads chased me. I knew I couldn't outrun one alpha let alone four. I still tried though.

Zaya was the fastest. He grabbed me and pinned me to the wall, putting his hand behind my head so it wouldn't hit the wall. I screamed in his face, startling him, but he wouldn't let go. His other brothers surrounded me. I kept very still. When they were sure I wouldn't run, Zaya released me, backing away to join the semi-circle of Quads cornering me. I folded my arms, hugging myself tightly. I fought back the tears and refused to make eye contact with any of them. They were all quiet for a few moments.

"Talk to us, Baby," pleaded Zaya. "Please!"
"About what?" I whispered.
"About anything, Princess...just talk," said Eli softly.
"I can't do this anymore," I admitted.
"What are you saying?" Asked Noah, his tone tense.
I shrugged.
"Star! Just tell us what you want!" Specified Jonah exasperatedly.
He made me the most furious of all.

"I, Hannah Star, rej-," I began, but Noah and Eli launched themselves at me with Noah reaching first.

He covered my mouth with his hand, cutting me off mid-declaration. Zaya and Jonah had made sudden jerking movements too, but stopped when they saw I'd already been successfully silenced.

"You promised!" Said Eli, his tone accusatory. "You said you wouldn't reject Zaya and me. You said you'd give us a chance despite our douchebag elder brothers!" Eli sniffled.

I felt so guilty. It had been a knee jerk reaction.

"Didn't you hear anything Jonah and I said? We explained it all to you!" Said Noah, his voice strained.

"Explained what?" Asked the youngest Quad, Zaya, sharply.

"Nothing!" Snapped the eldest Quad, Jonah.

I sighed against Noah's hand. He uncovered my mouth and stepped back.

"I'm sorry, Eli and Zaya. I did say I wouldn't reject you," I said softly. "But I never agreed to being humiliated like that."

"Didn't I tell you Angelique would take any opportunity she got to humiliate you?!" Retorted Noah.

"She wouldn't have any opportunity if my mates were all on one page!" I cried.

It was so hard to hold it all in. The tears streamed down my face. I was trembling. All four of them tried to hold me, but I shrank against the wall and put my palms up.

"Don't touch me!" I insisted. "Please!"

"Ok," mumbled Jonah.

"Did you guys really make fun of me for being poor behind my back?" I asked, my voice cracking.

"No, Baby, of course not," cooed Zaya.

"Princess, we would never betray your trust like that," insisted Eli.

"How did she know about the groceries then?" I asked pointedly, my voice thick with tears.

Jonah sighed. "That's my fault. I overheard Eli and Zaya telling Chet that you were really humble and hadn't had any demands on your birthday.

Chapter 10

You just wanted to go grocery shopping for your Granny. I thought it was sweet. I mentioned it to Noah in front of Angelique, which was short-sighted of me," admitted Jonah.

"Is there gonna be a sorry in there, cause I didn't hear one?!" Growled Eli.

Jonah sighed again. "Star, I'm sorry. Truly, I am. I don't like seeing you hurt, not one bit," he said.

He sounded sincere, but I really didn't trust him.

"Ok," I said softly.

"And where's the apology to me and Zaya?! You almost made our mate reject us!" Snapped Eli.

"Zaya, Eli, I'm sorry," muttered Jonah.

The younger two rolled their eyes.

"So, are we all good now?" Asked Noah.

Of course not.

"No! What the hell is going on? Why'd you call Star by the wrong name just now in the dining room? By being mean to Star, you're encouraging Angelique to mistreat her too," retorted Eli.

Noah was silent. Why were the two elder Quads keeping their plan regarding the curse a secret from the younger ones. If their Mom had really been affected by the curse, like Jonah and Noah had said, wouldn't Eli and Zaya already believe in the curse? I was too emotionally drained right now to cross-examine anyone just yet.

"Are you gonna answer?!" Demanded Zaya, looking back and forth between Jonah and Noah. "What's with the two of you? You clearly don't want Star to reject us, so why are you being jerks to her? It makes no sense!"

"Now is not a good time to reveal our true fated mate," stated Jonah.

"That's a bullshit excuse," muttered Eli.

"We don't want Star making a ton of enemies," lied Noah. "You know what a target the intended Luna always is... jealous girls, disapproving servants, scheming pack leaders and warriors..."

Eli and Zaya wore blank expressions, their eyebrows slightly raised. They weren't buying it. They both folded their arms, their jaws set, their eyes narrowed. Jonah and Noah sighed in unison.

"The curse..." began Noah.

"Oh Fuck, Noah!" Exclaimed Zaya. "Not this again!"

Eli groaned exasperatedly. The younger two knew about the curse!

"You two knew?!" I asked, looking at Zaya and Eli. "So, you're not the least bit worried?!"

"We would never let anything happen to you, Princess," purred Eli. "But the curse is an old wives 'tale in our family."

"It's not!" Protested Noah.

"Ugh, yes it is!" Grumbled Zaya.

"Two of Mom's best friends died, her maid of honour and her bridesmaid. Her parents are also dead!" Snapped Jonah.

"Mom's parents died before she even met Dad!" Retorted Zaya.

"What about the two best friends?" Reiterated Noah.

Eli shrugged. "Coincidence."

I thought of Jillian and Tobias. I couldn't risk them like that if there were any merit to this.

"Isn't it better to be safe rather than sorry?" I mumbled, feeling moronic for siding with Jonah and Noah.

"So, what do you suggest, Princess? That we just go our separate ways?!" Growled Eli.

"No!" I cried. "I just... I don't want to be the reason anyone gets hurt..."

"I gave you that ring for a reason," said Zaya. "It really is enchanted to cast a protection circle around you."

I glanced at the shimmering opal on the yellow gold band on my left ring finger. My heart warmed even more to Zaya.

"What about my family and friends? What or who will protect them? My grandmother lives all alone!" I said.

"I don't believe in this stupid curse, but I did station warriors to do patrols outside your grandmother's house!" Said Eli to my surprise. "She's your only real family and I don't want anything to happen to her."

My heart was so full.

"What about Jillian and Tobias?!" I asked.

"Well, Jillian has Chet to protect her. He's our intended Beta, you know. He's really tough, trust me!" Said Jonah.

"And Tobias stays in one of the private suites like ours, where there's great security!" Said Noah.

I nodded.

"So, this same old curse nonsense is why you're making our mate miserable?" Yelled Eli.

"Believe what you want, but Noah and I are going ahead with our plan!" Jonah said firmly.

"Which is what exactly?" Zaya asked, rolling his eyes.

"We're going to trick the witch who put the curse on our bloodline into thinking Angelique is our Luna and not Star. We won't let Angelique get killed, don't worry!" Explained Noah.

"I wasn't worried," said Eli.

Jonah growled. I felt a sharp pang. He really did care for Angie. He saw me wince.

Chapter 10

"We've been together a year. I consider her a friend…" said Jonah quickly.

"…with benefits," scoffed Eli.

I winced again.

"You guys broke up almost every other month during this year!" Said Zaya.

"I never said we were compatible!" Said Jonah simply.

"Right, so, Angelique will be the bait, and we'll get a powerful good witch to nullify the curse put on our lineage," continued Noah as if he hadn't been interrupted.

"What's the point of involving Angelique? Can't we just hire the good witch to try to take the curse off without bait?" Asked Zaya.

"We need to draw the witch out," said Jonah.

"It seems a bit cruel to use Angelique even though she's a huge bitch," said Zaya.

Jonah snarled and folded his arms. I flinched. He didn't say anything in response to my reaction this time.

"Would you rather use Star?" Asked Noah.

"NO!" Chorused Eli and Zaya.

"Exactly! That's what I thought!" Said Noah with a smug look on his face.

Eli sighed. "Let's say we believe you…" he began.

He was interrupted by the school bell ringing to signify the end of recess and the beginning of fourth period. At Viper Moon Academy, each class was usually one period long. A period lasted one hour. We started the day promptly at seven in the morning, followed by three classes or periods, recess at ten in the morning for half an hour, two more periods, lunch at half-past noon for one and a half hours, and then three afternoon periods, so that the school day ended at five in the evening. Students were scurrying off to class now, many of them pausing to blatantly stare at us. The Quads were like celebrities at this school.

Eli lowered his voice. "Let's pretend Zaya and I believe you, can a curse even be fooled? And how are you gonna make sure Angelique doesn't…die?"

"I think the curse can select the wrong target if we pretend she's fated to be our Luna. Also, the curse won't be able to claim the life of the wrong target, or, at least, that was what the witch we want to hire explained to me," said Noah. "By the time the witch's ghost, or remnant of her energy, or whatever it is that carries out the curse, realises that Angelique is the wrong target, it'll be too late, and we'll trap and purify it."

"You're forgetting one thing!" Said Zaya.

"Which is?" Asked Noah.

"The curse can claim Angie's life," said Zaya.
"No, she's not really our…" began Jonah.
"Based on the fact that she's the real fated Luna's relative!" Said Zaya.

Chapter 11

Tuesday 15th September, 2020.

Hannah Star's Point Of View

I heard Jonah's sharp intake of breath. He really did care for Angie on some level. That sick feeling I associated with Angie and Jonah was coming back. I needed to go lie down. Having four mates was stressful.

"But Angie and I aren't close at all! The curse is meant to cause misery. Won't it only claim family members and friends who I have a strong connection with?" I asked.

My social circle was already so small. I couldn't handle losing anyone.

"Not always. It kills people in close proximity to you, except for your alphas, meaning us, obviously," said Noah. "People you like or love have a higher chance of being claimed over your enemies. The curse is meant to cause misery like you said."

My wolf was happy hearing Noah call them our alphas. She was easily impressed when it came to the Quads. I, on the other hand, felt Noah and Jonah left a lot to be desired. I sighed. I hadn't told them about my premonition dream yet and I wasn't sure if I wanted to tell them.

"What if Damocles died because of the curse? Wouldn't that mean that the curse already knows I'm the one?" I asked.

"The curse is confused already!" Said Jonah confidently.

"How do you know that?" I asked quickly.

"Because Angie dreamt of Damocles' death last night," said Jonah.

Noah nodded. "Good. It'll all be over soon, okay, Star," murmured Noah.

I felt nauseated. How did Jonah know what Angie had dreamt? Had he been sleeping in the same bed as her, or had she told him this morning? I had had the same dream as Angie, so the curse was confused, but it was half-right.

"I'm not marrying Angelique!" Snapped Eli. "I don't give a fuck what you two say," he muttered.

Zaya snickered. "I can't pretend to be into Angelique. No offence Jonah," Zaya said dryly.

I knew there were much more important issues at hand but I couldn't help it. My wolf was whimpering. She needed to know.

"Jonah," I said.

"Yeah," he said, locking eyes with me, surprised I actually wanted to talk to him.

"How did you know about Angie's dream? Were you sleeping together?" I asked softly.

Jonah tensed.

"We... were sleeping next to each other," he admitted.

I drew a sharp intake of breath.

"I'm not rejecting you guys, okay. That should be enough for now. I need some time by myself. I won't bother you, Noah, or you, Jonah in public anymore, but please refrain from being jerks to me. I'd rather you just ignored me," I tried to leave, but Noah and Jonah grabbed my arms gently by the elbows.

"Star, please believe me! I care for Angie. We have a history together but... it's nothing compared to what I feel for you. I want you. Please, give me time to fix things so we can safely be together," whispered Jonah fiercely in my ear.

"Please, Star, try to understand," Noah said softly.

"I am trying!" I said, close to tears again.

"Let her go," demanded Zaya.

Jonah and Noah reluctantly released me.

"I'll walk you back to your dorm, Princess" said Eli.

"No, thanks," I said.

"It wasn't a question, Princess," said Eli, smirking.

I grumbled inwardly and started walking quickly back to my dorm. All four Quads followed behind me, their faces forlorn. They waited until I had closed my door and locked it before they left. I could tell when they had actually left because of their fading scents. I was missing fourth period, but I couldn't handle class right now. I called Jillian and asked her to please tell the teacher I was sick. She agreed. I cringed at the pity in her voice. She had probably witnessed Angelique insulting me. Just about

Chapter 11

everyone had seen and heard it. I buried my head in the pillow and finally let the tears fall freely.

Monday 7th September, 2020

Noah's Point of View

It was the first day of senior year. I pulled into my reserved packing spot at school. As I got out of the car, I felt many pairs of eyes on me. Being the Alpha's son meant always being under scrutiny, whether other males were sizing me up, or she-males were eyeing me. I had turned eighteen over the Summer break, but I had yet to find my fated mate. I wasn't in a hurry to find her. My family didn't have the best track-record when it came to mates.

Someone caught my attention. It was a short girl with golden skin and shiny chocolate brown ringlets walking up the hill towards Viper Moon Academy. She had almost reached the top. My eyes followed her. I recognised her vaguely. She was in my year. I had never really noticed her before. She looked different, more womanly, now. I followed her, trying not to make it obvious. It was usually the other way around, with girls stalking me.

I waited for her to reach the short flight of steps just before the double-doors. She was struggling with her suitcase. I felt compelled to help her, so I did, hoisting her bag up the stairs easily. She looked up, and I could tell she immediately knew who I was. I stared at her face. She was beautiful with her big warm brown eyes lined heavily by long dark lashes. She had full pink lips and a button nose. I offered to take her suitcase up to her dorm for her. She seemed shocked but grateful that I was helping her.

On the way to her dorm, any time she would lean closer, I would catch a whiff of her scent. She smelled amazing. I wondered if she were eighteen already. I looked at her intently, trying to remember her name. I spotted an oil painting of witches dancing in the woods at night. That was it! Star! Her name was Star! I had heard in class during roll call. Other than that, she wasn't really in the same social circle as me. If my memory served me correctly, she was one of those scholarship students. We reached her dorm. I didn't bother to introduce myself. My mind was suddenly filled with racing thoughts.

As I walked away, she called out to me, "My name is Hannah."
Hannah Star.
"Noah!" I responded.

I couldn't help but grin. I found myself hoping she'd say my name back to me so I could hear it escape her lips. I hoped this didn't mean what I thought it meant! I would have my hands full.

I met my brothers in our private suite. We were identical Quadruplets as if being future alphas didn't get us enough attention. Due to there being four of us, we were always the topic of discussion at school. The eldest of us was Jonah, then me, then Elijah, and finally, Isaiah. Elijah and Isaiah went by Eli and Zaya respectively. We were only a few minutes apart each, but things like that mattered with multiple alphas. I needed to talk to Jonah. I pulled him away from Zaya and Eli.

"Jonah," I said, keeping my voice low. "I...I think I might've found our mate."

"Might've? What do you mean? How could you not be sure?" Asked Jonah, furrowing his brow.

"I don't think she's eighteen yet, but there's something there," I said in hushed tones.

Jonah sighed, folding his arms. He knew, as did I, that our mate wouldn't have it easy.

"Don't do anything yet. Wait until you sure!" He said authoritatively.

I nodded.

"Angie's throwing a party tonight, by the way. A back to school bash is what she's calling it," said Jonah.

Ugh. I knew I would be expected to go.

"Ok," I said unenthusiastically.

Jonah laughed at my tone, clapping me on the back. At first, I didn't agree with the idea of any of us dating before we'd found our mate, but this was a special case. Angie would prove herself very useful. I grumbled inwardly as I got ready for Angie's party, hoping to high heaven that Star wouldn't be there.

Chapter 12

Monday 7th September, 2020.

Jonah's Point Of View

Angie's parties were pretty much legendary at our exclusive boarding school, Viper Moon Academy. The only students who threw better parties than Angie were myself and my brothers. We were sons of the Alpha, so we knew how to entertain. I was tense, despite looking at ease, sitting in a huge jacuzzi, on the back porch of Angie's house. There were four girls in the tub with my brothers and me.

I wondered if our suspected mate would show up. I hoped not. I'd been dreading her arrival for years. Being the eldest of the "Alpha Quadruplets" wasn't easy. A lot fell on my shoulders. It wasn't that I didn't want a mate, I just didn't want to love that deeply only to lose it. Losing a mate was the most painful thing a werewolf could go through. I'd known since the age of sixteen that my chance of losing a mate was much higher than other werewolves. My grandfather had called me to his study one day at our family's manor. I remembered it so vividly.

Flashback

"Good, you're early," drawled my Grandfather.

Even after retiring as Alpha, he still radiated power and authority. He was tall. We were eye to eye. He had dark wavy hair and an impressive dark beard flecked with grey. His eyes were a deep green. His face was hardened and always set in a serious expression. He was a joyless man, for the most part, but I couldn't blame him. He had lost his mate, my

Grandmother, when they were young, forcing him to have to raise my father on his own.

"Dad told me to be early. He said you consider on-time late, and early on-time," I said.

Grandfather chuckled. I gazed around his study. It was a huge room with curved walls instead of sharp corners. Oil paintings of past Alphas and Lunas graced the wall. There were other portraits out in the hallway.

Grandfather got up and motioned for me to follow him. He led me down the hallway, all the way to the very end. There was a door there leading to a room that was not in use. The room was bare except for two paintings on the wall both covered with tapestries. He gestured towards them. I unveiled the one on the left.

"Georgianna," I read.

That was all the caption said in gold-plated lettering on the frame. The painting was of a young, beautiful, raven-haired woman, with one violet eye and one brown eye and a slight smile playing about her full lips.

I unveiled the second painting.

"Alpha Alto," I read.

This was of a young man who greatly resembled my brothers and me. He had light ash brown hair and green eyes with a sly smile and a mischievous glint in his eyes.

"This is your great, great, great, great Uncle," said Grandfather. "His younger brother was named Oleander. Oleander was your great great great grandfather."

Why was he telling me this?

"Ok," I mumbled.

"You think I'm wasting your time?" grumbled Grandfather.

"No, no, not at all," I lied.

Grandfather chuckled sadly. His eyes looked faraway.

"When Alpha Alto met his Luna, Georgianna, he was shocked. Do you know why?" Asked Grandfather.

"No," I said.

"Because she was a witch!" Answered Grandpa.

A chill crept through me. Werewolves tried to avoid witches where possible. I only knew of one Alpha fated to a Witch. That was the Alpha of Ambrosia, but that was after a lot of modern-day progress. I could only imagine the scandal it had been back then if it was still shocking to this day.

"What happened?" I asked Grandfather.

"They fell in love! The mate bond is inexorably strong!" Grandpa said.

I nodded.

Chapter 12

"And then?" I asked.

Clearly, there was more.

"Our forefather, Oleander, was furious. A witch luna! Over his dead body!" Said my Grandpa. "So he poisoned his own brother, Alto, with silver and wolfsbane in his wedding goblet."

My eyes widened. "That's despicable!"

"Yes, yes, it is," muttered Grandfather.

"What happened to Georgianna? Was she poisoned too?" I asked.

"No, she lived on. She was greatly aggrieved though. In despair, she cursed Oleander and his lineage to never feel the love she was denied!" Said Grandfather.

I had heard about the "family curse" before. I wasn't sure I believed it. Supposedly, the curse claimed the lives of any luna joined to our family through marriage. For that reason, my parents remained unmarried, meaning my mother was an unofficial luna. She was my Dad's fated mate, but he'd refused to run the risk of marrying her. Grandfather, on the other hand, had married his mate shortly after my father had been born.

"You believe in the curse?" I asked.

Grandfather laughed humourlessly.

"I didn't when I was your age. I should have," he whispered, a single tear escaping his eye.

End of Flashback

I hadn't taken him seriously. However, now that I had a potential mate, I was worried. "What if" wasn't good enough.

Angie could tell my mind was faraway. We'd been dating a year. We had been friends first, partying together often. She had been after me the whole time and was thrilled to be more than friends despite us not being mates. I hoped she would find her mate, before I found mine, because she really didn't take rejection well. She was in her glee tonight though. The centre of attention. Her favourite place to be. She grabbed my face and pressed her lips to mine.

I felt Noah stiffen beside me. I followed his gaze when Angie and I parted. That had to be her! She was beautiful. She was short for a she-wolf with a shapely figure. My eyes trailed over her curves. Her long dark lustrous hair fell all around her. Her pink full lips looked soft as did her golden skin. I wondered why I'd never noticed her before. She had probably never partied until now. To my surprise, she came over. She was gazing at Noah. As she neared the jacuzzi, her scent hit me. It made my mouth water. I felt inexplicably drawn to her, though, there was still some confusion in my mind. She was probably nearing her eighteenth birthday.

The mate-bond hadn't hit fully yet. Noah had told me her name was Hannah Star.

"Hey there, uh, Moon?" Angie said.

What did Angie have against this girl? Could she sense I was into her already. The girl didn't correct Angie as though she was used to Angie's jibes. Angie did give certain people a hard time.

"Hi, Angelique," said Star.

Angie put a hand on Noah's shoulder.

"What brings you here, Cloud?" Angie said.

I laughed half-heartedly at her feeble joke. Star glared at me. I flinched. I didn't want to upset her, but I didn't want to piss off Angie too soon either.

"Tobias insisted I come," said Star softly.

My wolf growled, jealous. I quieted him. Tobias was gay.

"Ohhh, yeah, Toby, you must be thrilled, huh, to get to see how the other half lives?" said Angie snidely.

That was so unnecessary. Star frowned.

She spoke to Noah instead, "Hey, Noah, thanks for the other day."

"What happened the other day?" Asked Angelique, the jealousy evident in her voice.

I knew Angie would love to be Luna. She was a bit power-hungry.

"He..." Star began.

"Nothing!" Said Noah suddenly.

Star looked hurt. Noah seemed upset too. I knew he wished he could woo her like a normal alpha-luna bond. I noticed him going over to talk to her when we were drying off after the jacuzzi. He was touching her arm.

"I thought you didn't know her, little bro," I said.

He knew better than to confuse her by being hot and cold. We were supposed to keep our distance until we'd sorted out the curse. We'd decided to be safe, rather than sorry. Eli and Zaya were none the wiser. They just didn't believe in it. It was no use trying to convince them.

"I don't," said Noah, letting go of her arm. "I was just telling her to keep her distance."

I felt a sharp pain in my chest. My wolf whimpered. That must have hurt Star, because it was hurting me. I needed her to get away from us.

"Run along, okay, Cloud," I said, adding insult to injury. "You weren't invited."

Zaya and Eli came over. I hoped Star would listen but she remained put. She seemed rooted to the spot. It was probably overwhelming for her, being around the four of us and not being sure what the pull towards us meant.

Chapter 12

"I told you to go," said Noah, trying to snap her out of it.

I wondered if Zaya and Eli could feel the mate-pull. They'd both been drinking a lot, so, perhaps not. The bond hadn't been established yet.

"Hey!" Snapped Zaya. "The eldest Alpha told you to fuck off!"

Eli and Zaya laughed as though that were funny. I forced myself to laugh with them.

"Seriously, bye," said Eli to Star.

Star's eyes were brimming with tears. A searing hot pain lanced through me. Fuck. This was why I wanted no interaction at all with her till we had figured shit out.

"Are you seriously about to cry?" Asked Zaya incredulously.

Did my youngest brother not feel the connection at all? Noah was tense, regretful. I stopped fake-laughing. Eli took a step towards Star in response to her tears. Eli was probably sensing it faintly. It wouldn't be long before we all felt it and could no longer resist the pull. She took a step away from Eli. She felt threatened. I wished I could hold her.

"No," she said softly.

I was relieved to see her go.

"Fuck. Why am I such an ass?" Muttered Zaya to himself after Star was out of earshot.

I chuckled genuinely now.

"That girl was kinda cute," said Zaya. "What do you guys have against her?"

"Nothing. I told you, I don't know her," Noah said.

He was a terrible liar.

"She just didn't listen the first time I told her to leave. That's all. We need all pack members to respect us," I said, giving a feeble excuse.

It was chilly out tonight, even for a werewolf like me. I wished I were curled up somewhere under a blanket with Star. I hoped she wasn't cold.

"Sure," said Zaya, rolling her eyes.

"Did you guys hook up?" Eli asked.

"No!" Grumbled Noah.

"She's pretty," said Eli. "You made her cry, Zaya!"

"Me?! So did you!" Said Zaya, fidgeting uncomfortably.

"Whatever," said Eli though he seemed regretful.

Angie came over and dragged me onto the dance floor. My eyes kept darting all over the room, searching for Star. This was going to be torture.

Chapter 13

Tuesday 8th September, 2020

Noah's Point of View

As if we didn't have enough to deal with, last night, our best friend, Chet, had laid eyes on a girl named Jillian for the first time since they'd both come of age. They had discovered they were mates. Jillian was the best friend of Star. Great. Now, Star would be hanging around us all the time. Chet was not just our best friend, he was also our next-door neighbour. His family's manor was next to our estate, and his private suite at the academy was opposite ours. Jillian had gotten drunk last night, and Chet had given both her and Star a lift back to the academy.

I couldn't stop day-dreaming about Star like I was some thirteen year old in love with a pop star or something. I was showering, getting ready for class. The water came from all four walls and the ceiling in the huge shower. I imagined what would have happened if I had dropped Star home last night. I could've played with her long ringlets and touched her soft skin. She would have let me kiss her. I knew she would have. She was definitely attracted to me and my brothers.

I made myself and my brothers late for our first class. No one would dare punish us though. We met up with Chet and some girls from Angie's crew and went to class together "fashionably late", according to Angie's friends. My eyes immediately found Star in the room despite my brain begging me not to search for her. We locked eyes. I kept my poker face on. Chet went to sit next to Jillian so we all ended up in the same row as Star. My brothers 'eyes kept darting back to Star too. I was afraid of Zaya and Eli catching on early because there was no way of getting them to

Chapter 13

listen. They had been yearning for their mate a long time now. They played tough but they were softies.

Angie came back to class. She had gone to the bathroom to touch up her makeup for the third time this morning. Jonah obnoxiously whistled at her. Yuck. She sat among my brothers and me, two of us on either side of her. It would have been the perfect seat for Star. Angie started boasting about some modelling gig she had done. I couldn't take my eyes off of Star. She probably thought I was crazy, chivalrous one moment and rude the next. I overheard Chet invite Jillian and Star to our weekend getaway at his family's cabin. Shit.

"Saturday is Star's birthday!" Said Jillian brightly.

Please let her say she has plans already! I thought desperately.

"Awesome! There's no better place to celebrate!" Said Chet.

Ugh.

"*That* is coming with us to the lake, Chet," said Angelique.

Jonah laughed. He was much better at pretending to not be into Star.

"If Star isn't welcome, then I have no business being there," snapped Jillian.

Jillian was a loyal friend, deserving of being close to my Luna. I couldn't help but smile.

"I was just kidding, Jilli-bear!" Lied Angelique.

I resisted the urge to roll my eyes.

After class, I followed Star. It was now or never. I grabbed her by her arm. Tingles shot through me where our bare skin touched. I pinned her to the wall. Our lips were dangerously close. What was stopping me from kissing her? She smelled so good. Her voice was so sweet. She looked so beautiful as she looked up at me. Her skin was smooth and soft. I'd covered all the senses except taste. I wanted that so badly. I snapped out of it.

"Don't come to the Cabin this weekend!" I ordered her.

If she was really my fated Luna, the Alpha order wouldn't work, but, hopefully, she'd willingly obey me.

"Why not?" She whispered.

My wolf whimpered at the pain in her voice.

"Because Angelique will just use this as an opportunity to humiliate you, and Jonah will go along with it," I made up whatever worked.

"Why does Jonah hate me so much?" She asked, surprising me.

"Jonah?" I said. "He doesn't hate you. He just laughs at all of Angelique's antics. A better question would be why does Angie hate you so much?"

Angie probably sensed that Star was a major threat to her relationship with Jonah.

"Oh, she's my cousin. My Dad and her mother were brother and sister," said Star.

My wolf growled. Angie was an even bigger bitch than I'd realised. She was related to Star and still treated her terribly.

"Were?" I asked, wondering why she spoke of her family in the past tense.

"My Dad's dead," she said softly.

I felt awful. I was being such a jerk to her, but I didn't have much of a choice.

"Sorry to hear that," I mumbled.

"It was a long time ago," she said.

"So Angie doesn't want you to tell people you're related? Why?" I said, not wanting to fully believe that Angie was that shallow.

"The same reason you didn't want anyone to know you helped me with my luggage... ashamed of me I guess," she snapped.

She tried to brush past me, but I pressed her into the wall until she submitted to me. My wolf was excited, pleased with her submissive behaviour. I sniffed her hair. Delicious.

"I expect to not see you there! Don't disobey me!" I said for good measure.

She glared at me.

"It's for your own good, Hannah," I mumbled as I walked away.

Friday 11th September, 2020

Noah's Point Of View

Friday came quickly. I was looking forward to a weekend away from all the stress. Hannah would turn eighteen over the weekend, and I needed time to plan how to act when the fully-fledged mate bond hit me on Monday back at school. I was driving my favourite sports car to Chet's cabin, racing Chet. It was not the safest game, but it was fun, nonetheless. Zaya and Eli were carpooling with me though we all had several cars. We wouldn't need four cars this weekend, and Jonah was already taking his car too with Angie in his passenger seat. I glanced over at Chet's Maserati. He was gaining on me.

That was when I saw her, Star, in the backseat of Chet's car. I was livid. She'd disobeyed me. The moment we got to the cabin, I went to get Star. I found her in the kitchen.

"Oh, Alpha..." said Lana, the housekeeper, happily.

"Just a moment, Lana," I said, grabbing Star's hand and taking her to the pantry.

Chapter 13

I shut the door behind me. My wolf immediately filled my mind with pornographic images of what I should do to Star to punish her in this tight space. I pushed those thoughts aside.

"I told you not to come!" I snapped.

I felt my eyes turn black. I didn't want to scare her, but she drove me crazy. I could never react normally when it came to her.

"Jillian is my best friend and Chet is her mate," she said. "You're a stranger who won't even admit that we spoke once! Why should I listen to you?"

That hurt.

"I'm your alpha!" I said.

"Ok, Alpha, I'm sorry. It won't happen again..."

Ugh. I didn't want her calling me that. I grabbed her hand so the contact with my mate could help me calm down.

"You don't have to call me alpha," I said softly.

"But I have to obey you, so I may as well start now," she said.

"Fine! Suit yourself!" I said, getting pissed off again.

My eyes trailed over her form. I licked my lips. I stormed out of the pantry.

I went to join Angie and Jonah outside by the lake. I tried my best to enjoy myself, but all I could think about was Star.

Chapter 14

Friday 11th September, 2020

Zaya's Point Of View

That girl I'd told to fuck off at the party was apparently the best friend of Jillian, who was the mate of my best friend, Chet. It was a small world after all. I thought I'd be annoyed having her here on our weekend trip, but I was strangely excited at the prospect. I put on my swim trunks upstairs and headed down to the lake. I stopped on the landing. She was there, sitting in front of a large window, staring wistfully at the two couples canoodling by the lake.

"Why so glum?" I asked her, before I could stop myself.

She blatantly ignored me.

"Hey! I'm talking to you!" I said.

She looked up. "Didn't you tell me to fuck off the other day?"

She was feistier than I thought. Good.

"I was really drunk when I said that!" I admitted.

A lame excuse but whatever. I sat on the window seat next to her. She was wearing a black bikini under a really thin coat. She pulled the coat closed in response to me checking her out. Her curves were making my wolf howl.

"What're you hiding for?" I asked, disappointed she ruined my peep show.

"I just...I know you guys don't want me here, but I came to support my best friend, okay. She's always been there for me, and she's really excited to find her mate," she explained.

"I never said I didn't want you," I said.

Chapter 14

That came out more intensely than I'd meant it too, but, once the words left my lips, I knew they were true. I wanted her.

"Here?!" She added helpfully, thinking I meant to say I wanted her here, but I meant what I said.

I wanted her period. Maybe, it needed repeating.

Suddenly, it hit me. According to Chet, tomorrow was her birthday, her eighteenth birthday. What if she was my...

"You're turning eighteen tomorrow. We gotta stay up till midnight and ring it in," I said.

"Um, okay," she said as though she were suspicious of me for some reason.

"Okay," I said.

I got up and held out my hand. She tried to give me a handshake, but I pulled her up and ran, yanking her with me.

"Hey, n-no please I can't swim!" She cried.

I ran with her along the wooden dock and plunged into the water, dragging her with me. She screamed and began to splutter. I quickly grabbed her and held her, bridal style. She put her arms around my neck. My wolf was elated. He loved how she clung to us, needing us to protect her, counting on us. She wasn't getting out of this water anytime soon and I was going to make the most of it.

"Put your legs around me. It'll be easier," I said, hoping she would comply.

She did, wrapping her arms around my neck and her legs around my waist. Fuck. This felt good. I could see her bathing suit properly now. She'd left her stupid coat on the dock, thank goodness.

"I like your bathing suit...how it has little frilly sleeves," I said, chuckling.

She was cute, so innocent and sweet. I wanted to corrupt her a bit, but not too much.

"I don't like my arms," She blurted out. "So, I always wear sleeves."

Huh.

"What's wrong with your arms?" I asked, confused.

Girls were always insecure about the strangest things. Why was she self-conscious about her arms when she had an ass like that? Not to mention, round perky breasts. I tried to stop undressing her with my eyes.

"They're huge!" She informed me, still worrying about her arms.

Ugh.

"You're tiny. You're insane. What're you talking about?" I said, reassuring her.

She looked at me like I was crazy. I wanted to give her a few dirty compliments, but she seemed a bit prudish, and we hadn't known each other long.

Her curvy little body was pressed up against me, such a contrast to my large muscular frame. Perhaps, she wasn't that prudish. Her eyes were taking in my muscles hungrily. I laughed and flexed my pecs for her, making her blush. She wiggled around and ended up brushing against my hard-on. I wasn't the least bit embarrassed. I smirked at her.

"See I'm not lying," I said. "I like what I see."

I rocked my hips against hers. It felt amazing. If she really was the one, we'd soon repeat this sans our clothes.

"Don't," she said softly.

I stopped right away, not wanting to make her uncomfortable.

"May I ask why?" I said.

The attraction was clearly mutual.

"I'm saving myself for my mate," she said in a hushed tone.

"So, you're a virgin?" I clarified.

I could feel my eyes darken as my arousal increased. If I was that mate she was speaking of, I couldn't wait to bury myself inside of her.

"You knew that already. Can't you smell it?" She inquired.

"Yeah I can smell it," I replied.

Suddenly, we were splashed with water.

"Clingy much?" Said Angie.

Ugh. That stupid bitch had interrupted me and Star. We ignored her. Star was lost in her thoughts. I could smell her getting wet for me.

"Hey! Come on, come over here, we're having a splash war," said Angie.

"She can't swim!" I said loudly, hoping Angie would back off.

No such luck.

"So, both of you come here then!" Growled Angie.

"Fuck off!" I said.

I could hear Jonah laughing.

"Sorry," said Star suddenly.

"For what?" I asked, just managing to stop myself from calling her "Baby."

"For spoiling your fun," she said shyly.

She was so fucking cute. I laughed.

"You are my fun, you little idiot," I said.

"Hey!" She protested.

"What?" I growled playfully, pressing my nose against hers and showing her my black eyes.

I leant in so I could taste her lips.

Chapter 14

"Don't kiss me," she whispered.

I groaned inwardly.

"Why not, Star?" I whispered.

She seemed surprised at me addressing her directly.

"I'm saving it all for my mate," she said, reiterating her earlier excuse.

"Damn, that's one lucky mate!" I growled.

She giggled.

I kept her in my arms. By midnight tonight, I'd know for sure. I would most likely sleep in her room afterwards. There were four of us. Identical multiples usually shared a mate, but I was clearly connecting with her the strongest so far. I had thought she and Noah had had something going, but maybe not.

"Hey, you probably have a girlfriend?" She asked.

She seemed worried I'd say yes. My wolf was happy she was territorial over me already.

"No," I informed her promptly with a laugh.

"What about Angie?" She asked.

Yuck.

"She's Jonah's whatever the hell they are. They don't use labels or whatever," I muttered.

They were so gross together. Of late, whenever they made out, Jonah seemed not into it. Most of the physical stuff these days was initiated by Angie. She had been a one-night-stand that had turned into a fully fledged relationship.

After we connected in the lake, little Star avoided me all afternoon and all evening. She seemed shy, so I gave her her space. She would come to me when she couldn't take it anymore. Eli and I began doing shots as the night stretched on. Midnight couldn't come fast enough.

Chapter 15

Friday 11th September, 2020

Eli's Point Of View

That girl we'd been mean to at the party was here at Chet's cabin. Chet was our oldest friend. He had just found his mate, Jillian, a scholarship student. That girl was also a scholarship student, and best friends with Jillian. I found out her name was Star. Zaya had told me about how they'd "swum" together. She looked very pretty tonight. She smelled delicious, floral and innocent, with a hint of spicy seductiveness. I'd bottle that and sell it. She was an award winning fragrance just floating around.

I had been such a douchebag to her at the party. Some shots should break the ice nicely. I poured a shot of cafe patron and gestured to her wordlessly with the shot glass.

"I don't think she drinks," said Zaya.

She took the shot, seemingly out of spite, because Zaya had insinuated she wouldn't. I liked that. She downed it. She coughed a bit.

"Whoa," was her response.

I laughed. Zaya grinned at her.

"Why do people drink? It's awful," she said.

"Do another," I said.

She complied. She was loosening up a little, getting buzzed.

"Another, please," she said.

Whatever you want, Princess, I thought to myself.

My eyes kept trailing over her legs. I wished I could wrap them around my waist. I could pick her up and dance with her. The two couples were already on the floor. I made her a third shot. She giggled after that one.

Chapter 15

Lana, the housekeeper, came into the room, pushing a table on wheels with a huge cake on a platter. We sang Happy Birthday to Star. She cut the cake with Jillian. Midnight was almost upon us. I wondered, staring at her. Star.

Little Princess, are you mine? I asked myself, not able to take my eyes off of her

I would soon find out.

Jonah's Point Of View

Star ran off literally one minute before midnight. Fuck. I wanted to go look for her. I went outside. I could tell Zaya and Eli were catching on, especially Zaya. He never gave any of the she-wolves who swooned over him much of a chance. He enjoyed not being tied down. He was not a fan of PDA either. I'd never seen him so much as hold the hand of a girl he was seeing in front of us. Yet, with Star, whom he barely knew, he spent about an hour just lazily floating around the lake, holding her, like they were on their honeymoon, or something. I was a little jealous. I couldn't act on the mate-bond the way Zaya could, not yet anyway.

Angie pulled me towards the jacuzzi and begged me to get in. I obliged. She locked lips with me. I felt guilty, like I was betraying Star, but also using Angie. I needed her as bait for the curse though. I promised myself I wouldn't let any harm come to her. I was the eldest of the future alphas, so I had to safeguard everyone.

I sensed a pair of eyes on me while I kissed Angie. Then, I smelled the most alluring aroma. I broke away from Angie, and my eyes found Star, standing there completely nude. She had probably destroyed her clothes when she had shifted. It was after midnight now, and she had come of age. I took in her curls and her curves, her big brown doe eyes, her pouty pink lips. I'd do anything to be close to her. I wanted to be the sheen of sweat coating her golden skin.

Mate.

I locked eyes with her. She looked heartbroken. She'd seen me with Angie. It was the first time she'd seen me since turning eighteen and I was in a jacuzzi with another girl. Fuck. Fuck. Fuck.

"Put some clothes on!" said Angie. "No one wants to see that."

Angie wasn't stupid. She could tell how attracted I was to Star, so she'd say anything she could to discredit that. Star hugged herself, covering her beautiful body.

"Star," I said, my voice hoarse.

She ran away from me. Shit.

"Star!" I yelled, running after her.

This was a disaster. It was supposed to have gone down much more gently. She wasn't even supposed to be at the cabin. We would have just seen each other on Monday. Noah and I would've told her we needed time and space to figure some stuff out.

"Where are you going?" Cried Angie, following me.

Ugh. This was going to get ugly.

Zaya's Point Of View

I was on the landing, sitting on the window seat, where I had seen Star earlier today. I was waiting up for her to come back after her first shift. I smelled her before I saw her. My mouth watered. Fuck. She smelled so good. Her scent made me shiver in delight. I smiled at her as she came up the stairs in all her naked glory. I wanted to kiss every inch of her tender flesh while she writhed underneath me. I smiled at her, but she actually ran away from me.

She shut the door to her room. I banged on the door.

"Star! Star! Come on! Just get dressed and come out, okay! I'm waiting right here. Couldn't you tell earlier? Didn't you feel something... between us? Come out, Baby! Why're you hiding?" I called at her door.

Jonah joined me suddenly.

"Star, it's Jonah. Look, I'm sorry. Let's talk," called Jonah.

Sorry?

"Sorry?" I said, looking at Jonah with narrowed eyes. "What did you do to her?" I snarled.

"Nothing," replied Jonah. "She saw me with Angie."

I should have known. He knew better than that. Ugh! I shoved him. He growled and tried to shove me back. Eli and Noah came and parted us. Chet showed up with Jillian. Angie came up the stairs.

"You guys are fighting over that loser? Seriously?" Asked Angie.

I growled at her. Jonah needed to get his girl under control. I wasn't having it.

"Star, can we talk, honey?" said Jillian at the door, trying to coax Star out of her room.

"No, please, not right now," Star said, her voice cracking.

My heart broke for her. It was my first time hearing her talk since the official mate-bond had taken effect. Her voice sounded so sweet but so broken. Noah disappeared and retuned with the master key. It was an invasion of Star's privacy, but I needed to get into that room too so I let him use it.

"Noah!" Said Chet indignantly. "Not cool, bro."

Chapter 15

Noah walked up to Star. Would he be able to calm her down?

"You should leave," said Noah.

WHAT THE FUCK?! Had I entered the twilight zone or something?

"WHAT?" I snarled, storming into the room and grabbing my beautiful mate before Noah threw her out a window or something.

He was acting crazy! The contact with Star sent tingles through my whole body. I couldn't wait to sleep next to her tonight. I put her behind me and faced Noah. Eli entered and stood protectively in front of Star too. Thank goodness Eli was acting right. Jonah came in and sided with Noah.

"She can go, and we'll talk about this later," said Jonah.

Poor Star. This was so painful for her. I could feel it. She gripped my elbow for comfort.

Don't worry, Baby, I've got you, I thought.

"She's our mate. She's not going anywhere. Let your whore leave," said Eli.

Jonah growled.

Wow so he had it in him to defend Angie but not Star.

"I'll go!" Star said. "It's clear you guys don't want me."

Hearing my mate say that made me feel sick. Her little ass wasn't going anywhere ever. She was mine forever. End of story.

Eli's Point Of View

When Star came back from her first shift, it was apparent that she was ours. Our mate. Our Luna. Finally! I could smell her moving through the house. I followed the delicious smell. I wondered how far she'd let us go tonight. I tried to clean up my dirty thoughts, but it was to no avail.

I heard fighting. I ran upstairs, terrified Star could get hurt in the commotion. My brothers and I did fight from time to time, but we had to cut that out. We had a mate now. She was pretty tiny. She would be afraid, or worse yet, what if she were overly brave, and tried to part the fight and ended up injured.

When I got there, I was in for a shock. Jonah and Noah wanted Star gone from the cabin with immediate effect. Yeah fucking right. I told Jonah to make his whore leave. Star was our true fated Luna. Was he insane? She was perfect for us! Mates were designed to be our perfect matches. We would fit together exactly and satisfy each other with ease. We were made for each other, literally. I stood in front of her next to Zaya, my only sane brother at the moment. Now, she thought we didn't want her. She said it was clear we didn't want her.

"How exactly is that clear, Princess? I've just asked my brother to get rid of his whore so you'll stop crying!" I said, cupping her pretty little face in my huge hands, hoping the roughness of my calloused palms wasn't chaffing her delicate skin too much.

I used my thumbs to wipe her tears away. Jonah and Noah had made my mate cry. I had made her cry at the party. Shit. She would reject us if I didn't salvage this.

"Baby, relax, Elijah and I are not gonna let you walk out of here," said Zaya, placing his hand on her lower back, drawing her closer to us.

She stayed put. She seemed to be enjoying our touch and our warmth. Noah and Jonah were looking at her hungrily. Noah shook his head, clearly trying to fight the need. Why were they torturing themselves? They obviously wanted her too.

"Inviting her here was a mistake," said Noah.

Zaya shoved him. Jonah grabbed Zaya by his shirt. I shoved Jonah away from Zaya. It was two against two. I was glad I didn't have to stand up to all three of them alone, but I would have for Star. I'd do anything for Star.

"Noah, I thought we were okay," my Princess said to Noah.

He really didn't deserve her kindness.

"Star, I'm doing what's best for you, trust me," said Noah.

"And I get that Jonah wants to be with Angie," she said.

She started crying again. I couldn't stand this.

"It's not that," said Jonah.

"Ugh! Would you and Noah just get the fuck out of here? You're upsetting our mate. She's not leaving tonight. Over my dead body!" I said.

You're gonna make her have a breakdown! Please, guys! I said over mind-link to just the four of us Quadruplets.

I could tell they were listening and thinking it over.

Our elder two brothers glared Zaya and me. Angie pulled Jonah away. Star winced, but Zaya held her. Noah kept his eyes on Star as he backed out of the room. He took one last look at her, drinking her in, before he closed the door.

The moment he was gone, Star burst into tears, sobbing openly. Oh no! Zaya and I held her tightly.

We coaxed her into bed, under the covers. There would be no romance tonight that was for sure, but at least we could comfort her. She refused to talk about how she felt, but she welcomed our gentle caresses. We ran our fingers through her hair and kissed her tear-streaked cheeks and the marking spots on her neck. She had four perfect marking spots, two on either side. I could tell by the increased sensitivity there. She could bond to four mates. Fate. That was why it was this way. Fate knew what we would need. I massaged her back until she fell asleep. Zaya and I cuddled her, and eventually, we dozed off too.

Chapter 16

Tuesday 15th September, 2020.

Hannah Star's Point Of View

I missed every other class that day. I knew I would probably get in trouble. Viper Moon Academy was really strict when it came to the grades and attendance of scholarship students. Skipping class and getting anything less than an A were reserved for students whose parents had paid the hefty tuition and room and board fees.

The Principal, Mr Sanderson, was a jolly stocky older werewolf with permanently rosy cheeks, thick white hair and a snow-white beard. He honestly reminded me of Santa Claus. He was nice, but he tackled attendance and grade issues of VIP students. Not even regular rich students got to see him. The regular rich students went to the Dean, Molly Summers, a young she-wolf who had just finished her psychology degree and was rumoured to be Mr Sanderson's daughter from a past fling.

She was known for her lenience similar to her alleged father. Unlike her alleged father, she was also known for being incredibly scantily clad. Male students loved to misbehave for this reason.

Scholarship students with issues were handled by the Vice Principal, Megan Hitch, who many students called "Mega Bitch" behind her back. She was a middle-aged she-wolf, who put on a fake sickly sweet persona when dealing with fellow teachers and parents. She reserved her true venomous nature for students, especially those on scholarship. She seemed to abhor the fact that she dealt with the scholarship kids. I could tell she was somewhat jealous of Miss Summers, but I couldn't blame her. It did seem as though Miss Summers had gotten that job in an unfair manner.

There were many people already in the faculty with degrees plus experience who did not get the post.

Just as I'd suspected, I received a summons to the Principal's office come Wednesday morning.

Wednesday 16th September, 2020.

There was a sharp knock on my door around seven in the morning. I was contemplating whether or not to go to class. I just felt so out of it. I knew I would get in worse trouble the more classes I missed but part of me actually hoped to get suspended or expelled. That would crush my grandmother, which was the last thing I wanted, but I desperately needed a break from Angelique and the Quads.

I had to put down my spoon before I could even take a bite. Jillian had kindly made me some breakfast before she went to class early. I answered the door still in my night gown.

"Yeah?" I asked the girl outside the door.

I recognised her as Madison Fong, Head Girl, daughter of hotel-owner, Mark Fong. The Fong Family also owned a few of those huge cruise ships, where passengers could vacation fully on a ship, because of all the stores, shows and attractions available on board. I knew all of this because she was a friend of Angie's. My Grandmother always made me go to Angie's birthday parties. I was never invited to her regular parties though, but her mom ensured I was on the guest list every birthday. Madison was a regular attendee. She worshipped Angie and was constantly trying to be in her good graces. She was even crazier over the heartthrob Quads than she was over popular mean girl Angie. She usually ignored me. She was focused on me now. Her uniform was pristine, her sleek black hair in a high ponytail, her pale skin was blemish-free. She stared at me in my fuzzy onesie, holding a bowl of dry cereal.

"Um, you need to come with me now to the principal's office!" She informed me.

"Okay," I said, stepping outside.

"No! Change first!" She said, seeming shocked I would walk out my room like that.

I usually wouldn't, but, after yesterday, I felt like nothing could be more embarrassing, so I was free in a way. I showered quickly and changed in the bathroom into my uniform. I wore the uniform according to regulation. No more trying to be cute. I left my curls down as they were still damp. I followed Madison to the office. There was a huge common staff room one had to pass through to get to the vice principal or principal's office, so students had to walk through a room full of gossipy teachers, whenever they were in trouble. Everyone knew the troublemakers because

Chapter 16

of this. I was usually well-behaved and my grades were good. Many teachers looked at me in surprise when they saw Madison leading me to the office.

I spotted Dean Summers coming out of her office. She was in a low-cut black fitted midi dress today with red stilettos, red lipstick and her chestnut brown hair in a stylish bun. She smiled at me. I smiled feebly back. I sighed as I headed towards the vice principal's office. Mega Bitch was going to make minced meat out of me. As I put my hand on the doorknob, Madison stopped me.

"What are you doing?" She asked.

"I'm going to see the vice principal!" I told her.

"No, the principal sent me to get you!" Said Madison.

Huh.

"No," I said.

"How would you know? Were you there?" Asked Madison sarcastically.

Well, no, but...

"I'm on scholarship," I told her.

"I know," she said. "Go to the principal's office! He's waiting for you!"

What?!

Just then, Vice Principal Ditch came out of her office almost bumping into me.

"What is it, Miss Star?" She demanded.

Her shiny brown hair was in a tight bun. She wore square-framed glasses and a grey tweed suit.

"Um, I missed class yesterday..." I said.

"Why?!" She snapped.

"I felt unwell," I said.

"Why didn't you go to the Nurse then?!" She asked.

"I..."

She made an exasperated sort of noise.

"One period missed is a serious infraction for a scholarship student!" Said Miss Ditch.

"She missed five periods," said Madison.

"WHAT?!" Screamed Miss Ditch, making all the other teachers in the staff room jump.

"I...I'm sorry," I said.

Miss Ditch was seething.

"A week of detention!" Barked Miss Dean.

"Please, Miss Ditch I've never gotten Detention before, and if I get more than three days Detention per term, I won't be eligible for renewal of my scholarship next term," I pleaded.

"You should have thought about that before you skipped class!" Snapped Miss Dean.

"She didn't skip. She was sick," said Madison, shocking me by defending me.

"She's lying obviously," said Miss Dean. "I'm writing her up!"

"Talk to Mr Sanderson first! He's the one who sent me to get her!" Said Madison.

Madison always spoke to the teachers so casually. She was stellar in every subject not to mention sporty and outgoing. Her family also donated an art studio to the school. I was surprised she was trying to get me out of trouble. She was one of those girls who wished they could be part of Angie's clique.

"I think I can decide on a week's detention without Mr Sanderson's input, Miss Fong!" She snarled.

"His instructions were very clear! He wanted to handle this! I'll go get him," said Madison.

She quickly went towards the Principal's door and knocked twice, ignoring Miss Ditch's outrage.

"Just a second," called Mr Sanderson.

He came out of his office, laughing at something someone was telling him over the phone.

"No problem, no problem at all, Alpha Quaid! It's a joy to hear from you as always! Thanks for the new swimming pool! I was a swimmer in my day, you know! Yes! I play water polo! I know you play yourself!"

Mr Sanderson glanced at me. He motioned for me to go into his office. My jaw dropped.

"She's here!" Said Mr Sanderson to the person on the phone who seemed to be Alpha Quaid, the Quads' father!

"Yes, I'm meeting with her now!" Said Mr Sanderson. "Thanks again! The golf clubs work great too! I upped my score. I'll see you then. Take care!"

"Miss Star, go on in! What are you waiting for?" Said Mr Sanderson, chuckling.

His laughter shook his belly. He was in an expensive looking grey suit with a white shirt underneath and a grey and black checkered bowtie. I made my way to his office but Miss Ditch stopped me, putting her bony hand on my shoulder.

"Mr Sanderson, she's a scholarship student!" Said Miss Ditch with a little girlish laugh. "I'll handle this."

Chapter 16

"No, no, not this one. I will be handling any... issues concerning Miss Star from now on," said Mr Sanderson gently.

"Why?" Asked Miss Ditch blankly.

"The Alpha would prefer it," said Mr Sanderson.

"The Alpha?!" Asked Miss Ditch.

"Yes, yes, Miss Ditch, go get yourself some breakfast and relax!" Said Mr Sanderson cheerfully.

"I've given her a week's detention for her absenteeism though," said Miss Ditch.

"Oh! No, no, no. Scratch that!" Said Mr Sanderson, taking the detention slip in her hand and throwing it away.

"Thanks, Madison! Tell your Dad the new art studio is just sublime!" He gushed.

Madison smiled. She strutted off leaving a shocked Miss Ditch.

I had never seen the inside of the principal's office before. It was spacious. His desk and chair looked so refined. The type of wood alone must have been extremely expensive. There were framed photographs of high-achieving past pupils all over the walls including one of the current Alpha when he was a student here. My heart hurt. He looked just like the Quads, or rather, they looked just like their Dad. Mr Sanderson helped me into a seat in front of his desk. He sat behind his desk and placed a box of tissues and a box of gourmet chocolates near to me. I looked at him like he was crazy.

"How are you feeling today, Miss Star?" He asked kindly.

"Good," I lied.

"You sure?" He asked, handing me a slip.

I expected it to be another detention slip like the one he'd thrown away but it was a pass excusing me from yesterday's classes.

"Would you like one for today as well? Perhaps, you'd like to return to class this coming Monday! It's Wednesday already! The week is almost done. You'll just take the rest of it off," said Mr Sanderson, writing up passes.

"Um, no, I... I should be in class. I was just a little unwell yesterday. I'm sorry," I said.

"Want to see the Nurse? We can have an on-call Doctor brought in if it's something serious?" He said.

"No! Please! I'm fine now," I said.

"Right, just rest then!" He advised, handing me three more slips.

"I won't need these! I'll make the effort to go! Won't happen again!" I assured him.

"Hold onto them!" He instructed, refusing to take back the passes.

I slipped them into my pocket.

Billionaire Quadruplet Alphas

"Um... why did you want to see me, Sir?" I asked.

"To just check on you, that's all," he said, smiling.

"The Alpha asked you to do this?" I asked hesitantly.

"Perhaps," said Mr Sanderson.

"Let's say he did. Did he say why?" I asked tentatively.

Had the Quads told their Dad about me?

"You had a rough day, yesterday, I'm told," said Mr Sanderson, keeping his voice low.

I nodded.

"Take it easy from now on," he said.

"I'm on scholarship," I reminded him.

"Technically, yes... but... you are... special! Very special!" Said Mr Sanderson vaguely. "Of course all students are special but especially you!"

What?

The Quads had made their father bribe the principal into going extra easy on me so I'd be less stressed and more likely to forgive them. That was my best bet. Of course, the principal didn't want to directly admit to it but the school was allowed to accept "donations." The faculty could also accept certain "gifts."

"Thank you very much, Mr Sanderson," I said softly.

"Call me Eric!" Said Eric Sanderson with a wave of his hand.

WHAT?

"Ok... thanks Eric!" I mumbled, getting up to leave.

His phone rang and he put up an index finger to signify I should wait.

"Yes, yes, she's here, right now!" Said Eric.

Was that the Alpha again? The door swung open. Jonah came in with his phone to his ear. He put it in his pocket. Eric put his phone away laughing.

"You were right there! Why didn't you say anything?" Chuckled Eric, getting up and clapping Jonah on the back.

Chapter 17

Wednesday 16th September, 2020 (Continued)

Hannah Star's Point Of View

"You called your father?!" I asked Jonah, immediately annoyed just from the sight of him.
Eric raised his eyebrows. Jonah smiled slyly.
"No! Your lover-boy Zaya did," said Jonah.
"Oh," I said, blushing, but calming down.
"Oh!" Mocked Jonah. *"Now,* you don't mind! *Now,* you think it's sweet and thoughtful! When you thought I had called, it was probably invasive and pushy!"
I took a deep breath. Jonah just knew how to grind my gears. My she-wolf suddenly indicated to me that this meant he'd be amazing in bed. She was nuts. I pushed her to the back of my mind. I didn't need her horny thoughts distracting me.
"Thanks again, Eric," I said to Mr Sanderson, feeling embarrassed at what Jonah had said right in front our principal.
Mr Sanderson chuckled. "I had my hands full back in my day. My mate was something else. You ladies are not always easy to please!" Chastised Eric playfully.
I sniffed indignantly and made my leave with Jonah hot on my heels. I practically ran out the large staff room and into the hallway.
"You're supposed to leave me alone!" I hissed at Jonah. "Wasn't that you and Noah's masterplan?!" "We couldn't leave you to get expelled. Eli told us he heard scholarship students had to have perfect attendance. Then,

Zaya called Dad to make sure it didn't turn into a biggµµer deal than necessary! I came to make sure Eric was handling it," said Jonah.

"Eric?" I said, rolling my eyes.

This Academy was ridiculously unfair.

"Don't pretend like you're not relieved Mega Bitch didn't throw the book at you and ruin your scholarship!" Said Jonah.

I sighed. "Ok, tell Zaya thanks for me!"

"Tell him yourself!" Said Jonah. "I'm taking you back to our suite."

"How is that gonna confuse the curse?!" I snapped.

I was so annoyed with their constant push and pull. I wasn't a wind up doll. Jonah rubbed the back of his neck.

"Listen, Angie took it way too far the other day," said Jonah. "She took the day off school today to go to some spa. As soon as we get things sorted with the curse, Angie will be out of your hair, trust me."

"So, your girlfriend ditched school to go pamper herself, so, you thought you'd sneak me into your room while she's gone?!" I snarled.

He stepped towards me, standing very close to me, barely an inch away. "I thought we could use some quality time together to get to know each other," he said, pouting.

He was really handsome but I was really pissed off. I wanted to piss him off.

"Where's Zaya?" I asked.

Anger immediately coloured his expression.

"I'm Jonah and I'm standing right in front of you!" He said.

"Well, go get Zaya," I said, folding my arms. He looked furious. "And then I'll consider coming back to your suite to chill for the whole day."

Jonah looked eager now that I had said that. He pulled out his phone and called Zaya.

"She won't come unless you ask her," he said blankly over the phone.

He put the phone to my ear.

"Baby?" Said Zaya over the phone.

His voice calmed me down. Technically, he had the same voice as Jonah but Zaya's tone of voice was always so sweet with me.

"Zaya," I said, feeling embarrassed at how whiny I sounded. "Are you at your private suite?!"

"Yes, Baby! I'm here in my cold bed waiting for you," he said.

I smirked. Jonah looked so annoyed.

"And Angie isn't there?" I confirmed.

"Angie? In my bed? No, my room has been cleared by Pest Control!" Insisted Zaya.

I giggled. Jonah rolled his eyes.

"Is Eli there?" I asked.

Chapter 17

"Yeah," said Zaya. He gave Eli the phone.

"Princess?" Eli said.

I grinned. "So you're there too!"

"The only person not here is you, Princess!" Complained Eli.

"Okay, I'm coming," I announced.

"Noah wants to talk to you," said Eli.

I hung up the phone. I had spoken to the people I wanted to speak to already. I walked away from Jonah, but headed in the direikction of the Quadruplets 'suite.

"You don't have a key!" Said Jonah from behind me, following me.

"I don't need one," I said serenely.

Jonah snorted.

"So, how're you gonna get into our maximum security private suite?!" Asked Jonah.

"I'm going to yell for Zaya and Eli at the door," I said.

Duh.

"What if the doors are sound proof?" Jonah asked.

"I'm pretty sure you have surveillance cameras that you glance at from inside. They'll see me even if they can't hear me, and if not, they'll smell me, or is the door scent proof too?" I asked, rolling my eyes.

Jonah huffed and puffed like the big bad wolf, but he wasn't blowing my house down, that was for sure. I quickly made my way to the lobby of the wing that contained the private suites. I passed through the magic and metal detectors, and walked towards the elevators.

"Hold on!" Said a guard.

I stopped.

"Is she with you?" The guard asked Jonah.

Jonah smirked at me.

"Go ahead and say no! Good luck explaining to all three of your younger brothers why I didn't come when you get up there!" I said, smiling and folding my arms.

The guard looked confused.

"She's with me," muttered Jonah.

He grabbed me, and yanked me into the elevator. He pressed their floor number. He was quietly seething. I was actually enjoying myself a little. He walked me to their suite. He swiped his card in the door and then used a key too. There was a literal lock and a technological one. The door swung open, and the other three Quads almost tumbled out of it. They stumbled backwards to let me pass. I walked into the suite. It was just as lavish as I remembered from the weekend I had spent here with Zaya and Eli.

"Princess," said Eli.

He gathered me up into his arms, and kissed me slowly, cupping my face in his warm large hands. I sighed happily against his lips. He kissed the tip of my nose and my eyelids. Zaya snatched me from him, and kissed me urgently, his tongue snaking into my mouth and his hands roaming my body. He left me a little breathless. Noah was staring at me and so was Jonah. I ignored them and went over to the huge television and put it on. I curled up on the couch. Noah sat next to me on the couch. I glared at him. He pretended not to notice me glaring at him. Jonah sat in front of the couch on the plush carpet. He was leaning against the place I was sitting. His shoulder pressed against my knee. I wanted to kick him but I didn't.

"Hungry, Baby?" Asked Zaya.

"Yeah! I haven't eaten since breakfast yesterday. I was just about to have some cereal this morning when Madison, the Head Girl, showed up to take me to the Principal," I explained.

"You need to eat, Princess," cooed Eli.

Zaya and Eli were fixing me a plate of stuff. My tummy grumbled.

"You need to take better care of yourself. You're not eating, and you look like you haven't slept too," said Noah.

"Gee, thanks," I said sarcastically.

Noah smiled slightly. I put my legs up on the couch to get away from touching Jonah on the floor in front of me. Noah's hand found my ankle and stroked it. Goosebumps immediately sprang up on my skin. I yanked my foot away from Noah. I placed my feet back on the ground. My knee was brushing Jonah's shoulder again. Jonah turned and looked up at me.

"What?" I asked.

"Do you like this?" He asked.

Like what? I thought he meant us touching.

"No," I said.

"Oh, well, can I change it then?" He said, reaching for the remote.

Oh, he meant the show on the television.

"No, I'm watching it!" I said.

"You just said you didn't like it!" Said Jonah.

"That was a misunderstanding," I replied, grabbing the remote and keeping it close to me so he couldn't snatch it.

"You're so confusing!" Jonah said.

I snorted with laughter. "I'm so confusing!" Wow, he was a huge hypocrite.

"No! I told you what my plan was," said Jonah.

I sighed. I was tired of this back and forth with Jonah.

"Here," I said, handing him the remote.

He changed the channel. I got up and went to the bathroom. I could hear them arguing outside

Chapter 17

"Why would you do that?" Grumbled Eli.

"Do what?" Asked Jonah.

"Change the channel!" Yelled Zaya.

"Yeah!" Said Eli.

"What's the big deal?" Asked Jonah incredulously.

Noah spoke but a lot more softly than the others. I had to put my ear to the door to hear him. "She had to be coaxed into coming here. You should just let her watch what she wants," he said softly "You can watch the show you like anytime. If she gets fed up with us and leaves, I doubt you'll feel like watching it though."

I heard Jonah's loud, exasperated sigh.

"You're usually much more charming than this," commented Zaya. "Almost as charming as me!"

Jonah chuckled a little. "It's just difficult to be suave with Star," he mumbled.

"Why?" Asked Eli.

"I never gave this much of a shit before I guess. It's stressful," said Jonah.

"You always let Angie watch whatever she wants," said Eli, his tone annoyed.

"Yeah," said Zaya. "The channel stays on fashion shows all day when she's here. You won't let us change it either."

My tummy hurt. Of course, Jonah treated Angie better than me. Probably because he thought she was better: richer, more popular, skinnier. I sighed. Maybe, he wished Angie was his mate and not me. I felt sick. My wolf told me not to think that way. I couldn't help it. I came out of the bathroom.

"Hey, Star," Said Jonah. "I put the TV back on the show you were watching."

"I think I should go," I said softly.

"No! Please! Don't!" Said Jonah, getting up. "Look, just stay, please. If you want, I... I'll leave you to hang out with Zaya, Eli and Noah," offered Jonah, looking heartbroken.

My wolf was whimpering because one of her mates was sad and the other three were tense.

"No, that's ok, let's all hang out together," I said softly, hugging myself tightly.

"You cold?" Asked Noah.

"A little," I mumbled.

"Should we change the temperature in here?" Asked Noah.

"No, leave it," I said.

Noah gave me his jacket. I put it on. I sat back down on the couch with Noah next to me and Jonah still in front of me on the floor. Eli and Zaya came over. They gave me a plate filled with roasted chicken breast, macarons, chocolate cake and truffle fries. So random! I just smiled. Everything tasted delicious though. Zaya sat on the floor next to Jonah. Eli lifted me up and sat down, putting me on his lap. I felt flushed. He had his arms around me from behind. I relaxed into him. I stretched out a little. My feet brushed against Noah's thigh.

"Sorry!" I said, pulling my feet away.

"For what?" Asked Noah, taking my feet and putting them on his lap. I was too shocked to protest when he began massaging my feet.

It felt so good. I sighed contentedly. He focused on the left foot. Zaya turned around from where he was on the floor and started massaging my right foot. He tickled the sole of my foot a little. I giggled. Eli began massaging my shoulders.

"I'm glad I came," I murmured.

The guys all laughed except for Jonah who was just staring at me. I bit my lip, staring back at him. He grasped my right hand gently and began massaging the wrist. I smiled slightly at him.

"So... do you really have to marry Angie for the plan to work?" I asked.

I didn't want to ruin the moment, but I could think of nothing else. The thought of Angie smugly flaunting her marriage to all the Quads while I faded away into the background made me feel sick.

"The witch we hired said a fake engagement would be enough to draw the entity out to try to trap it or banish it," said Noah.

"So all of you will pretend to be into her soon?" I asked, feeling a bit tense despite being massaged by four guys.

"No!" Snapped Zaya.

"No the sequel," responded Eli.

Eli and Zaya laughed.

"Me proposing to her as the eldest should be enough to insinuate that we're all on board with making her our Luna," said Jonah.

Proposing? I sighed.

"So you'll have to buy her an engagement ring and plan some romantic proposal for her?" I said dryly.

Jonah shrugged, focusing on my wrist.

"Won't she be devastated when she finds out your real plan?" I asked them.

I felt a small pang of guilt. A fake proposal was a pretty mean trick even though it was being done to the Queen of Mean herself. I really wouldn't wish that on anyone, not even Angie.

Chapter 17

"The good witch actually said she can wipe Angie's memory," said Noah.

Wow.

"That's amazing," I said in earnest.

"Can she wipe mine too so I don't have to remember witnessing all of this?" I asked, half-joking.

"It'll be over soon," said Jonah softly.

He began working his way up one arm and down the other. He was really good at massages. All the Quads were. I sighed, feeling a bit happier now. I closed my eyes and leant back against Eli, enjoying the massage. Eli had begun to rub my temples with his fingers in little circles. Noah and Zaya had made their way up to my calves. Jonah was now massaging my forearms. Suddenly, a loud banging sound made me jump.

"What was that?" I asked sharply, keeping my voice low.

'JONAH!" Called a shrill voice. It was Angie on the other side of the door, back early from the spa.

Chapter 18

Wednesday 16th September, 2020 (Continued)

Hannah Star's Point of View

Angie banged on the door again.
"I forgot my key! I'm tired! I wanna lay down! Hurry up! Jonah!" She shrieked.
"She has a key," I whispered.
The Quads gave me an apologetic look. I sighed. It felt like Angie was a part of their day to day life and I was the intruder. I got up to leave.
"No!" Said Noah quickly, surprising me.
"What?" I asked.
"Let's go to my room," suggested Noah.
"There's no reason for you to go! You're here with Eli and me!" Said Zaya.
Eli nodded and squeezed my hand. I looked at Jonah who looked really tired all of a sudden. I actually felt a tiny bit bad for him. I still didn't trust him though. I stood on tiptoe and kissed the tip of his nose lightly. He grinned at me in surprise. He grabbed me and nuzzled me enthusiastically. I wiggled away from him but smiled. I decided to stay sitting on the couch between Zaya and Eli. Noah went to sit in the arm chair and sulk. He seemed annoyed with Jonah. Jonah let Angie in
"Ugh! What took you so long? What were you..." she stopped mid-question, spotting me on the couch between the younger two Quads. I kept my expression neutral.
"Get out!" She barked.
I rolled my eyes.

Chapter 18

"She's our guest. Angie, mind your business," said Eli.

"If you don't put her out, I'm going!" Threatened Angie.

The other Quads looked at Jonah.

"Go wait for me in my room," said Jonah quietly.

She stomped off and slammed the door.

"She's too much trouble!" Hissed Zaya in hushed tones. "Can't you pick a different fake fiancee?"

"At this late hour?" Said Noah incredulously.

"Oh, please, there's she-wolves lining up and down the block to be with a first-born alpha. They wouldn't even necessarily have to like him," said Zaya.

"Thanks!" Snapped Jonah sarcastically.

"Can't we hire someone to knowingly and willingly be the bait?" Said Eli.

"Would that work?" Asked Zaya anxiously.

"But Angie is already having the premonition dreams? Then I'll have to start all over, wouldn't I?" Asked Jonah exasperatedly.

"What's with your cousin, Star? Why does she dislike you so much?" Noah asked softly.

I shrugged. "She's a snob," I said.

"That doesn't make sense," Noah mumbled.

For some reason Noah's mild comment made me flustered. I blinked away tears. I was determined to compose myself and not cry. I had never expected having mates to be so stressful. I thought it would just be smooth sailings once the mate in question wanted you too. I certainly could have never anticipated all of this.

Noah was looking at me, his expression worried and apologetic. I glanced at him and smiled faintly. I tried not to think of Jonah placating Angie right now. What sort of things did he have to say to her? Did he say he loved her? Did he call her beautiful? Ugh. I needed to stop mentally exhausting myself.

Star!

Huh? It took a few moments to realise it was Noah who was mind-linking me.

Yeah, Noah, I said.

Can we please go to my room? Just for a little while? Noah pleaded. *Just you and me!* He added quickly.

I looked at him and he was making puppy-dog eyes at me. I smiled slightly. I got up. Zaya and Eli looked at me.

Noah wants to show me something in his room, I said to both of them.

Eli raised his eyebrows.

I have the exact thing Noah wants to show you right here! Zaya exclaimed with a grin.

Eli burst into laughter. I rolled my eyes, but kissed both of them quickly before following Noah to his room.

Noah's room was similar to both Eli and Zaya's rooms. It had very lavish in decor, but I could tell that Noah had removed some of the excess. It was probably not to his taste. He shut the door. He sat on the bed. I went towards him.

"What's wro-"

He cut me off mid-question, pulling me to him, so that I was straddling him where he sat. He crashed his lips against mine hungrily. Heat coursed through me. He tangled his hands in my hair and I wrapped my arms around his neck. He leant backwards, and I fell with him, until he was lying down, and I was on top of him, neither of us breaking the kiss. His hands gripped the backs of my thighs under my school skirt, and I moaned into his mouth as he snaked them upwards. He deepened the kiss, slipping his tongue into my mouth. I felt so flushed and excited. Maybe, mates were worth the stress. I broke away, feeling slightly breathless. I sat up, still straddling Noah

"Star?" He breathed.

"Yeah, one sec," I said, panting a little.

He chuckled under me. I giggled. He played with my hands.

Luna," he said more to himself than to me.

"That couldn't be me," I told him with a smirk.

"You know it is," he said, slightly annoyed.

"You are not very good at pretending I'm not your mate and Luna," I accused.

"You're only just realising this?" He asked.

I giggled. He rolled with me still straddling him so that I was pinned under him with my legs wrapped around him. He claimed my lips again eagerly. Heat formed in my tummy. I knew I should pull away, but I just could not. Were we messing up all the work they'd done to confuse the curse right now? I pushed against Noah's chest, and he broke the kiss.

"Luna," he groaned softly in protest.

I giggled. He kissed the tip of my nose, my cheeks and my forehead. He was grinding against me.

"Noah!" I said indignantly.

He actually blushed.

"What?" He asked sheepishly, knowing very well what.

"This isn't the master plan," I said.

"Star," grumbled Noah, caressing my cheek and stroking my hair.

His gaze was so intense.

Chapter 18

"Everything I do is for you," he said softly. "And you think I don't care about you."

"There's no reason to be rude to me!" I snapped, getting angry.

"I know!" He said quickly. "I'm apologising!"

I glared at him. He smiled.

"I'm sorry," he said, nuzzling me.

He was still on top of me.

"I'm so so so so sorry," he said, kissing me in between every "so."

I sighed, calming down a little.

"I'm going to make this up to you big time when I make you Luna," he said.

I rolled my eyes but I liked where this was going.

"I'm going to wait on you hand and food!" He promised.

I smirked.

"You'll win every argument by default!" He said.

His lips found mine again, kissing me more slowly than before. His hands caressed my cheeks.

"I have a headache," I mumbled, pouting when we broke apart.

I did. They had stressed me out this week. There was banging on the door.

"Oh, God, is that Angie?" I grumbled, turning onto my tummy and snuggling into the bed.

Noah opened the door. It was Zaya and Eli.

"It's not the big bad bitch, don't worry," said Eli.

Zaya laughed.

"What's wrong, Princess?" Eli asked.

"My head," I groaned.

"Baby," said Zaya.

He straddled me from behind and started massaging my shoulders, neck and temples. Noah brought me some painkillers and a glass of water. I took them and drank the water. Zaya resumed the massage, to my delight. Eli was massaging my scalp. Noah managed my lower back and legs. He kept squeezing the backs of my thighs which was making me excited. My wolf wanted Jonah. I was shocked when he actually showed up. I smelled him as he came in.

"Where is she?" Asked Noah, meaning Angie.

I heard him shut the door.

"I booked her another different spa appointment for today. She got in an argument with someone at the other one," Jonah mumbled.

He hopped onto the bed and quickly joined his brothers, massaging my calves.

"Where's my spa appointment?" I complained.

"I could book you one... or we could take care of you," suggested Jonah.

I smiled to myself as eight hands caressed me, soothing me. My headache was a thing of the past. My wolf finally stopped nagging me. She was elated. I still had my complaints, but at least I had four massage therapists for the day.

A phone rang.

"Ugh!" I said.

"You're gonna like this, don't worry!" Said Noah.

"It's Jamie!" Said Jonah excitedly.

"Who's Jamie?" I said. That could be a girl. "A girl?"

I was about to go off on Jonah. Angie was enough to deal with.

"A witch," answered Jonah.

I perked up. "*The* witch?!" I said. The one who was gonna help us.

"The one and only! She's a Luna too. She's someone you can talk to. I know she had a hard rise to Luna-dom herself," Eli said.

"A witch Luna," I said to myself.

I didn't know that existed. I could only imagine how difficult that might have been for her.

"Ready to meet her?" Asked Zaya.

Jonah was talking to her on the phone. She was coming in the next fifteen minutes.

"That leaves fifteen more minutes of massage, or I'm never booking an appointment at this spa again!" I mock threatened.

The Quads laughed and got to work. I sighed happily. I felt Noah's lips on my neck. He was out of hand today, but I wasn't complaining!

Maybe, I could get used to having four mates.

Chapter 19

Wednesday 16th September, 2020 (Continued)

Jessie's Point Of View

Jamie and I sat at the back of a limousine. We were being chauffeured to the Viper Moon Academy

"You're not going alone! We're already both here on the Viper Moon Pack lands! End of story!" I said to my Luna, Jamie.

I was an Alpha of another town and pack called Ambrosia. I was not about to let my little witch, Jamie, venture off into the unknown to fight some random old hag, and free the Quintuplet Alphas from their curse.

"The Quadruplet Alphas will help protect me, of course. It's really not a reckless plan. We've been discussing it!" She said, gazing up at me.

"I don't care what the Quintuplets say. All five of them have to share a brain and a mate," I grumbled.

"They're Quadruplets. All four of them want to make sure their mate, Star, doesn't succumb to the curse. They do not share a brain, Jessie!" Chuckled Jamie.

Whatever.

"I don't care how many of them there are," I mumbled. "*I* am your only Alpha, and I have to watch over you. You will not be properly watched over by other alphas. They will be preoccupied with their own mate plus their fake mate too!"

I disapproved of this whole fake mate scheme. I could never conduct a fake relationship once I had already met my mate, Jamie. The thought alone was gross.

"It's a really complicated situation!" Jamie said. "Give the Quads are chance!"

"The Quads?" I said. "What gym are we at? This whole situation is sketchy. Thank goodness, I had the foresight to come with you."

"Yes, thank goodness for my big bad wolf, as usual!" She said brightly.

She kissed my cheek. She was trying to butter me up.

"I would have liked for someone to stay behind with our own twins!" She added.

This was what she was truly upset about. Our children were being watched over by their four grandparents. She had wanted me to stay with them.

"I trust my former Alpha and Luna parents, and your mom, who was mother of your coven before you, and your Dad, a powerful wizard. They can more than handle our twins. I don't trust Quints I've never met!" I declared.

"Quads you've never met," she corrected.

"I'll count them when I see them for myself!" I said, folding my arms.

Jamie was laughing. She kissed my cheek again, and then she wanted to be nuzzled. I was not okay with this situation, but I nuzzled her anyway. I gave her a small smile and kissed her forehead.

"If they call again, I will speak to them," I said.

"Yes, Sir!" She joked.

"Jamie!" I chastised.

"Jessie!" She mocked.

I grabbed her and tried to put her over my knee to spank her. She squealed and swatted my arm playfully. I tackled her onto the carseat and tickled her mercilessly. She shrieked and then giggled.

"I give up! I surrender!" She said.

"Good," I said, sitting up.

She sat up too.

"We're here!" She exclaimed.

"Look at this snobby school!" I said.

"Our school was just as snobby!" She said, chuckling.

"No, we were so down to earth and cool," I said, reminiscing.

"What?" She yelped. "Chloe and Zack were huge snobs!"

"You love Chloe and Zack! And our twins love their kids!" I said.

Zack was my Gamma and Chloe was his mate. We had all gone to the same private school.

"Yeah, they're reformed snobs now!" She informed me. "They've turned their backs on their old snotty ways! They're cool now!"

Chapter 19

The chauffeur opened the door for us. She laughed and pulled me towards the building. The school's front lawn was hilly. We walked up a few feet and then climbed a short flight of steps. We went through the double doors of the academy.

"Alpha Jessie! Luna Jamie! Or, should I say Mother Jamie?" Said a jolly mall Santa Claus, who began following us.

What did he want?

"Principal Sanderson! Either is fine! Or just Jamie!" Said Jamie.

"It's Eric! Please call me Eric! I feel like we're old friends," said Eric, the principal of this snobby school, who we'd known for twenty-five seconds.

"I'll escort you straight to the private suite of the Quads," said Eric.

"We're actually here to see the Triceps!" I said blankly.

"Jessie!" Hissed Jamie.

Eric laughed and his whole belly shook. He gripped his jiggling belly. He really was like a mall Santa. I wanted to ask for a super soaker for Christmas, but Jamie would accuse me of being rude probably. Mall Santa Eric led us to the private suite, and winked at us, and did a strange dance as he shuffled off.

"I'm bored, let's go," I said.

"No," said Jamie, ringing the doorbell.

The door swung open immediately. There was a tall guy with light brown hair and green eyes. He had an alpha aura about him.

"I'm Alpha Jonah! Well, future Alpha, call me Jonah! I'm so happy you're here, Luna Jamie! Thank you!" Exclaimed Jonah. "And you've brought your Alpha, Jessie!"

I nodded mutely.

"Yes! This is my husband and alpha, Jessie! Please call me Jamie!" Said Jamie.

"Please call me Alpha!" I specified.

"He's kidding," lied Jamie.

Jonah laughed.

"Let me get my brothers and our Luna, Star!" Said Jonah.

There were four of them, but who cares? Star was shy and hid behind the younger two future alphas.

"You okay, Star?" I asked.

"I'm okay, Alpha Jessie, thanks for asking!" She said.

I smiled at her. I couldn't help but feel sorry for her. She had to watch one of her mates pretend to like another girl, and she had to deal with the curse hanging over all of their heads.

"Okay, let's get down to business!" Declared Jamie.

The Quads nodded, their expressions serious. Star seemed a bit apprehensive.

"Jamie is the most talented witch I've ever encountered," I assured Star. "She makes magic I didn't know existed."

Star's eyes widened and she smiled.

"Okay," said Star, nodding.

At least, we could all agree on something.

Star's Point Of View

The Witch Luna, Jamie, was about my height, with golden skin, long dark brown girls and hazel eyes. She had brought her Alpha, Jessie. He was Alpha of Ambrosia, a large rich wolf pack with a lot of human interaction. Humans did not tend to come to our pack lands, as they still feared our venomous bites, though we had been relatively peaceful in modern times. Jessie was just as tall as the Quads, with glossy dark hair down to his broad shoulders, olive skin and blue eyes. He was a bit buffer than the Quads, though they, too, were muscled. It was easy to tell he was a more experienced alpha, especially in battle, by his stance and his movements. The Quads were definitely sizing him up. Alphas were all so easily ruffled for such powerful beings.

"I hear you've fought a lot of demons?!" Said Zaya to Jessie.

Jessie smirked. "Jamie's fault. She kept summoning them," he said, teasing his mate.

"I knew you'd be bored otherwise so..." shrugged Jamie.

I laughed. I watched her draw a circle with chalk around me and then line it with salt.

"What are you doing?" I asked, intrigued.

"Casting a protection circle around you to help hide you from Georgianna," said Jamie.

"The witch, who put the curse on the Quinn family?" I asked.

"Yep," said Jamie.

"But I can't stay in the circle forever?" I asked, confused.

"No, but you will while I summon her, which will be in the next few minutes," said Jamie brightly but nonchalantly, like she was talking about buttering toast.

WHAT?! So soon! I sat in my circle, and took a deep breath. Here went a whole lotta something.

Chapter 20

Wednesday 16th September, 2020 (Continued)

Jamie's Point Of View

After I cast a protection circle around Star, I set to work summoning Georgianna. I wanted to know what would sate her. Every spirit with a grudge had something they wanted. Something that would satisfy them. Something to settle the score and end their reign of terror. I was willing to try to hear Georgianna out. I had to admit her story hit very close to home. She was the witch Luna of an Alpha whose family did not approve. That Alpha's own brother had *actually* done away with him, poisoned him! I did not know who I'd be if someone took my Jessie away from me, especially if the reason was connected to me. The line between good and evil was thin when it came to magic. It was all about intent. A "good witch" today could be a "wicked witch" tomorrow, and vice versa.

I cast a protection circle with chalk and salt around myself also. The Quads and Jessie remained outside of the main vicinity of the spell. I placed a shielding charm on Star's circle to conceal her from the witch.

The Quads had done as I had asked. They had brought me a portrait of Georgianna to focus on. It was on the floor nearby, leaning against the wall. I had a black candle lit in front of me, just outside my circle. I took a deep breath, and closed my eyes. I focussed on invoking Georgianna. My spell-work had become second nature to me. I no longer needed incantations. I still used them at times, out of habit, but my thoughts were enough. I thought about Georgianna, picturing how beautiful she must have looked on the night of her wedding feast. She had been thrilled to have found her Alpha Alto. She had loved him so much. How had it felt when she had watched him die?

I opened my eyes. I stood. I looked down at myself. I was in a dazzling gown, shimmery white with gold and silver embroideries. My shoes were clear and embellished with crystals. I walked towards a floor length mirror against the wall of my lavish surroundings. The mirror was right where the portrait had been. There, I gazed upon my own reflection. I was no longer Jamie. I was Georgianna in all the splendour of her Luna regalia, on the night before her coronation, the night of her wedding feast.

I gazed around me. I was in a high-ceilinged wide hallway. This had to be inside some sort of palace. There were crystal chandeliers overhead, and the tiles and walls were so ornate. The varying patterns and colours of every item dazzled my eyes.

"There you are!" Said a husky voice.

I looked up, and immediately, warmth flooded my body just from the sight of him. He was tall, muscled and broad-shouldered, under his green and gold velvet robes. He walked over to me, and pulled me into a tight embrace.

"Alpha Alto," I heard myself say in surprise.

My voice was silvery-toned, silky and sweet.

"What have I said, my Love, about calling me Alpha?" Growled the huge man playfully.

I stared into his green eyes. They were well complimented by his robes. His light brown hair fell to his mid-back, and his beard was full and impeccably groomed. The hoarseness of his voice suggested he had been drinking, as did the faint smell of ale, though it was not enough to overpower his musky masculine scent. The smell made me tingle all over. Alto pulled me into a grand room filled with people in the midst of revelry. They were celebrating.

"Sneaking away from me to do magic in the middle of our wedding feast," chided Alto. "That is so like you, Georgianna."

He kept a tight grip on my waist as he held me to his side.

"You will be sorely punished tonight," he purred in my ear, making me shiver.

His tone did not suggest this would be an actual punishment. I gazed up at him, and he winked.

We went towards the head table which was overladen with decadent dishes and goblets of ale. He put me to sit in a high-backed chair near the centre. He sat next to me in a similar chair.

The people were so rowdy, many of them drunk already. A few, who had passed out, were being attended to by servants. A handsome man stalked over to us. He was not as impressive as Alto, but he had to be from

Chapter 20

the same lineage, same eyes, same hair though beardless, and similar robes. He was a more boyish version of Alto.

"Brother, congratulations on your beautiful bride!" He said in a silky deep voice.

The brothers touched foreheads.

"Thank you, Oleander," said Alto.

Oleander smiled, but it did not reach his eyes. They were the coldest green I'd ever seen.

"Luna and Mother, Georgianna," said Oleander with a little bow to me.

I sniffed and looked away from him in distaste. He sneered. Alto seemed not to notice this brief unpleasant exchange.

"Ollie!" Said Alto, slapping the cheek of his younger brother playfully. "Fetch me some more ale! Let's toast!"

Oleander went to get the ale. Alto had indulged greatly already.

"Perhaps, it is time to retire, my Lord," I heard myself say sweetly.

"Nonsense!" Boomed Alto.

He grabbed me up from my seat and onto his lap. My cheeks flushed.

Are you so eager for your punishment, my Love? He said in my mind.

I looked at him indignantly, and he roared with laughter.

You have the most expressive eyes in the world! Said Alto.

I tried to extricate myself from his iron grip, though I could feel Georgianna's body getting excited.

And the tightest pussy! He added.

I flushed, my cheeks burning. My thighs quivered a little. Oleander returned with a servant, who was carrying a platter bearing two golden goblets, one encrusted with emeralds and the other encrusted with sapphires.

Oleander set the emerald goblet down before me, and handed the sapphire one to Alto. He had another ruby goblet he was already drinking from. The male servant remained standing nearby, holding the empty platter.

"Let us drink to Luna and Mother Georgianna's good health! May she bear strong heirs!" Said Oleander.

I felt my body stiffen. I left the emerald goblet there, as Alto and Oleander clinked goblets and then drank greedily, ale trickling down their chins. Alto finished his first. Oleander laughed, spluttering on his, but soon finished.

"I've bested you again!" Thundered Alto.

"You always do!" Said Oleander rather affectionately.

Alto was truly quite drunk now, which was a feat for a large Alpha like him.

"Will Luna and Mother not drink to her own health?" Asked Oleander, staring at my full goblet.

I felt myself resist the urge to roll my eyes.

"My Love, have a drink! You could use one!" Said Alto.

I looked at the emerald goblet distastefully. I picked it up. Oleander smiled. I brought it to my lips.

There was a huge crashing sound, as the Beta had lost his arm-wrestling match to a new warrior and had become enraged, smashing a table and many pieces of china. Oleander hissed, his eyes turning black momentarily. He stalked over to yell at the Beta. He ordered several servants to clean up the mess.

"Our mother will be furious!" I heard Oleander snarl.

All of this happened in just a few seconds. Meanwhile, Alto snatched me back up into his arms on his lap as he leant back in his chair.

"Don't waist good ale, little witch," he growled playfully.

I kissed the tip of his nose. He grabbed my cup from me, and downed it. I giggled as the ale ran down his chin, trickling through his beard. He slammed the goblet down. Oleander winced at the sound, an over-reaction. He practically flew over to our table, his eyes wide and fearful, panting as he stared at his brother, the empty cup and me.

"Who drank that?" Oleander said, his tone strange.

"Me, obviously!" Boomed Alto. "This little witch doesn't drink! She's a saint!"

"What sort of saint practices witchcraft?!" Bellowed the Beta, laughing loudly as he came over.

I smiled slightly. The Beta had a bad temper with most people but liked me.

Oleander looked pale and sick all of a sudden. He trembled slightly.

Alto laughed with his Beta. He began to cough. The Beta clapped him on the pack. He had a fit, coughing and hacking. The Beta kept rubbing his back, and so did I. A few warriors came over. The soon-to-be former Luna rushed over with a glass of water for her son. He refused it. His coughing gave way to retching. He heaved but nothing came out. He sank to his knees. The warriors and their mates gasped. A few she-wolves screamed. Many cried out, "Alpha!" In worry. The crowd grew, becoming increasingly distressed, as Alto's face reddened. His eyes were bloodshot.

"Alpha," I cried, getting on my knees to continue rubbing his back. His mother did the same. Oleander just stared in horror.

A trickle of blood came out of one of the alpha's nostrils. It felt as though a band was constricting around my heart. The alpha swayed on his knees. He collapsed onto his back, but his mother and I supported his head.

"Alto! Alto!" I whimpered, caressing his face.

Chapter 20

The Beta was on his knees too, feeling the alpha's forehead.

"He's roasting with fever!" Exclaimed the Beta.

A servant rushed to us and placed a wet cloth on his forehead. The healers and pack elders rushed to the alpha's side. The crowd was wailing. The servant with the platter was trembling, still standing nearby. Oleander was on his knees too, though a few feet away from his brother. The elders and healers began administering all manner of concoctions that the alpha weakly accepted or refused randomly. He began to wheeze. My magic failed me as that band constricted around my heart. I felt as though I were suffocating. I felt feverish too. I knew it was the mate bond. Alto's eyes met mine and I felt a rush of love intermingled with worry.

"He drank from your wedding cup!" Breathed Oleander suddenly, looking at me with so much hatred.

"The one you prepared!" I shrieked, understanding suddenly filling me with terror and rage.

I was murderous, but I was not the murderer. Oleander was, and he'd hit the wrong target. He'd missed me.

The Gamma roared. "I knew it! WITCH! You poisonous wench!" Snarled the Gamma, black-eyed and baring his fangs.

He lunged at me. The Beta tried to stop him, but the Gamma was too incensed. He threw the Beta off of him. The Gamma knocked me over. He was about to slash at my neck with his claws, but a sword was thrust from behind into his torso. Blood splattered all over my wedding feast gown. The Gamma slumped over, eyes white now. Alto withdrew his sword from the Gamma amidst the cries and commotion. Alto had used the last of his strength defending me. He sank back to the floor. I cupped his face in my hands, tears streaming down my face. Alto uttered one last decree.

"No one is to lay a hand on Georgianna. Anyone who tries is to be slain," he forced out the words, his voice incredibly hoarse but still deep and powerful.

The Alpha command was final even as he lay dying.

I pressed my lips to his eagerly hoping there was still enough poison on them for me. Life did not entrance me at all if it was devoid of Alto. He moved his lips against mine, and drew me closer. The elders rushed back to us, still trying to administer herbs. I wished I could live in the light in his eyes as he beheld me. That would be my heaven. He stared at me until he drew his last breath. The light faded and went out. The healers and elders pronounced him dead as the crowd wailed, the pack members beside themselves. No one dared to touch me.

My blood ran cold. No band constricted around my heart because it was gone from my chest. Alto had taken it with him.

"You poisoned him!" I muttered at Oleander as I rose.

I was a sight, covered in blood, still in my wedding gown. The crowd gasped, turning to Oleander

"Liar!" Bellowed Oleander. "It was you! WITCH! You are NO Luna of mine!" He hissed.

The crowd turned back to me. They seemed more inclined to believe Oleander, their second prince, but there would be no punishment. Alto had been greatly revered.

"You knew!" I cried, turning to the servant with the platter.

He trembled, and in his eyes, there was so much guilt. Tears streamed down his face.

"Admit it!" I shrieked. "Oleander prepared that cup with poison for me!" I screamed. "Alto drank it in my stead!"

The servant shook his head fervently. "No," said the servant. "You prepared that cup for your husband. I saw you."

I had never boiled with rage such as this. I shrieked, and as I did, the servant was reduced to his very bones as his skin and flesh pealed off and burst into dust. I did not even know how I had done that. I was still just a girl of nineteen despite my title as Coven Mother. The werewolves were horrified beyond belief. Half of the pack warriors literally ran from the room. Oleander was immediately silenced. I felt it all. The rage. The injustice. The despair. I could scarcely look at my love as he lay there lifeless. I stalked towards Oleander who trembled, paled and fell onto his back, scuttling backwards on his hands. I looked at his eyes, so similar to my Alto. I couldn't do it. I couldn't kill him. His mother begged for him, but the Beta held her back. He seemed the only one that believed me. As Oleander crawled backwards, his head and back hit the wall. There was nowhere else to go. I stood before him. I pressed a finger to his throat where his marking spot was. He was still unmarked. I had a fate worse than death in mind for him, my fate.

"You and all your sons and successors will never realise your mate-bond. Any Luna betrothed to you and your lineage will die, as will her kinfolk!" I said, not recognising my own ragged voice.

I carved an X on his marking spot with my own nail. He screamed in agony as the curse took effect. He felt the pain of generations to come. He lay panting, his eyes shut tightly. I closed my eyes. I didn't want to look at him anymore.

I opened my eyes. I was Jamie again, sitting in a salt and chalk circle on the floor.

"Nothing happened!" Said Jonah. "Did we do something wrong?"

Jessie was staring at me, his eyes intense. He had seen what I had seen through our bond. His eyes turned black. He was feeling Alto's rage. He shut his eyes tightly, trying to calm down.

Chapter 20

Star was panting. She had seen too. We had shared that vision. Star began to cry. She sobbed

"Luna!" Exclaimed Noah, rushing forwards.

'NO!" I bellowed. 'Don't break the protection circle! Georgianna lingers."

Chapter 21

Wednesday 16th September, 2020 (Continued)

Star's Point Of View

I could not believe what I had just seen. The quadruplet's forefather, Oleander, had been a monster! Not only had he plotted to poison his brother's mate, he had also framed her for the alpha's death, when the alpha drank the poison accidentally instead. I didn't want to die, of course, but Georgianna wasn't the villainess I had been expecting. I sniffled. I dried my eyes. I felt her heartbreak, her despair. She had felt so alone, so enraged. I understood her wrath.

"Luna?" Murmured Noah, who had decided to sit cross-legged just an inch or two outside my protection circle.

"I'm ok," I said softly.

"Can I touch her if I don't disrupt the circle on the floor?" Asked Zaya.

"No," said Jamie sternly.

Zaya sighed. I smiled at him.

"Can I give her a tissue?" Asked Eli.

"No," said Jamie, getting a little annoyed.

"Can we-," began Jonah.

"NO!" Said Jessie on Jamie's behalf. "All of you have to chill. We are summoning the spirit of a vengeful sorceress here. It's not family game night."

Jonah looked furious, but he wasn't about to act aggressively with Jessie. The Quads had not ascended to their Alpha positions yet, but Jessie had, and a few years ago at that. Hierarchy was extremely important among werewolves.

Chapter 21

"Noah, bro, I think you're too close to that circle Star is in. Your instinct will be to grab her if something weird happens, which it will, and then, you will disrupt her circle, and leave her vulnerable," explained Jessie.

Noah reluctantly moved away from me. I didn't mind. I was impressed with Jessie. He was the kind of Alpha who was neither a tyrannical dick nor a people-pleasing pushover. Believe or not, well-balanced pack leaders were a rare thing. Many fell into those two categories I had mentioned, with the tyrant one being more common, as pushover leaders led to the pack being absorbed, or conquered by another pack, so they didn't last long.

"Should we have sealed one of these guys in the circle with her, little witch?" Jessie asked Jamie.

"No," Jamie said. "Georgianna needs to be able to see all the Quads clearly. It's okay, because she doesn't wish to kill them, just to make them suffer forever."

"Oh! Only that!" Said Zaya, feigning relief. "Here I was worried for nothing!"

Eli laughed. Jessie smirked a little, then winked at Jamie, who nodded and closed her eyes. They had to be communicating telepathically. I didn't know witches could mind-link? In the vision, Alto had spoken in Georgianna's mind. It wasn't exactly mind-linking, but very close, a medium where mind-linking met magic through the mate-bond. I closed my eyes too. I had the urge to focus. I wasn't sure what Jamie was doing, but I decided to project my empathy for Georgianna. I wanted her to know that not everyone involved was against her. Oleander had just been an awful person, and he got his punishment already. I didn't want her to see fear or hatred or anger in me. I wanted her to see empathy, understanding, even commiseration.

It was silent. Jessie and the Quads were all standing a few feet away with their arms folded. Jonah puffed out his chest a little more when he saw me looking at Jessie, who was staring intensely at Jamie. I stifled a laugh, closing my eyes again. I hoped Jonah would grow out of being an arrogant asshole and into being an admirable alpha. I would love that.

A cold wind blew across the room. Goosebumps sprang up on my arms. A chill crept through me. I felt the displacement of air near me, as if someone were breathing nearby, but I knew all the Quads had been made to step away from me by Jessie. I dared not open my eyes. I was trembling. Jamie began to chant something in another language. I assumed it was latin. She repeated it over and over till it became almost a hum. The temperature dropped. I was shivering. My teeth chattered. I still would not look. I kept my eyes shut tightly. I knew if I opened them I would see my breath, because it was so cold, but I was not sure what else I would see. I heard a soft sound like fabric sliding across the floor, as though someone in a floor-length gown with a train was passing by. The sound stopped. I could feel eyes on me. The air shifted, as though something were bending down towards me. I felt my curls move as the breath-like wind touched the top of my head. I felt the wind only one of my ears. I stopped breathing. I held my breath. I was terrified. There was a deafening silence, during which, my ears rang. The silence was interrupted by a raspy soft voice, speaking right into my ear.

"I. See. You." Hissed the voice.

My eyes snapped open, and I wish I had kept them shut. Georgianna, in her blood-stained gown, knelt at my side, her claw-like nails just a few millimetres from the salt circle. They scratched across the hard wood floor leaving marks. Her eyes were wide-open and wild. They seemed to swivel in her head as she looked at the five alphas, Jamie and me. I glanced at the alphas. I could tell immediately that only Jessie could see Georgianna. The Quads couldn't. Why?

Jamie's eyes remained closed. I didn't want to speak to ask her to look. Georgianna reached for me. Her palm stopped against the air as if there was a literal glass there. There was! Some forcefield or magical shell projected by Jamie. Georgianna banged against the invisible barrier. My heart was racing. She couldn't actually touch me. She became frustrated and she jerked her head to the side. As if prompted by her sudden movement, I flew across the room towards the far wall. I screamed. The Quads saw and heard *that*.

"STAR!" Bellowed Zaya.

Noah rushed towards me. Jonah paled, and Eli was transfixed.

Jamie stretched her hand towards me, palm raised, and I stopped, suspended in midair, held telekinetically by Jamie. Noah stopped a few inches from me, panting, staring at me. I moved my feet. They were dangling in midair. I looked around for Georgianna. Jessie seemed non-pulsed, as though girls flew through the air all day everyday in his life. Jamie slowly brought me forwards and lowered me onto my feet back into the circle. She ignited a blue fire that didn't burn the word around me in the circle. The fire raged high and then dissipated. She had cast some extra spell on me.

"You can leave the circle now," said Jamie. "I put a few charms on you."

"You sure?" I asked, my voice shaky.

Jamie smiled and nodded. I stepped gingerly out of the circle. Noah immediately scooped me up, cradling my head against his chest. All the Quads pressed themselves against me. I realised I was crying still, and they

Chapter 21

were wiping my tears and stroking my curls and kissing my cheeks. It was overwhelming, but my she-wolf was howling with delight. Noah pressed his lips to mine suddenly. We broke apart and he kissed the tip of my nose and then nuzzled me. Jonah snatched me away from him and just enveloped me in his arms. He held me so tightly, practically crushing my body to his. The elder two were being so handsy. I wiggled out of Jonah's arms and went to Zaya and Eli.

Jessie had his arms around Jamie. He pressed his forehead to hers and even though they did not speak, I could tell they were communicating.

"We can try again, I suppose," said Jonah hesitantly, looking at Jamie.

"Georgianna just flung Star across the room!" Snapped Zaya. "This is even more dangerous than waiting and hoping. We just won't mark Star or marry her."

My heart hurt a little.

"Sorry, Baby," murmured Zaya, nuzzling me.

"We can still have a ceremony, Princess," offered Eli. "We just won't actually legally marry. And Jonah, you can get rid of your whore now. She served her purpose."

Jonah glared at Eli but did not protest.

"A ceremony would provoke Georgianna," said Noah, frowning.

"Don't get rid of the decoy just yet," said Jamie. "This was a success."

"It was?!" Said Zaya incredulously.

"Yes," said Jamie.

Eli raised his eyebrows, prompting the Witch Luna to explain.

"I know what Georgianna wants now!" Said Jamie, her expression solemn.

Chapter 22

Wednesday 16th September, 2020 (Continued)

Jamie's Point Of View

I had seen it just before Georgianna sent poor Star flying across the room. I supposed, even the vengeful Georgianna could not deny the similarities between us. She was the only other Witch Luna I had ever heard of, though she had not gotten a proper chance at being Luna. Perhaps, I was meant to free her. It had flashed through my mind. Alto's lifeless body. The mourning had gone on for days. Georgianna had locked herself away. Oleander had taken over the pack. He had besmirched Georgianna's good name. He had hid Alto's body from her, burying it somewhere Georgianna had not been able to find. Georgianna had been consumed by hatred, living a wraith-like existence. She had tried to do away with herself, but she could not pass on. She could not sleep, not without her Alto. We needed to find Alto's grave. We needed to lay her to rest with her mate. She had been denied him in life. She refused to be denied him in death too.

"We have a lot of work to do," I said. "And it's going to be dangerous, but we need to get it all done as soon as possible!"

"Tell us what needs to be done," said Jonah assertively.

"Alto's body was concealed, somewhere unbeknownst to Georgianna, by Oleander. It was Oleander's final insult to Georgianna: hiding her mate's body. We have to reunite their bodies so they can rest together," I explained.

Jessie raised his eyebrows. "So Georgianna is dead too?!"

Chapter 22

"Yes, but her she lingers on. Her curse remains. She is very powerful and restless. She can't rest without Alto!" I said, my heart breaking for her.

"But then, we have two bodies to find! Alto's and Georgiana's," said Jessie.

"Yep," I said, smiling at my mate for catching on so quickly.

I loved how much respect Jessie had for magic.

"Okay, so where do we start looking?" Asked Zaya.

"Alto's body might be easier to find, right? He's gotta be buried on one of our properties, or somewhere related to us, the Quinn family," suggested Jonah.

Jessie nodded. "It'll be Georgianna's body that'll be difficult and dangerous to find. She won't want us messing around her body at first. I guarantee you she won't trust us or think we're trying to help," said Jessie with a sigh. "For Alto's body, just ask your grandfather and other older pack leaders or members for leads."

"We'll need to research Georgianna a bit. Find out where she might have chosen for her final resting place!" I said.

"What about fooling the curse?" Eli asked. "Are we still doing that, or did we blow it? I'm pretty sure she knows our mate is Star now!"

"Don't get rid of the decoy just yet!" I instructed.

Jonah sighed. Noah nodded sadly. Zaya made an exasperated sound. Eli took a deep breath.

"We should probably bring Alto's body to Georgianna, and not the other way around. I doubt it would be wise to try moving her body when she's...around..." Jessie trailed off.

It was worth a try.

"Yeah, as soon as we locate them both, we'll bring Alto to Georgianna, once feasible," I said.

Star was very quiet.

"You okay, Star?" I asked.

She nodded mutely. Noah went over to her and enveloped her in his arms.

"You said the decoy is having premonition dreams, right?" I clarified with Jonah.

Jonah nodded emphatically. "She is! She saw Damocles 'death."

"Okay," I said. "What about Star? Is she having the same dreams or is she unaffected?"

"She's good," said Jonah, smiling. "She hasn't mentioned any dr-..."

Star cut Jonah off. "I...I'm sorry I didn't say this sooner, but I am having the premonition dreams too. Just like how I saw that vision of

Georgianna that Jamie saw, I must have shared the dream of Damocles with Angelique," Star said apologetically.

I nodded, sighing. Jonah looked crestfallen. Noah paled and gripped Star closer to him, as if someone would grab her at any moment. Zaya and Eli edged closer to Star. The younger two had been reluctant to believe in the curse, but they'd just seen Star levitate, so they were probably believers now.

"What does this mean?" Asked Jonah anxiously.

"It means Georgianna is a bit uncertain which girl is your fated mate and which is your not-fated girlfriend," I said. "I would've preferred if none of her targets were Star, but this could work. At least, she is unsure."

"Won't she be sure after today?" Asked Eli. "Star was here!"

"No, not necessarily," I said. "If Star was a decoy, we could include her in a ritual like this. People see the world how they are. They also factor in their past. Georgianna knows treachery, so she won't be quick to believe anything too straightforward. She'll be cautious, keeping an eye on both girls," I explained. "You know what would really help Star be in the clear?"

"What?" Asked Jonah softly.

"If she had another fake love interest to add to the mix," I said.

Star actually smirked. Noah tightened his hold on her. Zaya and Eli closed ranks a little, and Jonah growled.

Jessie roared in response to Jonah's growl at me, which made all the Quads step back a little, like a litter of frightened pups who had upset their alpha Dad.

"Sorry, it was a reflex. I don't mean your Coven Mother and Luna any disrespect," murmured Jonah.

Jessie stalked over and snatched me up, pulling me flush against him.

"Okay," he said, accepting Jonah's apology, but his tone suggested we'd be leaving sooner rather than later.

I pleaded with him with my eyes.

"I don't like this whole decoy mates thing idea, but Jamie is trying to help conceal Star. That would be confusing if Georgianna saw Star with a guy," Jessie admitted.

"Do you have any trustworthy male friend?" I asked, not the least bit perturbed by Jonah's growl.

Werewolves, especially alphas, growled and snarled all the time.

"Yes!" Exclaimed Star excitedly. "Toby!" She squealed.

Jonah growled again, this time at Star's words. Jessie sighed and rolled his eyes at this behaviour

"That's great," I mumbled, eyeing Jonah.

Chapter 22

"Toby is gay," Star added, looking pointedly at Jonah. "But he can be my fake boyfriend. He would find that hilarious. I know exactly what to do!"

Jonah was seething despite being the one who had a fake girlfriend. Alphas were so territorial, but still wanted to do their own thing. Jessie kept me snuggled against him, my cheek pressed to his chest and the top of my head in the crook of his neck.

"Operation fake boyfriend commenced!" I said with a laugh ignoring Jonah.

I felt totally safe with Jessie.

"Meanwhile, Quads, you guys talk to as many old relatives as possible to try to figure out where Alto was placed. You can also ask them if they have any idea what became of Georgianna. I'll do my own research too," I said.

I was thinking I could use a ouija board and try to contact Alto, or better yet, Oleander, as he might know where both were buried.

"Star! Come here!" I said, wanting to do one final touch for extra safety.

Star came over, her eyes wide. I kissed her forehead gently. The place where my lips had touched shone in the shape of an actual star. The blindingly white glowing star faded into her skin.

"I'll know when you're in trouble okay, and so will Jessie, through our bond! The Quads can't mark you yet, so this way, we can track you," I explained.

"Thank you!" Said Star, immense gratitude apparent on her face.

"Thank you, Luna and Mother Jamie!" Said Jonah.

"Thanks so much!" Said Noah.

"Thank you!" Said Isaiah and Elijah in unison.

"You can call me Jamie!" I insisted. "You're most welcome!"

I winked at Star and hugged Jessie's waist. I made us both teleport back to our chauffeur. I wished I could have seen the Quads 'faces as we disappeared.

Star's Point Of View

The Quads jumped as Jamie and Jessie vanished into thin air.

"Cool!" Said Zaya.

Eli waved his hands where they had been.

"She's nice, but her mate has so much attitude!" Grumbled Jonah.

"Who Jessie? Hmmm, he reminds me of another alpha I know whose name also begins with J," I said pointedly.

Jonah flushed but ignored my statement for the most part.

Noah was quiet and pensive. I wrapped my arms around him and buried my head in his chest. He hugged me back.

"If Star and Angie are both suspects, then, will Georgianna target people in both of their social circles?" Asked Eli.

"Yeah," said Jonah sadly.

My heart rate picked up. Noah held me closer. I sighed into his shirt. I was anxious, but I was a tad amused to make the Quads jealous. I knew Toby and I would have a blast!

Chapter 23

Thursday 17th September, 2020

Star's Point Of View

"I'm really sorry, Star!" Said Toby, placing his hand on mine, as we sat across from each other at a cafe near the Academy.

I sighed. "It's ok," I said.

Toby had just broken the news to me that he wouldn't be able to be my pretend-boyfriend, because he was going abroad in a student exchange program for a few weeks. He was an avid language student, and this was a great opportunity for him to practise his Italian.

"Eat lots of pasta and pizza for me," I said half-heartedly, smiling faintly.

Toby frowned.

"I should have told you and Jillian I got accepted into the program sooner. I'll be back in six weeks. Star, why exactly do you need a fake boyfriend? Are you trying to make the Quads jealous?" Toby asked.

I couldn't bring myself to tell him about the curse and my brush with danger in the form of Georgianna's vengeful spirit.

"Yeah," I said weakly.

Toby smiled mischievously.

"Atta girl!" He said. "The way they act with you, especially Jonah, is so rude!"

"Zaya and Eli are sweet though," I said, feeling protective of them.

"But, didn't you tell me they almost made you cry at that party?" Said Toby.

"Yeah, but as soon as they found out I was fated to them, they've been nothing but nice to me," I said.

"And Jonah just wants to be with Angie?" Asked Toby.

I shrugged. I was trying not to reveal myself and the whole messy confusing backstory.

"You're worth a thousand Angie's, Star! I hope you know that!" Said Toby.

"You know what?!" Said Toby with a determined glint in his eyes.

"What?" I asked.

"I'm gonna help you," said Toby.

"How?" I asked.

"Please, please, let me do this for you! You have to say yes, before you hear what it is!" Said Toby.

"I can't do that!" I chuckled. "What if it's something crazy?"

"Don't you trust me?" Said Toby indignantly.

"I do," I said. I meant that.

"Okay? So?" Prompted Toby.

"Okay, I agree, I'll let you help me," I said.

"Great! We're holding auditions then!" Said Toby.

"Auditions for what?" I asked, getting a sinking feeling already.

"Auditions for a new hot fake boyfriend!" Exclaimed Toby.

"I love that idea!" Squealed Jillian, as she carefully sat down, while balancing our three frappes.

I smiled to myself. It would be nice to finally get a little revenge, especially on Jonah, and Noah too.

"Let's do it," I said.

Jillian and Toby grinned.

"I'm paying for it, okay, and I don't want to hear any protests!" Said Toby sternly.

"How and where are we gonna find this dream guy?" Asked Jillian.

"Easy. The drama club," said Toby. "We'll pretend we're putting on some play and looking for our male lead. The play will be a romantic story, and the lead actor gets paid, even though it's a school production. We only tell the guy we actually pick about the real plan. We let them think they're auditioning for real," said Toby.

"That's brilliant!" Said Jillian, astounded.

"Thank you," said Toby with a little shimmy.

I giggled.

Friday 18th September, 2020

Star's Point of View

Chapter 23

The auditions were held the very next day, after Toby and Jillian spread the word about the "play" far and wide. Twenty-six guys showed up to addition. I was shocked. I didn't even know that many people at this school acted. Toby was a member of the Drama Club, but he didn't act, he was usually the costume designer. We sat in the dark theatre at the Academy, looking at the brightly lit stage. A few members of the Drama Club had come to watch the auditions.

"How many people are in the Drama Club?" I whispered.

"About forty-five," said Toby. "But some of these guys auditioning aren't members," said Toby.

"You think they're in it for the money?" Asked Jillian, sipping her mocha frappe.

"It doesn't matter," said Toby.

Jillian nodded.

"All right! Who's first?!" Called Toby, scanning the names on his clipboard.

A tall dark-haired boy got up on stage and introduced himself. He then did a monologue. He was somewhat convincing, but not exactly what I was looking for. He seemed too into himself to be a good fake boyfriend.

We went through the twenty-six guys auditioning pretty fast. Each was given only three minutes to impress us, so we were done in just over an hour. We narrowed it down to three guys and thanked the others. I studied the three finalists: Dane Wallis, Harper Jogie, and Evan Eagleton.

Dane Wallis was a jock, through and through. He played rugby, basketball, and football. He was on the rowing team, and he had a black-belt in karate. He was also a personal trainer on the side for extra income. His clients were mostly girls swooning over him. He didn't need the extra income though, because his father owned the gym franchise, Alpha Build, where Dane worked. Dane was muscular and tall with pale skin, a light sprinkling of freckles, light brown eyes, and light brown wavy hair. He had a chiseled face and was extremely energetic.

Harper Jogie was the Academy's very own rockstar. He was the lead singer and lead guitarist for his rock band, Pariah. He was the least nervous out of everyone auditioning that day. He was clearly comfortable on stage. He was tall and broad-shouldered with lean muscles. He got his olive complexion from his father, who was from Dubai and owned several luxury hotels over there. Harper's eyes were hazel and there was something soulful about them. He had thick glossy hair, as dark as a raven's wing, that fell just past his shoulders. He smiled at us, showing off his dimples. He had auditioned with a guitar in hand, playing a melody, while he performed his soliloquy.

Evan Eagleton was an overachiever. He would probably get into politics someday. He was class president and the leader of the debate team. He was a bit preppy, so he played tennis and did equestrian sports. He was a bit shorter than the others with a slight build, greyish-green eyes, dark brown hair and a chin cleft. He gave a speech instead of acting. The speech was actually surprisingly well-written and he had great delivery.

"Let's ask some more personal questions!" Suggested Jillian quietly. "To see if they'd be good at the job."

Toby nodded.

"What do you guys look for in a girl?" Asked Toby, his voice echoing in the almost empty large theatre.

"I like a girl who's not afraid to kick it with the guys. She pregames. She can outdrink me. She's sporty, athletic, cares about her health, outgoing," said Dane.

I nudged Toby. That was definitely not me.

"Evan?" Prompted Toby.

"I like a girl with big dreams. She's involved. She has school spirit and a thirst for change. She loves a good debate. She's well-rounded. She does extra-curricular activities. She can speak up and stand up for what she believes in!" Said Evan.

That sounded wonderful. I was academic, but I wasn't a go-getter, and I hated extra-curricular activities. As soon as the bell rang, I would rush back to my dorm. Why would I spend extra time at school?

"Okay, thank you," said Jillian. "How about you, Harper?"

Harper was quiet for a moment. "I'm looking for someone genuine. She would be kind, smart and fun to be around, whether we're at a concert or in front of a television," said Harper. "I want us to be comfortable with each other."

I smiled. I could manage that.

"How do you guys feel about PDA?" Asked Toby.

"Hate it! It's so juvenile!" Said Evan immediately, although Dane was supposed to go first.

"Dane?" Asked Toby.

"I learnt my lesson when it comes to PDA. My main girl's best friend snapped a pic of me at the mall with my side chick," said Dane with a laugh.

Okay, next.

"I think it's fine. You shouldn't hide your affection for your person, but you also don't need to overdo it. Either extreme is usually not a good sign," said Harper, stroking his chin with a faraway expression on his face.

Toby glanced at me. I nodded.

Chapter 23

"Okay, we'll be in touch with you guys via phone later today," said Toby.

As soon as all the guys left, Toby called Harper and had him meet us at the cafe near the Academy, where we had first discussed the fake boyfriend idea.

"You kept me in suspense for a whole five minutes," joked Harper.

"Harper's actually a member of the Drama Club! We usually release the cast list a week after the audition," said Toby.

"You guys must be crunched for time. How soon will the play be?" Asked Harper.

"There is no play," said Toby, cutting right to the chase.

"What?" Asked Harper, furrowing his brow.

"The play was just a front!" Said Jillian.

"Should I be scared?" Chuckled Harper. "You want my organs, don't you?"

Harper had an offbeat dark sense of humour, but I liked it.

"Please, allow our darling, Star, to explain!" Said Toby with a flourish of his hand, gesturing to me.

I was sitting in the corner of the booth, facing Harper. Toby and Jillian had insisted that I be the one to explain it to him as an ice-breaker.

"You will be acting!" I said apprehensively.

"Okay," said Harper slowly.

"But not in a play. You'll be acting in real life," I said.

"Improv?" Asked Harper.

"No," I said quickly. "I need you to pretend to be my boyfriend.

Harper raised his eyebrows. "Why?" He asked.

"To make her mates, the Quads, jealous!" Said Jillian.

"The Quads are your mates?" Asked Harper.

"Yeah," I mumbled.

"Look, I'm not looking to get my face rearranged by four jealous alphas," said Harper.

"You won't," I said quickly. "Jonah has Angie. Noah is indifferent. Zaya and Eli are cool with whatever. None of them are territorial over me," I lied.

"And you want them to be, so you're fanning the flames of jealousy?" Asked Harper.

Yeah, sure, why not? This lie was more believable than the accursed truth. I nodded.

"How much does this pay?" Asked Harper.

"A thousand dollars a week!" Said Toby.

I yelped. What?

"The threat of death is very real. How many weeks are we talking?" Asked Harper.

"I can't say, and it's not like you need the money anyway," said Toby. "Your father is a movie producer and director, in addition to owning hotels."

"I do, actually. He cut my spending off for the rest of the year, because he found out how much money I was spending on... recreational items," said Harper with a sly smile.

"How much money do you spend on recreational items?" Asked Toby quickly.

"I can make do with fifteen hundred a week," said Harper.

"Done," said Toby.

"Did I say fifteen hundred? I meant two thousand," said Harper.

"Nice try," said Toby. "Fourteen hundred it is!"

"Fifteen!" Said Harper, shocked.

Toby laughed. "Okay, you drive a hard bargain!" Chuckled Toby.

Harper laughed. He shook Jillian's hand enthusiastically. Then, he gave Toby a firm handshake. Lastly, he took my hand in his huge warm palm and brought it his lips. He brushed his lips across my knuckles. I bit my lip, a bit nervous about the whole prospect, yet excited at the same time.

Chapter 24

Saturday 19th September, 2020 (Continued)

Star's Point Of View

In the midst of all this chaos, Chet, who was none the wiser, decided to throw a party. Of course, the Quads, as his best friends, would be there, and I, as Jillian's best friend, would be there too. Angie would undoubtedly attend, hanging off of Jonah's arm.

"This is so cool, Star!" Exclaimed Jillian. "It's like you have a secret weapon!"

We were getting ready to go to Chet's mansion for this last minute party he was having. This was not an exclusive intimate affair like the weekend at the cabin had been. This was a get drunk and dance on the table tops kind of party, the kind of party all the VIP students would attend.

I painstakingly did my hair and makeup with assistance from Jillian. Toby had left for Rome early that morning. I hoped him being miles upon miles away would protect him from the curse. I had been corresponding with the Quads via a group chat, that Noah had started. Jamie and the Quads were still toying with the idea of confusing the curse. I really hoped Jonah wouldn't have to propose to Angie. The thought made me feel sick. I hadn't actually told the Quads about my new fake boyfriend yet. They didn't know Toby had gone away to Italy. They were expecting him to accompany me to the party.

There was a knock at the door. I opened it to find Harper standing there in all black: a black T-shirt and black jeans. His shoulder-length hair was down. He looked so handsome. I smiled.

"What're you doing here?" I asked.

"I know we said we'd meet at the party, but showing up together is way more convincing, trust me!" Insisted Harper.

He handed me a single red rose.

"That's so sweet, thank you Harper!" I said.

He winked and extended his arm to me. I linked arms with him on one side, and Jillian linked arms with him on the other. He led us down to the foyer.

"Wait here!" He said.

He drove his sports car up to the entrance of the foyer, so that we just had to descend the short staircase in our heels. Jillian was wearing gold stilettos, a backless gold sequin top, and fitted pale blue skinny jeans. I had on high-heeled black velvet ankle boots with a mini black velvet dress. We got into the car and sped off. Harper drove just as quickly as Zaya. We were at Chet's mansion in no time. I vaguely remembered the feral white wolf I'd seen before the last party I'd been to. I pushed the memory away. Chet's mansion was even bigger than Angie's. There was an olympic sized swimming pool out back with a grotto off to one side and a water slide. There was a huge jacuzzi. I recognised some of my classmates, hanging out in small groups, all around the pool. Some were in bathing suits, despite the cold weather. Werewolves tended not to feel the cold.

I walked inside with Harper and Jillian. Jillian immediately launched herself at Chet, who lifted her off her feet, and kissed her lightly on her lips and forehead. He kept her close to his side, putting his arm around her. I felt a pang, thinking about how I couldn't have these small joyous interactions with my own mates, without fear or worry. As if he sensed my sadness, Harper put an arm around me, drawing me close. I gave him a small smile of gratitude.

Just then, I heard a nasal high-pitched voice. Angie. She was laughing scandalously, as she walked towards Chet and Jillian, holding hands with Jonah. I couldn't help but notice their fingers were interlaced instead of just cupping hands. I wanted to scream. Devilique was in a tight bright sparkly red tube dress with red pumps and red lips. Her long blonde hair was down. She looked pretty, but her personality managed to detract from it. Noah was on her other side, and thankfully, he wasn't holding her hand or even paying attention to her. I'd made him promise not to be rude to me anymore, and to just ignore me instead. Zaya and Eli weren't with them. I craned my neck, hoping to spot them.

Chet clapped Jonah on the back, and then bounced knuckles with Noah. Angie gave Jillian and Chet a hug. She gazed at me disdainfully. Jonah and Noah were staring at me and Harper with wide eyes. They both stiffened.

Chapter 25

"Harper! What's up?" Said Jonah with a smile that didn't reach his eyes.

I had forgotten that most of the popular rich kids knew each other. Harper was usually the lead in most of the school's productions, and his band had a cult following at school. Of course, he would know the Quads, and vice versa.

"Nothing much, bro. What's up with you?" Asked Harper.

Jonah shrugged.

"Noah," said Harper, nodding.

Noah gave him a curt nod in return.

"Jonah, could you go get me something to drink? I'm parched," said Angelique.

I resisted the urge to roll my eyes. She just wanted Jonah's attention off of me and Harper, and back onto her.

"Star, Baby, do you want a drink too?" Said Harper, tucking a curl behind my ear.

The expressions on the two elder Quads' faces were priceless. I stifled a laugh.

"Yes, please!" I said sweetly.

Noah was glaring daggers at Harper. Jonah still hadn't responded to Angelique's request for a drink.

"Be right back, Movie Star!" Said Harper with a wink.

That nickname was so corny, but it made me smile.

"Coming, bro?" Asked Harper, looking expectantly at Jonah.

Jonah seemed a bit dazed. He left with Harper to go get the drinks. Angelique grabbed Noah and wanted to dance. Noah's eyes kept darting back to me. He looked so cute and confused. Harper returned with my "drink" which was just three shots of cafe patron tequila in one regular eight-ounce glass instead of three shot glasses. I downed it quickly for some liquid courage. I spotted Jonah, giving Angie her drink. She drank it in two gulps.

"Follow my lead, okay," murmured Harper.

I nodded.

He led me onto the dance floor. Jonah and Noah both had eyes the size of flying saucers at this point. Harper twirled me around and dipped me. He was a really good dancer. He put his hands on my waist from behind and pulled me flush against him. The music was upbeat and infectious. He swayed his hips, while he was grinding on me. I blushed. He had his hands on my hips now, as he encouraged me to sway them too. My cheeks were burning, but I followed his lead to the best of my ability. I giggled a little. The patron cafe was hitting me. Someone tapped on Harper's shoulder. Zaya. Shit!

Chapter 25

Saturday 19th September, 2020 (Continued)

Star's Point Of View

"What exactly do you think you're doing, Harper?" Growled Zaya, getting in Harper's face.

The young alpha's eyes were black.

Harper laughed. "Dancing. What's the issue?"

"Your mangy hands are all over my mate! That's the issue!" Snarled Zaya.

I pleaded with Zaya with my eyes, but he wasn't looking at me. Harper kept his cool, smirking at Zaya.

Toby couldn't be my decoy. He left for Italy this morning for a six-week trip! I hired Harper to help me confuse the curse! I mind-linked Zaya privately.

He was not the one I wanted to upset. Zaya stared at me, considering my words. He glanced at Angelique dancing with Jonah.

"Whatever," mumbled Zaya, walking away.

My heart plummeted.

"I thought you said they weren't territorial over you," said Harper with a gleam in his eyes.

"They're not... I," I began.

"I mean, obviously, I knew you were lying, but how many of them are territorial over you?" Asked Harper.

"Two," I said. "Zaya and Eli."

"Okay. Noted," said Harper.

I looked in the direction Zaya had stalked off in.

Chapter 25

"Don't feel bad, Star," said Harper.

"Why not?" I asked.

"Because they deserve to be the ones feeling insecure for once. You had your turn. Even if the younger ones have been nicer, did they march up to Angie and tell her to take her hands off Jonah? No, for the most part, they're at least complicit with Jonah's bullshit," said Harper.

"Well, Eli did try to make Jonah get rid of Angie that first night," I admitted.

"And what has he done since then?" Harper asked.

Nothing, really, I admitted inwardly.

Harper made a fair point. I squirmed a little. I didn't feel like dancing anymore. Harper took my hand, lacing our fingers together, and walked me outside to hang by the pool for a bit.

Zaya's Point Of View

I tried my hardest to remain calm. I went to the bathroom and washed my face. My alpha wolf kept trying to come forwards. How did Star manage to not rip Angie's head off? I was seeing red at the thought of her and Harper. I knew he was a paid actor now, but it looked so real. It *was* real in a sense. His hands were on my mate. I roared and smashed the mirror. It shattered. I looked at my bloody hand. Splinters were pushed out of the flesh, falling to the floor, as the hand healed perfectly in a matter of seconds. This was Jonah's fault. She was enjoying hanging out with her decoy to get back at Jonah. I just knew it.

Jonah's Point Of View

Angie was trying to encourage me and Noah to dance, but my mind was faraway. Noah and I were forbidden from talking to Star at all. She had made that extremely clear. We were supposed to ignore her and not be rude to her. She even made a little case for it in the paragraphs she had sent to the group chat, claiming our past animosity hinted at something more, and only indifference would truly show there was nothing between us. I kept rereading her words in my mind. Toby was nowhere to be found. She had shown up with that wannabe rockstar guy, Harper, who was a major player. He had dropped more panties than all four of us Quads combined. That whole deep, soulful rockstar shtick won girls over every time. I couldn't believe *that* was who Star had chosen to be the decoy. I focused on my breathing. I couldn't even drink now, because I'd be trying to fight Harper if I had a few shots. I just knew it.

Noah's Point Of View

I knew I wouldn't be able to handle Star having a decoy, and I was right. I felt like throwing up at the thought of her with Harper. Where was Toby? She had done this on purpose. I had thought we had really connected back at the suite, when we had finally been alone together. I knew I had a lot of making up to do. I kept reminding myself that Harper and Star's relationship was as fake as Jonah and Angie's, though it was much more convincing than Jonah and Angie's. Maybe, that was because only Jonah was acting, and he was growing tired of it. Angie was fake, in general, though. I doubted she truly loved Jonah. She wouldn't look twice if he was not destined to be alpha or if he was broke.

My thoughts were interrupted when Zaya marched right up to Jonah and shoved him. Angie screamed. Jonah fell backwards, but caught his balance easily.

"WHAT THE FUCK, ZAYA?! Roared Jonah.

"THIS IS ALL YOUR FAULT!" Growled Zaya, eyes black, canines bared.

Everyone at the party was staring at them now.

"Guys, come on, stop it," I said sternly, grabbing Zaya's arm.

"He started it!" Snarled Jonah.

Zaya laughed humourlessly. "I really didn't though," chuckled Zaya, his eyes still black.

He glanced at Angie.

"Where's Eli?!" I hissed.

Eli would help calm Zaya down.

"How should I know?" Muttered Jonah.

I knew it was killing Jonah's pride not to shove Zaya back, but he was trying his hardest not to retaliate, as he was the eldest. He was only a couple minutes older, but he acted like he were centuries ahead. He was, in all fairness, protective of all three of us. Likewise, I did feel a responsibility to Zaya and Eli who were both younger than me. I tried to grab onto Zaya, but he stormed off. I followed him, and Jonah followed me.

"Leave him," said Jonah. "He'll calm down eventually, when he realises he's acting like an ass."

Angie followed Jonah.

"What are you guys arguing about?" She huffed. "It better not be that skank!"

Jonah's eyes turned black. He took a deep breath, before he turned to face Angie. When he opened his eyes again, they were their usual green.

Chapter 25

"She's not a skank, Angie. She's your cousin. Why don't you like her?" Asked Jonah.

I really didn't need a deep dive into the workings of Angie's mind right now. I sighed. Angie laughed coldly. The drink Jonah had made her was really just liquor in a glass.

"Because, she's not my cousin!" Hiccuped Angie.

"What?" I asked.

"She's not my cousin. The stupid bitch doesn't even know who her real parents are," said Angie with a laugh. "She thinks my dead aunty and uncle are her parents, but they're not. They just took her in. My mom swore me to secrecy," mocked Angie, putting a finger to her lips. "Why else would she not have a venomous bite? She's not even from this pack most likely!"

Jonah stiffened. "And she has no idea?"

"None, whatsoever!" Laughed Angie.

Jonah looked at her distastefully. He sighed.

"So, who are her parents?" I asked.

"How should I know?" Snapped Angie, downing the rest of her drink, and tossing the empty cup aside.

It was plastic so it didn't shatter. I saw the look of disappointment on her face as the cup remained intact. She kicked it, almost losing her balance. Jonah gripped her arm, keeping her steady.

Jonah and I stared at each other.

"Should we tell Star?" I asked.

"On top of everything else?" Said Jonah.

"You can't tell her!" Snarled Angie. "She's not supposed to know. She's never supposed to know. She can't go looking for her real parents!"

"I thought you didn't know who they were?!" I said.

"I don't, but I do know she's not supposed to go trying to find them!" Angie said.

"So, they're alive?" I asked, my heart racing.

Angie shrugged.

I wasn't following Jonah's lead on this one. I was gonna tell Star!

Chapter 26

Saturday 19th September, 2020 (Continued)

Star's Point Of View

"So, you haven't met your mate yet, I'm assuming?" I said, looking at Harper.

He grinned.

We were sitting huddled together on a bench near the grotto. Harper had given me his jacket. There were fairy lights strung in the trees overhead. Whoever decorated Chet's family home needed a raise. There was beauty in every nook and cranny, and a great attention to detail. Even the bench we were sitting on had hummingbirds and flowers carved into the wood. I kept tracing the designs with my fingers.

"No," he said. "I doubt one woman could tame me," he added with a laugh.

"You'd be surprised," I said, smiling.

He smirked.

"What's the real reason you hired me?" He asked.

Whoa. Harper's perceptiveness could work against me in this case.

"To make Jonah and Noah jealous," I said.

"I know you're lying, but it's okay," he said, shrugging.

"I do want to make them jealous though," I reiterated.

"You do," agreed Harper. "But that's secondary, a bonus, so to speak. That can't be the main reason."

Harper looked away.

"You're not a petty person. I can tell," he murmured. "You wouldn't go through all of this just to get even."

Chapter 26

He looked into my eyes.
I sighed.
"It's okay. You don't have to tell me," he said, smiling.
"Okay," I said softly.
"Should we practise kissing now?" Harper said nonchalantly.
I giggled.
"What?" I said.
I shook my head. He tried to tickle me, but I got up, pulling him with me.
"No kissing," I said.
That was a rule! He was much taller than I was. He leant towards me. I gasped. His nose brushed against mine.
"Do you think Jonah tells Angie no kissing, because he has a mate," he breathed.
I could feel his breath on my face. He was right. Jonah didn't put limits on Angie. I blinked back tears.
"Hey!" He said. "Hey, don't cry," he cooed.
He cupped my face in his hands and wiped my tears with his thumbs.
"Shhh, Movie Star," he said. "Let's see that smile!"
I sniffled, but I smiled. That nickname was so corny! It was growing on me though.
"Okay, ready for your close-up?!" Asked Harper.
I knew he was asking me if I was ready to go back inside and face everyone again. I nodded.
"Lights, camera, action!" He said as he pulled me inside.
I giggled.
The music was even louder than I remembered. Jillian ran to me.
"Star! You missed it!" She exclaimed.
Chet was behind her, looking annoyed.
"Zaya came and shoved Jonah! They almost fought! Noah broke it up and the three of them and Angie went off somewhere," she said.
Angie. I sighed.
"What did they fight about?" I asked.
"You!" Snapped Chet, glaring down at me. "HEY!" Said Jillian. "Watch your tone with my best friend!"
Chet winced. He opened his mouth to argue, but Jillian launched into a lecture.
"You never snap at Jonah when he makes Star cry over his relationship with Angie! So why are you coming at Star over her friendship with Harper?" Said Jillian, folding her arms.
"Friendship?!" Sneered Chet.
Jillian glared at him.

Chet sighed.

"Sorry, Star," said Chet.

Harper rolled his eyes at Chet's apology. I smiled at Chet. I was a little upset that he was so quick to argue with me. He hadn't had this much energy when I was crying my eyes out over Jonah and Angie, but then again, he was the Quads 'best friend, not mine.

"I think we should go," I mumbled to Harper.

"No, stay!" Whined Jillian.

I shook my head. "Sorry, Jillian," I said.

I gave her a quick hug. Harper held out his hand to me. I took Harper's hand. I glanced back at Jillian, who was glaring at Chet with her hands on her hips. He looked apologetic. Harper opened the car door for me outside. I kept expecting to run into one of the Quads. I hadn't even seen Eli tonight. Had he shown up?

"Chet is a stupid name," said Harper as we got into his car.

For some reason, that made me crack up laughing. I kept laughing as we drove off.

"What?" Laughed Harper. "It is!"

I giggled.

"Is Jonah a stupid name?" I asked, curious to hear his opinions.

"No! Jonah is a stupid guy!" Said Harper.

I chuckled.

"Angie is, you know, technically pretty, but that's about it," said Harper. "You're actually beautiful inside and out."

"You don't have to say stuff like that," I said.

"I know," he said.

I smiled.

"Your mate, whoever she is, she's one lucky girl!" I said, smiling at Harper.

Harper winked at me.

Eli's Point Of View

I didn't go to Chet's party. I hoped he and my brothers wouldn't be too annoyed with me. I had something way more important to take care of, so I went home to see Dad.

"Eli!" he exclaimed, as I walked into his study.

"Honey!" Shrieked my Mom.

She had been sitting on Dad's desk. She launched herself at me.

"Mom!" I said, chuckling as she began fussing over me, fixing my hair and adjusting and smoothing my blazer.

"What're you doing here, Honey?!" Said Mom.

Chapter 26

"I came to talk to Dad about something," I said.
"What's wrong?" Mom asked.
"What's wrong, Son?" Asked Dad.
"I... um... " I said.
"I'll give you two a minute," my Mom said kindly.
She kissed my forehead. I smiled gratefully at her. She left the room.
"I'll bring back some snacks in a while," she called.
I went to sit in the chair in front of Dad's desk.
"How's school?" Asked Dad.
"Good," I said.
"And your mate?" Dad asked.
I sighed. "Dad... the Witch Luna Jamie... she's helping us. She might really be able to break the curse! She tapped into Georgianna's mind, or whatever, and figured out what Georgianna might want... for her and Alpha Alto's bodies to be laid to rest together!"
"I know," said my Dad, nodding. "Jonah told me. Zaya called me too. I have the pack historian trying to locate Alto's body."
"Yeah. Well, when Georgianna came, her spirit made Star fly across the room. I was so scared Dad. I froze. I couldn't do anything to help Star in the moment and... that's not good enough. What kind of Alpha will I make if I can't protect my own mate? If I freeze, when I'm supposed to react?" I said, shaking.
Dad sighed. "Eli, you're only eighteen. You won't be an amazing alpha on the very day you take up the post. You'll become one as you keep training. The fact that you have awareness about you is a good sign that you have what it takes," said Dad, smiling.
I smiled too. "Thanks, but I still want to be better now!" I said.
"What do you have in mind?" Dad asked.
"I wanna up my training. It was just a chore for us growing up, and I didn't take it seriously and always goofed off. I want to be serious about it. Starting now, I want to do extra training with the pack warriors. Sparring," I explained.
My Dad leant back in his chair. He seemed surprised.
"The luxury of modern life and peaceful times have made werewolves soft. Alphas used to train with the pack warriors as a rule. That's a great idea," said Dad.
I smiled. "So, you'll allow it?!"
Dad nodded. I rushed to hug him.
"Just so you know, the pack warriors won't go easy on you, just because you're their future Alpha! Quite the opposite actually!" Warned Dad.

Chapter 27

Saturday 19th September, 2020 (Continued)

Eli's Point Of View

Dad clapped me on the back. I nodded resolutely. I ate the snacks quickly, so I wouldn't miss too much of the party, and would still make my Mom happy at the same time.

When I got back to the private suite at the Academy, I was shocked to find all three of my brothers back from the party already. They all looked up at me.

"I was gonna change here, and come meet you guys at the party!" I said. "What happened? It's barely eleven."

Zaya looked like he was seething. He sat, rigid in the arm chair, with his arms folded. Jonah and Noah looked forlorn.

"Where've you been?" Asked Zaya stiffly.

"I went to see Dad and Mom," I said. "I just wanted to talk to them about everything that's happening. What happened?" I asked again.

"Star has a fake boyfriend now, to match Jonah's fake girlfriend," Zaya said, glaring at Jonah.

"Didn't we know that already? Toby's gay…" I began.

"Toby is in Italy. Star's new fake boyfriend is Harper!" Snarled Zaya.

"Harper Jogie?!" I asked.

"Yes," said Zaya.

Harper Jogie was a ladies' man. He was in a band all the girls at school went crazy for, and I was pretty sure that was his motivation, not the music.

"He was all over Star," said Zaya.

A growl escaped me.

Chapter 27

"She's doing this to piss off Jonah!" Zaya said. "Jonah overdoing it with Angie is gonna make Star wanna overdo with Harper," said Zaya.

"What do you mean overdo it?" I said.

My heart started to race.

"What was she doing with him?" I asked quickly.

"He was grinding all over her on the dance floor!" Snarled Zaya.

I took a deep breath.

"This decoy thing was a bad idea. On both ends! Neither Jonah nor Star should have one," I said.

"I don't like it either, but the decoys definitely help make it look like there's nothing going on between us and Star," admitted Noah.

"So, you're fine handing Star over to Harper?!" Zaya snapped.

"Of course not!" Hissed Noah. "But I'll do what it takes to keep her alive! Georgianna is extremely powerful. You saw Star fly across the room!"

The image flashed into my mind. I was trying to forget it.

"We need to keep Star safe," I said softly. I sank into a chair with my head in my hands.

"You didn't see them together. It was awful," said Zaya.

I looked at my younger brother. His lip quivered.

"I hope I never have to," I said.

"You'll have to, tomorrow," Jonah said.

"Tomorrow's Sunday though," I said.

"You forgot!" Zaya said.

"Forgot what?" I asked.

"Tomorrow is the Academy's fundraiser, the talent show," said Jonah.

Fuck. We had to go to that as future alphas.

"I checked the list. Lover-boy is performing," said Jonah dryly.

"So is Angie!" Said Zaya, glaring at Jonah.

Ew.

"Well, Harper is in a band, and he acts, so it makes sense, but what's Angie gonna do?" I asked.

Being a bitch was not a talent.

"Criticise the audience one by one until her five minutes run out. She's going for a world record," said Zaya.

I snorted.

"She's gonna dance," said Jonah.

"Can she dance?" Asked Noah. "Like properly?"

"She's a cheerleader, so she and the others are gonna do a cheer I suppose. Well, a cheer-dance. It's a group thing," muttered Jonah.

A small part of me felt sorry for Jonah. He would paying for this whole Angie situation with Star for a while. Noah seemed jittery. He got up suddenly.

"Well, I'm off to bed!" Said Noah.

"What?" I yelped.

"You're the biggest night owl out of all of us," said Zaya, eyeing Noah suspiciously.

"It's been a long day," said Noah.

Zaya sighed. "It has," he said exasperatedly.

"Night," said Noah.

I watched Noah head towards his room. Jonah sighed, and went to his own room. I was thankful Angie wasn't staying over tonight. I sat next to Zaya.

"What's the real reason you went to see Mom and Dad?" He asked.

I smirked. He knew me so well. I could never keep anything from him.

Noah's Point Of View

I didn't go to bed. I jumped out the window. I landed lightly on my feet and kept walking. I needed to talk to Star. She had a right to know! That was what I kept telling myself. Deep down, I knew the real reason for me going to her dorm was that I hoped for a repeat of our last bit of alone time, especially after I'd seen her with Harper.

Thinking of Harper made me see red. I punched a wall, making a hole in the concrete. Shit! I glanced around. The hallways were dark and empty. Good. At least, no one had seen that. Defacement of school property shouldn't be on a future alpha's school record. The school was an extension of our pack, and I respected the school rules, just as I respected pack laws. One of those rules was against co-ed sleepovers in dorms. Private suites were incredibly expensive, and part of that luxury was there was no "lights out" time, and no restrictions on sleepovers. I felt a bit more excited at the prospect of hanging out with Star after hours. My wolf wanted reassurance and to know that she'd break the rules for us. I knocked on her door.

Star's Point Of View

Harper had insisted on walking me to my dorm. Once we got there, he had asked if he could run something by me. It was a song he was working on for the talent show tomorrow. He was performing a song with his band, Pariah, and he was going to do a solo performance afterwards. It was the solo song he was nervous about. He played it for me on his acoustic guitar.

Chapter 27

It was so beautiful. He had a deep voice with a bit of a raspy sound to it that still managed to sound sweet simultaneously. It was a song about searching for the one. I clapped when he ended the song.

"You like it?" He asked.

"No," I said.

His face fell.

"I *love* it!" I said, emphasising the word.

He grinned.

"You're really talented," I said.

"You think so?" He asked.

"Yeah!" I exclaimed.

There was a knock on my door. I knew that smell! Noah. It was amazing how my wolf could tell her mates apart so easily. Strangely, my wolf wasn't hostile towards Harper. I was expecting her to view him as a threat and hold some animosity towards him, but she was quiet and peaceful around him. I, on the other hand, was freaking out right now.

Harper! I mind-linked, afraid to even speak.

Yeah? He answered, furrowing his brows, probably confused as to why I was mind-linking him from six inches away.

Noah is at the door. I can smell him, I said.

Harper was completely calm. He shrugged. He really was a rockstar. He had that vibe.

He usually visits you after hours? He asked curiously.

No, actually! This is the first time! I said, surprised myself.

What do you want me to do? Harper asked.

What *did* I want him to do?

I'm really sorry but do you mind sneaking out? You don't have to, if you don't want to, but I don't think it's fair for you to have to argue with my mates all the time, and they obviously won't be reasonable, I said, looking at him apologetically.

Harper always managed to surprise me. I thought he would get pissed, but I forgot the depth of his cool guy vibe.

Sure. Sneaking out of girls' rooms always gives me such nostalgia. My third favourite past-time, after music, and sneaking into girls' rooms, in the first place! Said Harper in an easy-breezy tone.

He was chuckling.

Thank you! I said.

I kissed his cheek, afraid to hug him in case that left too much of his smell fresh on me. I could blame it on the dancing at the party, but I didn't want to push my luck.

That's a wrap, Movie Star! He exclaimed instead of just "bye". So corny!

He leapt out of the window easily with his guitar in hand, before I had mentally prepared myself. I knew he was a wolf, but I still got worried about him! I ran to the window sill.

Harper! I whispered even in mind-link.

Yeah, he whispered back, chuckling in my mind.

I laughed out loud, but then clamped my hands over my mouth.

Get home safe ok! I said.

Always. Safety first. Thanks Movie Star, Harper said.

I sighed. The knocking became a bit more persistent.

Luna? Came Noah's voice in my mind. *I'm really sorry if I'm waking you.*

Oh! Perfect! I stripped off my clothes and pulled on a nightgown in record time. I shut off my light, though he had probably already seen the light on, from under the door. I would say I was getting ready for bed, so I could leave my makeup on and still be a little cute. I was pissed with Noah and Jonah, but they were still my mates. I wanted to look nice.

Hey? Noah? I was just getting ready for bed! I'm coming! I responded.

I lit a random scented candle I had, to help diffuse Harper's scent. The bed! Harper had sat on the blanket and used a particular pillow. He had a very expensive sort of smell, like shopping in an overpriced department store, that also printed money. It was hard to describe, but it was very unique, and I liked it. I ripped the blanket off the bed and took the pillow, and threw them both into my hamper. I put another blanket on the bed. I only had two pillows so the one left would have to suffice. I sprayed perfume on myself as an extra precaution. I opened the door cautiously, trying to hide how out of breath I was. Why did I have to hide the decoy he already knew about and we had all agreed to?

Noah's face lit up as he saw me. I couldn't help but smile. He was still in his clothes from the party. I suddenly realised that, in my haste, I had put on a slightly see-through night gown. I hugged myself a little, glad that the room was dark, but Noah was an Alpha, so he could see everything regardless. I let him in, and shut the door, locking it. He grabbed my hand, lacing his fingers with mine. He walked me over to the bed and pulled me onto the bed with him. My wolf was immediately excited.

Noah had me lying against his chest, while he rubbed circles on my back with his hands. It was so soothing.

"You just came to see me?" I asked, thinking that was actually really sweet.

Noah sighed.

"I wish I could say yes. I definitely wanted to see you, Luna, but there's more," he said hesitantly.

I looked up at him. He cupped my face in his hands. He looked so sad.

Chapter 27

"I'm sorry," he said.

"For what?" I asked.

"For everything! For your life being difficult, even before you met me, for making it worse, for hurting you, for being hot and cold, cause I couldn't stay away, for agreeing to this stupid plan with Angie! She's the worst decoy we could've picked! I'm no fan of Harper's, but you picked a much better decoy than us. At least, he's accommodating," said Noah.

Noah saying something nice about Harper stirred up some guilt within me.

"In all fairness, my cousin doesn't *know* she's a decoy. She acts like a jealous girlfriend, because, as far as she knows, she *is* one," I said, still feeling a bit sorry for her.

"That's just the thing," Said Noah.

"What is?" I asked, confused.

"Your cousin," said Noah apprehensively.

I furrowed my brows.

"She... she's not..." said Noah.

"Not what?" I asked. "Not a decoy?!" I asked, my heart immediately starting to race as I began to panic.

Did they prefer her to me? Was *I* the decoy? Wait! That made no sense. Calm down, Star. I was actually their mate. My wolf was sure of that.

"Of course, she's a decoy, Luna," murmured Noah.

He seemed to sense what I was insecure about and brought my face to his, kissing me gently. He seemed to savour it. He nuzzled me slowly.

"You're the one. You're all I want, forever," he said softly, as though he were thinking aloud to himself.

I blushed a little.

"Thanks," I said, extremely awkwardly.

Ugh, I could've chosen a much better reply than "thanks."

Noah laughed, really laughed, wholeheartedly. He had a really nice laugh. I'd never seen him be so open and relaxed with me.

"It's okay, Star," he chuckled. "You're welcome, I guess."

I giggled.

"I just hope you don't say "thanks" when I propose or say "I do" or something, but I'm gonna take it to mean "yes" if you do," joked Noah.

I smiled. He stroked my cheek.

"You're so beautiful, Star. That's the perfect name for you," he said softly.

"It's my last name though," I said sheepishly.

He smirked. He continued caressing my cheeks, and then, he stroked my hair, playing with it. He inhaled my scent, and kissed my ear. He kissed his way down my neck, until his lips reached one of my marking spots. He sucked the skin there, making me shiver. I moaned softly, as he gently teased the spot with his teeth.

"Wait!" I yelped, pushing him away.

"I wasn't gonna mark you yet, Luna. I know it's not safe yet," he said.

"I know," I said. "What were you saying about Angie? She's not what?" I asked, still a bit anxious.

Noah took a deep breath. He held me very tightly against his chest. He began massaging circles over my back again with both of his hands.

"She's not your cousin," he said gently.

Chapter 28

Saturday 19th September, 2020 (Continued)

Noah's Point Of View

"What do you mean she's not my cousin?" Asked Star.

My Luna was looking up at me, eyes wide. I sighed.

"Luna," I said gently. "A little while ago, at the party, Zaya was really upset about Harper dancing with you."

My little mate squirmed uncomfortably. She looked a bit guilty.

"Zaya pushed Jonah, and after a brief argument, he basically stormed off," I continued.

"Yeah, I know," she said softly. "Chet told me you guys fought over me."

I stroked her cheek.

"Chet was a bit annoyed with me," she added.

"What do you mean?" I asked sharply.

"He just snapped at me when I asked what had happened, because he felt I caused you guys to fight by bringing Harper," She said.

My wolf growled within me. The human side of me knew Chet meant that protectively as our best friend, but the wolf in me did not want any males having anything to do with Star. My wolf was offended someone else had tried to discipline her.

"Chet is not to tell you what to do, or criticise what you've done," I told her sternly.

She nodded.

"You get enough of that from me," I joked to lighten the mood.

She giggled. I nuzzled her. Telling Star anything was very difficult. I kept being distracted by how cute she was and forgetting my point.

"Right," I said. "Then, Zaya stormed off so Jonah and I went after him, and Angie followed us."

Star looked a bit upset at the mention of Angie.

"So then..." I began.

"Have Angie and Jonah had sex since he found out he was mated to me?" Star blurted out.

She gasped at her own outburst, clamping her hands over her own mouth. She hid her face in my shirt. I chuckled. She felt the vibration of it and peeked up at me. She raised her eyebrows, prompting me silently. I shook my head.

"Really?!" She asked, eyeing me suspiciously.

"Really!" I assured her.

Maybe, Jonah should have had this talk with her all along. He wasn't communicating with Star effectively, but I didn't have much ground to stand on to criticise any of the others with how they handled Star. I had sensed our connection first, and immediately began to confuse her.

"Jonah and I are close. We all love each other, of course, the four of us. We're identical quadruplets, so the bond is very strong, but Jonah and I have a special bond as the elder two, like Zaya and Eli have as the younger two," I explained.

She was listening intently. I greatly enjoyed this: talking to Star, while she listened, her full attention on me. It was also an excuse to stare at her a lot without it being weird. Almost every moment spent with her, I've usually had to ignore her, or discourage her from being around me, although all my wolf and I wanted was to just gaze at her. Just this simple interaction gave me so much pleasure.

"So, Jonah tells me things. The night he met you unofficially was at Angie's party," I said.

Ugh, we were completely off-topic again. You will be the death of me, Star. How was I going to rule as co-alpha when my luna numbed my mind with her charm?

"After that party, Jonah was upset we'd made you cry. Angie was trying to hook up with him," I said.

Star flinched.

"And he couldn't..." I said.

"Couldn't go through with it?" Star asked, looking so hopeful.

Jonah was gonna kill me for this. He was the eldest and prized himself on being macho, and this wasn't my secret to tell. I sighed.

Chapter 28

"He couldn't get hard," I whispered.

Star gasped.

"Do not ever admit you know this to anyone please!" I beseeched Star. She nodded emphatically, her eyes in earnest.

"Not Jonah obviously, not Eli, not Zaya and not Jillian either!" I said. Star looked a bit surprised when I included Jillian.

"She'll tell Chet, and he'll tell Jonah, and Jonah will know I told someone, most likely you," I said. "Okay, so that was before he was sure he was fated to you. On the night of your actual birthday, they were kissing in the hot tub or something, and Angie kept trying to initiate stuff, and then, your scent hit him and he saw you. And since then, he knew he'd never be able to be with anyone else, in that way, ever again, or, at least, that's what he said. I think Angie can tell, how faraway he is when they do kiss, and she went from hating you to well... really hating you," I said.

Star looked amazed.

"Now, I'm going to tell you about something important, okay," I told her, fixing her with a determined stare.

She nodded, assuming a very serious expression, to show me she was not gonna change the topic. I smirked. My Luna was so cute.

"Zaya left. Jonah and I were outside Chet's house with Angie, and somehow, Jonah ended up asking Angie why she hates her own cousin so much, meaning you, and... she said she doesn't hate her own cousin..." I paused.

Star raised her eyebrows. "So she likes me?" Star asked, looking a bit happy.

Ugh, Star, don't do this to me.

"No, Luna, I'm sorry. She says she's not your cousin," I said.

"She's always denying we're related because I'm poor..." Star began.

"NO!" I said, grabbing Star's shoulders gently. "Star, Angie was a bit drunk, but she was very serious, and she confirmed that you two are not biologically related. You're not cousins," I said.

Star looked worried.

"Because Angie's aunt and uncle took you in," I said softly. "You weren't their biological daughter."

Star's lower lip trembled. Her eyes were very glassy.

"She also said her mother swore her to secrecy, not to ever tell you, because you weren't supposed to go looking for your real family. Angie doesn't know who they are, just that you're not supposed to search for them," I explained.

Star was silent for a few moments. To my surprise, she lay on my chest and closed her eyes for a bit. I kissed the top of her head, and told her how sorry I was, for upsetting her. I felt my shirt getting damp, and I knew she was crying into it.

"Luna, talk to me, please," I whispered.

Star looked at me, her big brown eyes filled with tears. She bit her lip. She did something that shocked me. She grabbed my face and kissed me urgently. I kissed her back just as enthusiastically.

She settled herself on my lap, straddling me, her arms wrapped around my neck and her fingers tangled in my hair. I had my arms around her waist, drawing her as close to me as possible. I wanted not even an inch of space between us. She tasted and smelled and felt *so* good. I slipped my tongue into her mouth, as I gripped her by the waist, and rolled over with her, pinning her underneath me. She wrapped her legs around me tightly, never breaking the kiss. Her nightgown was almost sheer, and it was so thin that I could feel her erect nipples against my chest. I was grinding against her instinctively. My member was so hard. I could smell her arousal.

We parted only when she was totally breathless, and I immediately trailed kisses down her neck, heading towards her breasts. My hands found the hem of her nightgown and pushed it upwards, revealing her smooth tummy and her breasts. She was panting. I eagerly took her left nipple in my mouth. She cried out. I swirled my tongue around it, and sucked on it. She whimpered. I moved my mouth to the right nipple, sucking and nibbling it, making her squeal.

I kissed my way down her torso, enjoying how smooth her skin was. I reached the waistband of her underwear, and I hooked my thumbs in it, sliding it down over her perfect thighs and calves. I tossed it somewhere, and parted her legs, putting her thighs on my shoulders as my mouth found her most sensitive area. She moaned as I licked her folds with firm pressure, parting them slightly. I glanced up at her. She was flushed. I licked her again, darting my tongue in deeper this time, so I could taste her better. She was so sweet. I plunged my tongue deep inside of her, and she stifled a scream. I looked up and saw she was clasping both her hands over her mouth, eyes wide as she looked down at me. I grinned. I sucked on her vulva. She arched her back, still stifling her moans and whimpers. I found her clit and traced patterns on it with my tongue, before taking it into my mouth and sucking it.

While I covered her vulva with my mouth, I prodded her entrance with my finger. She was very tight, but so wet from all my attention that it was easy to slip a finger in. She cried out at the intrusion, and I sucked on her clit harder, while my finger pumped in and out of her. She couldn't take much more. I could sense the pleasure building up inside of her through our bond. It enticed me further. I sped up the motion of my finger, and

Chapter 28

increased the pressure of my tongue on her clit, as I teased it, sucking it into my mouth rhythmically.

"Noah," Star pleaded.

What, Luna? What do you want? I asked in her mind as my mouth was busy.

I knew what she wanted. I added a second finger, and picked up the pace, as my tongue continued to explore her. She rocked her hips, moving in rhythm with my fingers and tongue. I heard another stifled scream as she came. Her whole body shuddered. She moaned. I felt a rush of moisture against my face and I lapped at her eagerly. I kissed her inner thighs gently, while she came down, panting. I waited for her heart rate and breathing to slow, still trailing kisses up and down her thighs and across her lower belly. I lay my cheek against her tummy. Her fingers began playing in my hair.

"You ok, Star?" I whispered.

" Noah," was all she said softly.

I kissed the skin under her belly button where I was resting my head. We must have fallen asleep like that, with me resting my head on her belly.

Chapter 29

Sunday 20th September, 2020

Star's Point Of View

I slowly opened my eyes. Noah had come to see me last night, and he was still here, asleep, his cheek resting on my tummy. I was in my nightgown and underwear again. He had probably gotten up at some point, during the night, and redressed me.

I smoothed his hair. It always felt so silky. He looked so content. I smiled at him. I couldn't believe I'd practically thrown myself at him last night.

The news that I was probably unofficially adopted had stirred up so many emotions in me: despair as I was mourning the loss of my parents again, betrayal as my grandmother had lied to me, confusion over whether this could be a good thing or not and hope, hope that my real family wanted me. Even though I was not supposed to go looking for them, I felt that they might want me. I needed to be wanted in that moment, and Noah was there, and *very* willing to show me *exactly* how much he wanted me. I had certainly rushed things.

I had to add guilt to the emotions. I should have only gone that far with Zaya and Eli. I cared deeply for Noah, so a part of me was soaring, but I felt relieved we hadn't gone all the way. Things with the Quads were still messy, especially with Noah, and well, Jonah was in a league of his own. Things with him were a whole natural disaster cleanup effort, not a simple mess.

I kept thinking about Zaya and Eli. Why hadn't they come to check on me? Were they so pissed with me that they didn't even wanna see me? I

Chapter 29

also thought about Harper. Now, I wished I hadn't kicked him out. I hadn't controlled myself with Noah at all. Had we messed up the plan to fool the curse? What if I had let him mark and mate me? I couldn't trust myself around him, not when I was a wreck emotionally. Maybe I should be thankful it hadn't been Zaya or Eli, I would've probably gone all the way, and ruined the plan.

Noah's stirring snapped me out of my thoughts.

"Luna?" He murmured groggily.

He looked up at me, his hair ruffled. He looked so handsome. My heart leapt a little.

"I'm surprised the head girl didn't bust me!" I said, just to have something to say.

I felt a bit shy. The head girl had gotten girls in big trouble before for sleepovers in the dorms. Only private suites allowed for sleepovers, hence, the word private. Night-time company was strictly forbidden in the dorms.

"She'd never do that?" Said Noah, yawning.

Yes, she would!

"She'd be stupid to get her future alpha in trouble," he said absentmindedly.

Oh. He was probably right. If she had picked up his smell, there was no way she would want to upset the Quads.

Noah was staring at me expectantly.

"Yeah?" I said.

He cupped my face in his hands, causing a rush of warmth to flood through me.

"Star," he said softly. "I know you were... going through a lot last night, and probably wanted a distraction, but I'm still really happy you let me stay."

My heart warmed. Noah.

"Okay," I mumbled.

I kissed the tip of his nose and he grinned.

"I love you, Star," he whispered, his green eyes gazing into mine.

My wolf practically howled.

"Don't ever doubt that," he added softly. "You don't have to say anything back. Just take your time."

I felt sad, thinking about how we had to pretend not to care about each other later at the talent show. Noah got up and stretched. He was getting ready to leave. The same panic from last night gripped me.

"Don't, please!" I said.

He looked at me with concern. "Don't what, Luna?" He asked.

"Don't go," I said softly, feeling a bit embarrassed to ask that.

He immediately crawled back into bed without further question. He pulled me onto his chest, and massaged my back, like he had done before. I sighed. The panicked feeling was dissipating slowly.

"Do you need any extra special attention?" He asked hopefully.

I giggled.

"Not right now," I mumbled, burying my face in his shirt.

My cheeks were burning. Noah hugged me to him tightly, which really helped the panic to fade.

There was a knock at the door. Harper? I got up cautiously and went to the door. I recognised their scent immediately, and flung the door open. Zaya and Eli! I flung myself at them. They chuckled, both embracing me. The panicked feeling didn't stand a chance. Zaya and Eli did not seem surprised to see Noah, though Noah looked quite guilty. I ended up in bed with all three of them trying to cuddle me. My wolf was wagging her tail. I knew she was about to bother me. She wanted Jonah to complete her almost perfect mood. I told her to relax and be grateful.

"We knew you were lying!" Said Zaya to Noah.

"Going to bed, guys!" Scoffed Eli, mocking Noah.

I was sandwiched between Zaya and Eli. Noah was now in the corner and he looked unhappy about it.

"I wanted some alone time with Star," Noah mumbled.

"You got it!" Said Zaya, annoyed.

"I can smell how much you got," muttered Eli.

I knew he meant the smell of how wet I was. My whole face flushed, and I hid in Zaya's shirt. Zaya and Eli smelt so good. They were already dressed and ready to go to the talent show early.

"Are you ok, Princess?" Asked Eli suddenly, sensing something was wrong.

"What's wrong, Baby?" Asked Zaya sternly, making me look at him.

I knew they were sensing my panicked feelings, even though they had cooled. They must have come because of that.

"Did you guys come to check on me?" I asked.

"Yeah, I felt a strange pain in my chest, and I got worried," Zaya said.

"I felt it in my tummy," said Eli.

"That's your stomach growling," said Zaya.

"No! I ate!" Said Eli.

I giggled at them. I kissed Zaya slowly. Warmth coursed through me. Then, I kissed Eli. He kissed me gently at first then lightly nipped me, making me squeal. Heat stirred to life in my lower belly as Zaya and Eli began caressing me, their hands roaming my body. My core moistened itself further. This was exactly what I had been pondering on. I was in

Chapter 29

danger of going too far with them. I felt so needy, and I couldn't resist them when I felt this way.

"Zaya, Eli," I said softly.

"Yes, Baby," cooed Zaya.

"Talk to me, Princess," purred Eli.

"You guys know, too?" I asked, referencing the news that I was probably adopted.

"Know what?" Asked Zaya, confused.

I looked at Noah, who looked even more guilty.

"They don't know. Only Jonah and I were there, and we didn't tell them yet. I wanted to get to you and tell you first," said Noah.

"What don't we know, Noah?" Asked Zaya, looking at Noah.

Zaya seemed a bit exasperated. Eli sighed and looked at Noah. Noah fidgeted uncomfortably.

"Well... last night... Angie revealed to Jonah and me that Star was taken in by Angie's aunt and uncle. Star wasn't their biological daughter. That's supposedly why Angie doesn't treat Star very well. Angie's mother swore her to secrecy, but she was drunk last night when she told us. Star's not supposed to go looking for her real family, according to Angie's Mom, but she didn't say why," said Noah, looking away from Zaya and Eli.

There was some tension among the three of them, and I knew this, too, was my doing. I sighed. I felt overwhelmed. Zaya pulled me onto his chest, while Eli massaged my back.

"Baby, how are you taking all of this?" Asked Zaya.

"Um, I don't know. I need to talk to my grandmother," I said.

"Sure, Princess, Zaya and I will take you to her now, if you want," said Eli.

"The fundraiser talent show though?" Said Noah. "We have to be there as future alphas."

"We also have to care for our Luna as future alphas," snapped Eli.

"Noah cared for her last night," said Zaya offhandedly, making me hide in Eli's shirt. "Let Noah and Jonah go to the fundraiser. You and I will take Star to her grandmother's house. We've been there before," said Zaya.

Eli nodded.

"You have?" Asked Noah, surprised.

The younger two nodded. Noah looked annoyed. They were all very snippy and jealous of late.

"You've both met her grandmother?" Asked Noah.

The younger two nodded again. Noah sniffed, folding his arms.

"When was this?" He asked curtly.

"Her birthday morning, when you and Jonah were trying to toss her out of Chet's cabin, without communicating with either me or Zaya or poor Star as to why," snapped Eli.

Noah looked apologetic. His annoyance at not meeting my grandmother yet faded. How could I have introduced him anyway? Noah and Jonah had never claimed me publicly, though a few would have realised based on my interactions with Zaya and Eli, that I might be fated to the Quads. My grandmother knew too. I was about to say something Zaya and Eli wouldn't like.

"I want to go to the talent show too," I said softly.

"Why?" Asked Zaya, feigning innocence, though I knew immediately, from his demeanour, he was suspicious.

"She wants to see Harper perform," said Noah, folding his arms again and looking away.

I was livid. I stood up.

"DON'T you dare be angry at me!" I snarled. "I've had enough!"

"Do not speak to me like that Luna! I am your Alpha, no matter how many times Harper serenades you," Noah said softly, but his tone was cold.

I burst into tears. It was all too much. Noah's face softened. Zaya's whole demeanour changed. Eli snatched me back onto the bed. The three of them dragged me back under the covers, kissing my cheeks and forehead, and rubbing my temples and shoulders. Our interactions got heated. I was still in that thin sheer nightgown, so I felt every touch and kiss through the fabric, as the three turned their attentions lower, their hands and mouths roaming my body. I was so wet down there, because of them. A moan escaped my lips. I could feel the same pressure from last night, back again, in my lower tummy, and it was growing hotter and hotter. It kept building. My nightgown had gotten hiked up, and my underwear and midriff were exposed. Zaya's warm lips were trailing gentle kisses across my torso, sucking my skin at random places, while Eli kissed my thighs. Noah's lips came crashing against mine urgently, leaving me breathless. I whimpered as Eli put his palm between my quivering thighs, rubbing my most sacred spot through the fabric of my underwear. I whimpered, breaking the kiss with Noah, who began kissing my neck, unperturbed. Zaya squeezed my thighs, parting them further, while Eli rubbed my core gently through the soaked fabric. I was shivering. Noah teased my earlobe between his teeth, his hot breath on my ear.

"Guys," I whimpered.

They all chuckled.

"What is it, Baby?" Asked Zaya.

Chapter 29

"Do you want to come, Princess?" Asked Eli.

I nodded mutely.

"What did Noah do to you last night, Baby?" Asked Zaya as he pulled my underwear off.

I blushed deeply, covering my face. Eli gently removed my hands, so they could see my flushed face.

"Tell us, Princess," said Eli, his voice raspy.

Noah was smirking.

"Um," I said.

"You don't like us anymore, Princess?" Asked Eli.

"She doesn't care about us anymore, Eli," said Zaya.

"I do!" I squeaked.

Zaya and Eli flipped me over suddenly. Heat flooded my lower body, and my stomach clenched.

"You're not being a very good girl anymore, Baby," growled Zaya in my ear.

Why did his growl make me so excited? I could feel Zaya's hands on bare butt cheeks, squeezing them. I groaned.

"I'm so sorry, little Princess, but we're gonna have to teach you a lesson!" Purred Eli in my other ear.

Noah was sitting up on the bed. I could feel his eyes on my bare behind. I hadn't done anything wrong. They were all my mates, including Noah, though I knew Zaya and Eli were a bit peeved about the sleepover, and all the extra special attention Noah had given me and gotten from me. I also knew Zaya was still pent up with rage over Harper.

"But, I didn't do anything wrong! Right, Noah?" I said softly.

'Begin," said Noah to Zaya and Eli.

Chapter 30

Sunday 20th September, 2020 (Continued)

Star's Point Of View

In one swift sharp motion, Zaya smacked my behind, making my butt cheeks quiver. I groaned, and my flower weeped. My stomach clenched. I clamped my thighs together. I moaned as Zaya massaged my behind.

"Relax, Baby," Zaya purred. "We're not gonna hurt you."

"Make sure she picks a safe word," instructed Noah.

A safe word?

"Hey Princess, unfortunately, you've earned yourself a spanking," breathed Eli in my ear. "You get to pick a word, any word you want, to be a safe word. You say your safe word when you really can't take it, and you wanna stop. Then, we stop. So, tell us your safe word, Princess."

I felt like Zaya and Eli were playing Bad Cop Good Cop. Eli was the good cop and Zaya was the bad one. Noah was their sergeant. Who would Jonah be if he were here? My wolf told me he'd be the police chief.

Another rougher smack made me squeal. It stung so good. I was not expecting to like this, or maybe even love it.

"You're taking too long, Baby!" Growled Zaya.

I felt his breath on me as his large hands gripped my thighs, parting them. He licked my flower. I gasped. When his tongue reached my clit. He took the little bud into his mouth and nibbled it.

"Oh, fuck," I heard myself whimper.

I was not one to swear much, if, at all. I was meeker than most, but Zaya had me cursing from one lick.

"Safe word, Luna! Now!" Ordered Noah.

Chapter 30

I felt Noah insert a finger into my entrance. My pussy clenched around it.

"Oh," I groaned, moving my hips instinctively as Noah pumped me with his finger.

He smacked me himself, right across the ass. I shrieked. I felt his lips planting kisses along the areas that stung.

"Aww, don't rush her," cooed Eli, chuckling.

My mind was numb. Did I even know any words? My wolf grumbled at me. She picked.

"My she-wolf picked Brink," I whispered, but they all heard me.

"Interesting," said Noah.

"Love it. You know, Baby, my Alpha wolf is so excited to meet his counterpart," said Zaya.

My she-wolf was practically howling with anticipation at the thought of meeting Zaya's wolf. He seemed the most dominant somehow, though he was the youngest.

"How many?" Asked Zaya.

"Ten," said Noah.

"Inclusive of the three Princess got already?" Asked Eli.

"No," said Noah.

A sharp smack from Zaya made me moan. My butt cheeks stung. Eli kissed my ear and rubbed my lower back. He whispered sweet nothings to me, while Zaya wrecked my behind, each smack a little harder than the one before it. The bed under my middle was damp from how excited I was. Between spanks, Zaya and, sometimes, Noah kissed and caressed the stinging areas. I had no interest in my safe word, which was something that shocked me. Halfway through, my thighs were trembling.

"Pause," said Eli to his brothers.

He brushed away wisps of hair that were sticking to my cheek. "You want your word, Princess? You remember what it is?"

I nodded.

"She wants her word?" Asked Zaya.

"No!" I squeaked. I was nodding to say I remembered what it was. "I remember the word."

Eli nodded. Zaya smacked me a little lighter this time, but by the seventh he had built up some force again and I was dripping. With the final smack, I came. I cried out and my legs shook. My climax shocked even me.

"Baby, you've got me rock-hard," murmured Zaya, as he rubbed his cheek against the globes of my behind. "You did so good! You've impressed us! You've superseded our expectations!" Said Zaya.

I knew by us he was including their wolves, the six of them total, each guy and his wolf.

"What a strong Luna you are," said Noah softly in the opposite ear to Eli.

He turned my face and pressed a gentle kiss to my lips.

You're perfect for us. That's why I love you so much, and I'm not gonna let anything happen to you, whispered Noah in my mind privately while we kissed.

Zaya flipped me over when he was done soothing my behind. I was panting. Zaya was putting my thighs on his shoulders. I knew what he wanted to do. I looked at him eagerly and expectantly. Eli claimed my lips and I cupped his face, pulling him to me, while I gripped Zaya shoulders insistently between my legs. I heard Zaya chuckle at my enthusiasm.

Suddenly, there was a knock on the door, followed by someone banging on the door, making the whole door shake. Eli sighed. Zaya groaned exasperatedly. Noah said "shit" under his breath. The person broke down the door literally. I screamed.

Jonah!

Jonah's black eyes faded, returning to green. He was panting. He stormed into the room. He took his shirt off suddenly. My eyes trailed over his rippling muscles and rock-hard six pack abs. My stomach lurched for one split-second, thinking there would be a fourth guy attending to me. However, he offered me the shirt.

"Star," he rasped, shaking the shirt in my face.

I put it on hastily. Noah, Eli and Zaya all stood. Zaya grumbled as he went to put the door back in the frame, though it remained unattached from the hinges. I could tell he wanted to cover the entrance in case someone walked by. He returned to his brothers. I stood too, awkwardly. Jonah's shirt almost reached my knees and the sleeves were too long for me. We all waited with bated breath as Jonah stood there, seething.

"ARE YOU ALL OUT OF YOUR FUCKING MINDS?!" Bellowed Jonah, using his Alpha voice for the first time in front of me.

The room literally shook. Some dust sprinkled down from the ceiling.

"Mon ciel étoilé, go get ready for the talent show!" He said, dropping his voice to a normal volume with me.

"Um, ok," I mumbled, slipping into my bathroom, my heart pounding.

I could hear him, yelling at his brothers.

"YOU CLAIM TO CARE ABOUT STAR, BUT YOU'RE WILLING TO RISK HER DYING BECAUSE YOU CAN'T KEEP IT IN YOUR PANTS!" yelled Jonah.

"WE DIDN'T MATE HER!" Bellowed Zaya, adding his Alpha voice to the mix.

Chapter 30

The bathroom shook. I slipped, but caught myself. I tried to shower hastily. Maybe, if they saw I was ready to go, they'd stop arguing.

"DON'T TOE THE LINE!" Snarled Jonah.

"YOU DON'T GET TO TELL US HOW TO HANDLE STAR! IF IT WASN'T FOR ZAYA AND ME, STAR WOULD'VE HAVE REJECTED US BY NOW!" Boomed Eli, also using his Alpha voice.

The tiles were quaking. I hurriedly washed and conditioned my hair, detangling my curls. I was afraid to go back out there but even more afraid of leaving them to fight each other.

"AT LEAST, SHE WOULD BE ALIVE!" Thundered Jonah, his voice cracking a little.

Was Jonah crying? My wolf began to whimper. He was! I threw on a robe and ran out.

"Jonah!" I said softly.

He opened his arms to me and drew me to him. He held me tightly against his chest. Tears were streaming down his face.

"Don't die, don't leave, don't go, please," he breathed in my ear. He sniffled. "I can't take it, if something happens to you," he whispered.

He held me at arms-length suddenly, as if catching himself, before he lost control. I knew Alphas' instincts to mark and mate their Luna were incredibly strong, but so was their instinct to protect her. They were all at war within themselves constantly, especially Jonah.

"Let's go," he said to his brothers.

They didn't fight him on this one.

"Let's escort Star to the show, even if we walk a few feet apart to seem separate," said Noah.

"I already ordered guards outside her room. They'll watch her from a distance, as she makes her way to the show. Are you wearing your ring, Mon ciel étoilé?" Asked Jonah.

He had stopped crying. He was business as usual suddenly.

"Yes, Jonah," I said, nodding. "Always!" I showed him the enchanted ring Zaya had given me on my finger.

Jonah rubbed the back of his neck.

"Your door will be fixed, while you're at the talent show. Is Harper meeting you here?" Jonah asked.

I shook my head. "No... not that I know of... but he sometimes shows up, even if he says we'll meet somewhere else," I said honestly.

Jonah nodded. He walked out, without saying anything else.

Noah looked at me with wide eyes.

Luna, I'm sorry! I'm been so reckless. I just couldn't stay away. I'm so sorry, Noah said in my mind.

Please don't apologise. I really needed someone here with me and thanks for telling me... about my family... right away. I don't wanna be in the dark anymore, I said in his mind.

Noah chuckled suddenly.

When you're in the dark, remember you're called Star for a reason. Darkness can't consume you, he said.

I smiled. Noah left reluctantly, staring at me till the very last moment.

"I don't give a fuck what Jonah says, nothing is gonna happen to my Baby. I have some extra things in place," muttered Zaya to Eli.

Zaya kissed my forehead.

"Dress up extra pretty for us, Princess, so we can admire you from afar, though you'll be with your actor," said Eli, also kissing my forehead. "You wear a lot of black!" Eli added. "I want something I can see from afar."

"Okay, Star?" Said Eli.

"Okay," I said, winking.

Eli winked back.

Chapter 31

Sunday 20th September, 2020 (Continued)

Star's Point Of View

Shortly after the Quads left, I turned my closet inside out, looking for something sparkly to wear for Eli. I found a dress Toby had given me as a Christmas present last year. It was a blush coloured dress that sparkled with multicoloured glitter all over it. It was rather short, but it flared out at the waist and had a sweet-heart neckline with long loose sleeves that were tapered at the wrists. I put it on and admired how it shimmered with every movement. I had never worn it, because of how short it was. I just couldn't bend over in it, that's all, I told myself. I had just finished fixing my hair and makeup, when there was a knock on my broken door.

"Um, who is it?" I asked.

"Ready for your close-up, Movie Star?" Said a familiar voice.

Harper!

"Come in!" I said.

Harper pushed the door open and caught it before it fell flat. He chuckled. He didn't seem the least bit surprised by the door. Did he know what had happened?

"Jonah has quite the temper, doesn't he?" Chuckled Harper.

"You know about what happened?!" I squealed.

Harper pulled me into a tight hug. He massaged my back soothingly. He kissed my forehead gently and smoothed my curls.

"Jonah told me," he murmured.

What?!

"What?! Why?! When?! How?!" I blurted out, sounding like a broken record.

Harper chuckled. He answered every question in order. "Yes, he told me the whole story. Because he wanted me to come get you and take you safely to the show. He told me fifteen minutes ago. It was over mind-link."

I was shocked.

"Ready?! You look the part, Movie Star," said Harper.

"Yes, ready," I said.

Harper always had this calming effect on me, like I'd known him before I even met him, as though I knew I was safe with him. He extended his arm to me and we walked down to the massive theatre at the Academy together. Harper was in all black as usual, a black silk shirt with black trousers. I caught many girls admiring him as we walked past them. My heart almost skipped a beat when I spotted the Quads making their way to the front row to sit near the Principal. Jonah had changed his shirt. Angelique was with them. I wondered if my smell lingered on the younger three. They turned around at the precise moment Harper and I reached them. I tried to steer Harper away from them, but, as always, he did not seem afraid of them.

Zaya stiffened. Eli smirked at my glittery blush-coloured dress, knowing it was for him. I looked down habitually as my cheeks reddened. Eli continued to stare at me with bright eyes. Jonah's body became more rigid, but he did not look my way. Noah looked right at me. He smiled slightly. Angelique looked me up and down, as if I'd grown a second head. She was sneering at my dress. She was wearing a red velvet dress that accentuated her cleavage and her hips.

"Angelique," said Harper smoothly.

"Hey, Harper!" Said Angie, smiling more genuinely at him.

"Jonah, Noah, Elijah, Isaiah," said Harper rather formally.

Zaya nodded and took a deep breath. Eli grimaced. Noah forced a smile.

"Harper, Hannah," said Jonah stiffly, smiling at us without meeting our eyes.

At least two dozen girls from Harper's fan club at school were squealing and swooning nearby. His band actually seemed to have groupies. I spotted pictures of him and the other bandmates in their hands. They were waiting for autographs.

"What song will you be performing today, Harper?" Asked Jonah.

"My band, Pariah, will perform the fan favourite, Fated," said Harper.

The fans overheard this, and a few of them screamed and jumped up and down. Others did little celebratory dances. I grinned at them. I wasn't jealous. Harper deserved those fans. He was truly talented.

Chapter 31

"I haven't heard it," said Zaya offhandedly.

"You'll hear it soon," said Harper with a grin. "I can't wait to finally introduce the band to my girl, Movie Star," purred Harper.

I blushed.

Zaya looked livid.

"You're just doing one song! A big school talent like you," said Eli.

Harper laughed his silky laugh. "No of course not, we're doing three as a band, and then I'm gonna sing one song solo, accompanying myself on acoustic guitar. That one is intimate, personal, from me to my Movie Star."

Eli was gripping the arms of his chair with a rather intense amount of force.

"Do you ever sing to Angie, Jonah?" Asked Harper.

I raised my eyebrows.

"We're not so showy. We're more low-key," said Jonah.

"Sure," said Harper dismissively.

Chet came over with Jillian. Jillian squealed and launched herself at me. We hugged. She had slept over at Chet's mansion, while I had been with Noah, and then Zaya and Eli, and then Jonah, who broke up the party.

"Harper!" Said Chet. "Good luck! Break a leg!"

"Break both," muttered Zaya.

Harper chuckled.

"You're gonna be amazing! I love Pariah!" Said Jillian enthusiastically.

Chet frowned.

"Hannah, what's your favourite Pariah song?" Asked Noah, expecting me to not know any of them.

"Luna," I said, the song not me.

Noah frowned.

"That song is amazing! But I like Fated better," said Jillian.

"How do you guys know these songs?" Muttered Zaya incredulously.

"You don't like music, Zaya?" Asked Harper.

"I'm very particular about my music!" Said Zaya.

"So is Movie Star," said Harper, kissing my forehead and pulling me close to his side. "She made sure I had my song for her just right." Harper nuzzled me.

Zaya looked like he was going to shift or faint. I wasn't sure which.

The head girl, Madison Fong, got on stage. "Please take your seats, everyone. Five minutes till the start of the show!" She said.

I liked her a bit now for not busting me last night, during my sleepover. I was sure she had heard or smelled what was going on during her patrol.

I also respected her for not being afraid of Miss Hitch, our scary Vice Principal.

Harper led me backstage.

"Excited to meet the guys?" He asked.

"Yeah!" I said. I really was.

Some of the other performers were nervously practicing or anxiously staring in their mirrors, adjusting their outfits and costumes. He walked me over to a group of extremely calm guys.

"This is Chester," said Harper as he clapped a guy on the back.

Chester was tall, lean and pale, with long auburn hair literally down to his back. He had one blue eye and one brown one. I stared at him, until I realised how rude I was being and looked away. Chester grinned. He was strikingly handsome, but in a very unusual sort of way.

"He's our drummer," said Harper.

"What's up, Leading Lady?!" Said Chester.

He had a sleepy way of speaking, like he was groggy from having just woken up. His long hair was lustrous and thick but tousled, as though he had, in fact, just rolled out of bed. Even his ripped jeans and Tee shirt were crinkled, but he smelled nice, sort of spicy, so I knew he had probably gotten ready. Grunge was just his preference.

"Nice to meet you," I said excitedly shaking Chester's hand.

Instead of shaking my hand, he pulled on it, spinning me around. The other band members cheered. I giggled.

"This is River," said Harper, nodding in the direction of a wavy-haired blonde guy.

He had green eyes that reminded me of the Quads. He had high-cheekbones and a dimple on only one side.

"Come through, Movie Star!" He said with a grin.

They were being so nice to me. Did they know I was only a fake girlfriend? These guys were very popular at the Academy, though somewhat unfamiliar, as they rarely attended class. I was used to popular rich kids being so mean, but they seemed genuinely thrilled to meet me.

"Hi!" I said shyly to River with a wave. He beamed.

"You play bass guitar right?" I said, trying to make conversation.

Harper had told me a little about each of them on the way here, because I told him I was nervous to meet the band.

"Guilty," said River with a wink.

"And this is Brink!" Said Harper.

I almost fell over. My safe word.

Brink was the tallest guy in the band, probably six and a half feet tall with medium brown skin, hazel eyes and long dreadlocks. He was incredibly buff. He suited his name.

Chapter 31

"Is your name really Brink?" I asked softly.

Brink laughed, and so did the others.

"His name is Clarence," said sleepy Chester.

"Clarence Williams the third," added River.

"Shut up, Sleepy and Drippy," said Brink, laughing but rolling his eyes.

His friends cracked up even more.

"Please, call me Brink, Star!" Insisted Brink.

I wasn't about to say no to him. He was built like an alpha. I nodded eagerly.

"I don't really see you guys around much. I wish we had some classes together," I said.

They all roared with laughter.

"Movie Star, we have like every class together!" Said Harper.

"What?" I said, shocked. "So you go to... none of them?"

They were almost in tears.

"Our parents paid off the principal. We have perfect attendance!" Said River.

Chester nudged him. "Don't admit to that!"

"Who cares?" Said Brink, pulling out his lighter to light a cigarette for a cheerleader nearby.

I heard that high-pitched nasal voice that I recognised so well.

"Moon! You're performing?! Backstage is only for performers," Angie said, as she strutted over, holding her cheerleader uniform on her way to change.

"Are you on the security team? That's a weird uniform your patrol squad has," said Brink, looking at Angie's cheerleader uniform.

The cheerleader Brink had lit the cigarette for laughed and so did a few others. Angie smiled faintly. She forced a laugh.

"Movie Star is my Muse!" Said Harper theatrically. Several cheerleaders swooned at this. "She is part of the Band!" Explained Harper. "She inspires me by her very existence. Her life is her performance as a Muse."

His bandmates nodded as if that were the most profound thing ever said. I heard a cheerleader whisper, "Wow." They were in awe of him. Angie was pissed, but trying to hide it, rather than seem uncool even for a second.

"Of course," said Angie. "A-Muse-ing." Angie laughed.

The bandmates were quiet.

"Humour is not your thing, Babe," said Chester, leaning back in his chair.

Everyone laughed, even the cheerleaders, though Angie was their captain. She glared at them, and they quickly stopped.

"I need to go change," said Angie with a fake smile.

"Safety first," said Chester.

A cheerleader snickered, but quickly shut up when Angie fixed her with a murderous stare. The cheerleaders left. The last one to leave was the one with the cigarette. She glanced over her shoulder at Brink, winking at him. He smirked at her.

"Is that your mate?" I asked, curious about the two of them.

The bandmates roared with laughter.

Chapter 32

Sunday 20th September, 2020 (Continued)

Star's Point Of View

"No, twinkle-twinkle-little-star, she's not!" Said Brink.

"She's so innocent!" Commented Chester. "What's she doing with you?" He said, grinning at Harper.

"Getting corrupted," said River.

They laughed, but Harper didn't. He surprised me. He spoke to them in another language I didn't quite recognise. They all clearly understood him, and stopped laughing. They didn't make anymore suggestive jokes with me, but they remained friendly and lighthearted, for which I was grateful.

The show started. The Principal, Eric Sanderson, schmoozed during his introductory address, mentioning several prominent families, name-dropping a few famous past pupils and acknowledging that our future alphas were with us, and that the pack's alphas have always attended this Academy since its inception.

The Vice Principal, Miss Megan Hitch, aka Mega Bitch, stood to his left and was as intimidating as ever, in an impeccably tailored black pantsuit. She sneered at a few overly loud students, when they cheered too much. She caught sight of me standing in the wings, and raised her heavily penciled eyebrows at me. She turned away from me with a huff.

Molly Summers, our young Dean and Principal Eric's alleged daughter, was all smiles, flipping her hair, and waving at each student who called to her. Dean Summers looked amazing honestly in a fitted turquoise turtleneck and a matching micro-mini skirt. She could pull off anything.

"On a sombre note, the faculty and pupils alike were so saddened by the untimely passing of our very own Mr Damocles," said Eric, sighing into the mike. "We'd like to have a moment of silence in his honour now."

I saw Angie in the opposite wing of the stage, folding her arms, looking sad at the mention of Damocles. She had been one of his favourites. I felt sorry for her. It must have been even more awful for her having the premonition dream of his death, as she cared for him. She caught me looking at her, and made a face, as though horrified that I was there. I sighed and looked away.

After the moment of silence, there were a few more introductory remarks, and some more buttering up of people who had donated funds to the Academy. Finally, Madison Fong came back to announce the first act.

"This next girl and her squad put the sass in sassafras!" Said Madison.

Excuse me, what?!

"Give it up for the Viper Moon Cheerleaders!" Cheered Madison.

The cheerleaders were up first! I resisted the urge to roll my eyes. I watched from backstage. They were good! Angie was good. I had to admit it. They danced to two different upbeat pop songs in their tiny sparkly green, black and white uniforms. I could see VMA for Viper Moon Academy emblazoned on the front of their crop tops while their names were on the back. The crowd went wild for them, especially the guys. Some of the male students were howling like wolves and wolf-whistling. I peeked out a little, trying to see Jonah's face. I spotted him looking down at his phone, smiling. What was he smiling at? He didn't have a third girl around, did he?

The cheerleaders ended their dance on a high note, posing and freezing in a pyramid formation, while the audience cheered. Many of the guys gave them a standing ovation, along with a few catcalls. The girls seemed thrilled. They strutted off the stage. Brink was standing behind me. He and the smoking cheerleader made eyes at each other. He lit another cigarette for her, now that she was finished performing. She puffed it and walked away slowly.

"Maybe if you like her a lot, you should encourage her to quit?" I asked hopefully.

Brink snorted with laughter. I flushed, feeling like a dork for saying that. I really didn't like smoking though. My grandmother's human friend had died of cancer all the while refusing to quit. She was honestly a kick-ass granny to the end, but I wished she would have just quit. Werewolves thought they were invincible though, so they were even less likely to curb any bad habits. I felt a pang, when I recalled that my "grandmother" wasn't actually my grandmother. I would deal with that later. I wanted to see Harper perform first.

Chapter 32

"Star is Smoky the Bear!" Chortled Brink.

"Only you can prevent forest fires!" Exclaimed Chester, coming up behind us.

I rolled my eyes, but made sure they didn't see.

"Star is just concerned. She's sweet," said River.

I smiled at him, and he winked.

"Star is trying to salvage the backstage at least, cause we're about to burn down the main stage!" Said Harper.

His bandmates cheered. A few groupies squealed nearby. How were they allowed backstage? Angie had made a big deal about me being here. Maybe, they were the other guys 'Muses.

After the cheerleaders, there was a break-dancing group. They span on their heads and did some cool tricks. I was amazed at all the talent at school. I usually didn't come to the talent show or any show put on by the school. It was always more trouble than it was worth, and I had been more afraid of Angie and her reign of terror back then.

There was a ballerina next. Zaya seemed really impressed by this routine, which made my she-wolf snarl. As the ballerina neared me while she came off stage, I recognised her as one of the hot tub girls from Angie's party with the Quads. I glared at her which was unlike me, but I couldn't help it. There was something fierce arising within me. A stage-light above us sparked suddenly. A few sparks fell on the ballerina, singeing her tutu. The girl jumped, startled and scurried off.

"Whoa! Star's right! Fire is dangerous guys!" Said Chester.

Chapter 33

Sunday 20th September, 2020 (Continued)

Star's Point Of View

It was finally time for Pariah to perform. I squealed with excitement. The guys took the stage. The crowd was screaming. The shrill screams of the groupies rang out over all the rest.

"Go Harper!" I cheered from the wings.

"Hey guys, we're Pariah!" Said Harper into the microphone, eliciting a deafening chorus of more screaming.

He grinned and signalled to the band. They played my favourite song, Luna, first. Their sound was alternative rock. Harper's unique voice was so alluring, and his onstage presence was captivating. All eyes were on him. Even the disgruntled looking Quads were staring at him. Harper played lead guitar and sang. Brink also had a few guitar solo segments. River's bass guitar and Chester's drumming kept the tempo. The song was infectious.

They moved smoothly into playing the fan favourite, Fated. The girls were dancing and singing along. The guys 'theatrics on stage were quite amusing. I couldn't look away. They finished with the song Rejected, which was a slower more sombre song, requiring a greater vocal range. Harper sang it flawlessly, belting out the notes. They finished on a high note and the screams shook the theatre. The girls continued to scream mindlessly as Pariah the band left the stage.

Harper returned to the stage with his acoustic guitar, and sat on a stool. The spotlight was just on him. A hush fell over the theatre as he began to strum his guitar, playing a beautiful melancholic song. He sang just as

Chapter 33

sweetly as he had last night. The girls were swooning. This was the song he had ran by me, The One. Everyone listened intently. He played the last few chords, and as the music stopped, the spell of silence he had cast on the spectators was broken. Another round of shrill screams longer than all the others rang out. I screamed too, and jumped up and down. He had done brilliantly. I had edged close to the side of the stage and was within view of the Quads, who noticed me squealing over Harper. I was met with four frowns and eight narrowed green eyes. I stifled a laugh, and slipped further back into the wings, so that I was obscured from view.

"I just wanna dedicate that performance to my Movie Star, Hannah," said Harper to the cheering crowd.

His declaration was met with aww's. He ran towards me in the wings and scooped me up, spinning me around. I giggled. He hugged me tightly whilst my feet were still lifted off the ground. He released me, and kissed my forehead.

"What did you think?!" He asked.

"Absolutely amazing! I loved it! Both the band and the solo song!" I said.

"Thanks, Movie Star!" Said Harper.

Harper nuzzled me again, and then touched his forehead to mine. For some strange reason, this made me emotional. I flung my arms around his neck, and he held me tightly.

What's wrong, Movie Star? He asked in my mind.

Mind-linking Harper was always so seamless, as easy as breathing.

I have to have a very difficult conversation with someone I love very much very soon, I said, meaning talking to my grandmother about my parentage.

That's a lot of very 's! Exclaimed Harper.

I giggled.

I felt so... complete, whole despite everything that had happened in a short space of time.

"What the fuck do you think you're doing?!" Yelled a familiar voice.

Zaya's Point Of View

I jumped, startled. I removed my arms from around Harper, but he kept his around me protectively. He looked at Zaya with a bored expression on his face.

"This whole thing is supposed to be charade, and yet I find you embracing in a dark little corner, where no one can see?!" Hissed Zaya, stalking up to us, his eyes black and his canines bared.

He was right. It did look suspicious, but it really wasn't. I just didn't know how to explain it to Zaya.

"Zaya, please, Harper is just a close friend," I said, feeling close to tears at the thought of them fighting.

"Get the fuck away from him!" Snapped Zaya.

"Not if you're going to charge at him!" I said.

Zaya roared. He was shaking. Oh no! I heard the sound of fabric ripping and bones breaking as he transformed, growing larger and sprouting fur. Zaya's wolf was massive, light brown in colour with the same piercing green eyes. Most werewolves retained their eye colour in their wolf forms, and their hair colour usually became their fur colour. Deviations from these rules were exceptionally rare and usually held great meaning. Despite the gravity of the situation, my she-wolf marvelled at her strong beautiful mate. Harper quickly placed me behind him. He shifted too in mere seconds just as quickly as the youngest alpha. My jaw dropped. Harper's fur was snow white.

Chapter 34

Sunday 20th September, 2020 (Continued)

Star's Point Of View

Harper's snow-white fur was reminiscent of the wolf on the mountainside the night of Angie's party, but that wolf was even larger than Harper's. I was sure of it. They weren't one and the same, but they were exceedingly similar. Did Harper know the identity of the white wolf? Harper and Zaya charged at each other. My heart threatened to cleave in two. I felt like I was at war within myself.

"STOP!" I screamed.

I heard the buzz of electricity as a surge of current shot through the overhead lights. Sparks flew everywhere. Thankfully, none of the sparks singed either of the beautiful wolves. The lights flickered on and off, as they ran towards each other. They paused mid-charge, both glancing at me, sensing something.

I felt woozy. I swayed on the spot. The ground came up to meet me.

****

"Star! Star!" Came a familiar voice.

"Huh," I murmured.

I was lost in darkness. It was warm and cozy, rather than cold and uncomfortable, like I thought it would be. I groaned. I slowly opened my eyes. Bright lights made me close them again, turning my face to the side. I slowly opened them again. Harper.

"Hey, Star," he said.

Billionaire Quadruplet Alphas

I smiled.

"Baby, I'm so sorry," murmured another voice.

I looked to the other side. Zaya! He had my hand in both of his.

"I'm sorry I frightened you," Zaya said softly.

"What happened?" I asked. "Where am I?" I added, realising this place did not look like the wings of the theatre.

"You fainted, Princess," said a voice. Eli. He was near the foot of the bed. His hand clasped one of my ankles. He squeezed it.

"You're in the infirmary at the Academy," said Noah. His voice sounded strained. He was at the foot of the bed also.

"Where's Jonah?" I asked. My wolf had begun to nudge me immediately.

"I'm right here," said Jonah softly. He looked pale and tired.

I was pretty sure I had terrified the Quads when I fainted.

I tried to sit up but it was difficult. My body felt so heavy. Harper sensed what I wanted to do, and helped me. Zaya helped too. They propped me up on a pile of pillows.

"Please, guys, don't fight," I mumbled. "I can't take it."

"I'm sorry," whispered Zaya.

Harper was quiet.

"Is she ok?" Asked someone behind Harper. It was Brink. River and Chester were behind Harper too.

"Star!" Squealed a voice. Jillian!

"Star! I just stepped out to use the bathroom! You're awake! Thank goodness!" Said Jillian, launching herself onto the bed and hugging me. I heard Chet chuckle.

"Are you ok, Movie Star?" Asked River.

"No more doing your own stunts ok? We'll get you a body double," said Chester.

I smiled at the bandmates. "I'm ok, guys, thanks."

"Zaya, Harper and I are..." I paused, realising Harper's bandmates might not know we were a fake couple.

I didn't want to reveal Harper's acting job. It was supposed to be a secret. I had been about to say Harper and I were just friends, but I couldn't mess up the charade so openly. Zaya and Eli had already called me Baby and Princess in front of the bandmates, but perhaps they thought those were more nicknames like Movie Star. They certainly hadn't reacted to the terms of endearment strangely.

"Harper!" I exclaimed suddenly.

Everyone looked at me, including a surprised Harper.

"Yeah, Movie Star?" he said softly.

"Um... your wolf... it's white," I said.

Chapter 34

"Yeah, that's quite rare," commented Jillian, eyeing Harper and then me with interest.

I wondered if Jillian remembered the white wolf from the night of the party. I had been with her and Toby. I had told them about it.

"Yeah," shrugged Harper.

"I never knew you had a white wolf," said Jonah.

"Harper never knew he had a white wolf either!" Joked Chester.

His bandmates laughed.

"What do you mean?" I asked.

Harper brushed a curl out of my face, tucking it behind my ear to the chagrin of all the Quads.

"He only shifted for the first time this month," Brink said.

"He's the youngest one in the band, though he acts like the eldest," teased River.

"By a few months only," said Harper, rolling his eyes.

"When did you turn eighteen?" I asked quickly, my heart racing.

"On his birthday," said Chester.

River smacked Chester on the forehead playfully.

"Dude," said River, "As opposed to when."

"She means when is his birthday, Chester," said Brink.

"I know," said Chester. "I was just kidding."

I wasn't sure if Chester had actually been kidding, but I turned back to Harper who was looking at me intently.

"September 12th, Movie Star," said Harper with a wink. "I'm a Virgo."

"Yeah, he's a virgin," said Chester, clapping Harper on the back.

Harper rolled his eyes again. My heart was beating so fast. Noah was staring at Harper, like he'd never seen him before. I could practically see the gears in Noah's mind turning.

That was my birthday too. That meant Harper had not been the massive white wolf on the mountainside, because neither Harper nor I had shifted yet on that day, before we both turned eighteen. Harper wasn't the white wolf, but what if he was...

I pushed those thoughts from my mind. I had so much to do to get to the bottom of things. I had to find the while wolf, and I had to have a chat with my grandmother. I didn't have time to be lying around. I sat up and swung my legs out of the bed.

"Hey!" Said Harper and the Quads and the bandmates in unison.

"Chill out, twinkle-twinkle-little-star, you're not going anywhere!" Said Brink sternly.

"Don't tell her what to do!" Barked Zaya. "Star! Get back into bed!" Added Zaya.

"Harper, are your parents white wolves?" I asked.

"No, actually," said Harper.

"So, you don't know any other white wolves?!" I asked.

Harper shook his head.

"Are you the only white wolf at school?!" I asked.

Harper shrugged.

"Most likely," said River.

"Star," chuckled Jillian swatting my arm.

"What?" I yelped.

"He's not the only white wolf at school, silly!" Jillian said.

Everyone gasped and turned to her.

"Don't you guys know?" She asked incredulously, eyeing the Quads.

"Oh, that's right! You only saw her after she shifted back! I was the only one who ran out to look just as you ran out the cabin after we cut the cake together!" Jillian said.

"What are you talking about?" I asked, getting frustrated.

"Star! Didn't you even look at yourself in the lake or notice your own paws or anything when you shifted?" Jillian asked.

I shook my head.

"Star! You're a white wolf too!" Said Jillian.

Chapter 35

Sunday 20th September, 2020 (Continued)

Harper's Point Of View

My eyes snapped open. I had fallen asleep practising the guitar on my bed in my private suite. In just a few hours, I needed to be fully ready to rock n 'roll. I would be playing at the fundraiser talent show with my band Pariah, and then I would play my solo song for Star.

I sighed. I had so many conflicting feelings about Star. She was literally the girl of my dreams, though I wasn't sexually attracted to her. I found her beautiful, but I found myself wanting to ensure that she remained innocent, untouched. I was kind of glad she turned down my kissing practice offer.

The day I met Star, I had not intended to audition for Toby's play, but I had tagged along with some of the other drama club wolves to watch the audition. Then, I spotted her, sitting between Toby and another girl. My jaw dropped. It was her! The girl from my dreams. I had dreamt about her countless times. She would always be the same age as me in every dream. I felt as though we had grown up together in my dream world. I couldn't believe I'd met my "dream girl." I had known then and there that I needed to audition and get that part to get close to her. Thank goodness, I knew how to turn on the charm. My answers undoubtedly impressed her, because she picked me. Toby and the other girl were there on the panel, but I just knew it was her. She had to have made the final decision.

When I found out about the fact that there was no play, and I'd just be hanging out with Star, I was thrilled. I played it cool though. Asking for more money was a nice touch. It made me seem reluctant. Eagerness was usually a turn-off in a situation like this. I would seem like a weirdo doing this without reservations, so I had to pretend I had some. I had said I was worried about the Quads trying to fight me. I truly didn't give a fuck though. Yeah, there were four of them, and one of me, but I had... special abilities... let's call them that.

My cellphone vibrated. Toby again?

"Hey Man!" I said calmly. I yawned. "What's up?" I asked.

I knew what was up. He kept harassing me about the weekly salary we had agreed upon ever since I had decided I didn't want it. I had lied and said my parents had cut me off. I needed some dumb excuse. After Toby wire transferred the first payment, I just sent it back. He had called right away to make sure I hadn't left Star hanging. I had reassured him that that was not the case. I just didn't want the money. I never did.

I made him swear he wouldn't tell Star I was doing this for free though. That could potentially creep Star out. I managed to fend off Toby by saying I would take cash when he got back to the Academy, because I didn't want my parents noticing the deposits. That lie would work for now. I didn't want Toby becoming suspicious of me and alerting Star.

Star. She was a mystery to me. Why did I feel so at ease with her? Why did I feel so... complete when I was with her? She was practically still a stranger to me. Why did I feel so drawn to her? In my dreams of us, we loved each other, but it was never romantic. We were playmates as children, then best friends as teenagers in my dreams.

I was restless this morning. I usually wasn't nervous about performing, but I felt jittery now. I called my Dad. We were pretty close. I had been meaning to ask him a few things, man to man.

"Son! What's up? Everything ok?" He asked, the concern evident in his voice.

"Yeah," I said slowly. "Dad... can a she-wolf be my... soulmate without being my fated mate?"

Dad was silent for a moment. "Why do you ask? You think you've found your mate?"

"No, she's definitely not my mate, but I feel a deep connection with her all the same. I feel this weird urge to protect her, to be around her. My wolf really likes her. He might... he might love her, but he's not in love with her ... " I trailed off, not sure if I was making any sense.

"What's her name?" Asked Dad, his tone cautious.

"Star, well, it's Hannah technically, but..."

I heard a sharp intake of breath on the other line, followed by a heavy sigh.

"Dad?" I asked.

Chapter 35

"We need to talk, son. Face to face, as soon as you're able to, come see your Mom and me!" Specified Dad.

"Okay, yeah," I answered.

"When will you come?" Asked Dad.

"I'll try to come after the talent show tonight!" I said.

"Okay, great!" Said my father, though he didn't sound as though this was great. He seemed anxious.

"You okay, Dad?" I asked.

"Me...oh...yes...I'm...wonderful!" Said Dad, sounding completely unconvincing.

"Okay, how's Mom?" I asked.

"Great! You'll see her tonight too," Dad said.

"Dad, can't you just tell me what you want to tell me now?" I asked, feeling a bit anxious.

"No, no, it's nothing to worry about...it's just better said in person. You know, um parental advice!" He said. He was lying. I always knew when someone was lying. Just like I had known that the reason Star hired me was a lot more than just making her mates, the Quads, jealous. I enjoyed making those assholes squirm though, especially Jonah. He was the eldest Quad, meaning he had been an asshole the longest.

"Can I talk to him?" Said a feminine voice. It was Mom.

"Hey, Honey!" She said.

"Hey, Mom!" I said brightly.

"I miss you!" She cooed.

I chuckled. "I miss you too!"

I'd never admit this to the bandmates or Star or anyone for that matter, but I was kind of a Momma's boy. When I wasn't at the Academy or playing shows, Mom and I hung out together a lot. I considered her my best friend outside of the band.

"Honey, make sure that you... are um, taking your time with this new friendship with Hannah, okay!" She said.

"I am, yeah, of course," I said.

"I overheard you and your father talking about how special she is to you. It's easy to confuse one feeling for the next when you're young, especially when you don't have all the puzzle pieces. You're a teenager, and you're still figuring things out! There's no need to rush," she began lecturing me.

"Mom, it's okay," I said, cutting her off. I knew what she was worried about. "Hannah and I aren't hooking up."

I heard her breathe a sigh of relief. With any other girl, I'd be in a rush to get them all hot and bothered, but it just wasn't like that with Hannah. The thought of her being with the Quads disgusted me though. It wasn't really jealousy… it was more complicated than that. I didn't want anyone touching her like that, including me. It was weird. I'd never quite felt so fiercely protective of a girl before, not even ex-girlfriends.

"Mom, Dad, I'm gonna go, okay! See you tonight!" I said.

"Love you Harper!" Cooed Mom.

"Love you, Mom," I said.

I had told Star I'd meet her at the theatre, but I was going to go get her and walk her over there. I wanted her backstage with me anyway, where she wouldn't have to mope over seeing that devil's spawn with her mates. While I was getting ready, I heard a voice calling me.

Harper! Harper.

Huh.

It sounded familiar. I turned the shower off. I stepped out. It sounded like a guy's voice.

Harper! You there?! It's Jonah!

Jonah? I rolled my eyes. What the hell did he want?

Yes? I asked curtly.

Noah visited Star after hours last night, said Jonah.

I already knew that, but why was he telling me this?

And Zaya and Eli went to visit her this morning. We're supposed to be um giving Star her space right now, so I was a bit angry with them, not with Star though. When I went over there, I ripped the door off its hinges, so watch out for that. I'm having it fixed though, don't worry! Said Jonah.

What the fuck?!

So I was wondering if you could do me a small favour. It's something that would benefit Star also! He added quickly, trying to sweeten the pot.

What is it? I asked.

Escort Star to the theatre please! Meet her at her room. I don't want her being alone at all right now, said Jonah.

I had been about to do that anyway, but I wasn't going to tell him that.

I'll have to hurry up and finish getting ready but fine, I said in an exasperated tone.

Thanks Harper! Said Jonah, sounding genuine.

You owe me one! I said, pretending like I really was doing him a favour.

I met Star at her room and was careful with the broken door. She looked absolutely radiant. I told her a little bit about my three best friends and fellow bandmates: Chester, River and Clarence. Clarence was nicknamed Brink, but I didn't tell Star that, hoping she would call him Clarence to his face. He would hate that!

She met them and they seemed to be hitting it off. Angelique came out of nowhere and insinuated that Star shouldn't be backstage, because she

Chapter 35

wasn't a performer. Ugh. Couldn't she mind her business for once? I let her know Star was part of the band as my Muse. My bandmates agreed, and even the other cheerleaders on Angie's squad seemed to like the idea of Star being my Muse. Girls ate that stuff up. My Movie Star actually was my Muse though. I was glad to see Angie go.

Star spotted Brink lighting a cigarette for the cheerleader he'd been banging and immediately assumed they were mates. That right there was the innocence I was trying to protect. The guys made a suggestive joke about Star, something about me corrupting her.

"This one is off-limits! You're not to disrespect her, even in jest!" I said in Arabic, flashing them my black eyes so quickly I knew Star would miss it.

They spotted it though. The guys had grown up with me in Dubai in the human realm. There were pockets of wealthy werewolves in various affluent human places, especially modern cities, gated communities, or sleepy suburbs. We had all lived in the same rich neighbourhood, and our parents all went back and forth between there, and the Viper Moon Pack lands in Wolf Country.

Finally, it was showtime. We knocked it out of the park. The crowd was on its feet, cheering for Pariah. I mellowed the audience out with my ballad for Star afterwards. It wasn't exactly a romantic song, but it wasn't friendship either. It was something else. I felt like we were the same person in a weird way. I spotted my little Movie Star, cheering in the wings for me. She was so cute. Those Quads needed to start acting right if they expected to be with her. They also needed to pack Angie's bags and send her on her way. I dedicated the performance to my little Movie Star. I went over to her in the wings, while the crowd was still screaming. I loved the sound of screaming fan-girls. Now, that was music to my ears.

I picked Star up and spun her around. I bear-hugged her. I kissed her forehead, and then nuzzled her, pressing my forehead against hers. Nuzzling and forehead-touches were signs of great affection between two wolves. Zaya spotted us with our arms still around each other. He seemed pissed. I didn't get what the big deal was. Where was all this animosity towards Angie? They were so hypocritical. It irked me. I wasn't backing down. Zaya shifted and so did I. I wasn't going to hold back. I was about to go for the jugular when Star became lightheaded. I felt it as it happened. I felt the darkness encroach upon her like it was me who was fainting. Zaya felt it too as her mate. We both shifted back and caught her before she hit the ground.

Chapter 36

Sunday 20th September, 2020 (Continued)

Star's Point Of View

The Quads and the bandmates all gasped. Even Chet raised his eyebrows in surprise.

"I do?" I said.

"Yes, you do!" Said Jillian. "I saw you shift outside the cabin about a week ago. I guess I didn't say anything, because I assumed you already knew your wolf was white."

I felt so moronic. It had been more than a week since I had first shifted, and I didn't know the colour of my own wolf. My cheeks burned.

"You shifted for the first time about a week ago? So your birthday is in early September too, Movie Star?" Asked Harper.

I nodded.

Everyone was staring at Harper and me.

"It's the same day as yours, September 12th. We both turned eighteen on September 12th," I said, staring at Harper. He was gazing right back at me. I couldn't read his expression.

"And we're both white wolves," he added. I couldn't decipher the meaning behind his tone of voice either.

"So... what does this mean?" Jillian said.

"It could mean nothing or... it could mean that Harper and I are..." I paused.

"Twins," said Harper, finishing my sentence. "It could mean that we're twins."

Chapter 36

"That's preposterous! You would know if you were twins! Star's parents are dead!" Blurted out Chet.

I couldn't help but wince. Jillian swatted Chet's arm.

"Sorry, Star! That was... I'm sorry. But, Harper's parents are alive and they're extremely rich so why would they give up their daughter? And then, what about Star's deceased parents? Who were they?" Said Chet, thinking out loud.

Jonah looked slightly panicked for some reason.

"Well... I... I just found out that I'm adopted most likely," I admitted.

Harper raised his eyebrows. The bandmates gave me sympathetic looks. Jillian looked shocked. All the Quads nodded, except Jonah who furrowed his brow.

"Who told you that?" Jonah asked.

Before I could respond, Jonah turned to Noah. "You told her, didn't you?!" Asked Jonah, his eyes wide. Jonah gasped as though something had just dawned on him. "That's the real reason why you ended up over at Star's dorm after hours! You were in a rush to reveal what we'd learnt!" Said Jonah.

Noah looked away from Jonah.

"You weren't gonna tell me?" I asked Jonah. "Is that what you're saying, Jonah?"

I was horrified. How could he think of keeping something like that from me?

"No... no, Star! I was gonna tell you eventually! I wanted to wait until we fixed at least one problem first before I added to your plate. I was just worried! I just..." Jonah trailed off, noticing the look I was giving him.

My eyes were wide and glassy.

Jonah sighed, shutting his eyes tightly.

"No matter what I do, I'm always the bad guy when it comes to you. I give up. Think whatever you want," said Jonah.

Jonah walked out of the infirmary without another word.

"Star! I'm coming back! Just give me a few minutes to talk to him! He's just overwhelmed, that's all!" Said Noah.

Noah went after his elder brother.

I didn't know what to think anymore.

"We find out our parents aren't who we've always believed them to be, and Jonah manages to make it all about him," muttered Harper. "You deserve much better, Movie Star!"

I sighed.

My mind was reeling. My wolf was whimpering, trying to make me go after Jonah, but I was tired of trying so hard only to be let down. I had other things to figure out right now.

"So... you think something's up with your parents too?" I asked Harper.

"They said they needed to have a chat with me after I told them about you," Harper said.

"You told your parents about me?" I asked, feeling flattered.

Harper nodded. "Yeah," he said sheepishly. "And then they said we needed to have a talk in person tonight, and they said not to rush things."

"Your parents probably had a heart attack thinking you might already be boinking your own twin sister?!" Said Chester incredulously.

Harper, Zaya and Eli all growled.

"Whoa, tough crowd. Sorry, Harper. That just slipped out!" Said Chester.

"Watch it from now on," Harper said.

Chester put his palms up like he was under arrest which made me giggle. Harper and the two younger Quads calmed down when they saw that I wasn't upset.

"So what should we do now?" I asked.

"Play twenty questions with my parents?" Suggested Harper.

"And my grandmother! I have a lot of questions for her too!" I said with a small sigh.

Harper nodded.

"Do you really think we're twins?" I asked.

I didn't wanna get my hopes up for nothing.

"Can't you feel it?" Asked Harper.

I looked into his eyes. I knew what he meant. Harper wrapped his arms around me tightly. I held him just as tightly.

"Twinning!" Said Chester in a voice that reminded me of the cheerleaders.

"Can't spell twinning without winning!" Said River in that same voice.

Harper and I broke apart, and both rolled our eyes at them.

"My parents are expecting me around seven tonight," said Harper.

"What time is it now?" I asked.

"Half past noon," said River.

"Let's go see my grandmother first... together!" I said.

Harper nodded. "Together," he said.

Before we'd even left the parking lot of the Academy, Zaya, Eli and Harper had begun to argue over whose car we should take.

"Does it matter?" I asked meekly.

All three guys were on edge, and I wanted to calm them all down.

"It's not confirmed that Harper is even related to you yet, Princess!" Said Eli.

Chapter 36

"That's why we're going to her grandmother's house, and then to my parents 'place! To find out!" Said Harper matter-of-factly.

"If you are related, brother and sister, or even twins, aren't you creeped out, Rock Star?" Said Zaya, glaring at Harper.

His bandmates were with us too. I kept looking around, hoping to see Noah bringing Jonah back. I sighed. Jillian and Chet were holding hands, and staring at the three guys arguing.

"Why? Should I be?" Retorted Harper.

Zaya's eyes were wide in disbelief. "You were grinding on her at Chet's party!"

Harper shrugged. "I didn't know then. I don't even know now. It makes sense, but we have to find out first, right Eli?" Asked Harper with a smug smile.

Eli scowled.

"I thought you'd be happy," I said softly, looking at Eli and Zaya.

"Of course we are," murmured Eli, cupping my face in his hands.

"We want you to be happy!" Insisted Zaya.

I smiled.

"Then, let's go!" Said Harper sternly, grabbing my hand and leading me towards his sports car.

Eli and Zaya jumped in the back of Harper's car. Harper looked back at them surprised. His bandmates shrugged their shoulders and piled into Brink's car instead. Jillian went with Chet in his car.

"As if we'd let her go with the likes of you alone," muttered Zaya.

Harper rolled his eyes. "If I really am Movie Star's twin, you're gonna need my blessing to be with her, so watch your mouth!" Snapped Harper.

Zaya looked outraged, but his eyes widened as though he hadn't considered that. Alphas were very old fashioned a lot of the time when it came to courtship. I knew my alphas would, in fact, want the approval of my closest male relative. That was usually a girl's father, but I might have a twin. They would definitely need to impress him. He didn't even know about the curse yet I realised. How were we gonna explain that to him?

Harper followed my directions to my grandmother's house. I steered him wrong by accident and we had to double back.

"Sorry, I'm not very good at directions!" I said, frowning.

"Don't be so hard on yourself, Movie Star! It's not a big deal," said Harper soothingly.

I smiled.

We were silent for the rest of the trip. Harper pulled up to the tiny house where I'd grown up, the only home I could recall knowing. He took my hand, to the chagrin of the younger Quads. We walked up to the door. I stood on the cramped little wooden porch. I took a deep breath and knocked. My grandmother, Hella, answered the door in her floral house dress and yellow fluffy slippers. She regarded Harper warily, her eyes trailing over our joined hands.

"Granny, hi, this is Harper and well, you already know Zaya and Eli," I said.

Harper smiled slightly. Zaya and Eli waved.

"Hey Gran!" Said Zaya.

She smiled. "Come in, come in. Excuse the mess," said my grandmother.

The house was very small, but incredibly neat as always. There was no "mess." Granny Hella was a bit of a neat freak. There was, however, some clutter in the form of knick-knacks, ornaments, toys and doilies. Granny had decorated and adorned every corner with cute dainty items. She had a penchant for frills and pastel colours. The walls of the living room were cream-coloured with a floral trim running along the top of the wall. The floor was wooden, creaky and in need of vanishing, but swept clean. Harper and I shared a sofa with a few large spongy dolls. Zaya sat on the arm of the sofa next to me, and Eli stood behind me.

"What can I get you, Alphas and young man?" Said Granny.

"Please, call us Zaya and Eli," said Eli.

"We're fine, thanks," said Zaya.

Granny looked at Harper.

"I'm okay, thanks," murmured Harper.

"Okay. Hannah, what made you stop by? Everything all right?" Said Granny.

She was sweating. It wasn't particularly warm in the house. She dabbed her forehead with her handkerchief, and then when that wasn't enough, she used the kitchen towel that had been swung over her shoulder instead.

"Granny... I know," I said, staring at her.

She looked at me with wide eyes. "Know what?" She tried.

I looked at her pointedly. There was silence.

"I know my parents weren't biologically related to me... they took me in, and I wanna know more. I deserve to..." I said, trailing off.

Granny sighed. She shut her eyes tightly. "Your parents were good people," she began.

"I don't doubt that! But I have a right to know what really happened," I said.

"I'm not the right person to tell you," she mumbled.

"Then, who is? You raised me!" I said, my voice becoming shrill with emotion.

"Okay, okay," she said softly.

Chapter 36

"I never expected your parents would pass away after they took you in," said Granny, dabbing her teary eyes. "I didn't expect to raise another child, but I was so thankful for you, even though I didn't have much to offer you."

"Granny," I said, my heart hurting for her and for myself. "I love you, and I wouldn't trade you and the time we had together for anything else, but it's time for me to know the truth!"

She nodded. She got up and went over to her bedroom door. She went in and shut the door. I heard the lock click. Ever since I was little, her bedroom was always strictly off-limits. She came back out holding a normal-looking brown cardboard box. Harper looked at me. I shrugged. She put the box down and opened it. We all bent towards the open box. We gasped in unison.

Inside was a marvellous snow globe. Inside of it, a wintry white storm raged around a magnificent castle that sparkled as though it were made only of jewels. I could spot tiny figures moving in the snow globe. They looked like guards patrolling the outside of the castle. It was so real.

"What is this?" I asked.

"Take it," said Granny.

I lifted the snow globe carefully.

"What is it, Granny?" I asked.

"It's a portal," she said. "A doorway."

"To what?" I asked.

"To the kingdom you and your twin brother came from…"

Chapter 37

Sunday 20th September, 2020 (Continued)

Jessie's Point Of View

Jamie was on the couch, poring over some ancient map that might lead us to Georgianna's body, and I was on babysitting duty. Our twins, Jade and Jake, cooed in their highchairs. They were very reluctant to eat the mush that Jamie had insisted was healthy for them. They were fraternal, but both had my blue eyes and Jamie's brown curls.

"How's it going, my little witch?" I asked Jamie.

She sighed.

"It's not going. It's not going at all," she grumbled.

I chuckled.

Loud squeals and giggles rang out. I looked at the twins. They quickly stopped laughing. They were hiding something. They weren't even one year old yet, and they already had secrets. Their powers had come in very early from their witch side, and their motor skills had come just as quickly as expected from their werewolf side.

I looked at them and they stared at me, all innocent and wide-eyed. I didn't buy it one bit.

"Guys! What are you up—" I was cut short by the shower of mush splattering onto my head.

The twins erupted into fits of giggles. Jamie covered her mouth in surprise, stifling her laughter. They had levitated the bowl over me and dropped slop all over me.

"I distinctly remember your mother doing something very similar," I said, pretending to be disgruntled, as I wiped my face and hair.

Chapter 37

I vividly recalled Jamie tripping and sending her bowl of cafeteria mush flying at me when we were high school seniors. She then magically got rid of the stain in the bathroom. I then pinned her to the wall, and we had our first kiss. Her steamy thoughts had lit a literal fire in the bathroom that day, setting off the fire alarm and triggering the overhead sprinklers on us.

"You guys better learn some cleaning up spells," I growled at them playfully.

I tickled both of them. They shrieked and laughed.

"Who did that?" I asked them.

Jade pointed at her twin brother, Jake. Jake pointed at his twin sister, Jade.

"Who's lying?" I asked.

They again pointed at each other. Jamie giggled. She magically got rid of all the mess on the floor and on me.

"You left me struggling with the towel for a minute there," I complained.

"You looked so cute," she cooed.

"Yeah?" I said.

She nodded.

I sat next to her on the couch. I pressed my lips against hers. I grabbed her, and pulled her onto my lap so that she was straddling me while we kissed. She broke the kiss abruptly.

"Wait," she said.

"What? No break?" I asked.

"I have to find Georgianna's body, Jessie. I feel... like it's my duty to do it," she said.

"You didn't curse them, Baby," I said.

"I know, but I feel like I owe it to Georgianna," she said.

I pressed my forehead against hers.

"She deserved better," I whispered.

"You took the words right out of my mouth," said Jamie. "So did Alto."

I nodded, brushing my nose against hers.

"It's playtime for the babies," she told me, gesturing towards Jake and Jade, who were now trying to escape their highchairs.

"When will it be playtime for Mommy and Daddy?" I growled.

"Very soon," she said with a wink, brandishing the map so that it separated us.

I went over to the twins.

"Who should I take out of their highchair first?" I asked.

Jade and Jake each pointed to themselves this time instead of each other.

"Me, Daddy!" Squealed Jade.

"No, me! Me!" Demanded Jake.

I chuckled as I went to remove both of them from their chairs.

Star's Point Of View

"The kingdom my twin brother and I are from? You mean me and Harper, right?" I asked.

"Yes, Hannah," said Granny Hella.

Harper and I looked at each other. I glanced back at Zaya and Eli, who were staring at the snow globe.

"That looks like the kingdom of the Ice Moon Pack," said Zaya, looking at the snow globe in awe.

Eli nodded.

"How do you guys know that?" I asked, amazed.

"We're soon to be alphas," said Eli, shrugging. "We were taught about the leaders of other packs and other supernatural beings."

Zaya nodded. "Noah and Jonah would know ten times as much," admitted Zaya begrudgingly.

"Yeah," said Eli, nodding. "They're into that kinda thing. Politics and Pack structures and histories."

I didn't want to think about Jonah right now. I sighed.

"So I'm from the Ice Moon Pack and so is Harper?" I asked.

Granny nodded.

There was a knock on the door that startled everyone.

"Star," came a voice I recognised. Noah!

I ran to the door and opened it. Noah was standing there with Jonah.

"Why are you crying, Luna?" Asked Noah.

"Are you ok? Are you hurt? Did something happen?" Asked Jonah, his eyes worried.

I shook my head. I hadn't even realised I had been crying until they mentioned it. I realised the bandmates and Jillian and Chet had also arrived.

"Hey! You're all here!" I said.

Noah started drying my tears with a tissue. I sniffled.

"Yeah," said Chet. "Zaya asked us to give you a moment over mind-link, that this would be a difficult conversation for you... so we were waiting outside for a bit."

Oh.

Chapter 37

"Harper essentially said the same thing over mind-link, to give you a little time while you and your Granny talked. He said things were a bit tense when we pulled up," said Brink. River and Chester nodded.

I wiped my eyes. I was grateful for Zaya and Harper asking for some privacy for me and my Grandmother.

"It's okay now. Everyone can come in, if they want," I said, managing a smile.

Five minutes later, we were all smushed together in my Granny's tiny living room. I had never had friends over growing up. I had always been a little embarrassed of my humble abode, and now four soon-to-be alphas, four rock stars, my best friend and her billionaire mate were all squashed into the small space with my Grandmother at the centre of it.

All eyes were on the snow globe. Jonah and Noah were enchanted with it. They looked at each other with wide eyes.

"This is a portal to the Ice Moon Pack Lands!" Said Noah.

"Yeah, Zaya and Eli told us," I said. "They said you and Jonah were really into this stuff."

"You're acknowledging my existence?" Asked Jonah, sounding shocked.

"I could say the same for you," I said snidely.

Jonah sniffed. "In werewolf country, up north, where it's almost always snowing, there are four packs that inhabit the wintry terrain. There's the Winter Moon Pack which is run by triplet alphas. They're actually cousins of Alpha Jessie whom you've met," said Jonah, looking at me.

"Triplets?" I said.

Noah nodded. "Alpha Alex, Felix and Calix Thorn and their Luna Chasity."

I needed some pointers from this Luna Chasity. This multiple mates thing wasn't easy.

"The next two packs are closely linked: the Snow Moon Pack and the Cold Moon Pack. They're run by brothers. Elder brother Alpha Orion and younger brother Alpha Perseus," said Jonah.

"No Lunas?" I asked curiously.

Noah smiled at me. "Not yet, but there's been rumours recently that suggest they've both found their mates..."

"Ooooh gossip! Spill!" Said Jillian.

Noah chuckled. "All I heard is Alpha Perseus has an elusive she-wolf mate, and Alpha Orion is rumoured to have found a human mate," said Noah.

Zaya burst into laughter.

"What?" I asked.

"Alpha Orion with a human?! He's the most brutal Alpha I've ever met. He's more wolf than man," Eli said, clearly sharing Zaya's sentiments.

"Poor girl," remarked Zaya.

"He's hot though and rugged," said Jillian.

Chet frowned.

"Let's focus," said Jonah. "The last of the four northern packs is the Ice Moon Pack, the one in the snow globe. They... haven't had an Alpha in years..."

"What?" I whispered.

"The last Alpha, Alpha Otto, had only one child, a beautiful daughter named Hesper. She was a formidable she-wolf, blessed with unique gifts because that pack's history aligns with that of Winter Faeries or Winter Fae. So many Ice Moon wolves have magic in their blood," said Jonah.

"The she-wolf, Hesper, was actually a quarter Fae herself. Her maternal grandmother was the Winter Faerie Queen. The Winter Fae Queen had an affair with a pack warrior from the Ice Moon Pack and gave birth to a daughter who was named Orsa. The half fae, half werewolf Orsa was fated to Otto, the last Alpha of the Ice Moon Pack. The daughter of Orsa and Otto was Hesper. Hesper was the favourite grandchild of the Winter Fae Queen, despite the fact that Hesper was three-quarter werewolf and only one quarter Fae. In the Fae kingdom, a woman can rule alone, but in the Werewolf pack, she cannot. A Luna needs an Alpha. Every pack needs an Alpha," said Noah.

"But you just said the Ice Moon Pack hasn't had an Alpha in years?" Said Harper.

"Exactly," said Jonah. "Rather than be forced to marry her own cousin, the son of the Alpha's brother, Hesper fled."

"Wait, why was Hesper asked to marry her cousin?" I asked, alarmed.

"Because she was the only child of the Alpha, and they wanted a male heir of the same bloodline. Thus, she had a choice between marrying her youngest Uncle, or one of her male cousins, all of whom would be physiologically alphas, and from the same bloodline. That particular pack used to practice that sort of thing within noble families. It wasn't unheard of," explained Jonah.

"She ran away with her mate who wasn't an alpha. He was an exceptionally strong pack warrior though. He managed to bring down dozens of guards, so they could escape. People say he likely died of his injuries," said Noah.

"So then what happened?" I asked. "Wouldn't Alpha Otto just let his nephew take over? Why were there no more alphas?"

Chapter 37

"That's the thing," said Jonah, "Hesper and her mate escaped, but they were never seen or heard from after that. No one is certain what became of them. Otto and Orsa had been reluctant to agree to marrying Hesper off to her cousin in the first place. This cousin and his brothers overthrew Otto and Orsa, after Hesper fled because they were determined to have control over the pack one way or another. When the Winter Faerie Queen discovered that her illegitimate but beloved daughter Orsa had been killed and her favourite granddaughter Hesper was missing, her wrath knew no bounds. She had always been a tyrant of sorts. The Winter Fae Queen declared herself the ruler of the Ice Moon Pack after slaughtering all the usurpers of the throne, namely the other males from the Alpha's family, uncles and cousins of Hesper. The Winter Faerie Queen in grief swore that she would sit on the Alpha's throne till the day Hesper came back to claim it."

"What if Hesper is dead?" Asked Brink.

"She probably is," said Noah sadly.

"Granny, why were you given this portal? Who gave it to you? My parents?" I asked eagerly.

Granny shook her head. "No one gave it to me," she said.

"What do you mean?" Asked Harper.

"You were left on our doorstep, and this snow globe was left with you. Your adopted mother thought you were the answer to all of her prayers!" Said Granny, tears streaming down her face. "She had been struggling to conceive, and then, one day, poof, a baby shows up. A beautiful baby girl. She and her mate were overjoyed. They loved you, always remember that," said Granny.

I smiled and nodded.

"So you have no idea who my biological parents are?" I asked sadly.

"They must be from this pack," said my Granny. "That's all I can say."

"So why did Angie say I wasn't supposed to go looking for my parents?" I said.

Granny raised her eyebrows. "She said that?"

"Yes! Angie said her mother swore her to secrecy, saying that Star shouldn't find out she was adopted, because she wasn't supposed to go looking for her family!" Said Jonah.

"Angie's mother... huh you know Angie and you don't seem very close, but Angie's Mom and your Mom were like two peas in a pod. They adored each other," Granny said, looking at me.

"My Mom must have told Angie's Mom something more than what she revealed to you," I said.

A loud hip hop song filled the room suddenly.

"Sorry, my ringtone," said Jillian. She quickly went out on the porch to take the call.

"Fuck, we're gonna need Angie's help again," grumbled Zaya.

"Not Angie, just her Mom," said Jonah.

"And we still have Harper's parents to talk to. They might know more," said Noah.

"Okay, let's go to Angie's Mom first, and then we'll go to Harper's parents at seven," said Zaya, looking at his wristwatch.

"That was Angie on the phone!" Said Jillian as she burst back into the room.

My heart constricted painfully. Of course Angie had given "Jilli-bear" her number.

"So?" Said Harper, shrugging.

"An overhead stage light fell on Vice Principal Hitch!" Exclaimed Jillian.

My heart plummeted. There were several gasps.

"Is she ok?" I asked.

Jillian shook her head. "No, the light snapped her neck."

Chapter 38

Sunday 20th September, 2020 (Continued)

Star's Point Of View

A chill crept through me. Another person was dead. Another teacher. First, Mr Damocles. Now, Vice Principal Hitch. My heart was racing. The curse was progressing, probably after the escapade I had engaged in with Noah, Zaya and Eli. This was my doing. I shut my eyes tightly, and put my head in my hands.

"Honey, I'm so sorry!" Exclaimed Granny. "What a horrific thing to happen! Did you like that teacher a lot?"

I didn't actually, but the guilt was unbearable. I didn't think I could take the grief coupled with the guilt if I caused the death of someone I genuinely loved or even just liked.

Does your Granny know about the curse? Asked Jonah in my mind.

I was confused for a second, because he had never mind-linked me before. I glanced at him to make sure he was talking to me, and his eyes were boring into me.

No, I answered.

She didn't know. She deserved to know that. It impacted and potentially endangered her.

Does Harper know? Jonah asked with a furtive glance at Harper.

No, I said simply.

Keep it that way, insisted Jonah.

Okay, for now, I said, wanting some peace between Jonah and me for the time being.

He nodded, his expression impassive.

"That's such a freak accident!" Commented Brink.

"Yeah, it's like from some horror movie or something," said River.

"It happened in front of the whole school then? On stage?" Asked Chester.

"Yeah, she was presenting the next number, and the light fell on her! Isn't that just so freaky? Poor Miss Hitch," said Jillian, sighing.

Jillian didn't know about the curse either, and I wanted to keep it that way.

"Weird... how Damocles died in a car accident, now Hitch snaps her neck... who will be next?" Wondered Chester aloud.

"No one!" Said River. "It's just a horrible coincidence!"

"We need to call Jamie," said Noah under his breath to Jonah.

Jonah nodded.

"I'm sorry for what happened to Miss Hitch. That's awful but... the snow globe... you said it's a portal? How do we use it?" Asked Harper.

Granny seemed uncertain.

"It's simple enough," said Jonah. "It's a snow globe! You just shake it up and say the incantation that's usually inscribed on the bottom."

"Wait so you know this because... there are more snow globes like this?" Asked Harper.

"Yeah, there are a couple portals like this. They're rare, but our Dad has one in his office that leads to Marigold. That place is a fortress, but he's a trusted Aly, so he was gifted one by his close friend, the former alpha, Malachi," explained Jonah.

I nodded. Something didn't add up.

"Granny..." I said.

"Yes, Pumpkin," she said.

"If you don't know anything about my biological family other than the fact that they left me with this snow globe portal, then how come you said this was the kingdom my *twin* brother and I were from?" I asked.

My grandmother fidgeted uncomfortably. Was she concealing something from me?

"I... now... don't get upset!" Said Granny.

"I won't! Just tell me!" I said.

"When you were little, a rich family approached me, asking to adopt you. I don't know how they found us but... they offered me a lot of money in exchange for you, but I couldn't part with you. You were all I had. My daughter was gone, but she would never have let me give you up like that..." said my grandmother. Her hands were shaking.

"And the rich family told you about Harper?" I asked.

"The rich family had already adopted Harper!" Said my grandmother.

Harper stiffened beside me.

Chapter 38

"I never bothered to try to find out more. I just wanted to live a peaceful, quiet life with you," my grandmother said, her tone apologetic. "Please, try to understand."

Harper stood up abruptly, and walked outside.

"He's upset," whispered Granny. "I've upset him!"

"No, Granny, don't worry, thank you so much! I'll be back!" I said, scrambling to my feet and snatching the snow globe.

I hurried after Harper. He was standing on the small porch with his back to me and his arms folded.

"Harper," I said softly.

"Let's just go see Angie's Mom and my... whoever those people are and get this all over with..." mumbled Harper.

"They're still your parents, Harper! They took care of you! They raised you. They love you. That counts for something," I reminded him.

Harper shrugged. He wiped a stray tear from his cheek. I pressed my forehead to his.

"I know you're not exactly thrilled about all of this but... I... I'm so glad I found you. I think I loved you from the moment I met you and it didn't make sense. Now it does," I said softly.

"Same," said Harper.

I chuckled.

"Twinning," I said.

"Ugh! No, please! Spare me, Movie Star!" Groaned Harper.

He grabbed my hand and pulled me towards the car. Everyone trickled out of the house, following us.

Harper drove in silence for a while. He was pensive.

"Wanna talk about anything?" I asked.

"Your Granny found out about me from my parents... they were trying to raise both of us together! Your Granny said no, and kept you. Aren't you upset about that?" Harper asked.

"No, she couldn't just hand me over," I said.

"She could've told you that you had a twin!" Harper said, clearly annoyed.

"Your parents could've told you too," I said, shrugging.

"Your grandmother... no offence, Movie Star, but your grandmother seems as though she's struggling financially. You would have had an easier life with me. We would have been together, and money wouldn't have been an issue," said Harper.

He was upset with my grandmother.

"She's elderly, Harper. She lost her daughter. She was probably afraid to be alone and lose me too," I said.

Harper looked at me, his eyes filled with tears. Zaya and Eli were silent in the backseat. Suddenly, Zaya broke the silence.

"Harper, I'm sorry for... shifting and... trying to attack you," said Zaya quietly. "In all fairness, you seemed so into Star. I thought you were trying to steal her."

"I was trying to steal her," Harper admitted.

Huh.

"Sort of," said Harper. "I mean... I didn't want Star to have mates. I wanted her all to myself, but not in a romantic way, in a protective way so the more pissed off you guys were, the better for me. I tolerate you two, but I won't give my blessing for you Quads to be with Star until Noah and Jonah show me that she's their number one priority."

Everyone was silent.

"She is their number one priority! They're just naturally bland, so it comes across wrong," said Eli.

Zaya snickered. I chuckled. Harper smiled faintly.

"It's not seven o'clock yet," I said.

"Yeah, far from it. It's only four," said Eli.

"So, are we going to talk to Angie's Mom first?" I asked.

"Yeah," said Harper. "Jonah called her and asked to drop by."

"How do you know that?" I asked.

"Mind-link," said Harper, tapping on his temple with his index finger.

"So where's Angie?" I asked.

"I didn't ask," said Harper.

"She's back at school still. There's a news piece tonight on the deaths of both teachers at the Academy, and Angie is going to be interviewed," said Zaya.

"And how do you know that?" I asked, feeling like a broken record.

"Mind-link," said Zaya.

I sighed. "Okay."

"You okay?" Asked Harper.

"My aunty isn't even my aunty and she knows that. She's always known that. I guess I just hope she tells us the truth," I said.

"She should. She owes it to your adopted Mom as her friend," said Harper.

"I thought you said your Dad and Angie's Mom were brother and sister!" Said Eli.

"Yes, they were, but my Mom and Angie's Mom were friends. That's how my Mom met my Dad," I said. "Basically, my adopted Mom had a crush on her best friend's elder brother."

"Makes sense," said Harper. "But Angie's Mom is wealthy, so wasn't your adopted father from a wealthy family?"

Chapter 38

"Um, yeah, I guess," I said.

I had never pondered why Dad hadn't had millions to leave behind for me.

"Maybe, because he passed away, they just gave his share of the family money to Angie's Mom?" I asked.

"No way, rich families don't work like that," said Zaya.

"Yeah, the money would have become part of your inheritance, Star, and you would've had access to it when you turned eighteen, so basically you would have inherited it about a week ago, if there had been any," explained Harper.

"Yeah, and your legal guardian, in this case, your Granny, would have probably had some access to some of it to help care for you until you came of age. At least, that is how most people set up their affairs. Every family differs, I guess," said Eli.

That made a lot of sense, but perhaps my father had not had any money of his own to leave me. Maybe Angie's Mom had been the favourite or something.

The wrought iron gates of Angie's home loomed before us. We drove down the mile long driveway. Harper didn't seem particularly impressed. Perhaps, his house was even grander than this. The sprawling mansion came into view. We got out of the car, and knocked on the double doors. A formally dressed butler answered the door.

"Hi, Mrs Plastique is expecting us," said Harper.

"Ahh, Mr Jogie, Alpha Zaya, Alpha Eli and err Miss, welcome," said the butler in a refined deep voice.

How does he know your name? I asked.

My father is chummy with Angie's Dad. They're in the same Boys' Club. Our mothers attend the same Country Club too so I see her around. We stole their chef once! Said Harper over mind-link.

What?! Really? I asked laughing. *How can you steal a chef?*

Well, we convinced him to work for us instead! My Dad offered him more money and better working conditions. Angie and her family are awful to their staff and try to low-ball them with their wages, said Harper.

The butler led us to the drawing room, which was basically a fancy living room with expensive-looking couches, elegant armchairs, a grand fireplace and macabre oil paintings lining the dark grey walls. Jonah and Noah arrived soon after us, and they were followed by the rest of Pariah, and Jillian and Chet. We all waited for my aunt.

"Wow, full house!" Drawled a voice.

My aunt, Arcadia Plastique, had always dreamt of being a movie star. She never made it, but she continued to live the life of one. She dressed in designer duds and kept her dirty blonde hair bleached platinum. The cheek on which her large mole was drawn changed everyday. She always had a full face of makeup, including glowing dewy skin, glossy eyeshadow and seductively full red lips. She loved low-cut figure hugging dresses like the white one she was currently in. I had always found her so glamorous growing up. She seemed to neither like nor dislike me. She had an airy sort of personality and was the same with everyone, a bit detached, but pleasant enough. She was constantly cheating on Angie's Dad, according to my grandmother.

"Jonah, darling, what a surprise!" She said as she descended the sweeping staircase, walking slowly towards us in her six-inch stiletto heels.

"I told you we were coming," said Jonah.

"Did you? And you've brought Noah! And Harper, of course. My husband will be thrilled to see you, Harper. He hasn't been to one of your Dad's card games in a while. Isaiah and Elijah, I think this is the first time we've had you over," said Arcadia.

She seemed to be talking as if she were performing a scene from a script she'd been given just this morning. She always behaved like that. My grandmother had told me she had a pill problem and that was why she spoke so slowly. She was supposedly trying not to slur her words.

"Hi, Aunty," I said, with a little wave.

"OH! Hannah! My, my, how you've grown. Angie will be delighted to see you," said Aunt Arcadia.

"Angie is here!" I said, my pulse quickening.

"Yes, of course, she's going to be on the news tonight. She invited the filming crew here, so she could do her interview in her room, in front of all her beauty queen trophies. A fancy backdrop never hurts," said Arcadia.

"Alistair! Wine please! NOW!" Demanded Arcadia in a completely different tone, dropping all her airy pretences when speaking to her butler.

"Now, where was I," she said, regaining her sultry demeanour.

Alistair poured us all glasses of white wine. Arcadia downed hers immediately, and held out her glass for another.

"Um, we can't drink, we're too y—" I began.

Everyone looked at me pointedly. I stopped speaking.

"Arcadia, we needed to ask you some difficult questions," said Jonah softly.

"Ask away, I love a good interview," said Arcadia.

"Okay," said Noah. "Tell us about Star's parents."

Arcadia frowned. "What is there to tell?" She said.

Chapter 38

"We found out that Star's adopted," said Zaya, cutting to the chase. "And you didn't want her to know, because you didn't want her looking for her family. Why? What do you know?" Asked Zaya.

Arcadia laughed nervously. She downed the second glass.

"Hannah's parents, well they... they were down on their luck, and they gave Hannah up for adoption. Hannah's Mom was just a teenager, and the father wanted nothing to do with..."

"You're lying," growled Harper.

"Pardon me," said Arcadia. "Harper, darling..."

"You're. Lying!" Snarled Harper.

"How do you know?" Asked Noah.

"I know when people are lying," said Harper simply.

His bandmates nodded.

"He's never wrong about that," said Brink. "Our lead rocker can sniff out a lie better than a detection dog sniffing out drugs at the airport."

"What cause would I have to lie?" Said Arcadia.

"I don't know. You tell us!" Demanded Harper.

There was silence. The tension in the room was so palpable you could cut it with a cheese knife.

"We'll find out eventually, so I suggest you start talking," said Harper.

"Arcadia, what Harper means is..." began Jonah.

"I said what I meant! No one speaks for me! Now, tell Hannah the truth now!" Said Harper.

"Very well," said Arcadia, dropping her airy tone again. "I don't know who Hannah's parents were exactly. All I know is that Hannah's Mom died, and Axle and Edith took her in," said Arcadia.

I felt a stabbing pain in my chest. I had been hoping our birth parents would both be alive.

"How did she die?" I managed to whisper, while Zaya rubbed my back. I was fighting back tears.

"She killed herself..."

Chapter 39

Sunday 20th September, 2020 (Continued)

Star's Point Of View

I felt that stabbing pain in my chest again, right where my heart was. Harper wiped the tears that had begun to stream down my face.

"Is she telling the truth?" I asked him desperately.

He nodded. A sob escaped me.

"Why? Why would she do such a thing?" I asked, trembling.

Jonah came over and kneeled in front of me. He took both of my hands in his.

"Shh, it's ok. You're gonna be ok," he said. "It's better to know, and get to the bottom of things. I know it hurts, but you're so brave for deciding to find out..." said Jonah as he stroked my cheek. Zaya was rubbing my back. I could feel Eli and Noah close to me, but I hardly noticed them as tears blurred my vision.

"Jonah, darling, you and Hannah seem...close," said Arcadia, looking at Jonah in surprise.

Jonah squeezed my hands, then got to his feet and returned to his seat.

"Well, I suppose it makes sense...Hannah will be your cousin-in law eventually, when Angelique becomes Luna," said Arcadia.

I forced myself not to flinch at those words.

Eli snorted. Noah glared at him pointedly. Zaya sighed exasperatedly, but said nothing. Jonah was silent, his expression unfathomable.

"Why did our mother kill herself? Answer Star's question. No changing the topic," said Harper, narrowing his eyes.

Chapter 39

Arcadia glared at him. "Her mother was grieving over her mate whom she believed was dead?"

"Was he? Was he dead? Was he our Dad?" Asked Harper in rapid succession.

"I don't have the answer to any of those questions. All I know is he was missing, and she believed him dead," said Arcadia.

"What was our mother's name? Do you know?" Harper asked.

Arcadia shook her head.

"Do you know anything about our father?" He asked.

"No," said Arcadia simply and somewhat coldly.

"Well, if you have no other information, we'll head over to…" began Brink.

Harper shook his head. "Wait! Your brother is Hannah's adopted Dad? Right?"

Arcadia fidgeted uncomfortably. "Yes," she said.

"Were you two from a wealthy family or is all of this your husband's wealth?" Asked Harper, gesturing to the ostentatiously luxurious room we were in.

"I have my own inheritance from my parents. I was their favourite so naturally I inherited everything, but my husband is also an heir to his family's fortune," said Arcadia.

Harper stared at her.

"Okay, thanks for talking to us," said Harper rather quickly.

He got up abruptly to leave, pulling me with him. The others followed suit.

"Oh, Jonah, stay a while and say hi to Angie," said Arcadia.

"Oh…I really do have to get going, Arcadia! I'm sorry," said Jonah, extricating himself from the vice-like grip my aunt had on his forearm.

When we were outside, Harper pulled me away from the others, out of earshot.

"Why were you in such a hurry to leave all of a sudden?" I whispered.

"She's lying about the inheritance!" Said Harper softly. "She told the truth about our parents after I put pressure on her, but she's lying about inheriting everything, because she was the favourite. Also, I highly doubt she was the favourite!"

"So…what do we do?" I asked.

I had so many mixed emotions. I wasn't fully grasping where Harper was going with this.

"Well, I didn't wanna confront her about that, like I did with the lie about our parents. I don't want her to think we're suspicious, because we're going to break into the house and search for your adopted grandparents 'will!" Said Harper.

I wasn't sure if the Quads would agree to let me do something risky like that, and I still didn't trust Jonah, because of his history with Angelique.

"When?" I asked.

Jonah came over to us.

Tonight! After we talk to my parents! We're gonna get our whole lives sorted out, especially yours Hannah! We're twins! You win. I win. You lose. I lose and I don't like to lose so I never do, said Harper over mind-link with a wink.

I grinned at him, though there were tears in my eyes. I could feel him holding back his sadness regarding our biological parents and being strong for me. I hugged him tightly. He hugged me back.

"Hey, so off to Harper's house now?" Asked Jonah, taking my hand.

I wanted to ask him about even my aunt knowing that Jonah would propose to Angie, but he had already told me that was part of his plan to confuse the curse, so what would be the point in arguing with him? However, Harper was not in the know about that.

"What was that bullshit about you making Angelique your Luna? Isn't Hannah your mate?" Asked Harper, keeping his voice low so his bandmates wouldn't overhear him.

Harper spoke to the Quads as though he equaled them in rank which they hated, because they were alphas. I looked at Harper quizzically. What rank was he? He certainly didn't act like someone without a rank, not even like a Beta or second in command. He reminded me of Alpha Jessie honestly.

"I don't have to answer to you," said Jonah coldly.

Jonah turned away, but Harper grabbed his shoulder. They glared at each other with black eyes.

"If you don't have to answer to me then fine. Hannah and I will be going to see my parents alone. It's a private issue, anyway, not a field trip. Come on, Movie Star!" Said Harper, pulling me towards the car.

I could tell Jonah was seething, but he didn't say anything. Harper turned to Zaya and Eli in the backseat.

"Hannah and I, as twins, have decided that we need time to process the loss of our parents, our biological ones. It might have happened years ago, but it feels fresh to us. We only just found out about it," said Harper, his voice actually cracking a little.

He really was upset, but I was certain most of this was to piss off Jonah for refusing to answer his questions.

Zaya and Eli looked at me, their eyes filled with sympathy.

"What do you want, Baby?" Asked Zaya.

"Whatever you want, Princess," said Eli.

Chapter 39

"We wanna go alone to see my parents," said Harper. "I've already mind-linked my band, so they're not coming either."

"Are you my Princess, Harper? You're not my type, okay!" Said Eli, annoyed.

Harper rolled his eyes.

Eli looked at me.

"Yeah, I'll tell you both everything, once we're done talking to Harper's parents. It's a little difficult with such a big group. I don't wanna ugly cry in front of this many people," I said with a forced smile.

Eli smiled sadly. He and Zaya got out of the car and opened my door. I rushed into their arms. They held me so tightly, rubbing my back and kissing my cheeks. The rest of Pariah had already left. Jillian and Chet were sitting in their car. Jonah was standing in front of Noah's car, glaring at Harper. Noah came over to us. He grabbed me and pressed his lips against mine urgently. I broke away from him, breathless.

"What if Angie or my aunt sees?" I asked.

Noah sighed. "Let them," he said, looking up at the mansion's many windows. "I guarantee you they only care about Angie being Luna, even if the marriage would be loveless."

Noah kissed the pathway of the tears that had begun falling from my eyes again. The three younger Quads walked away from me towards a pissed off Jonah. Shockingly, Jonah came over to me. He just stared at me, like he'd never seen me before, like he was memorising me.

"If you let anything happen to Star while she's in your care, I'll kill you," said Jonah softly to Harper without an ounce of hesitation.

Harper stared at him from the driver's seat.

"If anything happens to Star while she's in my care, it means I'm already dead. That's the only way I'd allow that," said Harper.

Jonah nodded.

I got in the car, and my twin and I sped off.

Chapter 40

Sunday 20th September, 2020 (Continued)

Star's Point Of View

"Star, remember I said I wasn't gonna rush you to tell me the whole story about why you hired me?" Said Harper, glancing at me.

I nodded. "Yeah," I said softly.

"It's getting to be about that time. That time when I need to know everything, because the stakes seem very high. Arcadia seems to think Jonah is going to marry Angie. Do you have any idea how painful that'll be for you if you're still linked to them?" Harper asked.

I sighed. "They're not gonna marry her," I said.

They just had to get engaged to her to draw Georgianna out supposedly, but I couldn't tell Harper that yet.

"You really wanna hide stuff from your twin?" Asked Harper, raising his eyebrows.

I smiled slightly. I shrugged. He grinned.

I couldn't help, but feel a bit happy. I had a twin! And it was Harper. I had been dreading the end of our "arrangement". I had really begun to count on Harper's support in my life and now I got to keep him without the Quads being angry. They would've never let me have Harper as a friend in peace otherwise.

I had a gross thought. I had almost kissed my brother. My twin brother! And I had definitely danced provocatively with him. I pushed that memory away. It was old news. I thanked my lucky stars we hadn't done anything else during our "make the Quads jealous" phase.

"What are you thinking about?" Asked Harper.

Chapter 40

"Nothing," I said.

"You're not good at lying," said Harper.

I laughed.

"I know what you're thinking," said Harper.

"You do?" I asked, raising my eyebrows.

"I think so... you're thinking about us dancing at that party, back when we didn't know we were flesh and blood," said Harper triumphantly.

I gasped.

"I'm right, aren't I?" Asked Harper excitedly.

I stared at him. "What is that? Twin telepathy?" I asked, in awe. Was it just a lucky guess?

"I can't read your mind but... I know what you're feeling like in detail, and I used it to guess your thoughts," explained Harper.

"Tell me more," I said encouragingly.

Harper laughed. "You were feeling happiness because you found me, sadness over our parents, a little bit of disgust and mortification over our suggestive dance moves and relief it wasn't worse. I'm glad you turned down my offer to kiss you. That would have made steam come out of the Quads 'ears, but it wouldn't have been worth it with what we know now," said Harper, chuckling.

I flushed. "Yeah," I mumbled. That had been a close call. We dodged a really awkward bullet.

"Am I that transparent?" I asked, a little embarrassed.

"Only to me you are, maybe to your mates," said Harper. "Not in general."

"Fair enough," I said.

"I wanted to say this to you when I sang you that song in your room, but I didn't understand myself and the situation then, so I'm glad I didn't say it yet," said Harper.

"Say what?" I asked, curious.

"I love you, Hannah," he said.

I smiled. Warmth spread through me. Not the overwhelming heat the Quads gave me. A slow safe warm feeling. I felt like I was home. Like I'd just come home after being away for years. I looked at my twin brother. He was everything a wolf and a brother should be and I was proud to be related to him.

"I love you, Harper," I said softly.

"Thanks, Movie Star," he said.

I laughed.

"I think I'm probably the elder twin," Harper said.

"I think so too, actually," I admitted. "How much older do you think you are?"

"Hmm, I'm extremely mature, so like five minutes," joked Harper.

We both chuckled.

"Here we are," said Harper.

We had pulled up to an extremely tall set of automatic gates possibly ten feet high. Harper drove down a wide long private road lined with forested areas on either side. The estate was huge. He parked in front of a colossal building with white stone walls and a magnificent fountain out front. Wow. Harper's house was even more impressive than those of Chet and Angie. Harper and I walked up a short set of steps. Harper let us in with his keys. We entered a room with marble floors, taupe walls and two winding staircases that met at the top. There was a huge dazzling chandelier overhead. A man in a suit approached us.

"I would've gotten the door for you, Harper!" Scolded the man.

"It's fine, Regis, take a break for once," said Harper.

"I'll bring some snacks for you and the young lady," said Regis who seemed to be the butler.

"No, Regis, please, that won't be necessary, thanks though," said Harper.

He dropped his voice down to a lower volume and said, "Hannah and I will be discussing a sensitive topic, so it's better to be undisturbed. You can go ahead and relax a bit."

Regis nodded and left the room.

Harper led me into another drawing room though this one was much more elegant and tastefully decorated than the one in Angie's house had been. The armchairs, loveseat and couch were immaculately white and the cushions on them were white too, but the material was textured so that they reminded me of little clouds. I was afraid to touch anything in this spotless house.

I sat gingerly on a white armchair. Harper chuckled at me.

"You don't look too comfortable," he said.

"I just don't wanna mess anything up," I mumbled.

Harper grasped my chin and made me look at him.

"My parents hid the fact that we were adopted and you're worried about their white chairs? You're way too nice, Star," said Harper with a laugh.

He sat next to me. "It irks me that they knew about you too. They approached your adopted grandmother for you, and because she said no, they just moved on. We could've still had a relationship," said Harper with a sigh. "I'm texting them and telling them to come downstairs. I don't feel like walking up there. Why make it convenient for them?" Grumbled Harper to himself.

Chapter 40

A tall man with olive skin and dark hair entered the room with a petite brown-haired, pale woman on his heels. Neither of them looked like Harper though it wasn't strikingly obvious. They both seemed extremely nervous, and the women kept practically hiding behind the man. Harper stared at them pointedly.

"Hi, Honey," said the woman softly.

"Hey, Mom, this is Hannah, but you already know that, don't you?" Said Harper.

He was speaking calmly and pleasantly, but I could tell he was quite upset underneath. There was an edge to everything he said which was unlike Harper.

"Hi Hannah, I'm Mia and this is my husband, Marco. It's so wonderful to meet you, Dear," said Mia.

She had a very soft, soothing voice. I smiled at her.

"It's nice to meet you Mr and Mrs Jogie," I said.

" Likewise, Hannah," said Marco.

His voice was the polar opposite to that of his wife: loud, deep, clear and commanding.

"We're sorry we're meeting you under such... er intense circumstances," said Mia.

"It can't be helped," said Marco so authoritatively that I nodded automatically.

Harper, on the other hand, was not so easily swayed.

"Oh, it couldn't have been helped?! Really?" Said Harper, raising his eyebrows.

"Harper, don't start," said Marco.

Harper stopped whatever it was he wasn't allowed to start. He folded his arms and was silent.

"You two have probably already figured out that you're twins and that we adopted you, Harper, but you are our son. We raised you and we love you," said Mia softly.

Harper softened. "I love you too, Mom. I just want to know the truth. How did you find me? How did you find Hannah? When Hannah's adopted grandmother said no to letting you guys adopt her, why didn't you still let me know about her?" Asked Harper, his voice strained.

"We were waiting for you to turn eighteen to tell you everything, because those were the instructions we were given by your birth father, and, in all fairness, you've only been eighteen a week," said Marco.

"Our father?" I asked anxiously. "Instructions? Like in a will? Is he dead?"

"No, your father is very much alive and he will be here shortly," said Marco.

Chapter 41

Sunday 20th September, 2020 (Continued)

Star's Point Of View

Our mouths literally dropped open. Harper took a deep breath.
"Why... what... why didn't he raise us? Where has he been? What the fuck?" Said Harper.
"Harper!" Said Mia indignantly.
"Sorry, Mom. Sorry! It's just a lot to process in one day," said Harper.
He ran his hands through his long hair, and put his head in his hands.
"Oh, Honey! I know, I know," said Mia, coming over to us to rub Harper's back.
I felt a bit shaky but I was... happy. I woke up this morning an orphan and now I had a Dad. One who possibly didn't want me, but I would cross that bridge when I got to it.
"Could you tell us a little more while we wait for him?" I asked Marco.
Marco sighed.
"Please," I said, joining my hands together as if I were praying.
"Okay, he wants to explain certain things himself, but... sure," said Marco.
I almost squealed with excitement. Harper looked up from his hands. Marco sat back in his chair. Mia was looking intently at her husband.
"Your father was the best warrior I had ever encountered. He was unmatched, unparalleled. I was in awe of him from the moment I met him. I went to his pack to specifically learn from him. That was how good he was! He became my friend, my dearest friend, like a brother to me. He

Chapter 41

found his mate and he was crazy about her! My former player of a friend was whipped," chuckled Marco.

Marco had our rapt attention. Harper and I were staring at him with wide eyes.

"He wanted to marry her, but she was already engaged," said Marco.

Harper narrowed his eyes. I frowned. This sounded a bit...familiar.

"Her family had promised her to someone else and they wouldn't budge an inch. She continued to see your father in secret and she got pregnant with you two," said Marco, smiling, as he swivelled his index and middle fingers pointing to the two of us.

A small smile formed on Harper's face though he looked a bit strained. I smiled too.

"She and your father wanted to elope before her forced wedding could take place. She had been concealing her pregnancy in the meanwhile. Her fiancé was a powerful man. He found out about her secret meetings with Marco, her pregnancy, and her plan to escape, and he sent fifty of his warriors after them. I was helping them. We were ahead, but then your mother began having contractions. Your father asked me to take her and his unborn children to safety, while he held them off. He took down all of them, every single one, but he sustained some injuries. Your mother had given birth to you, Harper, her baby boy. She named you and she gave you to me and she asked me to take care of you," said Marco, his voice cracking a little.

A tear escaped down Marco's cheek. His lip quivered.

"I did that. I took care of you, like you were my own baby boy," said Marco, sniffling.

"I know, Dad, thank you," said Harper softly, his eyes filling with tears.

Marco nodded. "There's no need for thank yous between the two of us," he said with a small smile.

He continued. "She was worried about your father's injuries. He was in and out of consciousness. She wanted me to get medical attention for him. The second baby was taking a while to come. She didn't want to go further and leave your Dad, but she needed a midwife or a doctor or something for the second baby and your father needed a doctor too. They couldn't go back to the pack doctors as things were so she devised a plan. She made me take your Dad to the nearest pack. He had a good reputation there. It was where they had planned to hide and rest for a bit, before they went further. Your father had a few allies there. She went back to her pack, to her pack doctors, showing them the blood on her dress and saying she'd lost the baby and she was having trouble with the afterbirth. Her fiancé felt some pity for her and agreed to take her back. She was very special and he didn't want to miss out on such a she-wolf. She had special powers that he knew his offspring would inherit if he was with her. Her father had a title that his future son could also inherit. She summoned her own doctor. An old man. She had known him since childhood and he delivered the "afterbirth"," said Marco, using air quotations with his fingers.

"Oh," said Harper. "She got the doctor to pretend there wasn't a second baby and they already thought I was dead!" Said Harper with a gasp.

Marco nodded.

"The afterbirth was the actual afterbirth and you, Hannah, swaddled in a blanket. The doctor was entrusted with the task of getting a safe home for her baby girl, her Hannah. She had already had both of your names picked out and stitched on little blankets. She didn't even tell the doctor your chosen name. The name Hannah was stitched in little yellow letters on a dark blue blanket. She had stitched yellow stars all over it too," said Marco, tearing up again.

"I had been there back when she made your baby blankets! Your father had said "Dark blue for a girl!"," exclaimed Marco, doing an impression of a gruff man with a very deep voice.

"Is that what our father sounds like?" I asked excitedly.

Marco laughed uproariously. "Yes, little Star. It's not the best impression, but you'll hear his voice for yourself soon."

My wolf was filled with longing and so was I. Would I really hear my Dad speak to me soon? I grasped Harper's hand and he interlaced our fingers and held my hand tightly.

"Now, I'm telling you all this about the doctor taking you Hannah to safety, but I did not know this at the time it was happening. I only found out much later. At the time, all I knew was she had gone back to her pack to try to have the second baby in secret. I took your father and you, Harper, to the next pack as planned. That pack was run by a lineage of Alphas who prized excellent warriors and they loved your father. They nursed him back to health in secret. Once conscious, he was desperate to get back to her, and the second baby, unsure of what was going on with them. Then... we got some horrible news..." said Marco.

Marco took a deep shuddering breath.

"A messenger from your father's old pack told us that... that... that your mother had killed herself. She believed your father dead, and in her grief, she leapt from the highest tower of the pack's castle into the treacherous icy sea. They hadn't found her body though. The only thing that made him believe it even a little was the fact that her pack held a funeral for her, but with an empty casket. There was an obituary too," said Marco with a sigh.

Chapter 41

Harper's arms encircled me. I was confused as to why at first and I looked up at him strangely. Then, he touched my wet cheek, and I realised tears were streaming down my face. I buried my face in his shirt.

"I should stop..." said Marco.

"No, please, continue," I begged, though it was muffled by Harper's shirt.

I blew my nose in his shirt.

"Thanks," said Harper sarcastically but he was smiling.

"We have the same DNA. We're twins," I said defensively.

Harper wiped his shirt with a tissue.

"We're fraternal," he said, chuckling slightly.

"Similar DNA then," I corrected myself.

He tweaked my nose.

"Ow!" I complained.

We both turned back to Marco. He was smiling at our exchange. Mia had now gone over back to Marco. She was rubbing his shoulders.

"Your father disguised himself with magic provided by the pack helping him, and searched the seashore, the rocks, the icy landscape. He wanted to search the alleged site of her suicide for himself. There was no trace of her. He feared she was imprisoned somewhere, still alive but this could not be. There had been infighting within the pack. Her fiancé and his relatives had been killed already, so there was no further vengeance for your father to take. He became depressed. He cursed at the wind. He asked me to care for you, Harper. Again, someone was bestowing you upon me as your mother had. I was already changing your diapers and feeding you milk as it was, so, of course, it made sense," Marco said.

Harper smiled slightly.

"Your father disappeared for a while. He didn't tell me where he was going. I met my mate and explained why I already had a baby boy. Turned out that made me even more of a catch," said Marco, chuckling.

"I can't have my own children," said Mia softly. "So when my mate came with a baby already, I couldn't believe it! I was so happy! I loved you from the moment I saw you, Harper!"

Harper's smile widened.

"Then, your father returned when Harper was a little boy. He didn't want you to rely on him, Harper. He didn't want to disappoint you. He was in bad shape. Losing a mate is like a second death. The wolf's spirit dies with its mate. He loved you though. He still loves you," said Marco in earnest.

Harper looked upset.

"Your father had found Hannah," said Marco, grinning. "We were overjoyed!"

I gasped.

Marco nodded. Mia nodded eagerly too.

"Another baby, a girl!" Squealed Mia. "A sister for Harper, a twin!"

Harper grinned at Mia's enthusiasm.

"Yes, but your adopted grandmother had lost her daughter and her daughter's mate too, so she just couldn't part with you too," said Marco sadly.

"Your Dad disappeared again. Sometimes, I would be watching you playing, Harper, and I would catch a whiff of his scent. He was stealthy, but I knew his scent well. He would watch over you. I knew he probably did the same with Hannah. Eventually he found out the story of how Hannah was hidden by the doctor. He tracked down the doctor's son and he knew. That's just about everything I know and can tell. The rest, because there is more, has to be told by your father," said Marco.

"Why?" Asked Harper.

"Because it's time for you to know why I wanted you both hidden until you were of age," said a deep voice from behind us.

My heart almost stopped.

Chapter 42

Sunday 20th September, 2020 (Continued)

Star's Point Of View

When I dared to, I slowly turned around. Harper was already looking at our father. I glanced up at him, a bit nervous to meet his eyes. He had a very imposing sort of aura. He was a little taller than Harper and the Quads, at about six foot six inches. He had the same thick, wavy, shiny, dark hair as Harper. It reached his shoulders, though it was shaggier than Harper's was. His eyes were dark and intense. He looked as if he were scrutinising us. He had a moustache and a beard. He had a very rugged sort of appearance, but I was sure if he cared to groom more, he would be classically handsome.

Seeing him, as if earning a corner puzzle piece, made me want to know and piece together more. Now, I wanted to know what my mother looked like, and what her voice sounded like, but she was, perhaps, lost to me. I tried not to feel heartbroken at that when my father was standing right in front of me. The sadness of my mother's supposed passing battled the happiness at finally meeting my father.

"Dad?" I said, unable to remain quiet.

"Hannah," he said in a measured tone, as if he were holding back some emotion.

He waited for me to say more.

"Father," said Harper stiffly, nodding.

"Son," said Dad, with a hint of pride.

"We don't know your name actually," I pointed out.

He stared at me without acknowledging what I had just said.

"What's your name?" Said Harper more loudly, snapping him out of his thoughts.

"Heath," he said in his deep rough voice with a slight smile. "Though I won't be called that by my own children," he said sternly.

Harper looked taken aback.

"You've only just met us, and already, you're laying down the law?" Asked Harper incredulously.

Heath, our father, was silent. He had returned to staring at me, in particular. I stared back at him, wondering what he was thinking about.

Harper grumbled quietly to himself.

"Dad? Dad!" Exclaimed Harper, annoyed and trying to regain his attention.

Dad looked at Harper. Without another word, he grasped Harper by the shoulder and pulled him into a big bear hug.

"I'm sorry," I heard him say.

I heard Harper sniffle. I could tell my twin was very emotional at receiving this apology from our father after all this time. Dad pulled me towards him after he had relinquished Harper. It was surreal to hug my father. He smelled a bit like Harper.

"You look just like her... just like your mother," he said quietly.

He kissed my forehead and released me.

When I turned back to the couch, I realised Marco and Mia had left the room. I went to sit next to Harper and Dad sat opposite us in an armchair. Harper linked arms with me. I could tell he was emotional and was trying hard not to show it.

"I owe you both an apology and an explanation," said Dad in his gruff deep voice.

It was so strange that he seemed so decent, but had such a voice. He was an intimidating man, but there was a softness to him.

"The apology first. I'm sorry, Hannah and Harper. I wish I could've raised you. Perhaps, I should've, but I've been living under the radar for the past eighteen years for a reason. Your mother's people think you are dead, Harper, and Hannah, they don't know you exist. They think that she had only one baby, a boy who was stillborn. That story has protected you both, so that you could come of age without enemies who are still lurking, trying to do away with you. All Hesper wanted was for you two to grow up, happy and healthy, and I tried my best to arrange that without me in the picture, so as not to compromise you..." said Dad.

My heart was racing. Did he just say Hesper?

"Wait! Did you just say Hesper?" Asked Harper.

I thanked my lucky stars for my twin and our twin telepathy.

Chapter 42

Dad nodded. Tears filled his eyes, but he quickly composed himself. He was still proud. His demeanour was definitely that of a top pack warrior. Stoic.

"Hesper, as in the daughter of the Ice Moon Pack's last Alpha?" Asked Harper.

He nodded.

"And the Winter Queen Faerie's granddaughter?" I added.

He nodded again.

"Hesper is our mother?" Confirmed Harper.

He nodded.

"And your mate?" Harper asked.

Our father sighed impatiently.

"Do you want that in writing?" He asked.

I had thought he was being sarcastic, but he actually pulled some papers out of his jacket pocket. He gave them to us. We leafed through them. There was an ultrasound scan labeled Hesper Hortencia that showed two foetuses. There were two birth certificates! One for me, one for Harper. Heath Waldron was listed as our father on both and Hesper Hortencia was listed as our mother.

"How did you obtain these birth certificates, if you were trying to hide Hannah's existence and pass me off as a stillborn baby?" Asked Harper bluntly.

Heath shrugged.

"Your mother was a princess essentially, a rich and powerful noble though her father's family schemed against her... she arranged it somehow, without having the records readily available. The records are shut, sealed off somehow," explained Dad.

I lay my head on Harper's shoulder. We had discussed our birth certificates in the car. They both said the names of those who we had believed to be our parents. Those must be counterfeit.

"What's the point of all of this?" Harper said, brandishing his birth certificate.

"I know Hannah's adopted grandmother told you the story of the Ice Moon Pack. How they wanted your mother to marry her cousin not me. How he plotted against us. How your mother and I tried to escape him. I took down all his warriors, but I was injured. Many of my loyal fellow warriors were wrongfully imprisoned actually. Unable to assist me and your mother. And I know Marco told you the other half about the two of you and how your mother hid you, but was forced to stay with her pack. They say she thought me dead and killed herself. I don't know if I believe that, but I have searched for her in the meantime. I don't think a day goes by that I don't hope to see her face," he said more to himself than to us. He paused and looked at me. He smiled.

"You're beautiful just like your mother," said Dad.

I blushed.

"Thank you," I said softly.

"Those half-wit Alphas don't deserve you, but who am I to come at this late hour and tell you what to do?" Said Dad with an annoyed look on his face.

Harper snorted with laughter.

"You mean the Quads?" I asked, my heart racing.

How did he know all of that?

My Dad responded as if he had heard my thoughts.

"I've been watching over you two. My wolf is white too, like your mother's, so I expected both of you to be the same," said Dad.

The white wolf on the mountain was my father watching over me! I smiled.

Dad smirked suddenly. "I'm glad when you hear the word half-wit you immediately recognise I must mean your mates, Hannah," commented my father with a wry smile.

Harper burst into laughter, but he stifled it as best as he could when I gave him an indignant look.

I was stunned, staring back and forth between the two of them.

My father smirked again. His lip quivered and then he too burst into laughter, but he didn't stifle his. He laughed openly and raucously.

"Dad!" I whined, shocking myself at how naturally and quickly we interacted.

"What?" He said.

"They're nice boys," I said feebly.

"They're young, so, hopefully, they grow up soon. Forget about them and their melodrama. You have your own pack and titles to worry about," said Dad sternly.

Harper straightened up in his seat. Dad was very difficult to argue with. He spoke of things as if that was how it was. End of story. I saw where Harper got his brazen attitude from.

"Wait, what do you expect of us?" Asked Harper.

"Isn't it obvious?" Asked Dad.

"Is it?" I asked.

"You're spending too much time with those stupid boys. They're rubbing off on you. You're usually sharper than this! Come on, Hannah," said my father impatiently.

He looked at Harper expectantly. Something dawned on Harper.

Chapter 42

"You can't be serious? You expect me to what… to… march into the Ice Moon Castle, and take over their pack as Alpha, though the Winter Faerie Queen has put herself on the throne?" Asked Harper.

"The Queen did that out of vengeance on Hesper's behalf. You will have your twin, Hannah, with you who is a dead ringer for her mother. The Queen will vacate the throne," said Dad confidently.

"And the people will just accept us? Just like that? Because we have birth certificates?" Asked Harper incredulously.

Our father roared with laughter.

"Documentation is great, sure. But they will accept you, because you are you. You are their rightful Alpha. They are wolves, Harper. They will know their Alpha, sense it, smell it. They will know it as one knows one's fated. Alphas are also fated to their packs, in a sense, as they are to their Lunas. You will both have Fae powers. They will know," said Dad.

"We don't have Fae powers!" Said Harper, annoyed.

"You do," said Dad simply.

"What? Lie detecting? That's nothing…" Harper began.

"Enough!" Said Dad.

Harper fell silent.

"Your mother put a spell on both of you to suppress your magic to help hide you. The Fae can sense Fae magic, and would be drawn to it. Some traitorous Fae could have revealed you, before you were of age," said Dad.

"How do we take the spell off?" I asked eagerly.

My Fae powers could help me fight the curse too! Dad smirked.

"It will be broken the moment you step into the Ice Moon Castle," said Dad.

Chapter 43

Sunday 20th September, 2020 (Continued)

Jonah's Point Of View

It was torture being away from Star all the time, especially during times like these. Trying times. Pivotal moments when I knew she could use the support of a mate. Most Alphas were able to sweep their Lunas off their feet immediately or within the month of meeting. It came naturally. We craved each other as Alpha and Luna, and nothing should be able to keep us apart. In my case, my very love for Star kept me away from her. I refused to be her death sentence. That wasn't love. Love was more than yearning. Love was wanting the best for the person. My younger brothers were a bit too frivolous to understand that. They were moping about. I could hear them plotting to go see Star. They wanted to go to Harper's family estate and wait out front.

"None of you are going anywhere," I said bluntly, interrupting their plans.

"We should be there to support her," said Noah softly.

"This is our opportunity to meet her father," said Eli.

"And impress him!" Added Zaya.

I had mind-linked Harper to ask how Star was doing, and he had informed me that they were anxiously awaiting the arrival of their father. He was alive and on his way to them. I had made the mistake of sharing this information with my younger brothers. Now, they wanted to barge in on Star's family reunion.

Chapter 43

"He won't be impressed by us, not the way we've stressed out Star, and if he finds out about the curse, he will drive a wedge between Star and us," I said.

"You've done a good job of that all on your own," muttered Zaya.

I sharply inhaled and exhaled. I would not be incensed by Zaya.

"Let's give them this time together. Tomorrow morning, we can all talk with Star about it," I reasoned.

Zaya shook his head.

"I feel as though she won't be at school tomorrow morning. I don't want to be there tomorrow morning either. I want to be wherever Star is," grumbled Zaya.

I sighed. I wanted that too.

"We can't get slack now. You three already undid some of the hard work we've done with your debauchery. Let's just be thankful that our efforts are not in vain. The curse seems to be confused. Star didn't have a second premonition dream for the Vice Principal's death but Angie did!" I exclaimed.

My brothers gasped.

"When were you going to tell us that?" Asked Eli, annoyed.

"I only just found out myself! Angie called me. She had another nightmare like the previous one. She saw that stage light fall on the Vice Principal the night before it happened," I informed them.

"Wait, then why didn't she warn the Vice Principal? I understand if she didn't believe the first premonition dream, but after that one came true, she would know by now how serious they are!" Said Zaya.

Even though Angie was in the dark about the curse itself, Zaya had a point. If I had dreamt of someone's death before it happened once, I would take any further dreams of death extremely seriously.

"Warning Hitch wouldn't have necessarily spared her from the curse. Maybe the death was inevitable one way or another," said Noah.

"And maybe, just maybe, Angie is so evil she could know the hour and cause of death of someone, and still not lift a finger. How difficult would it have been to ask Vice Principal Hitch to not do any announcing? Or she could have distracted Hitch as much as necessary and made her miss all her cues?" Explained Eli.

I shrugged. I wasn't sure why Angie hadn't tried to warn Vice Principal Hitch especially since Angie was one of the only students who had gotten along with the crabby Vice Principal.

I pulled out my phone. I smiled at my wallpaper. It was a picture of Star in front of her birthday cake at Chet's Cabin. Just before she had blown out her candles, I had felt compelled to capture the moment. That was mere moments before the full mate-bond had taken effect. Whenever,

Angie was not around, I made that picture of Star my wallpaper. I changed it, whenever I was expecting to see Angie to a picture of Angie and me from that same day, but from earlier, by the lake. I sighed. I hated living a lie like this, but it was necessary. I felt guilty. Angie wasn't what most people would consider a good person, but she wasn't completely heartless and soulless. I wanted her to make it out of this in one piece also.

"So, since the plan to confuse the curse seems to be working... are you gonna propose to Angie?" Asked Noah hesitantly.

"Do I have any other choice?" I said, shrugging.

"Has father located Alto's body yet?" Asked Eli.

"The pack historian said he would be in the Alpha Mausoleum on the zenith of Mount Viper," said Noah offhandedly.

"Well, as soon as Jamie finds out where Georgianna is buried, we can bring Alto to her," said Eli excitedly.

"Hopefully, no one else is taken by the curse in the interim," I said dryly.

"If the curse thinks Angie might be the Luna, then won't getting engaged to her provoke Georgianna even more?" Asked Eli.

"Yes, but we might need Georgianna to be provoked again," said Noah.

"What? Why?" Asked Zaya.

"Because Jamie is having trouble locating Georgianna's tomb. Last time, she summoned Georgianna, she, Star and Jessie all saw something, like a flashback of Georgianna's life, her memories," I explained.

"So, maybe, it's not Georgianna's memory we need to access to know where she is buried," deducted Noah.

"What do you mean?" I asked, intrigued.

"We just need to make contact with literally anyone who attended Georgianna's burial," said Noah.

Jessie's Point Of View

"Why are we here again?" I asked an already disgruntled Jamie.

"You know why, Jessie," answered Jamie. "This is the coven house of Georgianna's old coven. They took forever to track down."

"Why though? Isn't that sort of information readily available? In Ambrosia, everyone knows where the coven house is," I said, feigning innocence.

I already knew what she was going to say, because she had explained this to me several times, but I liked teasing my beautiful wife and Luna, Jamie. I also liked listening to her explaining witchy things. It was hot.

Chapter 43

Jamie told me the story again, describing how Georgiana's coven members had faded into the shadows after Alto's death. Although Alto's last command as Alpha provided protection for Georgiana, the same could not be said for the other witches and wizards in the area. They had been under considerable strain as the death of Alto increased every manner of vitriol against them from werewolves. They had felt unsafe, and thus, had decided to conceal their coven house with powerful enchantments. Jamie had been trying to find out if the coven in question still existed today. We had both been surprised to learn that they did, in fact, still exist, and continued to reside on the outskirts of the Viper Moon Pack lands. Jamie had cast every revealing spell she knew, until she uncovered the current whereabouts of the coven.

We were standing in front of a dilapidated-looking mansion, with its stone pillars crumbling, and its garden overgrown with weeds. The grass on the estate was waist-high in places and chest-high in others even for me. We waded through the green sea of grass as the long blades bowed to the wind. We stood at the foot of stone steps leading to large double doors. All the windows and doors had been boarded up. There were cobwebs in every corner and archway. Vines covered the walls and crisscrossed across the roof. Jamie offered a white rose as a symbol of peace, resting it on the doorstep of the house. She began to chant.

"Sacred charms of anonymity,
Spells of stealth and secrecy,
Reveal what you've concealed from me,
Revelare
So mote it be!"

There was a high-pitched hissing sound, reminiscent of how a kettle sounds right before it begins to whistle. All the wooden planks nailed to the windows and doors crumbled to dust before our very eyes. Meanwhile, the crumbling pillars were rebuilt and reformed. The vines shrunk away from the house and the spiders un-wove their webs, moving in reverse. In mere moments, the mansion was restored to its former glory.

"Awesome, my Luna! What now?" I asked, looking at her in amazement.

She grinned at me. She stretched her hand out, and simple knocked on the door.

Harper's Point Of View

"Do you have the portal in your possession, Hannah?" Asked our father, gazing at a nervous Star.

She nodded and revealed the snow globe, where the icy storm raged on outside the magnificent gleaming castle.

"How comfortable are you two with the cold?" Asked Dad.

Star and I glanced at each other. We shrugged.

"We're going there, right away?" I asked incredulously.

Dad looked at me strangely.

"We've waited eighteen years. You want to wait some more?" He replied in the same incredulous tone.

I looked at Star.

"What about the guards that appear to be patrolling outside the castle?" I asked him.

There were tiny guards marching about the wintry landscape. I spotted some of them in wolf form and others in their human forms. I even noticed a few guards who had pointed ears and somewhat iridescent skin. They skin seemed to glow from within in a most peculiar way. They were undoubtedly magic beings.

"Are some of the guards...Fae?" I asked hesitantly, as I gazed at the globe.

"Yes, indeed, a few are," said Dad offhandedly.

"How will we get past them? They had magic! Our magic doesn't come in until we set foot in the castle, right?" I clarified.

"Yes, you must enter the castle to activate your full powers, as your mother specified when she first told me of the spell," said Dad. "But, I will be with you to help you fend off the werewolf guards..."

"And the Fae ones?!" I reiterated.

Dad had a knowing smile playing about his lips.

"Your mother's favourite cousin, Prince Asriel, has agreed to help you evade the Fae guards as well. In fact, if all goes as planned, you may not even need my brute force, only his stealth. He means to conceal us all as we traverse the perimeter of the castle," said Dad.

"Prince Asriel? He's Fae?" Star asked.

"Naturally," said Dad.

I had to admit that my father had at least given this plan some thought. However, I still didn't like the way it was sprung upon Star and me. There was one other thing I wanted to do, before I went to the Ice Moon Castle. Star was being rather quiet, her expression concerned.

"When do you intend to do this?" I asked.

"As soon as possible, tonight even!" Said our father.

"And where is Prince Adriel?" I asked.

"He is to meet us here soon," said Dad with a smug smile.

"Might I propose a test run then?" I asked.

My father raised his eyebrows.

Chapter 43

"So that Star and I may see for ourselves how stealthy we actually can be with his help?" I asked.

My father did not look too eager.

"Surely, you wouldn't have our very first instance with Fae magic be the storming of the castle. We should, at least, have some practice first," I said.

Star smiled slightly. She knew exactly what I meant.

"Where do you intend to practice sneaking into?" Asked Dad, furrowing his brow.

"The Plastique Estate," I said, without hesitation.

Star bit her lip, but she did not protest.

You okay with this, Movie Star? I asked, to be sure.

I think it's a brilliant idea! She replied mischievously.

Chapter 44

Sunday 20th September, 2020 (Continued)

Star's Point Of View

Prince Asriel was completely not what I had been expecting. I had anticipated that a Winter Fae Prince would be the very picture of elegance and sophistication. I had expected him to be punctual, arrogant, and immaculately dressed. Asriel showed up a half hour later than the time given, wearing artfully ripped jeans with paint splatters on them and a rock band Tee shirt. His light blonde hair was down to his waist and had been streaked with grey and purple. He had pierced ears. I kept staring at his earrings. They were tiny hanging skulls that spoke. One skull earring whispered snide comments and the other was very complimentary and polite. He jokingly introduced the skull earrings as Asshat and Asshole, but their names were actually Erin and Rein, with Erin being the kind one, and Rein being the abrasive one.

"I'm so happy to learn you're a fellow artist!" Said Asriel immediately to Harper with no prelude or verbal introduction whatsoever.

Asriel pulled Harper into a hug.

"Awesome! Can't wait to hear your material," said Asriel.

"I don't want to hear it. I'm bored already with him. Let's go," demanded Rein.

"I'm a huge fan of Pariah! Will you sign my mandible?" Asked Erin.

Harper was so confused by the skull earrings that he just stared at Asriel. He was left totally speechless. I had no idea how even Erin, the kind Fae skull earring, knew about Harper's band, Pariah.

"Righteous," said Asriel to a dumbfounded Harper.

Chapter 44

"Come here, Hannah," insisted Asriel.

He bear-hugged me, literally lifting me off the ground with such ease. He was very tall like Harper, but more lean than muscular, so I was surprised at his strength. His face was symmetrical perfection. It almost hurt to look at him. That was the face I had expected of a Fae Prince, fantastically handsome in a refined way. He placed me delicately back onto my feet. He held me at arms length and cupped my face, turning it from side to side and up and down, admiring it from every angle.

"Astounding! Amazing!" He said more to himself than me.

"Isn't she just?" Agreed Dad.

I felt so shy with all eyes on me.

"A perfect likeness," said Asriel.

"Your mother was my father's favourite cousin, so I hope we will be best friends as they were," said Asriel.

I nodded eagerly. He kissed my forehead.

"You look exactly like Hesper," he said.

"You met my Mom?" I asked curiously.

"I'm a lot older than I look," he said with a huge grin.

Asriel looked about twenty-one at the most. I wondered how old he was.

"Let's rock n 'roll!" He commanded.

He marched outside. Dad followed him. Harper and I scrambled after them.

"What's the plan?" Asked Harper, getting into his car. I got in too.

Dad and Asriel stood outside the car, staring at Harper and me, until we simply vacated the car again and stood awkwardly in front of them.

"Right," said Asriel. "The car is evidence!"

"Evidence?" Asked Harper.

Asriel grinned. "You wanna break into the Plastique house? Don't you? Yeah, evidence!"

Harper and I were shocked. We had not explained our plan, or mentioned the Plastique house yet.

"How did you know that?" Asked Harper, before I could.

"These guys!" Said Asriel, pointing to his earrings.

"We're not just good-looking, we know a lot of things!" Said Erin.

"You're not good-looking, Erin!" Said Rein.

"I'm gorgeous! I was Mom's favourite!" Said Erin.

"That's awesome!" Said Harper excitedly, peering more closely at the earrings.

"Are they all-knowing?" I asked in amazement.

"Oh! Aren't you the sweetest!" Cooed Erin.

"Of course not! Are you sniffing glue?" Muttered Rein. "We know certain things!"

"Desires and intentions," said Erin.

"Lottery numbers, but only the human lottery, and that money is useless in the Fae world. It's only paper!" Complained Rein.

"Will Rein and Erin be... um... quiet when we get to the house?" Asked Harper tentatively.

"Anything for you, handsome!" Said Erin.

"He just told us to shut up! He doesn't even have a post officially yet, and he's giving orders!" Yelled Rein.

Asriel laughed, tossing his head back.

"What's the holdup?" Asked Dad, annoyed.

Asriel was still laughing. "They want to know if my earrings will be quiet, when we get to the house!" Chuckled Asriel.

Dad looked elated all of a sudden. "They're like their mother, you know. They have it! They definitely have it!" Said Dad.

"Have what?" I asked.

"Fae magic!" Said Dad. "I can't hear anything."

Asriel nodded. "Only the Fae can perceive Fae magic. These earrings are motionless normal skull earrings to everyone who isn't Fae," explained Asriel. "So the Plastique family won't hear them bickering!" Asriel added in a dramatic whisper.

Harper looked like he wanted a pair of those earrings ASAP. I was fine without them. They seemed like a headache. They quarrelled nonstop.

Asriel took a small vial from his jeans pocket. It was filled with silvery dust. He blew it into the air and it surrounded us. I felt tingly all over for a moment and then the feeling faded.

"What just happened?" I asked.

"You're invisible now!" Asriel informed me.

I took my compact out of my little crossbody bag and looked at myself. I smiled at the nothingness reflected there. I only saw the tree behind me in the mirror.

"Will we be able to do stuff like that?" I asked hopefully.

"Eventually," said Asriel.

"You just discovered you were part Fae five minutes ago! Why are young people always in a hurry?" Asked Rein.

"She's eager to learn! She will make a marvellous princess! I can envision the halls of the castle filled with suitors already!" Whispered Erin conspiratorially.

"I have mates," I said to Erin.

"Yuck! Those four. Four of them, and not even one likeable one! Now, that's just ridiculous!" Said Rein.

Chapter 44

"Yes! I almost forgot! Jonah, Noah, Eli and Zaya. Oh, I love Zaya! I like Eli too. Noah and Jonah are... great also!" Said Erin.

I felt like Erin struggled to say the word great when referring to the elder two.

"They aight," said Asriel.

He snapped his fingers, and we were surrounded by darkness. My stomach lurched as if I had fallen suddenly. I held onto Harper to steady myself. Dad seemed used to this method of travel. I had so many questions for him. Did Mom used to travel via Fae magic like that? Did Mom take him to Fae places? What was she like? What was he like? My Dad was a stranger to me still.

We arrived at the Plastique residence in just a few seconds.

"Wow," said Harper softly.

I knew he meant the magic.

"Wait," I said. "How come we didn't... um... poof inside the house?" I asked out of curiosity.

Asriel chuckled. Dad smiled.

"We are Fae. We must be invited inside. Once invited, we can return as we please. You two were let in earlier. I was not. This is where I leave you for now. You're invisible. Go in and retrieve what you seek," said Asriel, with a knowing smile. "Your Dad can go with you. He's a werewolf. He doesn't need an invitation!"

"Not like vampires and faeries," barked Dad, laughing to himself.

"You'll wait here for us?" I asked, not ready to part with cousin Asriel.

He winked. "I'll wait forever if I must," he said dramatically.

"He'll wander off to the nearest fast-food joint for a bean burrito if you take too long," said Rein.

"Forever and ever, Princess Hannah!" Chimed Erin dutifully.

"He'll come back. Snarf down the burrito. Stand here and act like he never left!" Added Rein.

"Until the mountains crumble to dust and the stars fall from the heavens!" Erin practically sang.

"Thank you, Erin! You're a real one! Rein, you've got jokes. I admire that too," said Harper.

Rein was stunned into silence by Harper's compliment. Erin promptly began praising Harper and Pariah again. He then started asking Rein and Asriel to look for a pen so they could all get autographs.

Dad, Harper and I went around the side of the house, searching for an easy way in. Dad spotted an open window on the first floor. He and Harper were good climbers. I was not. They helped me shimmy up the drain pipe and climb into the first story window. I tumbled onto the floor. Dad quickly picked me up.

Are you ok? He asked over mind-link.

I nodded. He released me. I followed him and Harper around. Harper seemed to know where he was going. Harper went into a study. He searched all the drawers. I looked through a cabinet.

What are you hoping to find? Dad asked us.

A will from Hannah's adopted Dad! Said Harper.

You won't want for money, said Dad, confused.

It's the principle behind it all! Insisted Harper.

Harper became frustrated, and stole out of the room into the hallway. He edged along quietly, moving stealthily though we were invisible.

This invisibility spell wears off in about a half hour, okay, kids, so hurry! Said Dad.

What?! I pictured Asriel telling me he'd wait forever. I rolled my eyes. He knew his spell only lasted thirty minutes! I needed to start paying closer attention to Rein's comments.

Harper tiptoed into a dressing room of sorts, where there was a vanity overladen with creams, perfumes, and other beauty products.

Harper! How do you know the layout of this place so well?! I asked privately.

Harper grinned sheepishly.

I'm not proud of this, but it was before I met you, and saw how Angie treats you! Angie cheats on Jonah and their situation-ship all the time, before you came into the picture. They've been a sorta couple a year now, said Harper to me only.

I felt sick, thinking about where this was going.

You hooked up with Angie?! I asked outright.

Our Dad was leafing through some drawers nearby, unaware of our exchange.

Yeah, said Harper, avoiding my gaze.

I stormed out of the room. Dad came after me.

What are you doing? He asked.

Leaving, I said.

I found the window, climbed out of it, and almost screamed when I slipped. My feet were dangling in midair. I looked up and Dad was holding me by the hood of my jacket. He pulled me back inside.

We can't leave your brother, he said in a tone that did not allow for protests.

He gave me a stern look that I knew meant "stay put" and went to get Harper. Harper came hurrying out.

Star! I know you hate me, but I got it! I got it! Said Harper excitedly.

He practically leapt out the window, landing easily, crouching on his feet, and standing up smoothly.

Chapter 44

Why couldn't I do that? Dad helped me climb down, and Harper waited with his hands stretched upwards to help me too. I avoided Harper's help, and began walking towards the front.

Asriel was there. He hastily put away an empty burrito wrapper. He looked alarmed at my expression.

"What's wrong, Honey?" He asked softly, putting an arm around me. I sighed.

"She hates me now," said Harper quickly and dismissively. "But, that's ok! Because I got it!"

"What?" Asked Asriel with a smile.

"You know what!" Said Rein, annoyed.

"The will!" Shrieked Erin.

I almost shushed him, before I remembered only those who were Fae could hear him. Asriel snapped us back to Harper's house in a flash.

"And it says Hannah is the beneficiary!" Continued Harper, as if nothing had happened.

"What?" I asked.

"You know what!" Snapped Rein.

"Yay! We're rich!" Cheered Erin.

"We're already rich! We belong to a Prince! You act like you've never been anywhere! We should start leaving you home," said Rein to Erin.

Harper chuckled. He handed me the will. I reluctantly took it. My heart still stung so badly. Why were Angie's claws all over *everyone* I loved all the time? My mate. My *twin*. My... inheritance. I gasped. I had always thought my father had been exempted from his parents 'money, but that was apparently not the case. My adopted Dad had listed me as the sole heiress to his fortune, his billion dollar fortune. I fainted.

Chapter 45

Monday 21st September, 2020 (Continued)

Star's Point Of View

When I came to, I was greeted by the anxious faces of my Dad and my twin brother, along with the calm face of my cousin.

"She's fine," Asriel announced, as he finished sprinkling me with a shimmery dust that made me sneeze a shower of glitter.

Asriel wiped some glitter sneeze spray from his shirt.

"Hannah, how're you feeling?" Asked Dad, patting me delicately on the head.

"I'm ok," I mumbled.

I sat up slowly. Harper tried to help me, but I scooted away from him. I was lying down in a bed in an unfamiliar but welcoming setting. It was a spacious bedroom with cream-coloured walls and a hard-wood floor. The drapes were a chocolate brown and the bedding was lily-white. The room was simple yet luxurious. Where was I? Harper guessed what I was wondering.

"We're at my house again," said Harper.

"How is she feeling?" Whispered Mia, as she peeked into the room with Marco right behind her.

"I'm okay, thank you," I said to her. "Sorry to alarm everyone," I added.

"Will she be ok enough to go to the castle?" Asked Dad.

He was looking at Asriel who nodded.

"The castle?" Said Harper incredulously. "But, we need to confront Angie's Mom first! She stole Hannah's inheritance!" He said indignantly.

Chapter 45

Asriel stroked his chin, thinking it over. The earrings were quiet. In fact, they appeared to be sleeping. I leant a bit closer to Asriel to observe them. Erin was sleeping soundly, and Rein was snoring softly.

"Shouldn't a lawyer handle that? Look at the will," grumbled Dad in his deep voice.

Everything Dad said sounded gruff, even if he did not mean it in such a way. It was the bass of his voice, and his entire demeanour. He was intimidating without even trying.

Marco agreed with his best friend. "Your father is right! Don't worry, Harper, I'll have my lawyer look at the will and make an inquiry," he said firmly.

Harper reluctantly agreed. "Okay," was all he said. He was looking to me to object further.

"Okay," I said.

I was still so upset over Harper's history with Angie. I wasn't sure how to process it. When had he been planning on telling me? Would he have ever told me? I knew it was before he had even met me, but it was so frustrating that Angie seemed to have marred every aspect of my life in some way.

"We're going to the castle right away?" I asked, as the butler set a tray with a bowl of soup on it in front of me.

Steam rose from the spicy-smelling liquid. I sipped a few spoonfuls carefully, after blowing on them. The warmth filled my tummy. I began to feel better.

"We'll go within the hour. Better to go as soon as possible," said Dad.

He was in such a hurry for us to claim our birthrights. I supposed he had already waited eighteen years, so he was entitled to be a bit impatient now. I was eager to claim my Fae powers. They could be of great use against the curse. Surely, a magical luna would not be as susceptible to a curse. I hastily drank the soup and used the accompanying glass of water to take some painkillers. I had a throbbing headache. I got to my feet and put on my shoes.

"Let's go!" I said.

Harper looked at me disapprovingly, but did not object. Dad and Asriel grinned at each other. It dawned on me that I should alert my mates, before I left the pack lands.

"Take these!" Insisted Marco, handing a coat to each of us.

"Oh, wait I-," I began, but Asriel had already muttered a few words, whilst holding the snow globe portal.

This method of travel was smoother than the previous one. We seemed to glide through a kaleidoscope of colours for less than a second. After the whirlwind of colours, I found myself in a wintry landscape, surrounded by blindingly white snow. The blast of cold air prompted me to put on my coat. Everyone else donned theirs also. I blinked as my eyes adjusted to the light and the glare. My shoes crunched through the fresh snow. Snowflakes were falling from above steadily thickening the white blanket of snow beneath us. The castle could be seen in the distance. Asriel put another invisibility spell on all of us. I took a deep breath. I couldn't believe how my life had changed so suddenly. I was about to meet the Winter Faerie Queen, my own great-grandmother.

Dad held my hand and helped me meander through the rocky, snowy expanse. Harper kept holding out his hand to me also, but I refused it each time until he gave up. I felt a pang of guilt for being so hard on him, but I pushed that aside. My mind was already swirling with dozens of thoughts. What would the Fae Queen think of me? What would she think of Harper? Would she relinquish the pack to him? Would the pack members themselves accept us? Would Angie's Mom be found guilty for anything regarding the will? Would the money actually come to me? How would the Quads react to the news of my inheritance being stolen by the Plastique family? Particularly Jonah! How would they react to me being a Princess?

Erin and Rein snapped me out of my thoughts. They had woken up.

"It's so cold! Where's my coat? You selfish Fae you, Asriel!" Grumbled Rein.

"Wow, look at this winter wonderland! Isn't it a dream come true, everyone! Who has watched the human movie with the snowman and the princess? Shall I sing the song from it?" Asked Erin.

"Please don't! I'm miserable enough as it is!" Yelped Rein.

" LET IT G—" began Erin but Asriel promptly shushed him.

"The Fae can hear you two, remember?" He chastised them.

They were silent.

"There," whispered Asriel.

I gasped. A huge grey stone castle loomed before us. Now, that we were closer, I could see how magnificent it really was. It was a colossal maze of towers with pointed domed roofs and stained glass windows. The stained glass reflected their colours onto the nearby snow making the scene all the more brilliant. The castle was surrounded by a grey stone wall. There were walkways high up at the top of the wall like floating bridges. I could see guards in full armour patrolling them. A piercingly loud and fierce screech almost made me fall over in shock. I looked further upwards until my eyes found it. At the highest tower was a dragon. He was curled around the highest dome. His scales looked like they were made of ice. He was almost translucent and he sparkled brilliantly in the light. He seemed excited about something. He emitted another screeching sound as he

Chapter 45

stretched out his wide wings. He had to be at least one hundred feet long from snout to tail, perhaps larger.

He senses you two, said Dad over mind-link to Harper and me. Dad seemed thrilled.

Shouldn't we be worried? Won't he attack us? Asked Harper.

No! He was your mother's dragon! Said Dad.

My mother had kept a dragon for a pet!

If Mom had a dragon, how was anyone able to cross her and you, Dad? Demanded Harper.

Dad sighed. *That was eighteen years ago! He was a hatchling then! He is about the same age as you two!*

What's his name? I asked eagerly.

Haven, said Dad.

Haven raised his magnificent head, snout facing the sky. He opened his wide jaws and roared. A fountain of ice sprang from his mouth forming an icy curved bridge from just above the tallest tower descending outwards all the way down to the snow before us. I marvelled at it.

Haven is helping us! Exclaimed Dad. *Hurry! The guards will be suspicious now but the bridge will be the fastest way! Shift! NOW!*

I shifted without a single thought about my coat or clothes. I shredded through them as my form changed shape, growing. I looked down at my white furry paws, really noticing my coat properly for the first time. There were two other white wolves before me. Harper and Dad. Asriel motioned for us to follow him as he ran lightly up the ice bridge. We scampered after him. It was slippery but Harper and Dad grasped the scruff of my neck carefully with their jaws whenever I slipped. We were still invisible but a guard suddenly leapt onto the ice bridge midway, blocking our path. He peered into the thin air, swiping his hands out at nothing. He was onto us. Haven suddenly sent a blast of ice his way, knocking him off the bridge. Guards began to swarm the bridge, but after a few more ice blasts from Haven, they became very reluctant to investigate the new bridge. Many scurried off of the bridge, clearing our path. We reached the very top where there was a jagged edge hanging in midair. I could see the pointed tip of the domed roof below us. Asriel blew silver dust downwards forming a rope bridge that resembled a glistening silvery spider's web. We gingerly crossed it. We crashed straight through the stained glass window of the highest tower, tumbling across the stone floor. We were in the castle! We had made it! I looked over at Harper's white wolf, his fur dotted with pieces of coloured glass. He seemed okay. I couldn't shift back without clothes. I looked at my father's wolf, and at Asriel, who wore a wide triumphant grin on his face. Before I could ask either of them what to do, a chill crept through me.

My body was bathed in light as was Harper's. A surge of energy coursed through me. I opened my mouth to scream, but a howl escaped me instead. A tornado of shimmery dust swirled around my twin and me, faster and faster. Something was rushing through me, changing me. I was disoriented, but I did not feel unwell. I felt... powerful.

Chapter 46

Monday 21st September, 2020 (Continued)

Zaya's Point Of View

I spent the whole night pacing, thinking about Star. Eli did the same. I felt a bit loopy at some point during the night, but, as an alpha, I'd never admit to that. I knew Jonah and Noah had been having trouble sleeping too. I had heard their voices throughout the night. They had been discussing Star and the curse. I knew that Jonah had mind-linked Harper a few times to ensure all was well with Star. He had said yes, but he had not given any details.

Dawn came too soon. I really did not want to go to class, but the thought of seeing Star was a great motivator. I was ready in a matter of minutes. My brothers were all just as eager. Damocles 'class was now being taught by a substitute teacher. My brothers and I sat in the same row as Jillian and Chet. Angelique came over to sit next to Jonah.

"Where's Star?" I whispered to Jillian as the substitute teacher turned the lights off and put on an educational movie.

She shrugged her shoulders. "She never came back to the dorm last night," said Jillian, a worried expression on her face.

My blood ran cold. "Why not? Have you talked to her at all?" I asked quickly.

"I mind-linked her, and she told me she had met her father!" Exclaimed Jillian.

What?! We all gasped.

"Her father? Her biological father? He's really alive?" I asked in rapid succession.

"Yeah, her biological father is alive, and he came to see her and Harper. She said something about visiting her parents 'old pack," said Jillian.

"Star left our pack lands?!" I asked.

Jillian nodded. "Most likely. That's probably why she is out of range for mind-link," said Jillian.

I was livid. Star had left the safety of her alphas 'pack lands without so much as a message or phone call. How could she do that without telling us?! We were her mates! I took a deep breath as I tried to calm myself and cool my temper. Jonah was staring at me with worried eyes. Noah looked tense. Eli paled a bit.

"We need to go after her!" Insisted Eli.

I nodded resolutely.

Angelique was eavesdropping.

"Your little Cloud is missing, huh Zaya and Eli?" She asked snidely.

I glared at her.

"Harper's not in class either!" Added Angelique with a sly smile.

"Harper is never in class," said Noah blankly.

"They probably ran off somewhere together!" Said Angelique.

I remained quiet. Harper definitely could not be Star's decoy anymore, but it was not my place to start telling everyone they were twins. It felt as though they should be the ones to do that. I tried to focus on Star, trying to find her amidst thousands of voices. I couldn't mind-link with her. She was either unconscious or too far away. I desperately hoped it was the latter.

"Let's go," I said when the teacher's back was turned.

I didn't care too much about getting in trouble, but I didn't want to draw more attention to us than necessary. Eli and I got up. We glanced back at Jonah. He had a pained expression on his face. I knew he had to keep up his charade.

I'll catch up with you guys! Said Jonah over mind-link.

I'm going with them now, said Noah, rising to his feet.

Angie glanced up at us suspiciously.

"Ugh, puh-lease, tell me you three are not going after Cloud?" Snickered Angie.

I ignored her. She honestly wasn't even worth growling at. Eli and I got into his car, along with Noah. We sped off to the last place Star had been, Harper's house.

Jessie's Point Of View

Chapter 46

When I opened my eyes, I was momentarily puzzled by my surroundings. Jamie and I had slept over in the Coven House. This Coven had been Georgianna's many years ago. I rubbed my eyes. The bedroom we had been offered looked so different in the light of day. The wooden chairs and table in the corner were unvarnished giving them a rustic appeal. The bedding was floral and so was the wallpaper, drapes and rugs. Something was wrong. I ripped the blanket off of me. Jamie was gone!

I burst out of the door and followed her scent. I found her in a dining room downstairs. I raised my eyebrows in surprise. There were about a dozen girls seated at a long table all dressed similarly, in black velvet dresses and matching bows in their hair. They were all of different complexions, hair and eye colours, clearly unrelated, though dressed alike. Understanding dawned on me. A school. This was a school. A small one contained in the coven house. These were pupils, here to learn magic from the Coven Mother. Yesterday, the Coven Mother, Nina Van Saint had welcomed us warmly. She had been more than willing to answer questions, and to give us lodgings for the night. She had promised to take us to Georgianna's tomb today. As far as I had known, she had been the only person in the Coven House last night.

Jamie smiled at me. I frowned at her. I went to sit next to her.

You scared me! I woke up in an unfamiliar place and you were gone! We should stick together! I complained, refusing to meet her eyes.

I stared sullenly at the empty plate on the table before me. Jamie kissed my cheek softly.

I'm sorry, my Alpha, she cooed.

Ugh. It was so difficult to stay mad at her.

"Where did these rug-rats come from?" I asked under my breath, nodding towards the girls.

They all looked to be between the ages of about eight and twelve.

"These are very special girls," said Nina Van Saint.

She was sitting near to Jamie and me, her cat-like green eyes regarding us with curiosity. She was a tall woman in her mid-thirties with jet black shoulder-length hair and olive skin. She was wearing a black velvet dress just like her students. She had a whispery voice that also seemed to echo on its own.

"Most witches inherit their full powers around age thirteen. They can do magic before that but their spells would be diluted. These girls have started training as witches early, because they are magical prodigies, inheriting vast amounts of power at a young age," explained Nina.

"That's awesome, but where is Georgianna's tomb, and when are you taking us there?" I said, getting back to the point.

Nina chuckled. "I promised to take you on the coming morn, didn't I?" She asked.

"Yes, you promised that yesterday so that favour would be due today," I said.

Jamie elbowed me. Nina laughed heartily.

"What a spirited husband you have Jamie!" Exclaimed Nina.

"I'm practically possessed," I said as pancakes, bacon and eggs appeared on our plates out of thin air.

Our cups filled with tea and coffee of their own accord. Two large pitchers filled with syrup and milk respectively, and cutlery and napkins appeared.

Nina laughed cheerfully. Jamie thanked Nina, and then began pouring syrup onto her pancakes. I looked at both of them expectantly.

"After breakfast, we will go to the tomb," said Nina.

"So, you know exactly where it is?" I confirmed.

"Not exactly," answered Nina.

I raised a brow.

"We believe she made herself a tomb in the woods behind our Coven House," said Nina. "Georgianna and Alto first laid eyes on each other in that woods or so the story goes."

"Mother Nina, is it true that Georgianna lived out in that woods?" Asked Jamie.

"It's rumoured that she stayed there, from time to time, in a cottage near the heart of the woods," said Nina, smiling.

Jamie nodded. I stared blankly at Nina. She struck me as someone with secrets for some reason. A memory of Eva flashed into my mind, and a chill crept through me. Jamie could be quite trusting of those who did not deserve it. Eva used to be her best-friend, but she had been conspiring against Jamie's whole witching family.

"Who is the crone of this coven? Perhaps, she might accompany us for further protection," I said authoritatively.

"Oh, Elspeth is sleeping. She's over one hundred years old now," commented Nina.

"Like this house," I muttered, under my breath. Jamie elbowed me again.

"Why do you have that Glamour on the house? The one that makes it look abandoned," I said.

I was accustomed to witches being open about their witchcraft in Ambrosia. The Coven House back home was not hidden away or disguised. Jamie had already told me that this Coven House was hidden as a precaution after Georgianna was wrongfully blamed for her Alpha's death. His dying order protected Georgianna herself, but the same could

Chapter 46

not be said for the other coven members, and werewolves were known to retaliate swiftly and savagely. I wanted to hear Nina confirm this reason though.

"It's a necessary evil, I'm afraid," chuckled Nina. "After Mother Georgianna was blamed for the Alpha's death, years and years ago, her Coven became quite secretive. They feared for their lives," explained Nina sadly.

"Understandably so," agreed Jamie. "Werewolves can be so hot-tempered!" Exclaimed Jamie, shooting me a glare.

I knew she was annoyed I had asked that question yet again.

My temper isn't the only hot thing about me. Do you need reminding of how heated things can get? I said to Jamie privately, as my hand found her knee under the table.

I snaked my hand upwards, slowly caressing her thigh. She glanced at me indignantly, and I winked. She blushed a little, looking away.

"Shouldn't we get a move on, Mother Nina. We wouldn't want to have to spend another night here," I said bluntly.

Jamie shot me another warning glance.

Nina smiled. "Yes, but the woods here are so beautiful at night. The girls and I often star-gaze in them, lying on the soft grass. There's a lake there that reflects the sky beautifully as well!" Said Nina.

"Okay," I said slowly. "I'm sorry, but we don't have the time for any leisurely pursuits. This visit is strictly business unfortunately," I said sternly.

Jamie was half-way through her pancakes. I suddenly realised something. I could hear the scrape of a knife and fork on Jamie's plate only. I had already finished my food. I glanced at the plates of all the girls and their Coven Mother, their pancakes perfectly untouched as though the food was a prop.

"Not hungry?" I asked Nina.

Nina laughed. "I'm a slow eater," she said.

I grinned half-heartedly. Slow eating was not the same as no eating. What was going on here?

Jamie, the girls and Nina aren't eating anything! I told her.

I was thoroughly regretting eating that breakfast. Had something been wrong with it? Jamie abruptly stopped eating.

If it's poison or something, I have an any-tidote on me, in my emergency magic bag, she said.

You mean an antidote? I said.

No, an any-tidote, basically a potion that transforms itself into the antidote of any poison ingested, Jamie explained.

Thank goodness for my clever little witch.

"To the woods, Mother Nina, before darkness falls," said Jamie in a serious tone.

"Very well," said Nina, rising to her feet.

She led us out of the dining room and down a long hallway. I noticed the little girls were following us in two straight-lines, perfectly arranged into six pairs. Each pair held hands.

"Is the woods safe enough for the children to venture into?" I asked in concern.

"Yes, quite!" Exclaimed Nina.

We exited the Coven House. There was a huge backyard with tall green grass. In the distance, I spotted the edge of the woods. It was particularly still. No wind blew. I grasped Jamie's hand tightly. She gave my hand a reassuring squeeze.

Georgianna here we come, she said to me.

Star's Point Of View

I blinked. The bright light hurt my eyes. I sat up slowly. I found myself in an unfamiliar bedroom yet again. I looked down. I was in an embroidered floral dress made of an airy sort of material. It was beautiful. I admired the pattern, tracing my fingers over the embroideries. They were clearly painstakingly hand-stitched. The material itself was a shimmery green.

Harper! I looked around. Harper was staring at himself in the mirror of a nearby vanity. My father and Asriel were sitting at a table nearby. They had been waiting for Harper and I to regain consciousness. Dad grinned at me. He seemed so proud.

"What is it?" I asked.

Dad shrugged, but he had a mischievous look on his face. I went over to Harper, who seemed to be in a daze, as he regarded his own reflection. I followed his gaze and gasped when I spotted our reflections. Harper and I had both grown pointed ears. Fae ears. Our features seemed a little sharper, our noses straighter and our cheekbones higher. Our eyebrows were thick and perfectly arched, our eyelashes fanned out and curled upwards. Our skin remained a golden colour, but it had an extra glow of health to it now. Our hair seemed shinier and longer than before. Harper's wavy dark hair was now down to his mid-back and my dark curls reached my waist. Harper was wearing a green outfit too, a blazer and pants with a white ruffled shirt underneath. Asriel had changed out of his grunge rocker look into a similar outfit to Harper's. Dad was still in his plain clothes.

"We're...elves," muttered Harper.

Asriel hissed so viciously I jumped.

Chapter 46

"You're Fae! How dare you?!" Yelled Rein.

Harper put his palms up defensively. "Okay, okay," he said.

"Even I don't have anything nice to say about elves," said Erin softly.

"Yeah, elves and faeries have a difficult history. Kinda like vampires and werewolves," said Dad.

I nodded.

"What happened, Dad? Who dressed us? Has the Queen seen us yet?" I asked.

I had so many questions.

"Your ladies-in-waiting dressed you," said Dad.

Ladies-in-waiting?

"Are we in trouble for breaking in?" Asked Harper.

"The moment you entered, you got your Fae powers," said Dad triumphantly. "I knew no one would trouble you after that! The Queen cannot deny you are the children of Hesper, but no, she hasn't seen you yet!"

"You must request an audience with her," said Asriel.

"What if she denies our request?" I asked.

"She won't. It's just a formality. She's got to be as curious about you as you are about her," said Asriel reassuringly.

There was a knock on the door. I glanced around the room properly for the first time, while Dad went to open the door. This bedroom was clearly for someone of royal birth with its lavish decorations. Every item was Fae-made, and thus, there was a great attention to detail. The bed had tiny carvings of pixies in the wood. It was a canopy bed and the white curtains around it sparkled. The tiles on the floor were white, silver and gold. The ceiling was high and bore a circular golden crest of sorts painted right in its centre. There was a lovely array of smells surrounding us as though we were in a perfume store. The Queen had clearly redecorated the Ice Moon Pack's Castle with Fae stylings. I imagined there was a ballroom in this castle. Perhaps, a ball would be thrown in our honour! Or maybe, we would be thrown in the dungeon. A voice snapped me back to reality.

"Her Majesty, Queen Rowena of the Winter Fae Kingdom, requests an audience with His Royal Highness, Prince Harper of the Ice Moon Pack and her Royal Highness, Princess Hannah," announced a Fae man dressed in a top hat and suit with coat-tails.

He had a large white moustache with curled ends, pale skin, white hair and amber eyes. His ears were much pointier than ours, and his cheekbones and jawline could carve a roast. They were that sharp. I gasped. Her Majesty was summoning us?

"Thank you, we accept her request," said Harper rather formally.

He took my hand. He was my twin and we were in this together, even if he had dated that devil spawn Angie in the past. The Fae man nodded, bowed, and left the room.

"Let's go meet Great Grandma," said Harper in his normal manner again.

I grinned at him and nodded.

Chapter 47

Monday 21st September, 2020 (Continued)

Jonah's Point Of View

I couldn't wait for class to be over. I practically ran outside once it was done.

"You're walking too fast! We're in heels!" Snapped Angie, strutting towards me with her sycophants in tow.

I didn't even know their names to be honest, but Angie always had two to five girls dressed similarly to her, flanking her as she walked the hallways. Today, there were four of them, two on either side. All four sidekicks wore four inch heels if my estimates were correct. I struggled not to roll my eyes. I needed to mind-link Noah and I wanted some privacy.

"Bathroom break, Babe," I said with a small fake smile.

Angie folded her arms.

"The last time I let you go to the bathroom, you ended up in the girls' one with Star!" She hissed under her breath, eyes black.

Oh, now she knew her name was Star, and not Cloud or Moon or whatever.

"So…should I never pee again then?" I asked innocently.

She shot me a warning glance, because of my normal volume, but her bobble-headed friends were preoccupied. They were discussing a recent music video instead of eavesdropping on us. Angie let out a high-pitched tinkling sort of laugh, tossing her head back dramatically. I sighed inwardly. She took a menacing step towards me, eyes narrowed. We were almost nose to nose as Angie was tall enough to reach my height in those heels. I smirked to myself, thinking that they were not heels tall enough to allow Star to reach my height. I felt a pang as though a band was constricting around my heart.

"There was a break-in at my house in the wee hours of the morning! Did you know that?" Snarled Angie.

Why would I know that?

"No," I said blankly.

Angie sneered.

"What did they take? Are your parents ok?" I asked.

The Plastique family was still a part of my pack. I didn't want harm coming to them.

Angie shrugged, avoiding the first question. "There were no signs of forced entry as though someone just let them in! My parents are fine!" She said.

I nodded.

"Girls! Go get me a skinny French vanilla latte!" Ordered Angie.

All four of them scurried off. Apparently, it took four people to procure one latte from the school's cafe. Once they were well out of sight and earshot, Angie rolled her eyes in their direction as though fed up with them. She turned back to me.

"Does this look familiar to you?" Asked Angie.

I looked down at her open palm and my stomach did backflips. It was Star's ring! The one Zaya had given her. The one with protection charms on it to safeguard her from the curse. The one she had promised me she would always wear and never take off. The memory of her comforting, me when I had gotten into a shouting match with my brothers, flitted through my mind. I had made sure she was wearing it. Now, it was in Angie's hand. We had gone to Angie's house the other day to question her mom about Star's parents. I saw it all in my mind's eye. Star had definitely still been wearing her ring when I said goodbye to her outside in front of Harper's car. So how had it ended up back at Angie's? Star wouldn't go back there. Had Angie done something to Star?

"How did you get that?" I asked, unable to hide my annoyance any longer.

Angie raised her brows at my tone, not liking the change. She wanted to be the one interrogating me and not the other way around.

"It was found at the scene of the crime!" Retorted Angie.

"What? If you found it at the scene of the crime, why do you have it? Why didn't the pack police take it?" I asked.

Angie fidgeted uncomfortably.

"We didn't bother reporting the break-in. There's no need. Only one thing went missing," hissed Angie.

"What was the one thing?" I asked, confused.

Chapter 47

Angie shrugged. "One of my Mom's belongings. Why does it matter? Star broke into my house and you're questioning me?" Asked Angie incredulously.

My blood boiled.

"Star did not break into your house. You're lying," I growled. "How did you get that ring?" I practically roared. I snatched the ring from her. "Where's Star? What have you done with her?"

Everyone in the hallway was frozen, looking at us.

"What the hell has gotten into you?" She screamed.

People were whispering around us. Angie loved to make a scene, and she wouldn't be out done, though I had started it.

"YOU'RE FUCKING MY COUSIN BEHIND MY BACK!" She snarled.

There was a collective gasp from the onlookers. Angie and Star were not even related technically.

"Bullshit," I said softly, my tone deadly. "You could care less about that."

I glanced at the hickey on her neck, that she was failing to conceal with a ruffled turtleneck, under her school blazer. She saw me look at it. She hastily adjusted her outfit, tugging at the neckline of her blouse. I rolled my eyes.

"And you don't even care that I have to go elsewhere for affection! That's your fault-," she began.

"Shut up!" I hissed.

She paled.

"Shut the fuck the up!" I said softly.

I was seething. She seemed more unnerved, now that I was whispering.

"Don't change the topic! I don't want to hear about your escapades. I'm not your doctor. Where is Star?" I asked through gritted teeth.

"I don't know," she snarled.

I looked at her. Carefully. We stood there a full minute staring at each other in silence. My wolf told me she was telling the truth.

"Call your mother and ask her if she knows where Star is!" I demanded.

"She doesn't-," Angie began.

"Now," I said.

She sighed. She called her mother, tapping her heel on the ground, while she pressed the cellphone to her ear. I heard her mother's voice on the other end.

"Did she admit to it?" Her mother asked eagerly.

Huh.

"No, Mom! Um, actually, Jonah wants to know where cousin Star is," Angie said.

"How should I know?" Asked her mother.

I could hear a male's voice, laughing in the background. That voice certainly didn't belong to her father. Like mother, like daughter.

Angie gave me a pointed look.

"She's not at school?!" Asked her mother, her voice panicked all of a sudden. "You need to find her! She's going to-," Angie cut her mother off.

"Okay, Mom, thanks!" Said Angie.

She hung up on her mother. I sighed deeply, my temper cooling.

"Sorry," I said.

I didn't like acting this way, even if Angie was no delicate flower.

"I need the ring back! It's evidence!" Said Angie.

I practically snorted with laughter. She wasn't getting this back. I was going to put this back on Star's finger myself, and have a stern chat with her about how it came off in the first place. Maybe, Star had broken in. My wolf told me Angie and her mother didn't have Star in a basement or something. He would know if his mate was imprisoned so close by. He would feel the helplessness, the fear. He told me Star was safe, but very far away. The band around my heart constricted again. I wished I could have marked Star. That would make finding her easy. That was the whole point of an Alpha marking his Luna, in my opinion, a biologically built-in tracking device. However, marking Star would leave her totally vulnerable to the curse.

"Zaya would kill me if I didn't return this," I told Angie.

"Is it an engagement ring?" Asked Angie, narrowing her eyes.

"No," I said simply.

"What happens if Zaya and Eli want to be with Star, and you and Noah don't?" Asked Angie impatiently, tapping her foot on the floor.

She was still convinced she would be Luna, whilst knowing I had a mate and she had a lover. Noah wasn't even here. It was pretty much just me keeping up the charade.

"It's Noah I need to talk to privately right now, but you don't want me to go to the bathroom so…" I began.

"I was kidding!" Squealed Angie in a sickly sweet tone.

Her stupid friends returned with the latte. She took one sip of it, and literally, spat it out.

"What?" I asked, alarmed.

"This is full fat milk!" She screeched. "I can tell!" She insisted.

Good grief. I didn't have time for this. I walked away, while she was distracted. She clearly didn't have any information on Star's whereabouts outside of finding the ring. Star was up to something after all. My wolf

Chapter 47

told me so. I heard another collective gasp, and glanced behind me to see Angie pouring the contents of her coffee cup on the girl responsible for the full fat milk. The girl ran away crying. Was Angie possessed by the devil or something? She had never been that nice, but she had not been this bad either. She was getting meaner every minute.

I hurried to the bathroom. Finally, some peace. I decided to call Noah instead of mind-linking, because I had a headache already from my argument with Angie.

"Hey," said Noah in his usual deadpan manner.

Silence.

"Hey?" Repeated Noah, confused.

"Ugh! Noah! It's me! I know you have caller ID! What do you think I want?" I snapped.

"Um," began Noah.

I knew I was being a jerk, but I was a bundle of raw nerves.

"An update on Star!" I demanded.

Noah sighed.

"She's gone," said Noah, sounding like he was fighting back tears, which was very unlike Noah.

My heart constricted painfully.

"What do you mean gone?" I asked quickly.

Gone... like dead? My knees shook. I felt like I couldn't breathe.

"She went to the Ice Moon Castle to talk to the Winter Fae Queen, who is apparently her grandmother!" Explained Noah.

I could hear Zaya arguing with someone in the background, whilst Eli tried to calm him down.

I relaxed. Relief spread through me. She was alive. I could breathe again. My brain began analysing what my little brother had just said.

"Wait. What?!" I asked.

Chapter 48

Monday 21st September, 2020 (Continued)

Jessie's Point Of View

We followed those weird witches into the woods, wondering where they were taking us. I kept glancing at the hands of all the girls and at Nina's hands, just in case someone was holding a wand or a knife or something. I just did not trust them, not even the little girls. Jamie seemed tense too, especially after I had pointed out the fact that we were the only ones who had eaten the breakfast conjured by Mother Nina.

"Where are we going exactly?" I asked, as I helped Jamie step over the twisted roots of gnarled trees.

The canopies of the trees were so large and grew so close together that the forest was dark in the daytime.

"To Georgianna's cottage," said Nina in her usual serene manner.

We had been walking for about fifteen minutes when Nina stopped suddenly.

"This is where we leave you," she announced.

I stared at her and the girls, who were still in their perfect lines, following the buddy-system. We were in a clearing in the woods where light streamed through, a bright circle amidst the darkness. I glanced at Jamie.

"Where's the cottage?" Asked Jamie, seeming a bit annoyed.

"You must find your way to it on your own. It is hidden by magic, and just as you uncovered our coven, so too must you reveal the cottage," said Nina.

Chapter 48

"Well, are we hot or cold?" I asked. "The woods is huge. The coven house was different. It was blatantly there but dilapidated-looking."

Nina chuckled. "You have until nightfall to find the cottage! You're not the first to come looking for Georgianna's body, you know. Others were intrigued by her story for different reasons, and some come to visit the mysterious coven itself," explained Nina.

I was so focused on Nina, I had taken my eyes off of the little girls for just a moment. I glanced back to where they used to be. My blood ran cold. They were gone!

"Where are the students?" I asked, my tone accusatory.

Something wasn't right. Nina just smiled.

"Nina! The little girls! Where did they go?!" Demanded Jamie.

Nina was silent.

"Those girls are much too young to have teleported magically, prodigies or not," said Jamie, narrowing her eyes.

Nina grinned. She had a wild sort of grin. Some of her usual refined manner had begun to fray at the edges.

"See you at dusk," she said, backing away from us slowly, until she was cast in shadow.

Instinctively, I rushed forwards, but she had disappeared. I snarled in frustration.

"What the fuck?!" I growled.

"Jessie, relax," cooed Jamie.

She put her arms around me.

"Something's not right, Jamie!" I said. "This feels like a trap!"

"We'll get out of here as soon as we find Georgianna's body ok?" She said.

She stroked my hair, running her fingers through it, trying to soothe me. I pulled her close to me and nuzzled her. Thank goodness, I had had the foresight to request backup!

Dalton's Point Of View

Our Witch Luna, Jamie, wanted to go save some people from some ghost or something like that, same old story. Subsequently, Our Alpha, Jessie, was extremely worried for Jamie. Classic Jessie. He had asked his Gamma, Zack, and me, his Beta, to stake out at a crumby motel nearby. He wanted us to be within a fifteen minutes of where they were going. I was winning at cards and Zack was pissed. Zack, Jessie and I had been best friends since we were pups, and now we were pack leaders, all with mates and pups of our own. I had left my little human mate, Zoe, back in Ambrosia. This was much too dangerous for her. Chloe, who was pregnant yet again, was back home too. Chloe was undoubtedly the most hilarious pregnant she-wolf. After each pup, she swore that she would never ever get pregnant again, only to happily announce her pregnancy at the next pack meeting. Zack was determined to have five pups and to beat me at cards. He was failing at the latter currently. He demanded a rematch.

"I don't get why Jamie wants to help the sextuplets or whatever," grumbled Zack. "I should be home working on pup number four. Instead, I'm here waiting for Jamie to vanquish another demon. It's not like they really need the backup."

"I think they're quints. And it's a ghost I think, not a demon," I said.

"Quints?" Asked Zack. "Wasn't that a movie?"

"I dunno, but quints like quintuplets," I said.

"How many is that? Five?" Asked Zack.

"Yeah," I said, nodding.

"No, there's six of them. Sextuplets!" Said Zack.

"Sextuplets? Why's it called that? I would call it Six-tuplets!" I said.

"It's definitely called sextuplets!" Chuckled Zack, rolling his eyes.

Dalton! Zack! Jessie's alpha voice resounded in our heads over mind-link.

You ok, bro? I asked.

What's up, bro? You need us? Asked Zack.

Yeah! Jamie and I are lost in the woods but... not a regular kind of lost... a magical kind... she can't teleport us out, and we haven't found Georgianna's body or her cottage, said Jessie, his voice fading a little. His mind-link voice was usually powerful and clear, not this faint distant echo.

Where are you? I asked, grabbing my jacket as Zack and I headed out the door.

We're in the woods behind the address I gave you. The house looks abandoned out front, but trust me, that's where the coven is! It's a spell to throw people off. Don't come into the woods. You'll probably get lost. You'll need to figure out what the witches are up to! There's twelve little girls and one Mother. You'll need to take Fox with you! Be stealthy! Said Jessie, his voice fading in and out, like an overseas call with a bad connection. We had to hurry.

I knocked on the door opposite to ours in the dark hallway of the motel. Fox had wanted a separate room. He had been really low in spirits since Evangeline's death. Sure, she had been awful and she had picked a literal demon over him, but he had loved her to the end and killed the same demon to avenge her death. It was a long story. The door creaked inwards and Fox peeked out, his two different coloured eyes regarding me with concern. Heterochromia was a sign of great magical power in wizards and witches. Fox's hair had grown down to his mid-back. If he could have

Chapter 48

grown a beard, he would surely have one. He hadn't had his hair trimmed since Eva's death. In my opinion, he needed to get laid.

"Are they ok?" He asked.

"They're lost in some magical woods or something, and the coven house looks abandoned, but it isn't. There's some spell that makes it look that way," I said.

"A Glamour," said Fox.

He followed us downstairs to the car. We all got in. Zack was driving one of his many sports cars. I was in the passenger seat. Fox sat in the backseat. He was already chanting to himself. Although, he had been down in the dumps since Eva's passing, his magic had flourished. He was on his way to becoming the next Grand High Wizard, and he seemed not the least bit excited about any of it. Jamie and Fox were probably the two most powerful young practicers of magic around right now. Zack sped down the street, taking corners swiftly and sharply.

"Easy, Zack! I'd like to have dinner with the family tonight!" I said.

Zack grinned. "A tough Beta like you. Scared of a little speeding," he said.

The tires screeched to a halt at the end of an empty street. No people were in sight, but several parked cars lined the road.

"I didn't wanna park directly in front of the place," said Zack.

Fox nodded. He took a flask out of his jacket pocket and downed a small amount of liquid. Clearly, it was pungent, from the way he contorted his face. I chuckled. He passed the flask to me.

"Whiskey?" I asked, joking.

I knew it had to be a potion of some sort.

Fox smiled. "Not quite," he murmured.

"Bottom's up!" I exclaimed.

I drank some of the liquid, and passed it to Zack. The liquid burnt all the way down. I rubbed my chest.

"Cheers!" Said Zack raising the flask in a toast to us, before drinking it.

"What, pray tell, does this potion do?" I asked innocently.

"Isn't it a little late to ask that?" Chuckled Zack.

"It conceals us completely," said Fox with a sly smile.

"An invisibility potion!" Said Zack.

"No!" Said Fox, grinning. "I call it my Complete Concealment Concoction!" Said Fox triumphantly. "We won't just be invisible. They won't be able to see us yeah, but they also won't be able to smell or hear us."

"What about taste and touch?" Zack asked immediately.

"No, those two aren't covered, so be careful not to bump into anyone, or move stuff around," warned Fox.

"Yeah and don't let anyone lick you either, and you should be fine," I said to Zack in a very serious tone.

Zack rolled his eyes.

We approached the dilapidated house. Fox lifted the Glamour. The house transformed, before our very eyes, like extreme home makeover, magic edition. I gave Fox a thumbs-up. The door swung open to reveal a dark haired woman with cat-like eyes dressed in black velvet. This must be the Coven Mother Jessie had been talking about. She looked alarmed as she stepped out onto the porch, peering around suspiciously. We grabbed Fox's arms, and then Zack and I zoomed into the house swiftly and silently at werewolf speed and stealth. Phew. The creepy little girls were nowhere in sight. There were supposed to be twelve of them. The Coven Mother came back into the house. We were all crouching on the stairs.

"How come you don't have to look like this?" Croaked a voice from the next room.

The Coven Mother frowned in the direction from which the voice had come.

"You know why," she said succinctly.

She turned on her heel and marched in the opposite direction. I edged closer to the room where the voice had come from. I peeked inside. I stifled a gasp, but then I remembered that the spell was a complete concealment. Fox was a genius honestly.

There were twelve withered old women sitting at a dining table. They all seemed very tired. Some were falling asleep on themselves. Their features varied, but they all wore black velvet dresses that resembled school uniforms.

"Are these the... little girls? The students?" I asked softly.

Fox nodded. "A very powerful Glamour must have made them seem young to Jessie and Jamie. They expended a lot of energy, trying to fool Mother Jamie," noted Fox.

"But why?" Zack asked. "And how come their Coven Mother is younger than them."

"I have only guesses as to why, but I can tell you their Coven Mother is not younger than them. She is probably just more adept at keeping the Glamour in place," said Fox. "Unless, she actually is younger."

"Is it sunset yet?" Whined one of the old witches.

"No, you old fool," croaked another.

"I'm hungry and I'm tired!" Rasped another.

Chapter 48

"We'll feast soon," said one of them, swaying a little in her chair, and doing a celebratory dance.

"Cannibals?" Asked Zack under his breath.

It was difficult not to whisper, although we knew we didn't have to.

"I don't think so, but close," said Fox.

"Huh," I said.

"They probably feed on energy, not the people themselves," said Fox.

"Youth!" Exclaimed Zack. "They feed on youth!"

Zack had walked down the hallway, and was now standing in front of a collection of newspaper clippings, that had been pinned to a notice board. They had their crimes hidden in plain sight. Anyone passing by would assume genuinely that those clippings were notices, but they were article clippings about missing people, all young.

"Why do they need to do this?" I asked. "Aren't witches immortal?"

"Not these ones," Zack mumbled, pointing to one article that differed from the others.

This one was not about missing persons. It featured a photograph of twelve girls, all screaming, their faces contorted. The heading read: *The Twelve Crones of Thistle-woods.* I read further. The caption said: *Twelve witches react in horror when sentenced to death by senescence for crimes against their coven. The thirteenth witch involved is still at large.* The thirteenth witch, photographed alone, was the Coven Mother! I scanned the article itself.

The witching council was unanimous in its ruling to sentence all twelve Thistle-woods witches to death by senescence. The girls were found guilty of over fifty accounts of magical disfigurement, having magically stolen the beauty of various witches, human girls and she-wolves, all of whom wish to remain anonymous. The victims are to have their appearances restored by members of the witching council. The thirteenth witch involved in the crimes fled the scene before she could be apprehended. The twelve were caught in a hotel room on the outskirts of Thistle-woods. A kidnapped human girl was found alive and well in the bathroom. She has been safely returned to her family. The twelve will be magically confined to a house of the council's choosing where they will await death. A spell was cast on the twelve to age them by a century each. Thus, the end of their days is near. This photograph was taken just before the ageing spell was cast.

"Wait? What? That's their big punishment! Just ageing and then passing away like humans do!" I said, outraged.

"Well, they were young immortals and were turned into mortal old women," said Fox.

I thought of my human Zoe. I had made her immortal with my bite, but her human family continued to age.

"That's not a punishment! That's not enough!" I said.

I could feel my eyes turning black. I should rip those witches' throats out.

"They're still stealing youth and beauty, even while under house arrest!" I said.

"The thirteenth girl must have found them and gotten rid of the sentinel. All situations like this where people are under magical house arrest involve a sentinel, usually a gargoyle who watches them from his perch until the punishment is over," explained Fox. "This house probably was abandoned, so the council decided to use it for house arrest. I bet you anything, they faked their deaths to fool the gargoyle!"

"Well, why didn't the council show up to check and bury them when the gargoyle reported that?!" Asked Zack.

"This kind of spell robs you of an after-life of any kind and of any kind of coming back! The witches will burst into dust when they die and that's it. No bodies. No ghosts. Nothing," said Fox.

Okay, now we were getting somewhere. That was pretty final. I guessed that was a punishment then.

"Let's kill them, rescue Jessie and Jamie and go for tacos," I said.

"Chill out, Dalton," said Zack. "Jamie will want them brought to justice when she hears all this even if their punishment will be death anyway. She'll want a proper investigation and hearing. You know how she is. Let's find Jessie and Jamie first."

I grumbled.

"Can we still get tacos though?" I asked.

Zack grinned. He nodded.

Star's Point Of View

Harper and I walked, hand in hand, down a majestic sweeping staircase. Each step sparkled brilliantly, even in the soft indoor lighting cast by the crystal chandeliers overhead. Harper stopped suddenly, when we were on the landing.

"What is it?" I asked, following his gaze.

I gasped. He was staring at a huge painting of a young woman, who looked exactly the way I looked right now. Her pointy ears, glowing golden skin, high-cheekbones and glossy ringlets were exactly like mine, but she had amber eyes instead of brown ones like mine. Honestly, the portrait could be of me with contacts. We were so strikingly similar.

"This is Mom," I said to Dad, who had come to stand behind us.

It wasn't a question. I knew it was my mother.

Chapter 48

He nodded. He had tears in his eyes. I hugged him and he hugged me back. He pulled a reluctant Harper into the family hug. Eventually, Harper settled down and hugged us. Asriel came to joint the hug.

"Eww, don't touch me. Social distancing!" Yelled Rein.

"What's social distancing?!" Asked Harper.

"Oh, wrong realm, Rein," said Erin.

I had no idea what the earrings were on about, but I laughed anyway.

"All right, that's enough," said Dad in his gruff voice. "Go talk to your Great Grandmother, that old bitch," mumbled Dad.

Harper snorted with laughter.

"Is she mean?" I asked.

"She's a Fae Queen and she's... imperious, as a Fae Queen has to be, I guess," muttered Dad. "She didn't like me for your Mom, but she was willing to accept me to make Hesper happy. She never wanted Hesper with her wolf cousin. She would think that was barbaric and uncivilised. So, we have that on our side," said Dad, sounding as though he were trying to convince himself.

The Fae who had summoned us cleared his throat. We followed him through a set of unbelievably huge double doors that almost reached the high-ceiling of the castle. It took several Fae to open them on either side. We were ushered forwards. I clutched Harper's arm. A long red velvet carpet led through the centre of the room straight to a short flight of stairs. The Queen sat in her throne upon the platform. On either side of the carpet, royals and nobles of Fae birth both stood and sat. There were a few werewolves among them, clearly pack leaders, though not Alphas. Harper walked in quite confidently, as though he owned the place and everyone had been waiting all their lives for him to show up, which was true technically if you thought about it. I marvelled at the clothes of the court. There were stunning. I had never seen fabrics so vibrant. The colours become more and more vivid as we got closer to the throne. The royals seated near to the Queen were practically dripping in jewels and finery. Every piece of fabric on their form sparkled or glimmered. The Fae clearly loved sparkly things. I felt like I was inside kaleidoscope made of jewels. The colours swam before my eyes. It took a while to adjust to a room so ornate with people so lavishly dressed.

"Why aren't they dressed for court?" Said a woman's voice.

Her voice was clear and powerful, but distinctly feminine. It rang out over the colossal room. A hush fell over the crowd. I looked at my father, who rolled his eyes in plain view of the queen. I raised my eyes to the queen.

Her ears were sharply pointed and her features were angular. She had silvery pale skin with rosy cheeks. Her face was beautiful but cold. Her eyes were a light grey and her hair was white. It fell to her waist in sheets. She wore a silvery white gown with gold embellishments. The skirt of the gown fanned out covering the seat of the high-backed golden throne. Her neck was covered in layers of beads and jewels. Her crown was made of white gold and studded with diamonds. It looked uncomfortably heavy. Heavy was the head that wore the crown indeed!

"Bow," whispered Asriel from behind us.

Harper bowed and I curtsied. It just felt more appropriate than a bow in my case. All I knew about royalty was from movies and books. The Winter Fae Queen was staring at us. We straitened and stared at her. We glanced at each other.

"Who are you?" She asked.

I heard my Dad sigh exasperatedly. I looked back at him. Asriel shot him a warning glance.

"I am Harper, the son of Heath and Hesper, who was your very own grand-daughter, Your Majesty," said Harper smoothly.

The court members and pack leaders gasped. They began to murmur. The chattering grew. I was too terrified to introduce myself.

"And," said Harper extremely loudly, signalling for everyone to be quite. They fell silent, following his unspoken order with ease. "This is my twin sister, Hannah," said Harper.

The room burst into a flurry of movement and noise. Some were actually crying. Others shook their heads in disbelief. The pack leaders in particular were regarding Harper curiously.

Should I tell Great-granny she's sitting in my chair? Said Harper in my mind.

I wasn't able to stifle my laughter. The Queen's eyes went straight to me. I stopped laughing immediately.

"SILENCE!" Barked the Queen.

Everyone was silent at once.

"How do I know this is not merely a Glamour placed on the girl to make her look like Hesper. It would be an easy scheme," commented the Queen.

Harper shrugged.

"My granddaughter gave birth to only one child, a stillborn male," said the Queen.

"How do you know that?" Asked Harper.

The court members gasped. One of the ladies-in-waiting, who sat near to the Queen, swayed on the spot.

"Your Majesty," added Harper as an after-thought.

The Queen smirked. "Princess Hesper said so herself," said the Queen.

Chapter 48

"She wanted to protect us, so she concealed us both, pretending she had a single stillbirth instead of live twins. I was given to my guardians, before our mother returned to this castle, and she bundled Hannah up, passing her off as the afterbirth, so the doctor could spirit her away," Harper explained, summing everything up quite easily.

The nobles and royals seemed to believe this. Many were smiling at Harper, especially the ladies present. The Queen was silent, though there was a faint smile playing about her lips.

"Are you not going to introduce yourself to us, Your Majesty?" Asked Harper.

The room erupted again. People seemed to like his brazen attitude, but were also scandalised by it.

"Clearly, you know who I am," said the Queen.

"In theory. Are you not happy to see your Great Grandchildren, Your Majesty?" Prompted Harper.

"If you are who you say you are, then prove it," said the Queen.

How were we supposed to do that? Harper and I glanced at each other.

"Task us with something then," said Harper.

"If you are in fact Hesper's children, you should be able to mount her dragon," said the Queen.

There was another collective gasp.

"Very well, I-," began Harper.

"Not you!" Said the Queen.

I trembled on the spot. I focused on taking one breath at at time.

"Why not me?" Demanded Harper angrily.

"Well, you certainly think you're royalty, don't you," said the Queen, shocked at his outburst.

I knew Harper was trying to protect me. He shot me a worried glance.

"I have another task for you to prove you are a worthy Alpha and Fae Prince, don't worry," said the Queen to Harper. "But your twin sister will perform this one. The Fae are matriarchal, unlike patriarchal werewolves. If she is to be a Fae Queen, she must command respect from all beings. Which being better to start with than a dragon?"

The royals, nobles and pack leaders were all nodding in agreement, finding the chosen assessment fair.

"Prepare Haven the Hellish, and take him to the arena. Let the people know their Prince and Princess are here," sneered the Queen. "Their Princess Hannah shall tame the Ice Dragon before their very eyes."

Chapter 49

Monday 21st September, 2020 (Continued)

Eli's Point Of View

Zaya was fuming. We had just found out that Star and Harper had used the snow globe portal to go to the Ice Moon Pack's Castle. We had also just discovered that Hesper, the Alpha's daughter and the Winter Faerie Queen's granddaughter, was Star's mother. Harper's too, obviously. The great warrior from the Ice Moon Pack was their father. Their father had come to take them back to their original pack, and they had gone without so much as a note or a text.

"I can't believe she went so far away with telling us," said Zaya for the umpteenth time, looking at me.

Zaya had been ignoring Noah and Jonah, who had just shown up. He blamed our elder two brothers for just about anything that went wrong with Star. I blamed them too. My Princess Star and I would be much closer if not for them. I sighed.

"How are we gonna get to the Ice Moon Pack lands?" I said. "What's the fastest way?"

"The fastest way would have been the snow globe that Harper and Star took," said Noah with a shrug.

"Plane?" Said Jonah.

"Luna Jamie," said Zaya.

"Yes!" I exclaimed.

Jamie was a Luna and a witch, a Coven Mother at that.

Chapter 49

"She could teleport us there magically, or even make us a new portal like the snow globe, so that we could travel there and go back and forth when we need to," I said.

"Why would we be going back and forth?" Asked Jonah, looking annoyed.

"Star's twin Harper will become the Alpha of that pack! I'm sure of it! Our pack needs to become allies with the Ice Moon Pack as soon as possible. It's our mate's pack and she's part of the alpha lineage," I explained.

Jonah sighed. "Yeah, you're right. I'm still wrapping my head around all of that," said Jonah. "So Star's brother will probably become the Ice Moon Alpha, and her grandmother is Queen of the Winter Fae. Do we have to be friendly with the Fae now too?" Asked Jonah.

Noah shrugged. "Why not? Fae are magical. They'd be useful allies," said Noah.

"No, witches and wizards are magical," said Jonah. "The Fae are a bunch of tricksters. We have to be careful with them. They use their magic for mischief."

Zaya roared in anger suddenly, startling Mia, Harper's adopted Mom. Mia yelped and hid in the arms of her mate, Marco, Harper's adopted Dad. It had been Mia and Marco, who had filled us in on everything. Marco gave Zaya a pointed look for scaring Mia.

"Sorry," mumbled Zaya.

"What's your problem?" I asked.

"Luna Jamie isn't answering her phone," Zaya said exasperatedly.

"Don't blow up her phone too much!" Warned Jonah. "That might piss off Alpha Jessie."

"Should I call Alpha Jessie instead?" Asked Zaya, scrolling through his phone.

"Yeah, try his cell," said Noah. "He's a good person to talk to about befriending the Ice Moon Pack too. They're a northern pack. His cousins are alphas of one of the other northern packs."

"Which one?" I asked.

"The Winter Moon Pack," said Jonah.

"Oh, the one with the triplet alphas!" I said excitedly.

"Yeah," said Jonah. "That's why the Ambrosia Wolf Pack and the Winter Moon Pack are such good allies. Those two alpha lineages are related."

"Alpha Jessie isn't answering either!" Yelled Zaya.

"Zaya! Don't!" I said sternly.

It was too late. Zaya had flung his phone against the wall, smashing it. Fuck!

"ZAYA!" I yelled. "What if Star tries to call?! She knows your number by heart!" I reminded him.

Zaya looked horrified as what I had said dawned on him.

"OH FUCK!" Exclaimed Zaya.

"Excuse me, do you mind?" Said Marco indignantly, his eyes narrowed.

Mia was sitting on a couch nearby with a cloth on her head, obviously nursing a headache.

"Sorry!" said Zaya quickly.

"We'll get out of your hair! Sorry, Mrs Jogie," I said.

"I'm worried too," she admitted. "I knew this day would come... when my little Harper would go back to claim his pack," she said, her voice cracking.

She burst into tears. Marco comforted her, shooting us a look that said "leave."

"Take care, Mr and Mrs Jogie! We'll update you when we find out more!" I promised.

"What now?" I said, as we walked outside.

Noah stopped dead in his tracks. "Dad has one of those things! One of the snow globes!" He exclaimed excitedly.

"That one goes to the Marigold pack lands, not to the Ice Moon pack lands," said Jonah with a sigh.

"Right! And Marigold is such a strong Aly of Berryndale, they're almost the same pack! Right?! Right?" Asked Noah.

"Ok...so..." I said, unsure where he was going with this.

"Let's snow globe hop!" Exclaimed Noah.

"What?" I said, snorting with laughter.

Zaya looked intrigued.

"Taking Dad's private jet would take hours! We use Dad's snow globe to Marigold. I guarantee you, there's a portal from Marigold to Berryndale. And in Berryndale, I know there's a portal to the Winter Moon Pack, which is the neighbouring pack of the Ice Moon Pack," said Noah.

"Noah! You're brilliant!" Exclaimed Zaya, speaking to one of our elder brothers again.

Zaya grabbed Noah into a hug.

"What if the other packs don't let us use their portals?" Asked Jonah worriedly.

"They will! Have some faith! Every alpha knows what it's like to have to go rescue your Luna!" I said, immediately liking Noah's plan.

"But, we're not rescuing her. She went to her original pack!" Jonah said, looking forlorn.

Chapter 49

I knew what he meant. He was worried she'd left us without any message, because she'd left us.

"You think she left us as in she's done with us?" I asked.

Jonah shrugged. His eyes were glassy. He was a softie, but he hid it well.

"She ain't leaving me. That's not an option!" Said Zaya theatrically.

Jonah smiled. Noah was grinning from ear to ear, probably nerd-ing out over all the packs he was about to meet. He loved pack history.

"Let's go!" I said.

"Say your crazy plan again," said Jonah, more determined now, as we piled into Noah's car.

"We get Dad's snow globe," said Noah. "That one goes to Marigold! We take a portal from Marigold to Berryndale! We take one from Berryndale to the Winter Moon Pack! The Winter Moon Pack is next door to the Ice Moon Pack! Simple!"

That was not simple.

"Are you sure there'll be a portal in Marigold that goes to Berryndale?!" I asked, worried.

"They share a Luna for goodness sakes! They built a joint pack house! Don't you guys read Alpha Anthropology?!" Groaned Noah, annoyed with us.

Alpha Anthropology was an educational magazine that came out once monthly with updates on each large pack.

"No, Noah! We don't! We have lives, but we trust you!" Said Zaya.

Jonah was lost in thought during the drive. "Star is a Princess," he said absentmindedly. "What if that changes everything?"

"Well, she's always been my Princess, so nothing's changed for me," I said pointedly.

"You mean like what if she rejects us?!" Asked Noah, coming down off his pack knowledge high.

"What if someone challenges us for her?" Asked Jonah. "That's what I mean."

"Challenges us?" Asked Noah.

"For her hand. She might have a betrothed. The Fae are a bit different. They like to arrange things and the Ice Moon Pack also does arrangements," said Jonah, looking like he was going to be sick.

"Arrangements?" I asked.

"Arranged marriages," said Noah.

A chill crept through me.

"I think the fuck not," said Zaya. "Not my baby. My baby belongs to me."

"To us," I said.

Zaya grinned and nodded.

"But mostly to me," said Zaya mischievously.

He was so annoying, but he was my favourite brother.

"Let's go get our Princess," I said.

"Princess Hannah," said Jonah more to himself than any of us.

He was smiling to himself. He took out his phone and smiled at it. I knew he had Star as his wallpaper and was always careful about hiding it from Angie. It was that picture of her blowing our her eighteenth birthday candles. I had sent it to our messaging group with the four of us.

"I can't wait to meet Alpha Maze. He's an academic alpha, who will understand me," mumbled Noah to his nerdy self.

I knew Star was probably safe as she was with her people, but I had this crazy anxiety that just wouldn't let up. She was safe, I kept reminding myself. She just had to be.

Chapter 50

Monday 21st September, 2020 (Continued)

Jessie's Point Of View

The sky was growing darker. The light was fading as daylight slowly gave way to dusk. Something told me we had to get out of these woods before darkness fell. It felt as if we had been going round in circles. All the trees looked the same, and we kept circling back and stumbling upon the clearing where Nina had deserted us. Jamie was not able to magically teleport us out of this woods. It just wasn't working. At first, I was able to mind-link with my Beta and Gamma, but the connection was weak. I couldn't reach them anymore. At least, they were on the way. I kept telling myself that.

"Do you think Georgianna's tomb is even in these woods? Or, is that just a rumour?" I asked Jamie.

"I think she's here," said Jamie so confidently that I stopped dead in my tracks.

I looked at my mate. She was pensive all of a sudden.

"We're doing the wrong thing, Jessie! We're trying to get out! We should try to get in!" She insisted.

"Okay," I said slowly. "Into what?"

"Into her tomb…and forget about escaping the words," responded Jamie.

I nodded encouragingly. I trusted Jamie's hunches. She sat cross-legged in the clearing. I sat with her, facing her.

"You're not a witch, but focus with me, because we're connected," she said.

I nodded. She took my hands in hers. We closed her eyes.

"Um, what are we focusing on?" I asked sheepishly, trying not to peek. Jamie chuckled.

"We're trying to talk to Georgianna again," she said simply.

This spooky cursed woods was not the safest place to conjure a vengeful witch's ghost, but whatever. I focused on the vision I had shared with Jamie, the one of Alto and Georgianna at their wedding feast, the one that ended with Alto's accidental death. Sadness consumed me. It was so unfair. Why couldn't they have left them alone, and let them be together? They were just like Jamie and me actually, a Coven Mother Witch and an Alpha Werewolf fated to each other, in love, linked. I tightened my grip on Jamie's hand. There was a rustling in the trees surrounding the clearing. The temperature seemed to drop. I heard a soft padding sound, like someone walking barefoot slowly towards us. Jamie's hands trembled in mine a little.

She's coming! Jamie told me through our link.

I tensed up. I wanted to grab Jamie and run, but I knew that was exactly what I should not do. I stayed put. From the displacement of air, I could tell someone was near to us, standing nearby, watching us. I could feel their eyes on me in particular.

Jamie, what now? I asked my little witch.

Wait a bit, instructed Jamie.

We waited with bated breath. The air shifted again, and the padding was fading this time. The person was now walking away from us.

Let's quickly and quietly follow her. No talking at all! Jamie said, her voice a little shaky.

I opened my eyes slowly. My blue eyes met Jamie's dark hazel ones. I smiled at her instinctively. She glanced over her shoulder. Chills ran through me, when I saw what she was looking at: a woman was walking into the woods, her back to us. All I could see of her was her sheet of long dark hair and her glowing white dress, dragging along the forest floor as she moved slowly through the trees. I pulled Jamie close to me. We followed the witch in silence.

Dalton's Point Of View

Fox was adamant on subduing all the geriatric witches before nightfall. They were criminals so they needed to be rounded up. Nina had returned to the dining room, and they were eagerly awaiting sundown.

"It's almost dusk," hissed one of them excitedly.

"The Weary Wandering Woods will deliver them to us soon," croaked another.

Chapter 50

"These ones are strong, an Alpha and a young Coven Mother. The woods may not be able to subdue them. They may still be conscious when we teleport them back here. Draining them won't be easy," muttered Nina.

Fox, Zack and I were standing just outside the dining room, still invisible. I gave Fox a quizzical look. I was worried for Jessie and Jamie.

"They're using the woods to their advantage I think," said Fox.

Zack nodded. "Seems like the woods is enchanted, well more liked hexed. Everyone who goes in probably gets lost and wanders around, while the woods drain their energy until they're weary. Weary Wandering Woods," said Zack.

"So, then they do what? Teleport their victims back from the woods to the house?" I asked.

"Yeah and finish draining them of energy and youth, while they're already too weak to fight back," concluded Fox.

"Let's just subdue the witches then, before they try to drain Jessie and Jamie!" I said.

"No!" Said Fox. "I don't know how to get into and out of the woods without getting trapped. The witches obviously know how to summon Jessie and Jamie back here," said Fox.

"So, let's wait for them to retrieve Jessie and Jamie for us, and then we strike?" I said.

Zack and Fox nodded.

Harper's Point Of View

Star was terrified. I could feel it through our bond as twins. I was scared for her too. I would rather face the dragon myself, but our so-called Great Grandmother had tasked Star with taming Haven the Hellish, the Great Ice Dragon. Our father did not seem the least bit worried. Asriel was also cool as a cucumber, as we walked with Star to the courtyard of the castle.

We were bundled up in very elaborate coats, boots, and gloves. Everything the Fae wore was bright and conspicuous. There was not a black, brown, or grey outfit in sight. I would need to get some dark materials for clothing and import them here. There was no way I was going to adopt this manner of dressing. I felt ridiculous in this green velvet coat with leaves embroidered all over. Star was wearing a similar one, but hers had both leaves and flowers embroidered into it.

We got into one of several royal carriages with snow-white and jet-black horses pulling them. I wanted the ride to the arena to be delayed somehow. I had no idea how to use my Fae magic to do anything useful, though I did feel different. Star didn't know how to harness her magic either. The horses were unbelievably fast. They must have been enchanted somehow. We crossed the snowy, icy landscape easily. We arrived at the outskirts of the arena. I could see throngs of Fae and werewolves alike, filing into the arena, chatting excitedly. I heard the deafening, high-pitched roar of the dragon.

"You will be fine," said Dad reassuringly to Star.

Star was pale and tremulous. I would jump down onto the arena's floor if I had to. I grasped her hand and we entered the arena.

The Queen had taken a separate carriage to us. She, her ladies-in-waiting, and her personal guards motioned for me, Dad and Asriel to follow them. Star was to go down to the arena escorted by two pack warriors. I hugged Star tightly.

"I'll come down into the arena if I have to!" I whispered to her as we hugged. "Don't be scared!"

She nodded fervently, but her eyes were glassy and wide with fear. She went with the guards, while the rest of us were led to the Queen's private area, a high platform, where the royals sat to watch whatever cruel thing was taking place in the arena. All the chairs on the platform were thrones. I sat in one without being granted permission. I saw the Queen scowl. I smirked at her. She sat in the middle throne with the highest back. Other royals were seated. Dad and Asriel chose to stand in front of us at the balcony. I glanced at the royals and pack leaders, wondering if I was related to any of these people.

The dragon was already in the arena. Haven the Hellish was wearing a huge silver collar with thick chains holding him on a short leash. It did not seem uncomfortable though. In fact, it seemed as though he could break those chains quite easily, but simply chose not to for the sake of theatrics. The Fae and wolves were a sea of bright colours, sequins and feathers, with everyone dressed in Fae garments. They were blinding me. I searched the floor of the arena for Star.

Suddenly, the roaring crowd fell silent. The Queen had stood to address them.

"Fae of the Winter Kingdom and Wolves of the Ice Moon Pack, this boy, you see here," she announced, pausing and gesturing towards me, " along with his sister, claim to be the children of Hesper, my granddaughter and the former Alpha's daughter."

A collective gasp resounded through the arena. I suppressed the urge to roll my eyes.

"Thus, he is here to prove his worthiness in future, as your alleged Alpha, and his sister shall attempt to prove her worthiness, as a Fae Princess, right now!" Boomed the Queen.

The crowd cheered in excitement, clapping their hands and stomping their feet, making the arena shake.

Chapter 50

"She will now attempt to tame Hesper's pet, the Great Ice Dragon, Haven the Hellish!" Announced the Queen grandiosely.

The cheering of the crowd reached a crescendo. I felt like the vibration of this noise was enough to cause an avalanche. They quieted down when the gate to the floor of the arena creaked opens. Star walked into the arena slowly. The crowd seemed to be holding their breath, as they anticipated the spectacle they were about to witness. Several guards began releasing the chains attached to Haven's collar, until he was completely unencumbered. Dad had a smirk on his face. Asriel wore a smug look. They certainly had a lot of faith in Star. I tried to feel the same way. Before I could collect myself, Haven roared, shooting forth a shower of hail that rained down on the entire arena. Just as the brief hailstorm ended, Haven charged at Hannah.

Noah's Point Of View

We sped home and scrambled up the stairs to our father's study at werewolf speed.

"Dad, we need your snow globe portal to Marigold!" I yelled at our confused father, interrupting his meeting with a few of our pack leaders.

Rather than waiting for an answer, Jonah spotted the snow globe on a bookshelf nearby and snatched it. He turned it over and scanned the incantation on the bottom, while Zaya, Eli and I crowded around him.

"What is the meaning of this, boys?" Demanded our father.

"Star is a Fae Princess and an Alpha's granddaughter, so she and her twin brother went back to the Ice Moon Pack to reclaim it from the Winter Fae Queen, their great grandmother!" Said Eli extremely quickly.

"What?!" Asked Dad.

The other pack leaders looked just as bewildered.

"Never mind the details, we'll be back soon, Dad! Thanks!" Said Zaya quickly.

He grabbed the snow globe from Jonah and quickly read the incantation, while we put our hands on his shoulders.

"Be care-," began our father but the room fell away from view, as we hurtled through darkness.

It felt like being on a rollercoaster. The trip lasted only a few seconds. We found ourselves in a grand study, very similar to our father's own. It was devoid of people though.

"Where are we?" Asked Zaya.

"In the Marigold Pack House, I believe," I said.

I grinned at the huge study with its chestnut wood shelves and gleaming desks and chairs. There was a huge territory map that resembled a tapestry on the wall nearby. Next to it hung an oil painting of a pretty and petite dark-haired girl sitting between two hulking men, obviously Alphas from their builds. I looked at the dark-haired, grey-eyed man on the left of the painting. Alpha Maze. To the right, the lighter haired, blue-eyed Alpha had to be Thaddeus, the seven foot Alpha. In the middle was undoubtedly Luna Friday, who was once wolf-less, before becoming the deadliest she-wolf on any battlefield. I started explaining all of this to my brothers, but Zaya was not having it.

"It's not history hour! We need to find someone, and get to Berryndale! Focus, Noah!" Zaya said.

"I really hope we don't get told no. We would also need to return the snow globes," said Eli, taking the first snow globe from Zaya.

"We'll give them our word as alphas to return it," said Jonah.

Someone came hurtling into the room. He was tall and muscular with olive skin, grey eyes and long dark hair. Alpha Maze? A wavy-haired woman with golden skin peeked into the room. Luna Friday? She had a toddler grabbing onto her leg. He was the very image of the grey-eyed man in miniature.

"I told you to stay in our room, Baby, and to keep Maurizio with you!" scolded the man.

I looked at them more closely. No. They were older than Alpha Maze and Luna Friday should be. They were probably...

"What is the meaning of this?" Demanded the former alpha, clearly outraged at four random teenagers, bursting into his study unannounced.

Even though portals existed to show good faith between the packs, most of them were rarely used.

"Former Alpha Malachi," I said respectfully with a little bow. "I am future Alpha Noah of the Viper Moon Pack and these are my brothers. We are sorry for the intrusion, but we desperately need to get to Berryndale. It involves the rescue of our dear future Luna!" I said, pleading with my eyes.

Malachi softened a little. The woman, who I now recognised as Felicity, the mate of Malachi and mother of Luna Friday, edged closer to us.

"What's wrong with your Luna?" She asked softly, her eyes concerned.

"She's gone off to the Ice Moon Pack to take it back from the Winter Fae Queen," said Eli. "She's the daughter of Hesper, you see. I don't know if you are familiar with the story-," Eli was cut off by Malachi.

"You're Quaid's kids!" He exclaimed.

We nodded fervently.

"Look at how you're grown! Last time I saw you, you were in footie pyjamas!" Chuckled Malachi. He then adopted a more sombre expression.

Chapter 50

"I'm familiar with Hesper's... misfortune," he said softly. Felicity put a hand gently on his shoulder.

A squad of pack warriors suddenly burst into the room, led by a man with similar features to Felicity, though hardened and masculine.

"Alpha Malachi, you went to the check out the breach on your own?" Exclaimed the man indignantly.

"I can more than handle a breach!" Said the former alpha.

"Who are you?" asked Zaya, looking at the man leading the squad.

"Who am I? Who am I? Who the fuck are you? You came hurtling into our pack house! We'll be asking the questions!" Snapped the other pack leader. Beta Fang! He was known to be crass. This had to be him.

"It's alright, Fang," said Malachi. "They're my friend's kids. He's the Viper Moon Pack's Alpha."

Fang calmed down a little. The squad of warriors seemed a lot less tense.

"About that portal to Berryndale..." said Zaya.

Malachi chuckled.

"We promise to return the snow globe!" Eli said in earnest.

"Snow globe?" Said Malachi.

"The portal to Berryndale is an enchanted elevator," said Fang condescendingly, as though that should be blatantly obvious to everyone.

"A wizard arranged it for us!" Said Felicity with a smile.

"Is Maze here, by chance?" I asked sheepishly.

Malachi and Felicity chuckled. "Maze is in Berryndale actually with Friday and Thaddeus," Said Malachi.

I grinned from ear to ear.

"Fang, show them to the portal," said Malachi.

Fang begrudgingly led the way in silence. Two men, who resembled Fang, stopped us in the hallway. I realised they too were identical.

"Twins!" I exclaimed.

One of the twins snorted with laughter. The other said, "Speak for yourself!"

"Where are you going, Fang?" Asked one of the twins.

"To the elevator," grumbled Fang.

"So you're going to Berryndale?" Asked the other twin.

Fang blinked and continued to stare blankly at them.

"Well, I guess you've met our delightful brother! I'm Fallon," said Fallon, the younger brother of Fang.

"And I'm Fargo!" Said Fargo, Fallon's identical twin brother.

"We're-," I began.

"Oh, we've heard of you!" Exclaimed Fargo. "The Alpha Triplets!"

Fallon nodded eagerly. "Alex, Felix and Calix!" He added.

Fang snorted with laughter. "Your counting could use some work. There are four of them," said Fang dryly.

The twins considered this in obvious amazement.

"We're the future alpha quadruplets," said Zaya impatiently. "I'm Zaya, the youngest, then this is Eli, then Noah, and the first born is Jonah," explained Zaya, gesturing to each one of us in turn.

"But, we really have to go! It was nice meeting you!" Said Eli.

Eli tried to brush past them, but a woman, turning the corner of the hallway, blocked his path.

"Oh, sorry!" She said. "Fang, Baby, who are these people?" She asked. She had a toddler in her arms.

"Aww, look at him," cooed Eli, ruffling the toddler's hair. The little boy greatly resembled Fang, if Fang had the ability to produce a smile.

"This is Falcon," said the woman. "I'm Astrid. I see you've already met my mate, Fang. What brings you to-"

Fang interrupted her. "Astrid! They're in a hurry to rescue their Luna!" Said Fang, clearly annoyed.

I highly doubted Fang was rushing to help us. He was probably rushing to be rid of us, but I appreciated the speed nonetheless, when he practically ran down the rest of the hallway with us on his heels. We came to an elevator and got on it. The "floors", if one could call them that, read Marigold, Joint Pack House and Berryndale. I quickly pushed the Berryndale button.

"You're coming with us?" I asked Fang.

"I'm going to come straight back. This elevator is a fixed portal, unlike the snow globes, which go with you when used. Anyone can take the elevator back and forth in any direction, and the elevator is in all three places simultaneously," explained Fang.

This was the most he had spoken the entire time so far, for which I was a bit grateful. I needed an elevator just like this from the Viper Moon Pack House to the Ice Moon Pack Castle and back. That way, our Luna, Star, could come and go freely.

"How do we get one of these?" I asked Fang.

"Ask Maze and Thaddeus," said Fang curtly.

Back to square one with Fang. The elevator pinged and the Berryndale sign lit up. We scrambled out of the elevator. Fang led the way. The warm-toned colours of the Berryndale pack house were a complete departure from the cool-toned colours of the Marigold Pack House. We bumped into another set of twins. Fang sighed exasperatedly.

"You love us, don't you, bro-in-law?" Asked one of the twins.

"Yeah, you certainly visit us often," commented the other.

Chapter 50

They both snickered. They were both blonde and blue-eyed. These must be Timothy and Titus, the younger twin brothers of Thaddeus. I had read about all of these alpha lineages in my favourite periodical. Fang did not respond to their teasing and taunts.

"Where's Thaddeus?" Grumbled Fang.

"In the Luna's study," said either Timothy or Titus.

We scurried behind Fang to yet another study, this one was filled with a variety of knickknacks, and decorated in pastel colours and floral prints. A pretty girl in a floral sun dress was laughing heartily, while she watched two men arm wrestle, their elbows on the desk. The arm wrestling match seemed playful, not competitive. The girl watching them had a toddler on each knee. In response to our arrival, the men stopped arm wrestling, and the laughing girl frowned. Even the toddlers looked at us with puzzled expressions on their little chubby-cheeked faces.

"Luna Friday, forgive us, we beg your pardon," I said with a bow. "Alpha Thaddeus, Alpha Maze," I said. My brothers bowed respectfully. Since Marigold and Berryndale had combined their packs, they were easily the most respected and fearsome nation among werewolves. Fang was less impressed than my brothers and me.

"Friday, these Alpha Quadruplets want your snow globe thing the wizard the gave you, so they can go up north, where the Alpha Triplets are," said Fang.

"Absolutely not," growled Alpha Maze, without a second thought. I flinched. "The audacity!" Exclaimed Maze. Maze had an extremely refined accent and a haughty demeanour.

Alpha Thaddeus roared with laughter. "Maze, brother, you must hear the lads out," boomed Thaddeus. His voice was so deep, it was like the rumbling of an earthquake. I was awestruck. Zaya was not.

"Look, I need that portal to go rescue my Luna. Friday, surely, you understand!" Zaya pleaded.

Maze hissed at his Luna being addressed casually. Thaddeus growled. They were incredibly intimidating, but Zaya seemed unperturbed.

"You had the shittiest life ever before you became such a great Luna. My father told me all about it!" Exclaimed Zaya.

Friday snorted with laughter to my surprise at that comment.

Zaya continued, undaunted. "That is exactly how my Star is. She needs me... us. She needs a little rescuing, before she can be strong enough to rescue others as Luna. You were the same. I know you will understand. Star had nothing a few days ago, and now she has the world of responsibility, and she's been so fearless the whole time. I can't stand the thought of her facing everything alone. She's gone to the Ice Moon Pack, her original pack, all on her own, to try to reclaim it as Hesper's long-lost daughter," said Zaya.

Maze's eyes widened at that. Thaddeus stroked his beard thoughtfully.

"We need to go after her. We will return the portal, you can be sure of that. We intend to have one made eventually. But for right now, we need yours. Please, Friday. I appeal to you, not as a future Alpha to a Luna, but as a man in love to a girl who was once saved by love!" Said Zaya.

Friday smiled slightly. Her sons on her lap, one miniature Maze and one miniature Thaddeus, looked amused.

Maze and Thaddeus seemed slightly more willing, but still unconvinced. They looked at their beloved Luna, prepared to do whatever she wanted.

"Little Luna, what say you?" Purred Thaddeus, his tone of voice incredibly gentle when addressing her.

"What do you think, Baby?" Cooed Maze, also clearly besotted.

Friday stared at us for a few moments, her expression impassive, though a small smile played about her lips.

'Give them the portal," said Friday, without hesitation.

Chapter 51

Monday 21st September, 2020 (Continued)

Jonah's Point Of View

"I knew it," muttered Fang. "Do I know my baby sister or what?" He grumbled, as he went to retrieve the portable portal.

Relief washed over me. We were one step closer to Star. I had to admit, my youngest brother, Zaya, certainly knew how to give an impassioned speech. I wish I was as good at expressing my feelings for Star as he was. I sighed.

While Fang fetched the portal, I noticed Noah edging closer to Alpha Maze. Alpha Thaddeus offered us beers. Eli took one despite me shooting him a disapproving glance.

Zaya hesitated, then grumbled, "Why the hell not." He downed a beer in one long drink.

Thaddeus roared with laughter, and clapped him and Eli on the backs. Friday giggled at the three of them. Noah drew Maze's attention to a territory map on the wall, commending the distributions and management of the land. Maze smiled slightly. The little future alphas came towards me curiously. I smiled at them.

"Who are you?" Said one with dark glossy hair and wide grey eyes. He had the same refined accent as Maze.

"Jonah. Who are you?" I asked, stooping to be at eye level with them.

The other little alpha laughed mischievously. "He is Tiberius," said the lighter-haired one. "And I am Maddox," added the lighter-haired one. They burst into fits of giggles.

"It is the other way around," said Friday to me.

"Mom!" Whined the real light-haired and blue-eyed Tiberius, clearly the son of Thaddeus, upset at his prank being ruined by his Mom.

"It was a fib," Maddox, the dark haired son of Maze, told me, his tone solemn.

"That's ok," I told them. "You had me there!"

They grinned gleefully at me and then at each other.

"Our Mommy is pregnant!" Maddox informed me.

"Wow!" I said, widening my eyes. Did he even know what that meant?

"She is keeping our sisters in her tummy, until they are ready!" Maddox explained.

Tiberius announced, "We are naming them Monday and Tuesday!"

I laughed. The boys stared at me, their little faces serious. I stopped laughing.

Fang returned with the snow globe. He brandished it most unceremoniously, handing it to me.

"Thank you!" I said to everyone.

"Bye!" Called Zaya.

"See you later," said Noah.

"Cheers," said Eli, raising his second beer to our hosts.

"Bye, lover boy!" Laughed Thaddeus, clearly teasing Zaya for his dramatic declaration of love for Star earlier.

"He's whipped, that one," commented Maze.

The two alphas burst into laughter. Friday rolled her eyes. The little alphas were play-fighting. Fang was encouraging the play-fight.

Zaya, Eli and Noah held onto me, while I read the incantation. My stomach lurched as Friday, Thaddeus, Maze, Tiberius and Maddox disappeared from view. A blast of cold air hit us. We were up north now, in the Winter Moon Pack lands, the icy rocky landscape governed by the Triplet Alphas and their Luna Chasity.

Jessie's Point Of View

We followed Georgianna's ghost, as she practically glided through the woods. She had softly padded through the trees at first, slowly increasing her pace. Now, she all but flew. It was becoming increasingly difficult to keep up with her. Jamie was out of breath as I grabbed her hand, pulling her forwards. I was worried for my Luna. I shifted, transforming into a huge black wolf. Jamie promptly climbed onto my back, and we were off. I ran through the woods with my little witch on my back. She had flung her arms around my neck.

Hold on tight, little witch! I warned.

Ok, she said feebly.

Chapter 51

She was getting tired. This woods had a strange draining effect on her. It was affecting me also, but to a much lesser extent as an alpha. Georgianna stopped abruptly, and so did I. Jamie emitted a small squeal at the sudden movement. I flinched at the sound, hoping Georgianna would not turn around and look at us. I hadn't actually seen the ghost's face yet, and I really didn't want to. Her gauzy white dress billowed behind her in the wind. She stepped lightly along a curved pathway, and disappeared into thin air. I gasped. She had vanished through the wall of a small cottage in the middle of the woods.

This must be her cottage! It's real! Jessie, I think we found it! Said Jamie excitedly.

I walked hesitantly towards the cottage. It had white-washed walls. The entire structure was covered in overgrown flowering vines. The flowers seemed to sigh softly, as they unfolded in the moonlight. The sun had set, and the moon had come out. It was a starless night. The door was padlocked. Jamie enchanted the lock, and it clicked open, and fell to the ground. My wolf form could barely fit through the doorway, but I was determined not to shift back, in case we needed my full strength for something.

I walked into the cottage's cobwebbed living room. Jamie enchanted the dusty old candles, so that they lit on their own. Flames burst to life in the fireplace. I didn't need the light to see, but Jamie did. She studied the room.

What now, little witch? I asked her.

I'm not sure. I doubt she would keep her tomb upstairs, said Jamie, indicating to the tightly wound staircase in the corner. *There must be a cellar of some sort!* Insisted Jamie.

Jamie climbed down off my back. There was a large circular rug on the creaky wooden floor. She grabbed it and flung it aside. A cloud of dust rose up, causing my little witch to have a sneezing fit. When the dust settled, there was nothing there, but the plain wooden floor. Jamie tried a revealing charm. Nothing. We looked at each other. We went upstairs. The hallway was a bit narrow for me in my massive wolf form. Thus, my coat brushed against both walls. I made Jamie walk behind me. We found Georgianna's bedroom. This little cottage was her escape. Alto and Georgianna must have spent time here. There was a painting of them together hung on the wall. The drapes and bedding were coated with dust. The vanity was cluttered with unused potions and beauty products. The closet was filled with both feminine and masculine clothes, as though one day, the couple just never returned, without bothering to retrieve their belongings.

She never came back for their stuff? I asked Jamie.

She was probably too devastated after Alto's death to bear to look at any of it, responded Jamie.

A large floor-length ornate mirror stood in the centre of the room. I wondered why it stood out so much to me, and then it hit me. The mirror was perfectly clean.

Jamie, the mirror gathered no dust over the years! I pointed out to her.

She gasped. *It's enchanted. It has to be.*

Jamie walked up to the mirror. She peered into it. Clearly, I wasn't seeing what she was seeing. She grinned at me.

I knew it! She exclaimed.

Knew what? I asked, totally confused.

This cottage isn't befitting an Alpha and a Coven Mother. It's cute, but it's rather bland for them, don't you think? It was a ruse. A cover for their real hideout. Their actual escape, explained Jamie.

Jamie dragged her fingertips across the mirror's surface. The glass sublimed into silvery myst. The myst beckoned us forwards. A lovely smell wafted towards us.

Wait! I implored Jamie.

What's wrong? Asked Jamie.

I can't fit through the mirror like this! I said.

Oh! She realised, giggling at my massive shaggy wolf form.

Shift back! She said simply.

I shredded my clothes! I said.

She smirked at me. *Shift!* She commanded.

I shifted. I towered over her still, even in human form. My little witch trailed her eyes over my naked form. I grasped her waist and pulled her flush against me.

"Jessie!" She squealed out loud indignantly. "We can't—"

I silenced her by crashing my lips against hers hungrily. She moaned into my mouth, our breath intermingling. She pushed against my chest.

"No!" She squeaked. "We're on a mission!" She reminded me.

"I'm on a mission!" I growled playfully, grabbing her again.

"Jessie! Behave!" She implored me, making clothes appear on me.

"I don't like the outfit," I complained, attempting to take my new shirt off.

It wouldn't budge. The buttons could not be undone. I stared at her, my mouth agape in astonishment.

"You naughty little witch!" I hissed, attempting to grab her waist again, but she ran through the mirror of myst.

I grumbled as I chased after her. I found myself in yet another forest, this one strikingly beautiful. It was daytime here. Songbirds belted from

Chapter 51

the treetops. Every tree and blade of grass seemed to flower. The sweet smell was the combined aroma of thousands of flowers.

Jamie, I called through our link, searching for her in the silvery myst.

The flowers were emitting the mist, as if their scents could be seen. I realised most emitted a silvery mist, but some sprouted mists other colours, pink, gold, blue, yellow.

I'm right here! Said Jamie.

She made the mist clear a little, revealing herself to me.

Where are we? I asked.

She smiled sadly. *This must be a little haven Georgianna made for herself and Alto. It's abandoned now that they're both gone. The cottage we were in was just a decoy. Anyone who came looking for them would just find an empty cottage that looked lived in and assume they weren't home. A very clever way to protect their haven.*

I frowned. *I'm surprised it let us in so easily,* I said.

The protection charms might have faded over the years or... maybe we confused the doorway. We are a Coven Mother and an Alpha too, after all, similar to the previous owners, mused Jamie.

She was right. It felt almost meant to be for us to find this place. Perhaps, we were the only ones who would have been able to get in besides Georgianna and Alto themselves.

We walked a while through the scented mist and the fields and forest of flowers. There was a huge castle in the distance. That seemed more like where they would have been. I felt sad for them. They had not deserved such a fate. We walked into the castle. Jamie seemed entranced almost, as she made her way through the grand halls. There was no dust here. No cobwebs. Everything still sparkled and shone. Powerful magic indeed, to stand the test of time this way. Jamie began to walk faster, reminding me of the way Georgianna had glided.

Jamie, slow down! I commended.

Of course, my own Luna could not be commanded. She sped up. She broke into a run. I ran after her. She ran up a huge sweeping staircase. I followed her. We found ourselves in the bed chambers of Alto and Georgianna. Jamie stopped running. She stood still, as if transfixed. She was standing at the foot of a four poster bed, where the drapes were drawn.

Jamie! Jamie! JAMIE! I yelled in her mind. She seemed to snap out of it.

She's here! Said Jamie.

I took a deep breath. I gripped the curtain, and pulled it back to reveal the bed. Georgianna lay there, in the flesh, as though merely sleeping, but she had no heartbeat. Her body was perfectly preserved. The other side of the bed was empty. This is what she wanted, to rest in peace next to Alto. We had to bring him here, to her side, to stay forever.

Star's Point Of View

After Haven the Hellish had made it hail, he charged at me. Running was no use. I refused to run and hide. Where would I hide from a hundred foot dragon in an open arena? My heart almost stopped in fright as Haven's snout neared me. Was this the end of me? He opened his wide jaws. He could easily fit twelve of me in his mouth. His huge tongue snaked out. His breath was not hot, but ice-cold. I felt the blast of cold air. I shut my eyes tightly. Ice water touched my face. I shivered. I waited for the pain. None came aside from the blistering cold. I opened my eyes slowly. The ice water was Haven licking me.

"Stop!" I squeaked.

He stopped and seemed to whine like a scolded puppy. He sat, making the whole arena shake. I stared at Haven, and he stared at me. I had tamed him, hadn't I? That was it, wasn't it? I looked at the Queen hopefully. She starred at me, clearly unimpressed.

"Haven," I said loudly, feeling immensely relieved.

Haven cocked his head to one side.

"Come here!" I demanded.

Haven bent his head towards me again. I gripped his ear and hoisted myself onto his scaly head. I shrieked in surprise when he raised his head, causing me to slide down his neck onto his back. I held on for dear life, so I wouldn't fall from his back to the floor. The crowd was roaring madly. I knew what to do somehow. I got a secure grip on his scales, and leant forwards, as if I were riding a gigantic horse without a saddle.

"HAVEN!" I yelled.

Haven roared happily. I understood his emotions better now. I smiled.

"TAKE FLIGHT!"

Zaya's Point Of View

We were in the middle of a snowstorm of sorts. There was a mansion up ahead. We crunched through the foot-deep snow to get to it. We would have been hypothermic had we been humans. We reached a porch and climbed the short steps. We hesitated, wondering if to knock on the door. We were not completely sure if they would be a portal from the Winter Moon Pack Lands to the Ice Moon Pack Lands, or if we would have to find another mode of transportation from here. I glanced at the six SUVs parked in front of the huge house. I banged on the door.

Chapter 51

"HELLO! IS ANYONE HOME?! HELLO!!!" I bellowed.

"Hi," said a cheerful high-pitched voice from behind us.

We all jumped around to find a she-wolf standing there. She looked very young. She could be our age, or just a few years older. She had dark golden blonde curls down to her waist and huge brown doe eyes. She had an olive skin tone, a button nose and a small mouth with full lips. Her cheeks and nose were flushed pink due to the cold. She was very pretty in a delicate way. Of course, no one held a candle to my Star, but this girl sort of looked like a fairytale character. She had a sweet, innocent appearance. Star was sweet and innocent too. I sighed. I had to get to her quickly.

"Hi, little girl, we are the future alphas of the Viper Moon Pack. Our Luna is currently on the Ice Moon Pack lands, and we need the fastest mode of transportation there possible, a portal preferably!" I explained.

"Little girl!" Snapped the girl, narrowing her eyes. "I'm not a little girl, excuse you!" She said indignantly.

I didn't have time for her tantrum.

"Sorry, Miss! Young lady, do you know the fastest way to the next pack?" I corrected myself.

The girl was staring at us now in amazement, as though she had only just noticed something.

"You're the Quadruplet Alphas!" She squealed in surprise. She giggled. "I'm so glad I only have three. Four is crazy! Your Luna is missing! Oh no, I'm so sorry! Was she kidnapped?" Asked the girl.

"You're Luna Chasity!" Exclaimed Noah suddenly.

"Duh!" Said Luna Chasity, giggling again.

"Chasity, you have to help us please!" Begged Eli. "Our Luna wasn't kidnapped but she still needs our help!"

"There are two portals here, a fixed one and a portable one!" Whispered Chasity. We leant in to hear her better. "My alphas are... kinda jealous. I will sneak the portal to you, the portable one. My alphas are having a meeting with the other pack leaders in the cellar, where the fixed portal is, so you would have to wait to use that one and it'll take you to the edge of the pack lands, whereas the portable one will take you right outside the castle."

"Please Chasity! Let us use the portable one!" Pleaded Jonah.

"No prob! That's what I just said, guys," complained Chasity.

How did this tiny rosy-cheeked Luna boss around three humungous alphas? I had seen pictures of the alpha triplets, and they looked ferocious honestly. Alpha Felix, in particular, had one of the highest kill counts in the north. I didn't want to get her in trouble with her alphas, but I was desperate for that portal.

"Wait here!" She whispered. "Don't make anymore noise! You're lucky everyone was in the cellar!" She told us.

Chasity went inside. She quickly came back out. "On second thought, follow me!" She said.

She ran inside and up a large staircase. We ran after her, as lightly as we could. She ran into an upstairs office. She went to a shelf. She stood on tiptoe, but couldn't reach the snow globe on the highest shelf.

"Damn it!" She muttered.

I heard some heavy footsteps echoing in the hallway.

"Baby! What's wrong?" Called a deep, gruff voice.

"Luna, you in there?" Called a similar, but more refined voice.

"Are you playing hide and seek with us, Goddess?" Asked another voice playfully.

Chasity smiled in the direction of the voices, but then looked worried.

"Shit," she said out loud.

"Should we hide?" I asked, somewhat nervous.

Eli easily reached the snow globe.

Three huge men burst into the room. They looked livid when they spotted us. Chasity fixed them with a stern glare.

"I'm lending the Alpha Quadruplets the snow globe. They need to go to the Ice Moon Pack to rescue their Luna!" Said Chasity defiantly.

"Baby," growled one of them. He snatched her away from us, enveloping her in his arms. "How dare you talk to our Luna without us present?!" He roared at us, his eyes black.

"Felix," protested Chasity. "Calm down!" Implored Chasity.

Another triplet moved quick as lightning. He snatched the snow globe from Eli.

"This was a gift from our cousin-in-law! It's not to be borrowed," grumbled the alpha.

"Calix!" Squealed Chasity.

"Why can't they arrange their own transport to the neighbouring pack?" Asked another alpha.

"Alex! Lend them the snow globe! Please! For me!" whined Chasity. She pouted.

Felix kissed her gently. I felt a sharp pang. It felt like ages since I'd kissed my little Star and held her. Calix and Alex were looking at their Luna, stroking their chins.

"Ugh! You're wasting time! Remember how you felt when I was missing?" Said Chasity.

All three alphas flinched, clearly not over the bad memory of their beloved Luna's past kidnapping even though she was home safe and sound now.

Chapter 51

Alex sighed. "Okay, Luna, but we expect it back ASAP!" Said Alex.
"All right, Baby. You want it, you got it," said Felix.
"Next time, ask us first, please Goddess. Don't just steal it! You little thief!" Teased Calix.
Chasity looked livid. The triplets laughed.
"She's just like the actual goldilocks, snooping, taking people's things. Eating their porridge. Critiquing their furniture. Stealing their snow globes," grumbled Felix, his eyes alight with mischief.
His brothers laughed heartily.
"Yeah, yeah, you're hilarious! Have you put the boys to bed?" Asked Chasity.
"Don't try to change the subject, gorgeous!" Snarled Felix playfully, attempting to tickle Chasity's sides.
"We let you out of our sight for one minute, and you find Quadruplet alphas!" Said Alex, bending down to nuzzle an outraged Chasity.
Calix chuckled and ran his fingers through Chasity's hair. Chasity rolled her eyes.
"I only have eyes for my Star, and I'm sure Chasity is all about you three," I said, finding their banter amusing.
"Who the fuck are you four exactly? What're your names?" Asked Felix casually, snaking his arms around Chasity again, after she had wriggled away.
She giggled and tried to swat his arms away, but he tightened his grip, bear hugging her. They were so open with their affection. I smiled at that. I was pretty sure Felix had heard of us. We had certainly heard of them, but I introduced myself and my brothers anyway.
"I'm Zaya. This is Eli. Jonah. Noah. Our Luna is called Star," I said, pointing to each of my brothers in turn.
The triplet alphas were a few years older than us. They regarded us with curiosity.
"I'm Felix," said Felix. "This is baby boy, Calix!" Calix laughed. "Alpha of alphas, Alex," Felix added. Alex grinned. "And this little minx is my Baby, Luna Chasity," said Felix, giving Chasity's waist a squeeze.
"Where are the baby triplets?" Blurted out Noah.
Ugh. We didn't have time for this. I was anxious about being apart from Star. Alex grinned, and motioned for us to follow them. We entered a large nursery, where there were three toddlers dressed in the same striped outfit, but in three different colours: red, blue and green.
"I thought you said you had put them to bed before the pack meeting!" Said Chasity, shocked to find all her babies awake.
She smoothed their shiny loose dark blonde curls. They had gotten her hair and the blue eyes of their fathers.

"They were restless today, Goddess," said Calix sheepishly.

"We'll put them to bed now, Luna," promised Alex.

"Baby, I'll come with you to watch over you while you rest," said Felix.

"I'm not the least bit tired," protested Chasity.

"What are their names?" Asked Noah.

Alex grinned. "Luna named them," said Alex.

Chasity smiled. "My little blue boy is Adriel. Raphael is in green. Tzuriel is wearing red," explained Chasity.

" Goddess colour-coded our heirs," laughed Calix.

I couldn't help but laugh. "I love it," I said. I really did like the idea.

"Don't let those kids pull a fast one on you!" Said Eli.

"Watch them like a hawk," chuckled Jonah.

Chasity nodded. "Alex, Felix, Calix!" Said Chasity pouting. "Stop stalling. Give them the portal!"

The triplets laughed. Were they scamming us? Felix seemed like a handful. He laughed the loudest. His way of laughing made me laugh too.

"Our snow globe portal is time-sensitive. My cousin-in-law, Jamie, cast a spell on it. It doesn't work after a certain hour until the next day!" Explained Chasity.

What?! Shit!

"Is it too late?" I asked anxiously.

Chasity shook her head. Relief washed over me.

"Wait, did you just say Jamie?" Asked Jonah.

"Yeah," mumbled Chasity.

"She's the Witch Luna helping us! There's a curse affecting our Luna that needs be broken!" Said Jonah.

"Jamie's mate, Alpha Jessie, is your cousin, right, triplets?" Asked Noah.

The triplets nodded.

"Sorry about your Luna," said Felix, sympathising with us.

"Go get her!" said Alex, tossing the snow globe to Jonah, who caught it, his face lighting up.

"Good luck, guys!" Said Calix in earnest.

All the triplets were now sitting in the corner of the nursery, behind a huge desk on three separate chairs. Chasity was on Calix's lap. Alex and Felix were both playing with the Luna's long dark golden curls.

My brothers and I gathered around Jonah, who was holding the snow globe.

"Go kick some ass!" Said Felix.

"I intend to!" I said.

Chapter 52

Monday 21st September, 2020 (Continued)

Jessie's Point Of View

Wait, so we'll have to return here? I asked my little witch.
Yes, I'm afraid so! We can't move Georgianna's body from here and bring her to Alto. I believe she wants him brought to her. This was their getaway. These enchantments are all hers. She made this place for them. She won't want to rest in a cold Alpha's tomb with him on his pack lands, especially not after what his brother did! Explained Jamie.

I sighed. I understand Georgianna. She was not the villain I had been expecting. She was a hurt, scared, heartbroken woman. She was supposed to have been a blushing blissful bride, but Oleander took that all away from her when he framed her for Alto's poisoning. The poison had been meant for Georgianna herself, so, either way, Oleander was an unforgivable enemy in her eyes, and his lineage had produced the Quadruplets. The curse made sense. Why should Oleander and his successors fall in love and live in marital bliss, when she had been denied it? She deserved to have Alto brought to her.

What about Nina and her students? There's something off about them. When we return with Alto's body, won't they be in the way? I pointed it.

Jamie considered it. She tilted her head to one side, thinking. She looked at me, and opened her mouth to speak. Just as she did that, she vanished!

"JAMIE!!!" I bellowed, grabbing at the empty space where she had been.

Dalton's Point Of View

The Coven Mother and the old hags were performing a summoning spell, according to Fox. They had drawn a large chalk circle on the dining table, and lined it with salt and candles. Zack and I waited to pounce when necessary.

The hags chanted, their croaky voices echoing throughout the manor. There was something materialising in the midst of the circle. I watched it take form. My eyes widened.

"Luna Jamie!" Exclaimed Zack.

He attempted to rush forwards.

"Wait!" Said Fox. "Wait for them to summon Jessie too! Then we'll get rid of them!"

Zack nodded reluctantly.

As soon as Jamie had appeared within the circle, magical restraints held her in place, tying her to the table. She struggled against them, but could not move. There was a light around her that seemed to be her aura.

"Summon the Alpha now?" Asked one of the hags.

"No!" Said the Coven Mother sharply. "We'll need sufficient strength to deal with him! We'll drain his mate first! That way, he'll be weakened and devastated, and we'll have her energy! That'll be just enough to best him! Sisters, imagine how powerful we'll be once we drain them both!"

Zack growled lowly. I snarled.

"On second thought, we'll figure out how to get Jessie from the woods on our own. Do your worst, Dalton and Zack!" Said Fox.

Zack and I shifted in seconds. Just as the old witches began siphoning Jamie's energy, breathing it in, leeching from her, we pounced. We were still invisible, and they could not hear us either. I had never witnessed such terror as this. The reactions of the old wicked witches when Zack chomped the head off of one them was priceless, as to them, there was no assailant in sight. Nina looked on in horror. We were not cruel. It was clean and quick and over in a minute for the main twelve. We saved the Coven Mother for last. She was crouched in the corner, staring wildly at the empty air, casting random spells in random directions hoping to hit us, unsure of who or what we were.

"Wait!" Said Fox, as he released Jamie from her restraints and helped her down off the table.

We'd regrettably splattered our Luna with blood. We should have probably helped her down first. She didn't seem too disturbed. She was an Alpha's mate after all, so she had to be tough.

"A concealment charm," she said softly.

"Yeah," said Fox, sprinkling Jamie with something, so she could see and hear us, whilst the spell was still in effect. Jamie looked at the Coven Mother.

"Summon Jessie!" She instructed.

"Only if you'll spare me!" Said the Coven Mother.

Jamie thought about it for a few seconds.

"Sure. Zack and Dalton stand down," said Jamie.

We had to listen to her. She was the Luna and our Alpha was not present, making her first in command. I hoped Jessie would let us kill the Coven Mother when he arrived.

"Summon Jessie!" Said Jamie again.

"Vow," said the Coven Mother.

"What?" Asked Jamie.

"Magically vow that no harm will come to me if I summon Jessie, and then I will!" Said the Coven Mother simply.

Jamie's eyes widened. She looked a bit worried. Fox did too. Nothing worried those two usually. Zack and I exchanged a nervous glance. Maybe we should find Jessie the old fashioned way. Tie one end of a string to a tree and the other end to our waists, while we search the woods or something. Could that work?

Star's Point Of View

Haven stretched his magnificent wings out to their full span. The crowd gasped in amazement. I glanced at the area where the nobles sat. Harper was cheering and jumping up and down. My Dad and Asriel were cheering too. The Queen actually smiled. She stood to watch me as my dragon took flight. A rush of cold air whipped my curls about as we soared upwards and out of the arena. I let out a joyous cry. I felt so alive. This was reminiscent of the night I had shifted. I felt wild and free, and like my true self, no matter how fleeting the moment. Nothing could touch me in this moment. The world was a wilderness, but I was a wild creature myself, and thus, I belonged. I squealed. Somehow steering Haven was as easy as breathing. He moved based on how I leant my body weight, and he seemed to guess my thoughts. I called out to him.

"Look!" I shrieked.

There were moving dots in the snow. There were people down there at the outskirts of the castle moving as quickly as possible towards the castle itself. A breach? Well, I had been a part of a breach just earlier this very day. Haven roared. He swooped down towards the dots. I sensed them before I smelled them. My mates!

"Heel!" I bellowed.

Haven reared a bit. He landed, causing a cloud of frost and snow to rise up, as his gigantic claws hit the white blanket beneath us. I slid off his back, and landed lightly on my feet in the snow, mere yards from my four awe-struck mates, the Quadruplets.

Jonah's Point Of View

We arrived in the Ice Moon Pack lands. These lands were even wilder and colder than the Winter Moon Pack lands. The castle sparkled in the distance. We had done it! Noah's crazy plan had worked! We had snow-globe-hopped all the way to Star's pack lands.
"YES!" Screamed Noah.
"WE DID IT!" Bellowed Zaya.
Eli cheered.
My three idiotic little brothers jumped up and down, dancing around like mad men. They looked like they were playing ring around the roses in the snow.
"All right!" I said, though I was grinning at their antics. I was elated too, but we were far from finished.
"Now, onto the actual point of all this madness... locating Star!" I said.
They nodded eagerly. A high-pitched screech made us look up, startled. A massive dragon flew overhead. My jaw dropped. I had not been expecting that. Would we have to fight that thing to get to Star? I was prepared to do whatever I had to. I took a deep breath. Zaya was peering at the dragon, his eyes narrowed. Noah gasped. A huge smile spread on Eli's face.
"What is it?" I asked them, yelling over the sound of the dragon's roaring and the rushing of air caused by him circling low to the ground.
"STAR!" Yelled Eli. "STAR IS RIDING THAT DRAGON!"
WHAT?! My heart dropped into my stomach. The dragon landed a few yards away, displacing an awful lot of snow in a cloud of white. The dragon itself looked as though he were made of frost and ice, all his scales either icy blue or snow white. He camouflaged easily, once on the snow. I wouldn't want to step on him by accident.
I spotted Star. Her ears were pointy! She looked different, but it was unmistakably Star. She slid off the dragon's back and walked towards us smiling. Where was the shy scared girl who had cried when we told her to leave Angie's party? She was a dragon-riding babe all of a sudden. Her Fae heritage showed now. It had probably been suppressed earlier somehow. She had always been very pretty, whether she realised or not, but the small changes suited her well. She was even more stunning

somehow. She seemed somewhat more self-aware. She smirked at us, a tiny bit smug, waiting for us to say something.

Noah's Point Of View

My snow-globe hopping plan had actually worked! I was a real strategist now! Like Maze and Alex. And Jessie! I was so elated. I could practically smell Star. I gasped. I could smell Star. She was here. I was certain of it. A huge ice dragon drew my attention upwards with its battle cry. I gulped. How had I missed that? It did blend in well with the landscape. The magnificent creature landed nearby, and Star slid off of its back. She had ridden it here. My mouth was agape. We all stared at her in astonishment as she walked towards us. The dragon roared behind her, sending a blast of cold air our way, whipping our hair back. Star seemed unperturbed by it. As she came closer, I noticed her ears and her cheekbones were like that of the Fae now. I smiled. She seemed more herself. She was even more beautiful this way. I felt a bit lost for words. I wanted to say we had come to rescue her and tell her about my snow-globe-hopping plan had worked, but she had just pulled up on a dragon, so she did not seem to be a damsel in distress in need of rescue right now. I grinned sheepishly at her. I couldn't wait to tell her about all the Alphas I had met! I had the last snow-globe in my hand. Star needed to be there when I gave this back to Chasity's alphas. Chasity would be the perfect friend for Star! They could definitely relate to each other. I didn't know where to start so I just marvelled at Star in silence.

Eli's Point Of View

I felt like a kid at Christmas. This landscape certainly resembled the North Pole. We had done it. Noah's crazy plan had worked. Thank goodness, for my nerdy elder brother. I clapped him on the back. Zaya was staring at something. Noah gasped. I looked up.
"STAR!" I yelled, spotting Star atop a colossal dragon, an ice dragon!
"STAR IS RIDING THAT DRAGON!" I bellowed.
My Princess did not seem to need rescuing. I grinned as she landed her dragon. Her own rarity and magnificence outshone even the rarest of dragons. She was stunning as always, but now she had her Fae ears. Some of her features were slightly sharper. Her curly hair had grown longer and shinier. She looked the picture of health. She walked towards us. Words failed me. She seemed proud of herself for once, as she should be.

Zaya's Point Of View

Noah's nerdy ass had saved the day with his crazy snow-globe hopping idea. Thank goodness, we had listened to him. We usually didn't, but we'd been so desperate today.

I heard a whoosh above me. I smelled a beautiful floral scent, coming from above me. How strange. I peered upwards. There was a dragon flying towards us. I knew about ice dragons, but I had never seen one. They were quite rare. Dragons were rare already, and ice dragons were rare among dragons, so you could imagine my surprise. I was anxious to get to my Star, but it seemed my Star had come to me. She was on the dragon's back. She landed her dragon a few yards away. Since when was my baby such a badass babe. I let her out of my sight for half a day, and she changed her whole look, and adopted a pet dragon. I grinned at her as she approached us. My dorky elder brothers were quiet. Even Eli, the only other cool one, was acting shy.

"Come here, Baby! Don't think cause you ride dragons now, that you can just run off whenever you want! I'm not afraid to spank a dragon-riding Fae princess!" I told her.

She burst into laughter.

"I wanted to tell you, but…" she began.

"No excuses!" I said, still a little angry with her, but so relieved to see her.

The dragon heard the aggression in my tone and roared at me.

"Pipe down! I saw her first!" I told it.

Dragons were jealous and possessive pets. The dragon growled at me. I would bribe him with meat. I would walk with some steaks the next time. I didn't want this huge thing cramping my style when I was wooing my Baby.

Star ran to me. She ended up with eight arms encircling her, as we all hugged her tightly. She sighed happily. The dragon noticed Star's liking for us and sniffed us. It made a face as if we smelled gross. I was not surprised. I expected a Fae dragon to be just as snotty as the Fae were. I would win the dragon over.

"Come on," said Star. "I want you to meet my Dad!"

It seemed as though the dragon was not the only one I had to impress. I followed Star eagerly, as she led us into her new royal life.

TO BE CONTINUED…

ABOUT THE AUTHOR

Joanna J is a medical doctor, an animal enthusiast and an avid reader. She began writing short stories for her own entertainment as a child, and she continued writing into adulthood. Fantasy has always been her chosen form of escapism. Joanna has often drawn comfort and courage from books. She writes, hoping to pass on the favour to at least one person. She is from Trinidad and Tobago so she enjoys incorporating Caribbean folklore into her fantasy novels.

Visit Dreame to Read More Story by Joanna J

When A Witch Loves A Werewolf
The Challenge Two Alphas, One Girl
Her Triplet Alphas
Sold to the Billionaire Alpha
Luna Queen Pariah
www.dreame.com

ABOUT DREAME

Established in 2018 and headquartered in Singapore, Dreame is a global hub for creativity and fascinating stories of all kinds in many different genres and themes.

Our goal is to unite an open, vibrant, and diverse ecosystem for storytellers and readers around the world.

Available in over 20 languages and 100 countries, we are dedicated to bring quality and rich content for tens of millions of readers to enjoy.

We are committed to discover the endless possibilities behind every story and provide an ultimate platform for readers to connect with the authors, inspire each other, and share their thoughts anytime, anywhere.

Join the journey with Dreame, and let creativity enrich our lives!

Printed in Great Britain
by Amazon